CW00734658

Back in the Summer of '96 (oh yeah!)

Natalie Adele Mason

Published in 2009 by New Generation
Publishing

Copyright © Natalie Adele Mason

First Edition

The author asserts the moral right under the
Copyright, Designs and Patents Act 1988 to
be identified as the author of this work.

All Rights reserved. No part of this publication
may be reproduced, stored in a retrieval
system or transmitted, in any form or by any
means without the prior consent of the author,
nor be otherwise circulated in any form of
binding or cover other than that which it is
published and without a similar condition
being imposed on the subsequent purchaser.

Published by New Generation Publishing

This book started as a dream. No, really! I even dreamed of the title and upon waking, I thought 'I just have to get this down on paper', and so, 90,000 words and several months later, here it is. My first Novel.

I am an Artist by trade, so I suppose creative writing and art go hand in hand, hence my desire to write. I have already started the sequel to this book, and sincerely hope you enjoy reading it as much as I enjoyed writing it!

I have to thank YouWriteOn and Legend Press, for giving me a chance to publish my work. Thank you Ted, thank you, thank you, thank you!!

I also want to thank my wonderful family and friends for their help and support during my time spent bent over a computer going over and over and over the manuscript, and for giving me their very honest feedback. Thank you!

Thanks also to my Editor Johnny....thanks for spurring me on, helping me through the tough times, and being brutally honest with me. And thanks to Pam too, you know who you are!

I also have to say a special thank you to my wonderful sister Clair, and sister-in-law Jayne, for the memories and funny anecdotes. Without you, my memory would have been useless, and this book would not be nearly as funny as it could have been.

Here's to the Summer of '96....What a year!

For my beloved Daddy 1942-2005.

I hope I made you proud.

Chapter One.

Natasha woke early, eyes bleary, and temples that hurt from a hangover which was just surfacing.
It was still dark outside, and she squinted at the bedside clock. 6.25am.
'Oh no' she thought, another bloody boring day at work.

Shuffling around under the covers, she turned to look at the beautiful face of Anton, her ex fiancé. Just enough street light filtered through the curtains for her to see him. He looked lovely when he slept. She'd not forgotten how she used to stare at him for what seemed like hours. Often he'd sense her watching him and would say "Tasha, stop staring at me while I sleep will you." She smiled at the thought.

As if once again sensing her staring, Anton sleepily opened his eyes and focused on her, "Good morning gorgeous," he said.
"Ditto back. I enjoyed last night, Anton. Fancy round two before I have to get up for work?"
She laid back down, and he leaned over her, kissing her lightly at first, then more intensely, running his hands down her flat stomach, and then stroking her thigh.

She moaned at the pure pleasure, and gave in to him, "take me now Anton," she whispered. And so she opened her legs, and he mounted her, entering with ease and moving slowly in and out of her.

He covered her neck with little kisses and nibbled her ears, and Tasha felt herself becoming more aroused. Wrapping her legs tightly around his toned torso, she moved with him, faster and faster, until she heard his breathing change, she knew he was close to orgasm.

She felt hers coming too, and biting down on his shoulder, and raking her nails down his back, she moaned, "now Anton, now, I'm coming."

***

After their fervent love making, Natasha had left a sleeping Anton, quickly picking up her clothes which were scattered all over his bedroom floor, and made her way to the kitchen to get dressed, so as not to disturb him.

She called a taxi, before quickly dressing in last nights clothes, checked her appearance in a mirror on the wall, rubbing away the sleep from her eyes, and applied a little lippy. It was important to her how she looked at all times.

There was no time for coffee, she had to go home to shower and change for work.

She found a pad and pen, and scribbled him a note thanking him for the most wonderful night, and that she hoped he'd enjoyed it as much as she had, and signed it with three kisses.

Anton, as gorgeous as he was, was her past. One last night together, she'd enjoyed it immensely, but knew they had no future.

With that thought it mind, she walked out of the door, posted his keys through the letterbox, and waited in the crisp morning air for her taxi to arrive.

***

Natasha was bored out of her mind, and feeling just a tad guilty at her betrayal.

It was a typical mundane day at work, and how Natasha wished she were outside, instead of being stuck in this stuffy office.
Thinking back to the night before with Anton, she remembered the sex had been mind blowing, four times, in almost every position you could think of. She was sure her colleagues could see she was walking like John Wayne.

When she had first started seeing Anton, he had been coming up through the ranks of the youth team at Sheffield Utd, and had been on the bench twice for the first team.

Not bad considering he was only eighteen at the time, four years Natasha's junior.

He'd also had interest from some of the big clubs, including Liverpool, Arsenal and Manchester Utd, until one fateful day, when he was injured as he saved a goal, smashing his shoulder against the goal post, and badly dislocating it.

Hats off to Sheffield Utd, they'd paid for the best treatment for him, but his shoulder was damaged beyond repair, and his promising footballing career came to an abrupt end, sending him in to deep depression.

She'd felt so very sorry for him, but nothing she did or said helped him, and they'd split a year later. 'Shame' Natasha thought 'He was fantastic'.

She was just pleased that his depression which had torn them apart, seemed to have, lifted and he was back to his usual happy go lucky self, and he'd lost the weight which he'd gained whilst on anti-depressants. He looked amazing again, hence not being able to resist him last night.

She had absolutely no willpower whatsoever. Especially where men were concerned.

■■

The sex had been just like it had been at the start
of their relationship, before things
had started to go wrong. Natasha remembered,
and was still so very sorry for Anton. Who knows
where he could be now if that accident hadn't
happened?

She thought back to their relationship. It had been
so good in the beginning, so passionate, they could
not get enough of each other. Natasha had
revelled in the fact she was dating a handsome
footballer, who didn't have a roving eye. She
knew that was a rarity, and was so in love with
him. They were inseparable, and spontaneous,
often taking off for weekends away to Fowey in
Cornwall to see his cousin, or taken a week to
Brittany in France, whenever he wasn't in training.
They'd spent as much time as possible either in
bed or out socialising, and she had loved every
minute of it.

She was sure, had the gripping depression not
descended on Anton, they would still be together.
Yes, she'd enjoyed the status of being the
girlfriend of a footballer, but had stood by him
after his career had ended, because she loved him
for him, not what he did for a living, but he'd
pushed her away, snap at her for no reason, he
didn't want to know. So sadly, after a year of this,
Natasha had walked away, she'd tried and
▪▪

tried, but there was no getting through to him. She'd had enough, and even though it had hurt her like hell, she'd turned her back and walked away from their relationship.

Even after last night and the fantastic sex, there was no going back for them. Anton was her past, and knew in her heart it would never work if they got back together, she thought sadly.

***

Natasha worked as an International Buyer for a large Kitchen Company, and recently she had come to hate it.
The people she worked with were great (she'd even had a fling with one or two of them), but she was just so bored of it all. She even had a secret crush on Ben, one of the warehouse workers, but he was so young and cocky, it wasn't right to have such thoughts.

All this paperwork and deadlines, it was enough to drive a girl crazy.
She'd always wanted to be an artist, but knew that it was not a job likely to pay the bills, so here she was, sat at her desk, bored out of her mind, wondering if she'd ever get that promotion which had been dangling like a carrot for the last couple of years.
At least if she got that, she would get to travel to

the countries she purchased from, instead of only talking to her foreign contacts by phone or email. So frustrating, she knew she deserved that promotion and was sick of waiting for it. She'd have to say something about that to her boss, Paul, and soon.

It was a beautiful late March morning. The most glorious blue skies, white fluffy clouds, and a hint of warmth from the sun.
There were the first signs of spring and new life in the air.
From her open window she could smell the wonderful aroma of freshly cut grass and hear birdsong. It was wonderful to think that summer was just around the corner, she thought.

Why are workdays always like this, yet weekends are wet and windy, messing up her hair and outfits when she was out on the town?

Which of course, was every weekend.

As she sat at her desk, with her elbows on it with hands holding her chin up and in a world of her own, her thoughts flicked between last night with Anton and her soon to be dumped boyfriend, David.

David was everything any *normal* girl might wish for.
■■

He was handsome, with a mop of dark brown hair and he reminded her of a young Hugh Grant, Natasha had thought on more than one occasion. He was junior partner in a Stock Brokers, had a penthouse suite in *the* most fashionable place in the city, drove a top of the range Mercedes, wore only the very best tailor made suits, was polite, opened doors for her, took her to the best restaurants, came from very well to do parents - but he was, well – boring.

Natasha had tried to be the perfect girlfriend, which it seems, is what David wanted.
But what had been the final crunch was when he had appeared in a club he knew that
Natasha would be at and told her he had come to take her home.

The cheek of the man. She was twenty five for goodness sake, not some underage teenager who shouldn't be in the place!

Oh, and the fact that he'd asked her when she was stopping smoking only three weeks in to their relationship hadn't helped either. For goodness sake, she'd not even said she was stopping (secretly, she wanted to, but hadn't disclosed this to any one). Nope, he'd have to go.

■ ■

Natasha liked the high life, but she also liked a
man to have an edge, a little sense of danger about
him, and perfect David did not tick any of those
boxes.

It would have to be done soon, she thought, whilst
nibbling the end of her pen.
She wanted someone else, and didn't want to lose
her chance, that's if she ever saw
him again.

Hmm, how to do it?
She may be sassy and outspoken sometimes, but
hated dumping men. And then a thought jumped in
to her head.
She'd have to make him dump her!
Yes, she thought, that was the answer.

***

The trilling of her phone abruptly broke her
daydreaming. Oh how she wished she knew who it
was before she picked it up.
It was most probably work related, but it could be
him and she had already decided that avoiding him
would give him the message he'd been officially
offloaded.
She picked up the phone; "Hello, this is Natasha
Johansson, can I help you?"
Luckily, the caller was Samantha from the
company's Manchester office requesting some

stock information, so she was saved from any confrontation just yet.
Still, she knew she'd have to face him sometime, and soon.

***

Natasha was Swedish by birth, as were her parents, but they'd moved here when she was a baby, brought to England by her father's work.
Natasha's parents had moved back to Sweden when she was 20 years old, but Natasha had chosen to remain in England, having an established job and vast array of friends.
Still, she visited her parents and home country often, and they spoke on the phone all the time, so she didn't miss them too much, especially with her hectic lifestyle. Who had time for parents when there was so much else going on?

Her parents were quite well off, and often indulged Natasha with gifts and large sums of money, which they sent to her even if it wasn't her birthday or Christmas. Natasha thought they did this to make up for the fact they had moved back to Sweden, leaving her behind, even though it had been her choice to stay here.

■■

She was an only child, and had been spoiled
rotten. Anything she'd asked for as a
child, she had got, and had been the envy of her
friends, especially when she had
asked for and received her very own horse,
Grayson's Lass, a beautiful palomino. She'd only
been eight at the time, and not only did she receive
Gray, her parents had bought her a pony, Sheltie,
as company for Gray. Her parents had paid for the
best riding lessons for her, and had paid for the
horses to be looked after by the local stables, so
Natasha didn't have to do a thing apart from ride
her horse or pony, whenever the feeling took her.
Anything she wanted had been hers, and so she'd
grown up to expect nothing but the best. She was
spoiled, and she often acted it, even now, if she
didn't get her own way.

She was beautiful, and was acutely aware of this.
She had the most amazing mass of platinum hair,
which ran straight down her back like a beautiful
silk curtain.
She was not too short, a nice 5'6", and a perfect
size 10.
Who wanted to be too skinny? She knew that men
liked curves, and was proud of her toned yet
womanly figure.
She had the most unusual green eyes which she
knew were her best feature, they were so
penetrating, so beautiful. They were framed with
lashes that most women would have to buy in a

box.

Her lips were full, just the right size, and she had a smattering of freckles on her cheeks and nose, which came out like a mini army when she caught the sun. This was one thing she didn't like about herself.

The freckles seemed to join up like a dot to dot riddle and she ended up looking like Adam Ant with that ridiculous stripe across his face and nose. So, she tried to avoid the sun on her face at all costs, instead opting for a spray tan when the mood took her.

Her only other flaw was a little bump in the middle of her nose from where she'd broken it when she'd fallen off of a wall when she was little.

People didn't notice this though, how could they with everything else about her being so alluring?

***

By the time Natasha arrived home after having to work well over her 5pm finishing time to hit a deadline, Carrie, her flatmate, was already there with her bottom in the air and her head in the oven.

Natasha took off her coat, threw that and her bag on to a chair in the hallway, and walked over to where Carrie appeared to be gassing herself.

"What on earth are you doing?" she asked her
friend.
Carrie jumped up, banging her head on the top of
the oven.
"Ouch!" Carrie howled, rubbing her head, "didn't
hear you come in, I'm trying to scrape what should
have been a pizza off of the bottom of the oven."

Yes, there it was.
The distinct smell of burning in the air, and
Natasha knew that once again her friend
had tried to burn their apartment down.
Carrie was so good at so many things but cooking
was not one of them.

Her silky shoulder length golden hair was
dishevelled and she had what looked like
soot on the end of her nose.
Natasha couldn't help but laugh, although it was
worrying that her friend's continued misuse of the
appliance could one day raze their apartment to the
ground.

They were already on first name terms with the
local fire brigade!

"Just leave it will you - I'll clean it up and we'll
get a take out - you're a liability and should have a
'serious health hazard' sash around your neck at
all times." Tasha retorted, laughing.
Carrie, pretending to be hurt, flipped her hair away

from her face and stormed off in to the lounge where the stereo was blasting out "Cotton Eye Joe" by the Rednex.
Such a corny song but such a feel good song too.

After a rushed takeout pizza and a light chocolate mousse (they thought that by choosing a light mousse it would somehow counteract the calorie laden pizza) , the girls were in utter chaos trying to get ready.

It may only be a Tuesday, but they were out on the town as usual, and were running late, again, as usual.

They had a ritual of getting ready together in Tasha's room with a glass (well, bottle) of wine, a packet of cigarettes, and music blaring out. Not a great idea because Tasha's room always stank of stale smoke the following day, which only made her hangover worse.

Because they always got ready like this, chattering all the way through their ritual, it took twice as long to get ready, and after squabbling over clothes and many glances in the mirror from different angles, they were ready to hit the town, already half an hour late and already a little tipsy.

***

Natasha, looked especially gorgeous tonight, her long hair left loose, which flowed down her barely covered back, and she was wearing impossibly tight hipsters and a tiny top. Carrie, with her golden blonde hair tousled in that 'just got out of bed' look which men found so sexy, was wearing a long black dress which had a slightly wet look to it and clung in all the right places.

The girls looked stunning, and they knew it.

***

Annalise was waiting for them in their usual meeting place outside a bar called Bellina's, and she did not look happy.
"I am bloody freezing, what the hell took you so long?" Annalise quizzed with a glare that would freeze hell over, whilst rubbing her arms to warm herself.
"The taxi was late Anna, so sorry."
But it was clear that they weren't all that sorry, and Annalise was not impressed - great way to start the night!
"And anyway," Natasha said, "I'm not surprised you're freezing, you forgot your clothes!"
This broke the ice and sent the three of them in to fits of giggles.

Of course, Annalise looked amazing, as always.

She was very pretty, but not in a conventional
way. Striking was probably the most
appropriate word to use, Natasha thought as she
looked at her friend.
Annalise had hair the likes you have never seen.
It was naturally jet black, so glossy, with the most
amazing hints of electric blue streaked through
which cascaded down her back in the most
amazing curls.

She worked as a top stylist in a hair salon, which
paid her 50% commission on every hair cut or
coloured, so she was paid very well.
Because of this, her hair always looked like
something out of a glossy mag.
She had sky blue eyes, which were a wonderful
contrast against that hair, and standing at a
respectable 5'3", and a size six, she was so petite,
men wanted to look after and protect her. Not that
she needed it. She may be petite, but she was as
wild as her hair.

Anna was a very independent girl by nature, not
expecting handouts from her parents, she'd often
turned down their offers of help when she was in
need, often choosing to work Godforsaken hours
at work to earn her own money, in order to pay for
the things she wanted, or for her hectic socialising.
She didn't like being beholden to anyone, and
wanted to pay her own way in this world, even

though her parents were always willing to help her out, she simply refused their offers.

She had two siblings, Robert and Gabrielle. Rob was six years older than her, and Gabby two. She was the baby of the brood, but had never been spoiled because of this. She was very close to her siblings now, but that hadn't always been the case. Because of the age difference, Rob had not had much to do with Anna when she was younger, as he was too busy being a young lad, and had no time for his little sister. Gabby had resented Anna wanting to hang around with her as they were growing up, and the two would often come to blows if Gabby found out that Anna had pinched some of her makeup or borrowed some of her clothes. There had been times when hair and nails had flown everywhere, the two having to be separated by their parents, and sent to their rooms to cool down, and told to think about what they had done, before being made to apologise to each other, which they did, but of course, never meant it.

At least, as they had grown older, the three had become closer, and now she got along brilliantly with both of her siblings, and loved them dearly. She didn't see that much of them because of their busy lifestyles, but often chatted to them on the phone, and they always met up for birthdays and Christmases.

Her ex boyfriend had been an up and coming clothes designer and as a result of this, she had some amazing outfits, original one of one's which no one else had.

Tonight she was wearing the most gorgeous two piece. A tiny cream A line skirt and matching top which tied just under her bust, showing off her amazing cleavage and abs and all year round suntan (Anna liked her sun beds).
This she'd finished off with knee high cream boots, and with her mass of amazingly wild curls, ensured she was always a show stopper.

Party girls they were, and that's the way they intended to be for as long as their faces and figures would allow.

***

∎∎∎

Chapter Two.

Once ensconced in the warmth of the bar, the girls waded through the already dense crowd (it was only 8.30) and managed in their usual style to navigate to the front of the queue with more than a few admiring glances their way.

"God, this is a nightmare," Carrie remarked. "I've not seen it this busy on a Tuesday night before."
"Must be pay day," Natasha replied, "or the fact the weather is unusually beautiful for this time of year."
"It's still bloody freezing out there at night though," Annalise scowled, still not having forgotten how long she'd had to wait outside for the other two to arrive.
"Oh do stop moaning, you daft mare," Natasha retorted. "It's spring, and we weren't
that bloody late, any one would think you'd been standing there since Christmas!"
Annalise had to laugh, she couldn't stay angry with her mates for long.

***

Even though the bar was packed, Del, the cute barman, saw them straight away and strolled over.

"What's it to be tonight then ladies?" he asked in his cocky yet cute style.

"What do you say," asked Carrie. "Sex On The Beach or a Screaming Orgasm?"

Squealing with delight the other two announced they'd like both, in that order.

Del walked away, laughing and shaking his head.

***

The music was amazing, Jamiroqui's 'Space Cowboy' was playing and the girlswere dancing away to it even though it was only a bar and there was no dance floor.

Annalise was singing along to the lyrics, and Carrie listened intently.

"What did you just sing?" she asked her friend.

"I'm singing along, what's wrong with that?" Annalise said.

"Nothing," Carrie replied, "apart from the fact that the lyrics you are singing should be 'military good vibe zone, *not* military combat zone'!"

Fits of laughter broke out between them, much to the amusement of the crowd around them.

They couldn't stop laughing.

Natasha had tears rolling down her face from laughing so much and her abs hurt from laughing so hard, she'd almost ruined her perfectly made up face, but she didn't care.

▪▪

This was what life was all about!

They were young, free and single (well, Natasha wasn't but that was an afterthought).

***

Annalise noticed a very handsome man looking over the crowds and he seemed to be looking directly at Natasha. His eyes never left her.
She nudged her friend; "Hey Tash, have you seen that gorgeous bloke over there, he can't keep his eyes off of you."

Natasha glanced in the direction Annalise was pointing and saw that it was the man she wanted, and had done for the last year.
She could feel her heart beat faster, she felt her breath catch in her throat, and could hardly breathe with the excitement bubbling up inside.

"Oh my God, it's him, it's Marcus, what should I do?" Tasha asked quickly.
"Go to the toilets, they're that way, you have to walk straight past him." Carrie replied.
"I don't know if I can, I mean, I've not finished with David yet, and, oh God, I just can't!"
"Yes you *can*!" the others shouted over the noise.
"Just go for it Tash, you don't know when or if you'll see him again." Carrie said.

Taking a very large slug of her drink to calm her
nerves, Natasha decided the girls
were right, she had to at least walk past, give him
a chance, see if he tried to even talk
to her.

"Ok girls, here I go, wish me luck." ('I think I'll
need it' she was thinking to herself).

With that, Tasha, head held high, walked down
from the podium they were standing on and slowly
made her way through the crowds, navigating so
that she would have to move past him, but not too
closely so that it didn't look too obvious what she
was doing, although she thought, any idiot in their
right mind would see exactly what she was doing.

As she neared him, every step seemed like a
lifetime. Her heart was beating so fast she thought
it would burst out of her chest, but still she carried
on, she knew she needed to do this.

***

Before she knew it, he was there, stood in front of
her, blocking her way.
She looked up at him and as his eyes bore in to
hers, she thought she might faint.
"So," he said in that wonderful voice, which she
had never forgotten. "We meet again."
It took all of Natasha's strength to mutter; "So we

do."

There seemed to be a silence which went on forever as they stared at each other, and Natasha didn't know if she could bare it.

Then he spoke again; "Me and the lads are going next door after this, I don't suppose you're going too?" he asked lazily, his eyes roaming over her body.
With her heart about to explode she replied that they were, and slowly, he said; "Well, I'll see you there then."

And then he was gone, back in to the crowds.

***

Natasha forgot that she was supposed to be going to the toilets and rushed straight back to the girls.

"Oh my *God*, he's asked me if we're going next door, and I said yes, even though I know we said no, but if…."
"Slow down Tash!" shouted Annalise above the current track playing, 'Three Lions' by the Lightning Seeds. It was nearing the end of the footie season and everyone was excited about Euro '96 which was to begin in a few months. Surely this time, England would win.

Everyone in the bar was singing along to it, and the noise was deafening.

"Start again, you're making no sense!" shouted Anna once again.

"Ok, sorry," Natasha responded, "he wants me to go to the club next door, but I know we said we wouldn't because it's a week night, and with work and everything next day - what do I do?"

"Look," Carrie said, "we'll go ok, just for an hour, that's it. We'll see what happens.

I'm not ready for home yet anyway, so what the hell!"

So with that, Natasha's fate was sealed.

***

Chapter Three.

The club was heaving, as was the bar before,
which was unusual for a Tuesday night.
But as it was buy one get one free on most house
drinks and cheap entry to the club, it seemed
inevitable, especially with the students of the city.

As usual, the girls made their way to the bar,
easily getting through the throng of people by
wiggling and squirming their way through.
They avoided the women queuing, and no man
could easily refuse to let them through.
On the rare occurrence when they did, they were
soon charmed by the flirtations of the girls.
Tasha ordered them all softer drinks this time, just
an alcopop each, so they hopefully
wouldn't suffer too much in the morning.

Then she was keenly scanning the crowds for him.
She knew he must be here already, she almost
sensed it.

And then there he was, in front of her. Just like
before.

***

The thing with Marcus was, Natasha had met him
before. Exactly one year before, to be precise.

She remembered the date exactly, 15th March 1995.

She remembers what she was wearing. She remembers what he was wearing.

She remembers seeing him for the first time and locking eyes….those wonderfully penetrating eyes…she remembers everything.

She remembers talking to him, laughing until her sides split, and dancing until the early hours.

Then, he'd asked her back to his house, but she had declined.

That was the last time she'd seen him in person - until tonight.

***

He was a footballer, so she couldn't *not* see him on TV when his match was shown, but until tonight, she'd not seen him in person, although she had thought about him often over the last twelve months.

She had always wondered what would have
happened had she gone back to his house
that night a year ago.

Bringing her thoughts back to the present, Natasha
found that in the club, the hours had sped by, the
girls had long gone, pleading for their beds, but
Natasha could not leave, not this time.

And when he asked her back home again, she
accepted.

***

Her inhibitions were gone, thanks to the cocktails,
and when they arrived at Marcus's house, she fell
into his arms.
They kissed passionately. They couldn't get
enough of each other, Natasha had waited a year
for this moment.

Finally managing to pull themselves apart, Marcus
asked her in his husky voice,
"Would you like some Champagne?"
"That'd be great, thanks." she replied, thinking it
would be just the job to stop the
butterflies in her stomach.
She watched him walk through to the kitchen,
'God his butt looks good in those jeans' she
thought. Marcus was handsome, but unlike Anton,
he was aware of this, and flauntered it. Natasha

had seen it, had seen how easily he flirted, and how easily girls literally fell for him as soon as he turned on the charm. That same charm had hooked her, she knew that, and even though she would never entirely trust him, knew she had to have him.

Marcus took a bottle of Cristal out of the giant American style refrigerator, and two long crystal flutes from a display cabinet, and they moved in to the beautiful lounge which had one whole wall of floor to ceiling windows and the most amazing view of the city which seemed to be a floor of shimmering fairy lights, lit up, just for them. They just sat there in silence. Snuggled up on the couch, not talking much, sipping Champagne, enjoying the views and the company, and mostly the closeness.

When he got up from the sofa to lead her upstairs, she went willingly, where they had taken no time, ripping at each others clothes, kissing passionately, they couldn't get to each other fast enough. They'd waited a year for this moment.

The chemistry between them was electric and they made love for hours, time after time, she'd lost count. His body felt so right, it felt so right for him to be inside her, and she couldn't get enough of him. He made her feel like no man had ever made her feel before, every fibre of her being was

alive, her aroused state wanting more and more of
him, until they could take no more.

Hours later, they had fallen in to an alcohol and
post-coital fuelled sleep, bodies entwined.

***

When Natasha awoke, bleary eyed and feeling the
effects of last night, she instinctively knew that
she shouldn't be there, but didn't know why.

She had seen some women's toiletries dotted
around, and tentatively asked Marcus "Who do
these belong to?"
He had replied that they belonged to his mother
who he had recently lost and that
having them around comforted him.

Natasha accepted this, but something just didn't
seem quite right. She couldn't put
her finger on it.

Something else bothered her.
Instead of driving her home or ordering her a taxi,
Marcus had rung his friend Lee, and asked if he
could pick Tasha up.
What was that all about? she thought.
Marcus was capable of driving her home, he had
no training that day, so that really bothered her,
but she didn't ask him.

Deep down, she didn't think she wanted to know the answer.

Still, even though she felt there was something not right regarding Marcus, she knew she had to see him again. She knew she had to have him.

***

Carrie was not impressed.
It was 7am, she felt like hell, and was not in a good mood.

As she waited for the kettle to boil, she thought of the night before.
Natasha had failed to come home. She'd not even left a message for her, and Carrie
was now wondering what the hell was going on.
Well, she figured that it had something to do with Marcus, who for some reason, she didn't entirely trust, and she was genuinely worried about her friend.

Just as Carrie was opening her car door to go to work, Natasha showed up in a black BMW, and it wasn't Marcus driving.
Natasha got out of the passenger side, said something to the driver, smiled and closed the door.
▪▪▪

She looked like she'd been dragged through a hedge backwards with her normally immaculate hair in tangles and traces of last nights' make up smudged around her eyes.

"What the hell happened to you, and who the bloody hell was that?" Carrie demanded.
"I ended up going back with Marcus. It's a long story, I'm sorry, I feel like total shit, and need a shower, I'll fill you in later."
And with that Natasha was walking away to their apartment.

'Charming' Carrie thought. 'I feel like hell because she dragged us all to a club on a weeknight and all I get is a brush off'.

I'll deal with her later, Carrie decided, as she closed the car door behind her.

***

Carrie worked in banking.

A steady job with good prospects, her Father had told her when she'd first got the job as a junior clerk after leaving school (which in layman's terms meant tea and coffee maker, getting everyone their sarnies from the local deli, and general dogsbody).

However, she'd worked hard and was now a personal banker, but it was so bloody boring sometimes.
Still, it paid very well, and kept her in a decent(ish) lifestyle.
Yet she wished for more, who didn't?

Carrie came from a working class background. Her dad had been a long distance lorry driver, and her mum owned a little café bar. Her parents had worked hard all their lives, and had instilled in Carrie the importance of this, and of being frugal with her money. They'd been fair but strict parents, and Carrie had grown up to be a very caring young lady. She had just one sibling, Mollie, who was a year older than her, and they'd been best friends growing up, Carrie remembered back. They were still the best of friends, which was unusual for sisters – they'd hardly ever fought, even when growing up. It was just a shame that her family lived so far away, in Burton-on-Trent, she would have loved to have seen Mollie and her Mum more often.
Carrie had lost her Dad when she was only twenty years old, and it had devastated her. She had always been a Daddy's girl, so they shock of losing her Dad at such a young age had almost sent her over the edge. He'd had prostrate cancer, which hadn't been caught in time, and had travelled to his liver and lymph nodes. From

finding out about the cancer, to losing him, had been a matter of weeks, and Carrie was still finding it very hard to deal with the fact she'd never see her beloved Daddy again.

She tried to keep as busy as possible, so that she didn't have too much time to think about her loss. She also worked hard, as she always wanted to make her Dad proud of her. Even though he was no longer here, she liked to think he was watching her, and was around still. This spurred her on to work hard, and she tried to keep high morals, even though at times she found this hard.

Carrie was one of those people who were naturally beautiful, inside and out, but she wasn't entirely aware of it. Others had told her this, but she hadn't believed them. She knew she was fairly pretty (the fact was she was so much more than fairly pretty, but Carrie just didn't see it).

She was even more petite than Annalise, standing at only 5'1" tall, and a size eight, but seemed so much smaller because of her height and lithe toned limbs.
Her hair, unlike her friends, was totally natural. Beautiful golden waves, a la Meg Ryan, which she wore shoulder length most of the time. She has the biggest blue eyes you've ever seen. High, almost regal cheekbones, and plump 'kiss me now' lips.

Add a body to die for, thanks to her addiction to the gym, and the biggest heart you could ever imagine, and that was the package that was Carrie.

She would do anything for any one, and was a giving person, never expecting anything in return. She really was as beautiful inside as she was on the outside.

***

In her lunch hour, Carrie decided to browse the local shops.
One good thing about her place of work was that it was on the doorstep to all themajor fashion shops. Great if you had the money, but a carefully used credit card was just as good in Carrie's eyes.

As she sauntered up St. George's Street, casually glancing in shop windows at shoes and bags she couldn't afford, she clumsily bumped in to someone and her sandwich and bag went flying, scattering the contents everywhere.
There was just the usual stuff in there, her purse, her new mobile, some make up, her diary, and some odd bits and bobs. Luckily, no tampons.

"I'm so sorry." she heard a male voice say.

Looking up, she realised it was David, Natasha's soon-to-be-dumped boyfriend.

"Oh, Hi David, don't apologise, it was my fa
not looking where I was going, I'm sorry," C
gushed. "And oh God look, you've coffee all
down your shirt, I'm so sorry!"
"No worries," David said with a wry smile, "I've
heard many a tale of Carrie and her calamities, so
it's only to be expected."

Carrie couldn't help but laugh. That cheeky cow
Tasha must be telling all sorts of tales about her,
but she didn't mind, she knew she was like an ant
on acid most of the time.

"Look, can we go to a café bar? The least I can do
is replace your coffee, and you can use the men's
room to clean up some of the mess I caused, how
about it?" Carrie asked.
"How can I resist an offer like that young lady,
come on, let's go to Shenanigan's on Camping
lane, it's not too far, and I've heard they do a
mean tuna melt on soda bread, and right now I
could murder one!"

Carrie agreed, she had always felt comfortable
with David, he was 'posh' as that was his
upbringing, but was down to earth too, and she
never felt clumsy or out of place in his company.

***
As they headed towards Shenanigans, they made

small talk, and of course, inevitably, the
conversation turned to Natasha.
"So," David asked, "how's the elusive Natasha?
I've not heard from her for a few days, and am sort
of wondering what's going on."

Carrie felt herself colouring up, she knew this
question would be asked and didn't want to be
unfaithful to her friend (as she felt she would be, if
she talked about this), but didn't like to lie to
David either.
He was a nice, decent guy who didn't deserve how
Natasha was treating him, and he didn't deserve to
be lied to either.

What a predicament to be in.

"She's ok," Carrie replied not meeting his eyes,
"busy with work as usual, busy with socialising as
usual. You know Tasha."
She knew that David could see straight through
her pathetic attempt at covering for her friend,
she'd never been a great liar.
"Oh come on Carrie, tell me, what's she really up
to?" David continued, "I get the feeling I'm on the
way out as far as your mate is concerned."
"I don't know, David, you know what Tash is
like," Carrie tried to explain. "She's not one to be
tied down, she's a party girl, you knew that when
you started dating, what more can I say?"

David seemed to think for a moment before he replied, "I know, and I knew. I knew it wouldn't last, I suppose I was hoping, stupidly, that I would be the one to tame the Lioness, I think I failed, don't you?" he said with a sad smile. "Please don't get me involved in this, David, she's my friend, and I like you, so this is very awkward for me, I don't want to get involved." "Hey, no worries, there's plenty more ladies looking for an eligible bloke like me." he laughed it off, but Carrie knew it was bothering him. "I bet there are, you stud!" she said, and with this the awkwardness seemed to be broken and they spent the rest of their time together talking, laughing, poking fun at each other, and avoiding the subject of Natasha at all costs.

***

Carrie was said when lunchtime was over. She had enjoyed herself immensely, but then thought 'God, what am I doing! This is my mates boyfriend.' Okay, soon to be ex boyfriend, she mused.

As they'd hugged their goodbyes and promised to see each other soon, Carrie gave herself a mental kick up the ass. She should not have spent time with David, it was against the rules, even though Natasha didn't deserve him.

Carrie thought yet again, 'what was Tash thinking?'
He was gorgeous, eligible, rich, funny, everything a girl could want, and yet she
didn't want him, was the girl mad or something?

'Oh. My. God.' Carrie thought, as she walked briskly back to work.

I have a crush on my best friend's boyfriend.

***

Chapter Four.

■■■

It was now April, the spring had certainly sprung, and Annalise was in a great mood.
It was Thursday, she'd booked three days off from the salon, so had four whole days of '*Me*' time.

She thought about the day ahead, with butterflies in her stomach.
She knew that she was treading on very dangerous ground.

She was secretly seeing her friend Suki's fiancé, but couldn't help herself, Max was like a drug to her, one that's hard to stop. He was her addiction, and she knew she wouldn't be able to give him up of her own free will.
It was dangerous, *he* was dangerous, he was good looking, with dirty blonde hair and chiselled, almost sharp features, but best of all, he owned an Aston Martin Vanquish!

She was due to meet up with 'her man' at the trendy Quincy's, on the London Road, for brunch, and was hoping Tash would show up with Marcus, who she'd been seeing spasmodically since their night together in March.

Annalise was still quite nervous being alone with Max in such a public place, and if Tasha turned up, she thought, it would look better if any one was to spot them.

***

Oh what to wear, Annalise was thinking.

It was now late April, so summer clothes were still out of the question, but it was so beautiful outside.

After much deliberation, and about twelve outfits later, she'd finally settled on very flattering hipster multi-striped trousers, and a top that was just the right length to show off a tiny bit of her amazing midriff - enough to keep Max wanting more, and that is what this was all about.

She wanted him, and she was going to get him, no matter the cost.

She decided to keep her hair as it was, so long that it reached the small of her back, and yet so wild in colour, a shiny jet black with electric blue streaks which she'd just had redone at her workplace…it was wild, unruly, and amazing, just like herself, she thought wickedly.

She sprayed on a little XS perfume in all the right places, picked up her fake Gucci bag (Max may buy her a real one soon, she hoped), and strolled out of the door, head held high, and so full of the joys of life.

■■■

She was a female on a mission, and as they say,
the female of the species is more deadly than the
male.

***

When she arrived at Quincy's, Annalise was
relieved to see that it was not too busy.
She didn't even look around for Max, but
sashayed straight to the bar and ordered
herself a large white wine spritzer, with two
straws.

She always wanted two straws.
It was an oddity of hers, everything had to be in
two's, or fours.   Equal numbers only, ever.

She knew the reason why - her Granddad, God rest
his soul, had always insisted on everything two at
a time.
She remembered he ate humbugs, two at a time,
and his explanation had been, "It's so one doesn't
feel lonely in my stomach!"

Ever since, Annalise had stuck by this rule, two at
a time, it was a ritual now, a part of her, and she
doubted she'd ever change. She didn't want to.

As she flirted with the barman, she felt a presence
behind her and instinctively turned around.

■■■

Max.

"Hey darling, you look amazing as usual, and smell amazing, again, as usual."
"You know how to charm a girl." Annalise retorted, "not exactly the most original chat up line that one is it?"

She intended keeping him on his toes, and decided that if by being mean to keep him keen would do it, then that what's she would do. Max was not that easy though and didn't fall for Anna's pretentious front.

He grabbed her and kissed her passionately, running his hands down her back, and grabbing her pert little bottom in a tight grasp. She melted into his arms, all her sassy front had up and left, and she gave in to her feelings for this man, who she knew was so very wrong for her. Max, as if sensing her resolve melting away, made the most of it and as he continued to kiss her. He pushed his groin up against her, knowing she would feel his arousal against her.

***

A moment of control came over Annalise, and she pushed him away slightly. She wanted to keep him wanting her, and by giving in so easily, knew she would lose him.

"Hey Mr, that's some welcome, how's you?" she managed to whisper.

Max smiled easily. He knew what he was, He knew what he looked like, and what he had. He also knew how to treat a lady, and more importantly, read a lady…and this lady certainly wanted him. Anna knew all of this, it was part of his charm.

Playing the game, he replied, "I'm the same babe, you know me, as easy as the day is long."

This infuriated Annalise.

Her charms (of which there were many, and would usually work wonders on any *normal* man) were not working on Max, and she was out of her comfort zone here.

"So," she retorted, playing along, "you're the same, I can see that. Let me rephrase….how've you been, and how is your lovely fiancée, and my friend Suki?"

She could see straight away that this had wrong footed him, and went for the kill.

"Does the delectable Suki know anything about us yet, or am I still your very dirty, very sexy, and very available, little secret?"

Annalise had ensured she'd mentioned the 'available' part in her killer line,so that he knew she was on the market to anyone who came along, just in case he thought she would wait around forever.

Max looked awkward for a while, as if either thinking of an equally devastating statement, or was totally dumfounded. Hard to tell, he was only a man after all.

"Of course she knows nothing," Max finally retorted. "For a start, my balls are still where they should be and you look okay, so I doubt she's been near you either." he quipped.
Eager to keep the banter going, Annalise continued, "So, we're safe for now then gorgeous, what would you like to drink?"

And with that, they fell in to the easy banter they were used to.

***

As Anna and Max were sat in a window seat, enjoying the warmth of a promising Summer to come, Natasha and Marcus strolled in to the bar, arm in arm, as if they were soul mates, been together forever sort of relationship, staring adoringly at each other.

'As if', Annalise thought. She knew that Natasha had spent the last month wondering when he'd call, when he'd want to see her, why he'd not called, and everything in between.

Natasha, with her platinum blonde hair pulled
back into a high ponytail, was wearing the most
inappropriate clothes for the time of year ('what's
new there then', Anna thought.), with a micro
denim skirt on, which only just covered her
bottom, and a little red summer T Shirt with the
word "Bunnies" written across her breasts.
She was also wearing killer red heels to
compliment her T Shirt.
They looked like Jimmy Choo's, but Anna knew
they weren't, there was no way Tasha could afford
those.

Annalise had to admit though, even though it was
way too early in the year for that sort of outfit,
Tasha *did* look amazing, and her toned, tanned
legs seemed to go on forever, and every man in the
place was staring at her.

Marcus was dressed down in faded denims, and a
"granddad" style shirt, open just a little at the
top…very casual, but so sexy. His dark, almost
black hair, was a little tousled, and he looked fit,
healthy, and well, gorgeous. Anna could definitely
see why Natasha was so smitten with him.

Natasha saw them straight away, and after
whispering to Marcus and kissing him on the
cheek, she ran (as fast as her shoes would allow)
over to where Anna and Max were sat.

"Hey you two, budge up, make space for two little ones!" Tasha announced.

"Are you talking about you and Marcus, or those things?" Max asked pointing to Natasha's breasts. Natasha rolled her eyes, "Don't you men ever think of anything else?"

Max pretended to think for a while, and then answered, "Nope, I don't think so," with a cheeky grin.

Before Marcus arrived with the drinks, Natasha managed to regale Anna with last nights sexual acrobatics between her and Marcus. He was fantastic in the sack, and Natasha couldn't get enough of him, in bed, and out of it. "We never slept," Natasha said. "I'm surprised you can't tell!"

"Please Ladies. It's a little too much info for me, if you don't mind!" Max laughed, enjoying the girly banter all the same. "I just hope you don't talk about me like that when I'm not around."

"Of course I don't," Anna replied, secretly winking at Natasha, who managed to keep a straight face.
***

Annalise, having studied Natasha, thought she was being too 'nice'.

She didn't think this in a bad way, but just thought
Tash may be covering up, or papering over
something.

"Do you like my new shoes Anna?" asked Tasha
with anticipation, "They are the real McCoy,
Jimmy Choo's! Marcus bought them for me."
"Are you joking?" Anna asked in amazement, and
more than a little envious.
"Nope, these babies are the real thing, look." And
with that, Tasha pulled one of the shoes off and
held it in the air like a trophy for all to see.
"Okay okay, I can see, they are the real thing,
lucky you!" Anna replied, "how on earth did you
manage to get him to buy you those?"
"Oh, it's a little apology present, for not, well,
being in touch as much as he could have been he
said," Natasha replied looking down.

Okay, Marcus was a footballer, and was away a lot
of the time when he wasn't
training, but Anna was sure that he could have
made a little more time for Tasha.
"Still, these shoes more than make up for it."
Tasha said, and this seemed to brighten up her
mood, but not before Anna had noticed.

***

Marcus soon joined them, jovial as usual,
simpering over Natasha as if she was royalty, and

greeted Anna and Max in a, "you're my best mate ever" kind of manner.

The mood had changed significantly since Tash and Marcus had arrived. It hadn't been wonderful before, as Anna was on edge being alone with Max in such a public place. But now, Annalise was beginning to wish she'd not hoped her friend would turn up.

There were some much needed, but still unspoken words between Annalise and Max, but now it seemed much harder to even make polite conversation.
Even though the four of them tried mindless banter, there was definitely a difficultness about the situation.

"I'm just off to powder my nose," said Anna with a wry smile on her face. Natasha
picked up on the message and got up to follow her.

***

Once in the Ladies, Anna took no time in asking her friend what was going on.
"What do you mean?" Tasha asked defensively.
"Well, you don't hear from him for weeks," Annalise stated, "and now here you both are, all loved up like you're newly married. Have you even berated him?"

"And what about poor David?" Anna concluded, stood there, hand on hip, waiting for an answer.

Natasha felt more than a little uncomfortable, which was unusual in front of her friend, but she knew that in her heart, what Anna was saying was true.

"He's been busy, what with training and everything like away games etc," Natasha replied.

"That's not a good enough reason though is it?" Anna replied, "he's like that Paul Young song, 'Wherever I lay my hat, that's my home'" Anna continued, on a roll now, "Are you going to keep letting him treat you like that?" she continued, "I mean, yeah, the shoes are great, but it only goes to proves he feels guilty about how he's treating you."

Natasha was now very annoyed.

"He's said he's sorry, he's been busy for God's sake, that's all, and that's a good enough answer for me," she snapped back. "And as for David, he's done and dusted, I just avoided him, he got the message." She added sarcastically.
"Charming," replied Anna. "Nice way to treat such a great guy who treat you like a ▪▪▪▪▪▪▪▪▪▪▪▪▪▪▪▪▪▪▪▪▪▪▪▪▪▪▪▪▪▪▪▪▪

princess, and you don't even have the decency to tell him to his face," she continued, "and as for God's gift out there, you do know he'll break your heart don't you?"

Natasha was nearing boiling point now, and on the defensive.

"No he won't!, I won't let him, I know what I'm doing, and you've some need to take the moral high ground haven't you? With Max the *taken* man, who just happens to be engaged to our friend, Suki!" she snapped back.

And with that, Natasha turned on her heels, and marched out of the room.

***

Chapter Five.

Natasha decided it was time to leave, and now. She returned to the table before Annalise had even left the toilets, and without even sitting down, she quickly slugged back her drink.

"Come on, we're going," she said to Marcus.
"What? Why?" Marcus asked, confused.
"Don't ask, just come on, I want to go somewhere else." she snapped.

They made their excuses to a rather bemused Max, and had left the bar before Anna had even reappeared.

***

Once inside Marcus's Lotus, he turned to Tasha and said "What was that all about, I was enjoying myself?"
"Oh, please don't ask! Annalise is so infuriating, I just had to get away before I said anything further to ruin our friendship."

Marcus looked very concerned and after a short silence he asked her once again what was wrong.
"Oh for goodness sake Marcus, why the third degree? If you must know it was about you. She thinks you're taking me for a mug, and I defended you, simple as that. I wouldn't mind, but who's she to talk, knocking off her friends fiancé!" Natasha almost shouted, she was that angry.
"Oh, I see," was all Marcus replied.
"What?" Natasha snapped, "you *see*?, You don't *see* anything!" she continued, taking all of her anger and frustration out on him.
"And I think Anna's right, you are taking me for a mug. We spend a couple of nights

together, and apart from a couple of brief drinks and the odd phone call, I've not heard from you. Then I get these shoes, what are they for exactly? To stop the little lady from being annoyed?"
Natasha was in full throttle now.
"Well, get this Mr, this little lady *is* annoyed."
And with that, Natasha opened the car door to get out.

"Tasha, stop, please, we need to talk." Marcus pleaded.
"We'll talk when I can fit you in, see how *you* like the silent treatment for a change."

And with that, she slammed the door shut and stormed off.

There, she thought, that'll show him. He thought more about that bloody car than he did of her.

***

Great. Now she'd fallen out with one of her best friends, and her boyfriend, all in the space of five minutes. What a great day this was turning out to be - not.

***

Annalise returned to the table and was confused as to where Tasha and Marcus where.

"Where've they gone?" she asked Max.

"Don't ask me," Max replied looking up at her, "Natasha came storming out of the loo like a scud missile, grabbed Marcus and literally marched him outside the bar, he didn't even get to finish his drink."

This worried Anna, she'd gone too far, and she knew it. But she'd told the truth and had only done so because she was worried about her friend.

She could have gone about it in a much better way she realised now, and asked Max if he minded if she left.

She didn't want to leave Max, they had so little time together as it was, but this was important, and she needed to do it.

She wanted to find Natasha and apologise.

"No probs babe, I'll call you later in the week." Max responded easily.

She bent down to where he was still sitting and passionately kissed him (that should keep him sweet, she thought), and then went off in search of her friend,

Though she realised, she had no idea where to look.

***

Once out on the pavement, Anna realised the drink
she'd had had gone to her head, she felt a little
tipsy and it was only 12.30. Oh dear, that's what
drinking in the day, and on an empty stomach does
for you.

She looked around, but Natasha was nowhere to
be seen.
She rummaged in her bag for her mobile, and
tapped in her friend's number.
After a couple of rings, Natasha answered,
"What?" was all she said, and not in a very
friendly tone either.
"Where are you Tash, I need to see you, I am so
sorry." Anna said, soothingly.
Anna sensed that Tasha's anger was subsiding,
and she told Anna that she was in The Nursery
Tavern, across the road.

Anna made her way over to the Tavern, and found
Tasha sat in a corner on her
own, nursing yet another glass of wine.

"Oh babe, I'm so sorry, I really am, it's just I'm so
worried about you."
With this, and her frustrations over Marcus's
behaviour recently, she couldn't help it, Natasha
burst into tears.

"No, I'm sorry," Natasha managed to sniffle, "I shouldn't have spoken to you like that, and you're right, the truth does hurt, I'm so worried about Marcus," she continued, "I've tried to cover it up, but I think I'm in love with him, and it hurts like hell that he hardly ever calls, and I've only seen him a couple of times since our last night together. I don't know what to do Anna."

Annalise thought for a moment.

She had to word this carefully, as she didn't want to offend Tasha any more than she already had done.
"Natasha, please, don't get mad with me, but do you think there's any possibility that
Marcus may be seeing someone else?" she asked.
"The only reason I say this is because I've seen the signs. I'm 'the other woman' too remember."
Anna continued, "Only I know I am, whereas you don't."

She paused for a few moments before she continued, "I have no proof of course, but I just think there's something not right, I mean, look at you, you are absolutely gorgeous, yet he's as elusive as Jack the bloody Ripper, there's something not right here sweetheart." Anna concluded.

Natasha knew what Anna was saying could be true, she'd tried to deny it to herself, but she'd had her own suspicions on the subject.

She finally replied, "I didn't want to admit it Anna, but I think you might be right. I know how busy he is, especially at this stage in the season, but I know for a fact he could have made more time for me if he'd wanted or was able to."

Anna stayed silent as Natasha continued, "And there's something else I've not told anyone. When I was at his house, there were a few feminine things dotted around, not many, but a few. Enough to make me wonder," Tasha said. "I questioned him and he told me they had belonged to his Mum who he'd recently lost and that having that stuff around comforted him. Surely he wouldn't make that up, how sick would that be?"

Natasha blew her nose on a tissue Anna has given her and lit a cigarette (she was trying to stop, but was way too stressed at present).
As she took a long drag, Natasha stated, "Plus, he had his mate pick me up from his house when he could have driven me home himself, or even called me a taxi, don't you think that's a bit weird?"
■■

Annalise sat there, taking it all in.
Something was definitely not right.
She'd had the feeling before, but now Tasha had
revealed all this, she was sure that Marcus was up
to no good, but she didn't know how to help her
friend.

"I don't know what to say to make you feel better,
but I've never trusted him, Tash. I know I'm not
one to talk about trust, but you're my friend and
when it comes to friends, I am one hundred per
cent trustworthy and I am worried about you."
Annalise said.
(She conveniently forgot at this point that she
herself was seeing her friend's fiancé).
"He's a footballer," Anna continued, "always bad
news if you ask me, so all I can say is, if you insist
on seeing him, just be careful, I do think there may
be someone else involved in all this."
"I'm here for you ok?, that's all I can say. I can't
make you stop seeing him, but I would if I could,
because I think he's bad news." Anna finally
finished her lecture.

With that, Annalise leaned over and gave her
friend a much needed hug, which only
made Natasha burst in to tears again.

Oh dear, Anna thought, she really does love him,
and what the hell can I do to help?

***

Carrie had a conscience that was playing games
with her, and she wasn't happy with it.

She could not stop thinking about David, and
although he and Natasha were over, it was still
against the rules in her book, to date a friend's ex.

Anyway, who's to say David even liked her? She
knew he thought of her as a friend,
and they'd chattered on the phone several times
over the past couple of weeks, but that was all.

As she sat snuggled up on the sofa, with her
favourite old, but oh so comfortable
dressing gown on, and a mug of steaming hot
chocolate, the phone rang.

"Hello?" she answered in her usual quirky way.
"Hi Carrie," she recognised the dulcet tone of his
voice straight away, so needed no introduction, but
he gave one anyway.
"It's David, how're you?"
He must be a mind reader, Carrie thought, she'd
only minutes before been thinking
about him, and here he was, at the end of the
phone.
"I'm fine thanks, all snuggled up with a mug of
creamy hot chocolate, just the
■ ■

ticket for a girl sat in on her own on a Thursday night with no idea where her mates are," Carrie replied. (Natasha hadn't returned home, and Carrie was beginning to wonder where she was).
"Oh that's a shame, I was hoping I could tempt you out for a bite to eat?" he asked eagerly.
Carrie's heart skipped more than a few beats.

Did this mean anything, or did David like her too? What to do, he was her mates ex!

"Erm, what were you thinking, I'm not even near ready to go anywhere." Carrie answered.
"I just thought to that new Thai place on Glossop road, heard the food's amazing, do you fancy it?"
Carrie's conscience was now in overdrive…what to do, what to do!
Not wanting to think about it any further she replied, "How long were you thinking, I'd need an hour to get ready?"
"An hour? For goodness sake, why do women take so bloody long to get ready?" he replied laughing.
"An hour or nothing, that's it, up to you now, Mr."
"Okay, okay, I give in, an hour it is. I'll pick you up at 8.30 then, alright?"
"Yes, but make it 8.45, just in case."
He laughed, agreed, and hung up.

Oh dear, what am I getting myself in to Carrie thought, as she dashed to the bathroom to shower quickly.

***

Chapter Six.

That same old predicament.

What. To. Wear.

Carrie was showered and moisturised, sprayed liberally with her favourite Chanel No.5 perfume (hey, if it was good enough for Marilyn Monroe, it was good enough for her).

She had dried and tousled her beautiful golden mane quickly, applied seductive makeup, but still managed to look fresh faced, she had a knack with that. She was only twenty-three, so didn't need that much make up any way.
So, now she was stood in her bedroom, wearing her white balconette bra (which showed major

cleavage), a matching lace thong, and nothing else.

Where was Tasha when she needed her?

Mind you, thinking about it, Tash was the very last
person she should be asking about
clothes advice, seeing as she was going on a date
('was it a date' she thought?) with Tasha's ex.

S.H.I.T.!

Carrie glanced at her watch, it was 8.35, and
David would be here in ten minutes, or less, if she
knew him like she thought she did.
She didn't want to look like she'd made too much
effort, but he was taking her to a swanky new
restaurant, so she had to wear something
appropriate, and secretly, she wanted to impress
him.

There was nothing for it, she had to borrow
Tasha's red dress.
They were different sizes but as the dress was so
tight, she thought she'd get away with it. And even
though Carrie was a couple of inches shorter, she
was sure she could pull it off with the right heels.

She went to Natasha's room and retrieved the
beautiful dress from her wardrobe, just hoping
Tash wouldn't mind, but she'd worry about that
later.
■■

And anyway Carrie reasoned, her friend owed her one after that "night out" fiasco.

***

She was right, the dress fit like a glove, she looked beautiful, and she knew it.
The dress was a full length halter neck, beautiful flowing satin material which skimmed over her flat stomach and toned hips.
It was backless, a little too backless to be honest, it only just covered the top of her bottom. But it showed off her amazing back wonderfully. Being a gym fanatic, she knew her toned, slightly muscled back was one of her best features.

Luckily, because her hair was shoulder length, she didn't have to take it up to reveal the beauty of the back view of herself.
The bra had to go of course, but who cared, the dress was double lined in that part, so she was sure she'd be covered enough. Her firm, pert breasts didn't need to be held up, so going braless wasn't something she needed to worry about.

As she was adding some tiny diamond earrings, the doorbell rang, and she was suddenly flustered.

Oh Good Lord, this was it.

Grabbing her diamante-encrusted clutch bag, and taking one last glance in the mirror, and then checking she'd got all she needed, she headed downstairs.

***

"Wow!" was all David said, when Carrie opened the door to him. He just stood there, staring at her in wonder.
"Aren't you going to say anything else?" Carrie asked coyly.
"Yes, Wow again! You look amazing."
Carrie could feel her cheeks flushing, but luckily David didn't seem to notice.
"Are we ready to go then?" Carrie asked.
"Erm, yes, yes of course, sorry. You. You're appearance just threw me for a moment there. I didn't realise...."
"Realise what?" she asked.
"Just how, well, gorgeous you are."
He was silent for a moment and then said, "Well, I know you're gorgeous, but I've never seen you looking so gorgeous, if you know what I mean."

Carrie grinned like the cat who'd got the cream, and a helping of seconds to boot.

Yes, she knew what he meant.......

■■■

He held open the car door for her, which she found so chivalrous in this day and age, and she got in carefully, legs together, as she'd seen in the glossy mags.
The last thing she wanted to do was show him a flash of her, well, you know what.

He had the stereo on, playing soft classical music, which she found soothing, and soclassy. This man oozed class, she was amazed, Natasha could not see it.

"You smell lovely," he said, once they were driving. "What is that perfume you're wearing?"
"It's Chanel No.5, my favourite," Carrie replied and was about to say, "if it's good enough....." but David beat her to it. "Hey," he said, "if it's good enough for Marilyn Monroe, it's good enough for you, right?"
"Right." she smiled. She felt so in tune with this man, she hoped that she wasn't making a mistake. By doing so, it could break her heart, and damage a friendship she'd had since childhood.

She was prepared for this one night. It was make or break in her mind.
If things progressed, then she would have to tell Natasha and risk losing her friendship (not that she thought Natasha deserved this man at all after the way she'd treated him), and if things didn't, then she hadn't lost anything, had she? Apart from

someone who could possibly be the love of her life.

***

They pulled up outside the restaurant, luckily, one space left. In his usual manner, David opened the door for her to get out. Such a gentleman. As they walked to the restaurant, just a few steps, he took her hand, and she felt shivers down her spine, the tiny hairs on the nape of her neck bristled. She was falling for this wonderful man, and there was nothing she could do about it.

The doorman opened the door for them, and thanking him, they entered the restaurant.

***

Carrie was hugely impressed with the place. It had high ornate ceilings, Romanesque style columns, and was so eloquently decorated in creams and golds, in an understated, yet elegant style.

The restaurant was an old building, this had previously been a bank, only recently refurbished and changed into this stunning restaurant.

The Maitre D, who seemed to know David, greeted them, and they were shown to one of the best tables in the place, right by the windows, but in a quiet corner, which seemed so intimate.

The MD must know David well, Carrie mused, wondering how many women had sat at this table before her.

The service was excellent. A waiter brought over their menus and explained the specials of the night. Carrie had no say in her choice of drink, David ordered Dom Perignon for them both straight away, not that she was complaining. The bottle arrived quickly, complete with a silver ice 'bucket' on an elegant stand. David didn't ask her, he just picked up her glass and poured, bubbles brimming to the top. He did he same for himself, and settled back, staring straight at Carrie.

He lifted his glass and seemed to toast her. "To the most beautiful woman in here. No, to the most beautiful woman in South Yorkshire, at the very least!" and with that he took a sip of the very expensive Champagne. Carrie picked up her glass tentatively, and took a small sip. The bubbles danced wonderfully playful tunes on her tongue, and she languished the taste and feeling of the Champagne in her mouth.

"And to you, the most eligible bachelor in South Yorkshire, at the very least!" she toasted, teasing him back.

David smiled easily back at her.

***

Carrie intrigued him.

He admitted to himself that he had not given any other girl a second's thought whilst he was seeing Natasha, but now he knew for certain, Natasha was not the one for him.

He knew he would never live up to her, 'I want the fairytale, highly demanding' lifestyle. He doubted any man would, and pitied her for that.

Carrie was on a different level altogether, but you had to get through the layers, to realise what an amazing beauty, inside, and out, she was. And what was more intriguing, Carrie had absolutely no idea how perfect she really was, he mused.

***

The waiter returned to ask for their order, and Carrie, not being used to Thai food, said she would have the same as David.

Perusing the menu, David told the waiter what they wanted to order. 'Tord Man Plah' to start with, which was a delicious dish of Thai Fish Cakes, made with specially imported curry paste, and was served with a sweet chilli sauce and ground peanuts.

Carrie thought the name of the first course sounded like a Klingon, and giggled.

David looked at her enquiringly, but she just smiled, whilst trying to suppress her laughter by taking another sip of her drink.

For the main course, he ordered them both 'Pad Preow Wahn', which was a dish of crunchy pork, fried in a delicious, Thai style sweet and sour sauce.

Carrie thought the dishes sounded delicious, and her taste buds were already in overdrive in the anticipation of the arrival of their first course.

Taking a sip of Champagne, Carrie looked over at David, who was staring at her intently. "What are you thinking?" she asked him.

"Just how lucky I am to be here with you. I think I am the envy of every man in here.

I've been watching, and you've had more than your fair share of admiring glances." David smiled.

Carrie knew she was pretty, but was totally unaware exactly how beautiful she really was, and was suddenly feeling quite shy.

She wasn't used to such praise and didn't know how to answer, so she passed it off jokingly, "Oh, they're probably all gay and are looking at you." she laughed.

"Don't be so quick to pull yourself down." David replied, his eyes never leaving hers. "You're a stunner, surely you know that. I don't know why I ever went with Natasha when I should have pursued you."

"How do you know I would have been interested." Carrie quipped, "that's rather presumptuous, don't you think?" she said, teasing him.

"I don't," he replied, "but I have a feeling that you would have been. I have a feeling you are." he said, still staring at her.

Carrie was now feeling a little out of her depth. She didn't know how to deal with her feelings about David, mainly because of Natasha, and what her reaction would be.

"I may have," Carrie eventually replied, taking another sip of her Champagne, "but we're in a rather difficult situation aren't we?"

"Why are we?" asked David, with a confused look.

"Because of Natasha." Carrie deadpanned.

"Oh, I see," David seemed to think for a moment before replying. "But she has no interest in me, so why should there be a problem?"

'Men just don't understand the unwritten rule about not dating a friend's ex', Carrie thought ruefully, and told him this.

"But, I happen to like you Carrie, very much so, and I don't see why Natasha should
be a problem. She dumped me remember. Surely she will understand."
"Is there even an 'us'?" Carrie asked, suddenly feeling a little braver.
"I'd like to think so," David replied. "I would like to get to know you much better,and to be honest, I do think about you a lot, you take up a lot of space in my head young lady, especially when I should be working. It would be a shame if we didn't give this a chance Carrie."

Carrie was delighted to hear that she took up much of his time, and replied, "I suppose you're right, but I just hope Natasha see's it that way. She is very highly strung remember, and even though she was the one who did the dumping, she may still make a fuss about this, and that does worry me."
Still staring in to his eyes, Carrie finished by saying. "But I'm willing to take that chance David, if you are."

And with that, he leaned over the table and kissed her lightly on the lips.

***

The dinner had been delicious, Carrie had savoured every mouthful of the delicious Thai Fish Cakes and the Crispy Pork dish. She was now a converted Thai food fanatic, she'd never tasted anything like it.

If only she could cook like this, instead of her speciality dish of beans, cheese, and mushrooms on toast.

The conversation had flowed easily, as if they had known each other a lifetime, and Carrie could feel herself falling even further for the gorgeous man.

When the waiter returned to ask if they wanted to view the dessert menu, Carrie had declined. She was already stuffed, and didn't want to end up looking like a pot bellied pig with this clingy dress on.

Instead, they'd ordered coffee, and sat in quiet contemplation, both completely sated.

Carrie felt as if something special was just starting.

***

Chapter Seven.

By the time David dropped Carrie back home, it was gone 1am, yet it had seemed they had only been together for minutes. She could not get enough of him, and wanted so much to take this further and invite him in, but knew that was a very bad idea for two very obvious reasons. One, you never sleep with someone on a first date, and two, Natasha was in there.

Instead, they said their goodbyes.

He leaned over and kissed her very tenderly on the lips. Every single hair on Carrie's neck was standing on end, she was almost shaking with excitement. His kiss intensified and she responded, kissing him back passionately.

She knew, from this kiss alone, that when she did sleep with him, it would be absolutely mind blowing. She couldn't wait!

***

With regret, she said her goodbyes and got out of the car. David was going to come around to open the door for her, but she insisted there was no need. "I'll call you tomorrow, if that's okay?" he asked her.
"Of course it is, I can't wait, David. Talk to you tomorrow."

And with that, she shut the car door and walked towards her apartment, doing her best wiggle, knowing that he would be watching her.

David, being the gentleman he was, waited until she was safely inside before driving away. He watched her figure sway in that wonderful womanly way, and felt his arousal. He was falling for Carrie, he just knew it.

***

Carrie peeked in to Tasha's bedroom to check that she was back home safely, and was glad to see that she was tucked up in bed asleep.

She wasn't ready to talk to her about David yet. It was her little secret for now, and one she cherished.

But she knew that the conversation would have to happen soon, because she had the feeling that this was 'the real thing' between her and David.

She only hoped Natasha saw it that way.

Carrie tiptoed into her room, carefully took off the dress (hoping she could have it dry cleaned and returned to Natasha's wardrobe before her friend realised it was missing), and wiped off her make up.

After slathering her youthful face with moisturiser (she didn't really need it as yet, but believed that prevention was better than a cure), she got into bed, and instantly fell in to a wonderfully deep sleep, and of course, she dreamed of David.

***

Carrie awoke to the annoying noise of that bloody alarm clock, which meant work.

'"Bloody thing!" she mumbled grumpily.

Slowly, and without opening her eyes, she reached out her arm, and fumbled around in the dark for the off button.

It was 6.30am, and as she'd had little sleep and a little too much Champagne the night before, she

did not feel like working at all today, and was
seriously considering throwing a sicky.
She knew this was impossible though, she had an
important client to see today, so having the day off
was not an option.

Turning on her bedside lamp, she rummaged in
her bedside table, and found paracetamol, and
swallowed two with several large gulps from a
glass of water which she always kept on her table.

Dragging herself out of her still much needed bed,
and still more than half asleep, she remembered
the night before, and all her emotions came
flowing back. 'God he was gorgeous, how lucky
was she!' She thought as she threw on her faithful
dressing gown and made her way to the bathroom.

***

In the shower, as she stood under the powerful,
wonderfully soothing warm water, she couldn't
stop thinking about him. His eyes, so blue and so
penetrating, his sensual full mouth, his high,
almost chiselled cheekbones, that gorgeous mop of
dark brown hair, and that voice, so eloquent, and
so very sexy. She was amazed she'd managed to
bag herself a man like that!

"Hellooooo!" brought Carrie back to the present.

Natasha was in the bathroom and was peeking around the curtain.

"Oi!" exclaimed Carrie, "can't a girl have any privacy!" she laughed.

"Sorry!, just wondered if you wanted some tea and toast?"

Just the thing I need, Carrie thought, after last night.

She knew that black coffee was supposed to be *the* drink for a hangover, but also knew it just dehydrated you further.

"Yes please, I'll be out in a mo." she replied.

***

Padding through to the kitchen, she saw that Natasha was already sat at the table, nibbling on a piece of toast, with the radio on low in the background playing Toni Braxton's 'You're making me high'. Hmmm, Carrie thought, how appropriate.

"Good Morning, again." Natasha said, "here, sit down, everything is already here for you."

Carrie gladly sat down, and took a big gulp of tea. There, she was feeling better already.

"So" Natasha inquired, "what happened to you last night?"

Carrie hadn't expected this question straight away, and was hoping that Natasha had got in and just gone straight to bed without noticing her absence.

Thinking quickly, Carrie said, "Oh, Jasmine called, asked me if I fancied a drink, so we just went down to the Oak Tree."

God, she hated lying, especially to one of her best friends.
She'd have to remember to phone Jasmine this morning and ask her to cover, just in case Natasha asked.

"How is she? I've not seen her for ages." Natasha asked.
"Oh fine, you know Jasmine, she's always fine. I don't know if I know anyone who is that happy all the time! I wonder if she's on happy pills or something." Carrie laughed.
"Any gossip to tell me then, at least?" inquired Tasha, through a mouthful of toast.
"Well, she's got another new boyfriend," smiled Carrie wryly, "Apparently she's
having the best sex of her life. His name's Simon, and he works at Bellina's of all places. He's that cute new guy with the dimple in his chin, remember?"

"She knows how to pick them," Carrie continued, "Apparently, he's an absolute *God* in bed, and get this, apparently he his hung like a horse!"

The girls collapsed into fits of giggles, which Carrie couldn't stop. All well and good, but it wasn't helping her hangover.

Carrie knew all of this news already, as she'd spoken to Jazz only a couple of days before, which now proved to be a stroke of luck.

"We'll have to meet up with her and Mel soon, I've not seen them for ages," Natasha replied. "A good old girls night out again, huh, the whole gang back together?"

Just the ticket, Carrie thought, yes, just what she wanted.

***

Chapter Eight.

Annalise was in bed.

It was quite late on a Saturday morning, and the
late April sun was warm through her open
window. Oh the joy that Summer was only around
the corner. Another day off, when the salon would
be packed solid, she felt so lucky.
She turned over and looked at him still sleeping.
He was beautiful. Probably the wrong word to use
to describe a man, but he really was beautiful,
Anna thought as she continued to stare at Max.

As if he knew he was being watched, he opened
his eyes and lazily smiled that oh so sexy smile of
his, just for her.

"Morning sexy," he said, "how long have you been watching me?"

"I wasn't watching you," Anna replied indignantly, "I just happened to be looking at you when you woke up."

"Yeah, sure babe." he said, whilst pulling himself up on to one elbow, to be on eye level with her.

God, he was so infuriating, but that was one of the things that attracted her to him.

He reached over and grabbed her. Pretending to try to squirm away, Annalise giggled and gave in, allowing herself to be pulled in to his arms.
He kissed her deeply, and she could feel him becoming aroused. She'd never known a man with such a high sex drive.

He took no time for foreplay this time, he rolled on top of her and parted her legs with expertise.
Before she could complain, he was inside her, and she melted, he felt so good, it felt so good, and she moaned slightly as he began to move in and out of her.
She wrapped her legs tightly around his back and moved with him, biting him, sucking him, kissing him.
She could feel her arousal mounting and knew she was nearly there. "Oh Max, please, faster." He started to thrust in and out of her a little faster,

kissing and nibbling her neck and ears, and there it was, she was coming in massive waves of pure erotic delight. Max pumped even harder until he was coming himself.

Anna glanced up at him, taking great pleasure in the post-coital glow of his face.

He stayed inside her for a while, kissing her face and tenderly kissing and licking her neck which delighted her, and then pulled away, and lay once again, by her side.

"That was a nice surprise," Anna sighed, "the best start to my morning for a while." she smiled at him. His dark blonde hair was tousled, and she thought he'd never looked so gorgeous.

"And mine too, you sexy little minx," Max laughed. "Do you fancy round two, or a cuppa?"

"Charmer!" Anna laughed, "I think I'll settle for a nice cuppa for now, then maybe seconds a little later." she smiled back at him as she lay back down and snuggled under the covers.

***

Max staying over was a rarity.

Because he was otherwise 'engaged', he often found it hard to make excuses to stay out all night, but Suki was on a hen night in Prague, so he had the weekend free, and intended to spend as much as he could with Anna.

***

As Max stood waiting for the kettle to boil, he thought about her.
He'd not admitted it to her, he was way too cocky for that, but he was falling for her, even though he'd promised himself this was only ever going to be a fling.

Falling for Annalise had not been a part of his plan.

He loved his fiancée, Suki, of course he did, but his feelings for Annalise seemed to be taking over, and at present, he didn't know what he was going to do about it.

***

Taking the steaming mugs of tea up to the bedroom, Max suggested they go for a drive in the country later, as the weather was so beautiful. Maybe they could grab a bite to eat at a nice cosy little country pub somewhere.

This delighted Annalise. A day out in the country with her man, and in the Vanquish!
Did it get any better than this?

"Fantastic idea sexy, now come back to bed, I've something to show you."

And with that, seconds had arrived before they knew it.

***

As Max expertly steered the sports car around the bends in the country roads, Anna could not have been happier. She loved Max, she knew that, although she'd never tell him, unless of course, she achieved her goal and managed to steal him off Suki for good.

She liked Suki, but not enough to lose her as a friend, if it meant gaining Max full time.

Louise's 'Naked' was blasting out on the stereo, and Anna was in her absolute element.

Max was speeding, 'why have an Aston Martin and drive like a Driving Instructor' was his motto.

The beautiful, Derbyshire countryside flew by, but Anna hardly noticed, she was just so excited at being with Max for the whole weekend.

They arrived at Hathersage, a quaint little historic village in Derbyshire, in record time, thanks to Max's need for speed.

Choosing The Scotsman's Pack for a bite to eat, Max parked up, and they walked inside arm in arm, Max glancing back at the car one last time to ensure it was parked carefully and locked. It was his pride and joy.

Annalise went to find a table, whilst Max went to the bar to order some drinks. A glass of white wine for Anna, and a Coke for him. He wasn't risking losing his licence for any one, not with a car like that at his disposal.

As soon as Annalise walked through the lounge area, she stopped in horror, stuck to the spot, like a rabbit caught in headlights.

Over in the corner, were Suki's parents, Kath and Pete.

Oh. My. God.

What the *hell* do we do now! she thought.

She was about to make a rapid escape to warn Max, but it was too late. Pete had looked up and waved her over.

SHIT.

If she'd had a shovel, she would have dug herself
a hole there and then and crawled right in to it, she
literally had no idea what to do, and no way of
warning Max.

***

Putting on her best fake smile (even though she
was shaking like a leaf), she waved back and made
her way over.

"Hi Anna love, what brings you out here?" asked
Pete.
"Err, I, I mean we, we've just popped out for a bite
to eat. I'm with Max. He's alone cos of Suki
being away, and I offered to take him out to
lunch."

Pete frowned for a moment. Anna knew he must
be thinking that it didn't sound right at all, Max
being out with her, the minute Suki's back was
turned.

"So where is Max then?" Pete asked sharply.
"He's just at the bar, he'll be here in a minute."
"Well, sit down then, you may as well join us,
now that you're here." Kath said.

Anna knew she was only being asked to join them so they could keep an eye on her and Max, and was feeling the start of a panic attack coming on. She took a couple of deep breaths, and just wished she had a drink inside her to calm her nerves.

Max walked through smiling, that was, until he saw who Annalise was sat with. Anna turned and saw a flicker of panic on his face, but only a flicker. Max could compose himself when need be, she was sure he'd talk his way out of this for them both.

Without hesitating, Max strolled over to where they were all sitting with a big grin on his face.

"Hi Kath, Pete. How're you doing?" Max asked with a false air of confidence.
"We're fine thank you Maxim." Kath replied, "we were just wondering what you're doing out here, with Anna?"

Annalise shot him a warning glance, but she had no need to. Max was charm personified, and if any one could get them out of this sticky situation, he could.

Lying through his back teeth, Max replied, "I was due to be out with Anna's boyfriend Shay, but he's decided to go to the match which I didn't fancy, so I brought Anna along instead."

Anna didn't even have a boyfriend, so she gave herself a mental note to give him a pat on the back for his quick thinking.

Both Kath and Pete looked doubtful, but seemed to accept this explanation. What else could they do apart from outright accuse him of cheating on their daughter, thought Anna?

They had no proof of this, so could hardly do that, but this was still a dubious situation, and one she'd be glad to be out of.

***

The situation was highly tense, and Anna was not enjoying it. She was sure the others must feel the same. She felt way out of her depth, and more than a little guilty in the presence of Suki's parents.
She'd known them for a long time, and she was sure they could what she was up to with their daughter's fiancé.

Breaking the awkward silence, Max said, "Right then, any one for another drink?"
"No thank you." Kath replied, "we were just about to leave, enjoy the rest of your day won't you, and I'm sure Suki will be pleased to hear you're looking after Anna whilst her boyfriend is at the

game." Kath stated, her almost black eyes bore straight in to Max.

It was a warning, Max knew, and he also knew he was up the creek without a paddle when Suki got to hear of this.

***

Chapter Nine.

It had once again been weeks since she'd heard from Marcus, and Natasha was beginning to give up hope.

For goodness sake, look at her! She was amazing looking, a body to die for, and was usually so self assured and confident, and yet Marcus had managed to reduce her to this.

Every time the phone rang, her heart leapt, but it was never him, and she was deeply hurt by his silence.

***

It was a Friday, the 10th of May, and thank
goodness, work was finished in, looking at
her watch, twenty minutes. Thank God for that.
Two days off, and she needed them.
All this stressing over Marcus who was *awol*
again, was doing her no favours, and she could not
even begin to count the sleepless nights she'd had.

Still, she was looking forward to later. It was a
big girls night out! Anna and Carrie would be
there of course, but so would Jazz, Mel, and Lucy.
Six of them, it would be fantastic.

Carrie was already home when Natasha arrived,
but luckily she'd left the long suffering oven alone
this time.
"Hi you, are you ready for tonight, I am *so*
excited!" exclaimed Carrie.
"Sure am. It's just what I need, and I'm pretty
sure I won't bump into 'you know who' because
he's got a game tomorrow, and he's not allowed
out on the night before a match."

God, it made him sound like a naughty school boy,
which is exactly what Natasha was starting to

think, because that's exactly how Marcus was behaving.

Idiot, she fumed.

***

"I've got a surprise for you." said Carrie excitedly.
"What?" asked Natasha.
"This." Carrie opened a bag and held out the most beautiful dress Natasha thought she had ever seen. It was a shimmering silver full length dress, which obviously was meant to be skin tight. It had great big holes cut out of each side, and the only thing holding the top of the dress to the bottom of it, were two silver rings, one on the front, and one on the back.

"My God Carrie, what've you bought me that for, it must've cost you a fortune!"
"Well, not really, we have this guy who pops in work sometimes with some, shall I say, dodgy gear. Not sure where he gets it, but when I saw this, it said 'Natasha' all over it, and I just had to get it for you." Carrie replied.

Natasha was stunned, truly stunned. The dress was amazing, and she could not believe the kind gesture of her friend.

"You must let me reimburse you." Natasha insisted, but Carrie was having none of it. Instead, Carrie said she'd like a quick chat, and a favour, and asked, if at all possible, that Natasha did not get mad at her.

There it was. Natasha *knew* there had to be a reason for this gesture.
"Okay" she sighed. "What have you done now?"
"Before you try the dress on, just come and sit in the lounge for a bit, there's something I need to tell you, Tash".

Pouring them each a large glass of red wine, Carrie walked through to the lounge where Tasha had already parked her bum on the edge of the sofa. She hadn't relaxed back, she had a feeling she wasn't going to feel relaxed for some reason.

"Here, have this." Carrie said, passing Tasha the glass of wine.

Blimey, it must be bad, wine at this time, they usually only started drinking when they were getting ready.

"Okay" Carrie sighed, looking down, trying to compose herself, "I'm in love with someone, and I think they feel they same about me." Carrie blurted out.

_____

"Well, that's great news, surely! Why the dramatics over that, it's fantastic news Carrie!" Natasha was genuinely pleased for her friend.

"You may not think so when I tell you who it is." replied Carrie. Taking a gulp of her wine, and a deep breath, she looked up at an expectant Natasha and said, "It's David, your ex."

Natasha looked blank for a second, just sat there digesting this new information.

Eventually she asked, "What, When, How did this happen? How long has this been going on?" Carrie, looking very sheepish and more than a little guilty looked up and said, "Just a few weeks, I've only seen him on a handful of occasions, and we've talked on the phone," Carrie continued, "we grew close when you dumped him, I suppose at first I was a shoulder to cry on, but then we realised there was more to it, more between us. I'm so sorry Natasha, for deceiving you, but I can't help it, I'm in love with him."

Natasha was silent for what seemed like an eternity, and then finally spoke, "I'm not mad about that Carrie, I didn't treat him well, and he wasn't right for me. What does hurt though, is that you've only just told me. Why did you hide it from me, lie to me even?"

"I didn't want to hurt you, I didn't want to break the unspoken rule of 'never date your mates ex', I tried, honestly," Carrie continued, "and I didn't know if it was going any where at first, so I didn't tell you straight away, in case there was nothing to tell."

"Ok, don't worry, Carrie, I understand. I don't mind you dating David, in fact I think you're perfect for each other. But you should have told me, I thought you were my best friend." Natasha looked hurt.

"I am!" exclaimed Carrie. "Please Natasha, don't be mad at me. Like I said, I didn't tell you in case nothing came of it. I didn't want you getting mad at me for something that turned out to be nothing. But now I know for sure, I thought you should know."

"I do understand Carrie, but it just hurts that you couldn't confide in me, I thought we shared everything."

"I know, and I am truly sorry for that, really I am," Carrie said, "I wanted to tell you, but was so scared of losing you. I love you as if you were my sister Tash, please believe that."

Natasha knew that Carrie didn't have a bad bone in her body, and knew that Carrie would never betray her. With that thought in mind, Natasha stood up, walked over to her friend and gave her a big hug.

"What was that for?" Carrie asked in amazement. She had built herself up for a big confrontation, knowing that Tasha could have a fiery temper, but instead her friend had accepted, was calm and forgiving.

"Because I love you like a sister too, and know you'd never betray me, even though you should have told me sooner. Oh and because you bought me that amazing dress!" she berated but with a smile on her face. "So in future, no more secrets, deal?"
"Deal!" said Carrie, with a massive weight lifted off of her shoulders. She had everything now, the man of her dreams, and she still had her best friend.
The dress, (she'd lied about the price, it had cost a small fortune) had been worth it.

***

"Come on then, it's going on for 6pm, and you've still got the dress to try on!"

With that, the girls took their drinks, and the rest of the bottle, through to Tasha's bedroom, where they started to get ready.

***

Chapter Ten.

Natasha had not yet tried the dress on, but knew that Carrie certainly had an eye for what would suit, that was for sure, and Natasha made a mental note to do something to thank her friend properly.

She had no hard feelings about Carrie and David, but she did wish Carrie had felt able to confide in her sooner.

By some miracle, the girls managed to get ready in record time, only two hours. Even though they still weren't dressed.

Carrie was deliberating over her choice of clothes as usual, and of course Natasha wanted to wear *that* dress.

Wasting no time, she pulled on a tiny thong. That was the only underwear this dress would allow, and chose some silver strappy shoes to compliment the dress. She thought that she would put the shoes on first because the dress was long, and wanted to see the full effect of it with the shoes on, before looking in the mirror.

She slipped the dress over her head, careful not to disturb her expertly styled hair, which she was wearing half up, and half down, tousled, and with a backcombed quiff on top, it looked amazing, so shiny and healthy, even if the colour did come out of a bottle.

The dress was a little fiddly, with it having two parts to it, but Natasha arranged it, smoothed her hands over it to ensure it was on properly, and finally turned to her mirror.

'*Wow, wow*, and double *wow*.' she thought as she gazed at her reflection.

The dress was absolutely stunning, and clung in all the right places.
The huge holes on each side showed off her tiny toned waistline, and the only things that were covered were her legs, her breasts (but only just), her bottom, and her belly button, which was covered by the silver ring which held the two parts of the dress together. If you looked closely though, you could just see her belly button, through the silver ring, which was pierced with a little silver cross, and looked so sexy.

She turned to look at her back view, and was just as impressed.
How had Carrie managed to find something as amazing as this? Natasha was elated, and couldn't

wait for Carrie to see her, but she'd insisted Carrie wait outside the door until she was fully dressed. Natasha carefully chose some simple long silver cross earrings, a tasteful silver bangle and just one silver ring. She didn't think she needed anything else, as she believed less is more where jewellery was concerned.

Finally she shouted to Carrie, "Okay, you can come in now!"

***

The door opened immediately (obviously Carrie had been stood patiently just outside it), and she walked in.

"Oh my *God* Natasha, the dress looks amazing on you, you look like you should be on the Red Carpet!" Carrie stated, literally stunned by how beautiful Natasha looked, and how beautiful the dress was. It fit her as if it was made only for her.

Natasha grinned, "I know, even if I do say so myself!"

She ran over to her friend and hugged her. "Thanks so very much Carrie. I can't believe you bought me this. You have such an eye for outfits, you should've been a fashion designer, not a banker!" Natasha exclaimed, "and I meant it when

I said I am pleased for you and David, I genuinely am."

***

Carrie was so pleased with this news, she was bursting with pride and excitement.
Pride, over choosing such an amazing outfit for Tash, and excitement, because all the worry she had been carrying around for the past few week, had finally gone, and she was free to see David as and when she liked now. No more sneaking around and lying, which she had hated.

Carrie still wasn't dressed, so Natasha flung open her wardrobe doors and removed a shimmering midnight blue micro dress, which she knew Carrie absolutely adored, and said, "Here, wear this. No, in fact you can have it."
"No, I can't take it, it's one of your favourites!" Carrie replied.
"Yes, you can." Tash replied, "look what you bought for me, it's the very least I can do!"

Carrie was so pleased, she had loved this dress which Natasha had found in a little boutique on a recent trip to London, and had secretly wished it was hers ever since.

How fantastic was this! She hugged her friend whilst saying thank you over and over again, and rushed through to her room to get dressed.

***

The girls were all due to meet at Bellina's as usual.
It was their ritual to start there, which was a bit strange, because they would have a couple of drinks in there, then walk all the way up to the Mission bar, which was a decent walk, especially in heels. Then they would walk all the way back, to go to the club Euphoria, which was right at the side of Bellina's.
They did it that way, because everyone did it that way, and they liked to see the same crowd of people.

***

Natasha and Carrie arrived in record time, it was only 8.20pm, and they were the first there, and they waited outside for Anna who would be arriving alone, and were due to meet up with Jasmine, Mel, and Lucy inside the bar.

The doormen at Bellina's greeted them as friends. The girls visited the bar so regularly, they may well have been friends.

"Looking good tonight, Ladies." said Jake, one of the regular doormen, with a low whistle to them both. The girls laughed and thanked him, chuffed that he'd made the comment.

Annalise arrived five minutes later, and was amazed to see the other two already there.

"Bloody hell, who wet the bed?" she laughed.
"Don't ask us how we managed it," Carrie replied, "we've no idea how we made it in this time!"
Anna looked at Natasha. God she was looking good, she'd not seen that dress before, and thought her friend looked amazing, in fact both her friends did.
"Is that new Tash, I've not seen it before?" Anna asked.
"Yes, can you believe it, Carrie *bought* it for me!"
"Blimey." replied Anna, "what are you feeling guilty about Carrie?"
"Nothing, now. I'm seeing David, and was worried about Natasha's response. I bought this in the hopes that it would help when I broke the news." Carrie laughed.
It was clear to Anna that all was fine with the other two, obviously the dress had worked a treat.
"Isn't that Tasha's dress Carrie?" Anna then asked.
"Not any more," Carrie replied. "She just gave it to me."

"Well, it looks stunning on you, and makes those legs of yours look like they go on for miles!" Anna continued, "and the colour really suits your hair and skin tone, I think it suits you better than it did Tash."

"Oi!, thanks a lot mate, what's that supposed to mean?" Natasha asked, pretending to be mad.

"I'm joking, Tash, you know damn well you'd look good in a bin bag!" laughed Anna.

"Thanks, I know." Natasha replied a little arrogantly, "I love your outfit, very sexy little lady."

Annalise was wearing a white trouser suit. The trousers were hipsters, which flared out slightly at the bottom, and the top only just covered her breasts, again, in the style of being tied just under her bust, revealing that cleavage yet again. "Is that another of Dan's creations?" asked Carrie.

"Yes it is," admitted Anna, "such a shame I had to dump him, the scheming lying rat."

She'd found out that Dan had been two timing her with some little slapper from the bar 'Dexter's', next door to Bellina's. She wouldn't mind if she'd been traded in for a better model, but this girl looked like a cheap slapper, and probably was one.

Annalise had wasted no time in dumping him, even though he'd pleaded with her not to leave him.

Some chance.

Once a cheat, always a cheat was what Anna thought, conveniently forgetting that she was seeing Max, who was engaged to Suki.

She'd refused to return the clothes he'd made for her. He'd had the cheek to ask for them back.

Unbelievable after what he'd done, there was no way he was getting her outfits back, they were hers, and he could go whistle.
The girls finished admiring each other's outfits, and made their way inside the bar.

***

Chapter Eleven.

The place was heaving, and the girls were finding
it harder than usual to navigate to the bar.
As they nudged their way through the throng,
nodding and saying hello's to people they knew,
Natasha noticed Jasmine near the podium, where
they always stood. Jazz had noticed the girls
entrance too, and was waving madly at them,
grinning like a Cheshire cat on speed.

'Wonder what she's on', Natasha mused, although
she knew that Jasmine was just like that by nature.
The girls lived on a constant natural high, with a
drink every now and again to add to their
infectious likeability.

***

Anna made it to the bar first, the other two holding
back, as it was just so cramped.
Tasha could see that Anna had grabbed the
attention of Simon, Jazz's new 'squeeze',
and could tell by the look on his face that Anna
was flirting outrageously. Typical Annalise, just
to get served more quickly, she thought.

Tash just hoped that Jazz didn't see what Anna
was up to, as there'd be fireworks.

Both could be fiery, so God help Anna if Jazz was watching!

Of course Tasha knew, Anna didn't mean any harm, she was a natural flirt, and not even aware when she was doing it. But some girls would take offence to her and this had resulted in a few spats which had nearly turned into bitch fights.

Fighting her way back, Anna managed to return in one piece with three bottles of lager. They weren't going straight to the cocktails, it was going to be a long night, and they wanted to pace themselves.

"Bloody hell," She said, hair askew, "I feel like Zena after a battle."
"Come on," Carried said, pointing to the podium, "Jazz and the others are over there,
let's make our way to them."

***

"Tasha!" squealed Jasmine, "You're looking great, girl, I miss you, how've you
been?"
"Not too bad thanks," Natasha replied, "got man trouble again, but that's my own fault, I always go for the bad ones."
"You'll have to fill me in later, it's way too noisy in here to get down to the nitty gritty," Jazz replied, "plus, I've got a few stories of my own to

tell, it's been too long Tash, we mustn't leave it so long next time!"

"Yes, I've heard about Simon the Horse," laughed Tasha, "I need to hear more on that score at the very least tonight."

As the girls greeted each other and got reacquainted, Natasha felt so pleased this night had been arranged. Just the tonic she needed after thinking of nothing but Marcus for the last few weeks.

'Bastard' she thought, bitterly.

***

Jasmine was looking better than ever. She'd just returned from Magaluf, and had the most amazing tan.

She showed this off beautifully with a short white crocheted dress, which was a little see through. Naughty girl, Tasha mused.

She was very toned and Tash guessed, a very small size 12. She was also blessed with enormous breasts, the lucky mare.

Jazz wore her hair short in a funky, spiky style. It was naturally black, but she'd had a red dye put through it, and it shone beautifully under the lights.

Yes, Tasha thought, Jazz was looking good. Probably something to do with Simon, too. 'Must find out more about that later', she thought.

***

'Macarena' by Los Del Rio came on, and even though it was probably the corniest song ever written (well, since the birdie song, maybe), the girls couldn't help but sing and dance along to it. Jazz knew all the moves, and the others clumsily tried to follow her, which only sent them in to fits of laughter.

Carrie noticed much amusement from others in the bar, but she also noticed a group of girls clearly bitching about them. 'Oh well, that's their problem, and sad little lives', Carrie thought, if they had nothing better to do than watch and snipe about them. Carrie grinned in their direction, which only seemed to infuriate them more, which Carrie found great pleasure in. 'I am as bad as them' she thought, but hey, you're only young once, right?

Straight after 'Macarena' came Livin Joy's 'Don't stop moving', so the girls didn't, they carried on dancing, on their make shift dance floor, laughing and swigging beer. 'So ladylike – not', Carrie mused.

***

After the dancing fiasco, the girls settled in to
catching up on gossip again, and also nominated
Jazz to go to the bar this time, even though she
complained profusely about this.
She'd seen the queues, no way did she want to
wait in them. "Come with me, Tash,"
Jasmine asked. "I can't carry all those drinks on
my own, and I think we should double up,
so that we don't have to go back again." They
would have a couple more here, then head off to
the Mission bar (the name of that bar always had
the girls in stitches, what a name to call a place).
"Ok Jazz, no probs," said Tasha, and off they went
to try to wriggle their way to the front of the bar
again.

***

As they stood waiting to be served, Jasmine turned
to Natasha and said, "Things between me and
Lucy aren't right, I don't know if you've noticed?"
"No, I've not noticed anything, but with
everything going on, I wasn't really looking
for anything like that."
"It started in Magaluf," Jasmine replied. "All over
some tosser of a bloke, and things haven't been the
same since. We used to be so close, but now
things are so strained, and I get the feeling that it's
not over yet," Jazz continued, "you know what I'm

like, but as for holding grudges, Lucy takes the gold every time."

"Surely it isn't that bad?" Tasha almost shouted over the noise.

"Believe me, it is," Jasmine said. "She just can't let sleeping dogs lie, and with a few drinks down her, I bet she tries to kick off, I just hope it's not tonight."

"Oh, it won't," Tasha said, "I won't let it. We're out for the first time in ages as a
group, there's no way I'm letting her spoil it."
And before they knew it, they were being asked what they wanted to drink by Jasmine's man of the moment.

***

"Oh my God!" Tasha said to Jasmine on their way back to the others, "The electricity between you two is amazing, I almost got a bloody shock." she laughed.

"I know!" Jazz said, "he's nothing serious, but Lordy me, is he good in the sack! Enough to keep me occupied for a few more weeks at least," she laughed.

Typical Jasmine, she was more like a man in that department, and soon grew bored of her men, often overlapping them in her feat to find the next one. Natasha admired her ballsy-ness, and wished she could be more like that instead of worrying over Marcus all this time. She was beginning to think it was time to forget him and move on, and she had just the man in mind, she thought.

***

Chapter Twelve.

The girls were running late, having spent much longer in Bellina's than expected, so they chose not to traipse all the way to Mission, but instead go to the quieter Dexter's, which was next door to Bellina's.
Anna was a little dubious in case slapper was working tonight, but as they walked in, she scanned the half empty bar and could see she wasn't, and relaxed.

***

They were soon served, and as the bar was quieter, they managed to find a table to sit around.
As the girls were sat around chatting amongst themselves, Tasha finally noticed the frostiness between Jasmine and Lucy.
Lucy had sent more than a few stabbing glares in Jasmine's direction. God, what was wrong with the girl? Why hold a grudge over a man? They weren't worth losing a friendship over, Natasha thought, as she remembered Carrie's earlier revelation about her relationship with David.
Even she wasn't that shallow as to fall out over a man.

Tasha finally got around to explaining to the group about the whole fiasco that was

Marcus, and how miserable she had been. They had all been listening intently, and saying things like, "Oh my God, the Bastard," in all the right places. Tasha felt better for getting it off of her chest, but also wondered if it would be that easy to get him out of her heart.

Lucy, who had not said much until now, suddenly said, "Well, at least you weren't shit on from a great height by someone you thought was your best friend," whilst staring at Jasmine.

Oh no, Tasha thought, here we go.

"What's that supposed to mean?" Jasmine retaliated.
"You know damn well, you scheming bitch," Lucy slurred. She'd clearly had one too many already.
"Excuse me?" Jazz glared at her.
"You know what I mean," Lucy shouted, "nicking Tony off me on holiday. How could you?"

Others in the bar were now looking in their direction.

"Oh for the love of God," Jasmine sighed. "I didn't nick him off you, he wasn't even yours. In fact he wasn't even bothered about you, you silly cow!"

With that, Lucy sprang to her feet and threw her lager and black all down Jasmine's white dress.

"You stupid, stupid cow!" Carrie stepped in, "what on earth did you do that for?"
"She knows why," Lucy slurred, and with that, got up and staggered out of the bar. No one tried to stop her.

***

Jasmine looked so hurt. Lucy's outburst had put a dampener on the night, as well as her dress.
"Oh Jazz, I'm sorry, I said I'd ensure nothing like this would happen," Natasha said.
"It's not your fault, it's hers," Jasmine sighed, "she's got a right chip on her shoulder, and I knew it would come to boiling point sooner or later, I was just hoping it would be later."
"Look," Anna stepped in, "tonight isn't ruined Jazz, it's still early," she continued, glancing at her watch. "You can easily get a taxi home and change, we'll all chip in won't we girls?" to which everyone nodded.
"No, it's ruined, I can't be messing around like that," Jasmine replied.
"Well, in that case," Anna said. "She's won, hasn't she?"

This seemed to perk Jasmine up. She was not one to stay down, and knew Anna was right. There was no way she was letting that idiot, Lucy spoil her night.

"Ok, I'll go home and get changed. Luckily the silly mare missed my hair and makeup else I'd take forever to get back, but all I have to do is change. Hopefully the taxi will wait for me and bring me back. Thank God she was pissed, else she'd probably have got my hair and face too," Jasmine laughed, warming to the idea.
"That's my girl," Mel piped up, "go get your next best glad rags on and get back soon, we've some serious dancing to do."
Jasmine agreed to phone them when she was on her way back, and with that, went outside to hail a taxi.

***

"Unbelievable," Carrie said once Jasmine was out of sight, "what on earth is wrong with that idiot, Lucy?"
"She's bitter that Jazz got this gorgeous bloke on holiday," Mel replied. "He was never interested in Lucy, only Jasmine, but Lucy got it into her head that Tony was hers, God knows how, but that's what started all this, and Lucy being Lucy, just will not let it go."
"Well, with a mate like that, who needs enemies eh?" Carrie laughed.

"We're well shot of her," Mel replied. "She's a liability, and always gets us into some sort of trouble, I just hope Jazz sees sense now, and dumps her for good," Mel carried on, "but you know Jazz, heart of gold, and also forgiving. She'll give her another chance, but in my book, there's no way she deserves it." she finished, the others agreeing with her.

***

Tasha knew the DJ, Nathan, and went to ask him to play 'Three Lions'. She loved the song, both her and Carrie were mad footie fans, and as Euro '96 was just around the corner, she wanted to be in the mood for it.

"Ok love, but only cos it's you," Nathan replied. "Just give me a min to find it out okay?"
"Thanks Nath," Tasha replied, blowing him a flirty kiss and sashaying back to the others.

"I've just asked for 'Three Lions' Carrie, I want us in the mood for the Euro championship."
"Great, that's just what I need after that episode."

It took no time for Nathan to find the song, it came on straight after Underworld's 'Born Slippy'.
"Yay," squealed Carrie, who immediately jumped up onto the seat, bottle in hand, and started chanting along to the lyrics.

'So ladylike', Tasha thought.   Look at her, made
up to the nine's and yet acting like a ladette.

Carrie jumped up and down, singing along…

*"But I still see that tackle by Moore, and when
Lineker scored, Bobby belting the ball,
and Nobby dancing. Three lions on a shirt, Jules
Rimet still gleaming, 30 Years of hurt, Never
stopped me dreaming."*

She was contagious, and soon, everyone was at it,
"*It's coming home, It's coming home, It's coming,
Football's coming home,*" everyone in the bar
chanted.

Tasha looked over to Nathan and winked her
thanks, he winked back at her, grinning.

***

Mel's phone was ringing, "Hi Jazz, where are
you? Right, we'll head to Euphoria,
and meet you in there, up on the top stand as usual
okay?" They heard Mel tell Jazz.
"She's on her way back, I told her we'd meet her
in Euphoria, it's 10.30pm already," Mel said.

The girls, still all geared up from singing their
song, agreed, drained their bottles, and

headed out of the door, and to the club a couple of doors down.

***

Chapter Thirteen.

It was there again. Natasha was sure she had a
sixth sense. She was acutely aware that Marcus
was here, somewhere.

Looking around, she couldn't see him. It was only
early as far as clubs were concerned, and it was
only half full, so she couldn't understand why she
thought he was there.
May be it was just her mind playing tricks with
her, she knew it was unlikely as it was a Friday,
and he was playing tomorrow against Oldham FC,
if she remembered correctly (she didn't admit it to
any one, but still followed his career and fixtures).

Carrie passed her a glass of white wine, "I thought
we were staying on the lighter stuff," Natasha
stated, "I'll be on my back in no time at this rate!"
"You wish," Carrie laughed. "But, I don't see that
much talent in here yet, so doubt that will be
happening any time soon!"
"Oi, you cheeky mare, I'm not that bloody easy
you know," Tasha pretended to be indignant, "and
any way, I'm feeling a little uneasy, I don't know
why, but I get a feeling Marcus is here."
"Don't be daft," Carrie retorted. "You know he
can't come out on a night before a game, there's
no way he'll be in here tonight, you're safe babe."

"I hope so," Natasha mused, but she wasn't so sure. Her instincts were not very often wrong.

***

After a few dances to Tori Amos's 'Professional Widow' and Peter Andre's 'Mysterious Girl' (another corny one, but contagious all the same), Natasha excused herself and went to the ladies room.

Looking at her reflection, she saw perfection. This may seem arrogant, she thought, but she knew her assets. She also saw the sadness in her eyes, which, until a couple of months ago, had never been there.

Why did she want a man who made her so very miserable? she wondered.
She couldn't answer, she just knew that shaking Marcus off, would be much harder than she had originally thought.

Perfecting her makeup by adding a little powder to her nose which had become shiny, and adding a touch of lipstick, she fluffed up her hair, checked her appearance front and back, and deciding that she would 'do', headed back into the club.

Jasmine had arrived and was already catching up with them in the drinks department. She'd

changed in to a very flattering sky blue chiffon, tie
dyed micro dress, which complimented her tan just
as well as, if not more so, than the white dress
she'd had to change out of.

Jazz seemed in a much better mood, and was
bopping along to the current track, Mark
Morrison's 'Crazy'.

"Hey you, see, it didn't take you long, and you
look bloody gorgeous," Natasha remarked. "That
silly cow, Lucy is the only one who missed out in
all this, I'd give her a wide berth from now on."
"I'll see," Jazz replied. "She'll come around and
say sorry, no doubt, and hopefully this will be the
end of it."

Tasha sighed, when would Jazz learn?

"Where's Anna?" Natasha asked, scanning the
crowd.
"Some man came over to talk to her, she's up
there, talking to him," replied Mel.
Looking in the direction in which Mel had
pointed, Natasha stopped dead. Time
stood still, and the room seemed to spin.

Anna was talking to Marcus.

***

What on earth is she doing talking to *him*?"
Natasha demanded.

"Who?" Carrie replied, having heard her
conversation with Mel.

"Marcus." Natasha spat, "he's up there look, and
Anna is bloody talking to the git!"

Carrie looked up. Oh dear, Natasha was right, and
this was just what she didn't need right now.

Carrie had thought Natasha had seemed a little
more like her old self lately, and the last thing she
needed was this set back.

"Hang on Tash, I'll go and see what's going on,"
Carrie replied, and before Natasha
could stop her, she was heading towards them.

***

Natasha was fuming. Marcus *knew* she'd be here
tonight.

He'd not been in touch for ages, and showed up
like this, the bloody cheek of him.

She slugged back her drink, and without asking
the others if they wanted a top up,
went to the bar and ordered herself a large white
wine, which she gulped down as soon as it arrived.

She was so *mad*. How dare he. And how dare
Anna even give him the time of day after all he'd
put her through. What was he doing here anyway,
what's happened to the 'no night out before a
match' rule?

***

Carrie returned quickly, and pulled a very upset Natasha to one side.

"I need to talk to you Tash," Carrie said, "it's important."

Against her better judgement, Natasha agreed, and the two girls made their way to the foyer, where it was quieter.

Both girls took a seat, it was quiet out here, with only the odd couple of people sat here and there, and people walking to and from the loo's.

"Okay, before I start, you have to promise to listen to me, Tasha, I mean it," Carrie said.

Grudgingly, Natasha agreed.

"I just spoke to Anna. Apparently, Marcus is scared to confront you, but wanted to talk to one of your friends first, in the hopes that when he does talk to you, you won't go ballistic."

"I'm listening," Natasha replied.

"He's admitted all to her. He says he's fallen for you big time, and wants you more than anything, can't get you out of his mind apparently."

"Well, he's got a funny way of showing it," Natasha snapped.

"Listen to me for God's sake!" Carrie said. "It's complicated. He's not been honest with you, but apparently regrets that a lot. He's got a live in girlfriend, she's an Air Hostess, so that explains a few things."

'Now everything fits in to place.' Natasha thought, and felt like she'd been hit by a bolt of lightning.
The ladies toiletries dotted around, his absence for so long, him getting his mate to pick her up to make it look like she was with him and not Marcus, in case the neighbours saw. It all made sense now.

Now she understood, and the thing she hated the most was the lie about the toiletries. How could anyone say they belonged to his recently deceased mother, when in fact they belonged to his bloody girlfriend?

"The Bastard," Natasha spat, "how could he tell me about those toiletries being his dead Mother's, when they belonged to his bloody *girlfriend*!" she continued, "How *sick* is that, the twisted son of a bitch!"
"Calm down, Tash, he really is sorry. He seems to be smitten with you, and doesn't know what to do," Carrie tried to reason.
"Calm down?" Natasha retorted, "how can I bloody well calm down, after you've just told me all this? I put my bloody life on hold for that shit of a man, and now I find out he has a live

in girlfriend! I should've listened to my instincts,
I *knew* something wasn't right."
"But he's here now," Carrie said. "He shouldn't
be, but he is, and is talking to Anna, hoping that he
can eventually talk to you."
"Not a bloody chance in hell," Natasha was almost
chomping at the bit. "He lied, has left me for
weeks wondering, and now this! Not a chance, he
can fuck straight off as far as I'm concerned."

Carrie realising that she was fighting a losing
battle, gave up.
Natasha on a mission, was not one to be messed
with.

Natasha at least had the decency to apologise to
Carrie for her outbursts, but was now
going to end something that should never have
started.

***

Natasha stormed back into the club.

It was heaving now, and she literally pushed her
way through the crowds, knocking
through people so they spilled their drinks.

"Oi, thanks a lot!" someone yelled, but Natasha
didn't even hear, and even if she
had, probably wouldn't have apologised.

She was near him now. Anna was back with the others, and Marcus was stood with his team mate, Darren, up near the top bar.

Marcus must have sensed trouble looming, because he turned to look in her direction.

Without a word spoken, Natasha swung back her arm, and gave him a massive slap across his face. A red indented hand print sprang up immediately on his right cheek. It looked as angry as Natasha felt.

"That," she spat, "is for being the bastard of the Century."

"How *could* you do this to me you total shit?" she continued, "and all that crap about those toiletries being your dead mother's, what sort of sick fuck makes up a story like that?"

"Please Natasha, please listen to me, at least" he pleaded whilst rubbing his cheek.

"No way you asshole, you don't deserve one more minute of my time, I hope you rot in hell, and I feel sorry for that poor girlfriend of yours. Poor sod, I'd hate to be with a twat like you."

And with that, she turned on her heels and marched off, with a very hurt Marcus watching the woman he loved walk out of his life for good.

***

As Natasha neared her group of friends, they fell silent and allowed her back into their little crowd. They knew all the details, Annalise had filled them in, and they all waited in anticipation for Natasha to speak.

"It's over," Natasha snapped, "I just gave the lying cheating bastard the slap of his life, and told him I never want to see his face again. Hopefully that mark I left on his face will still be there when he gets home, then he'll have some explaining to do. I feel sorry for the poor cow."

She was shaking with rage.

"Yes, we saw that," Carrie said, "but, he's admitted he's been a git, he's comehere tonight especially, surely that counts for something?"

Carrie was an old romantic at heart, and liked happy endings, and always saw the best in someone, never their faults.

"You're joking aren't you? Who's side are you on anyway?" Natasha was amazed.
"Yours of course, but, well, I thought you'd give him a chance. You do love him, Tasha, remember, and he's made a mistake, has admitted it, and wants to be with you. He told Anna he's leaving his girlfriend for you."

"She's welcome to him," Tasha replied, "I could never trust him again. Anna was right when she said never trust a footballer."

And with that, Natasha went to the bar to order herself another very large white wine.

***

Chapter Fourteen.

Carrie couldn't wait. She was seeing David tonight, and had already made her mind up that 'tonight was the night'. She'd kept him waiting long enough, 'and herself', she thought.

It was Saturday, the day after the disastrous encounter between Natasha and Marcus. Oh how she'd hoped that had turned out differently. She knew deep down how hurt Natasha must be, but Tash could put on a very brave front when needed, and she was doing that now.

It was late morning before Carrie ventured out of her bedroom and made her way to the kitchen to put the kettle on. No sign of Tasha, she must still be asleep. No surprise there really, after the amount of alcohol she'd downed last night.

Carrie turned the radio on low and listened to the sounds of The Fugees rendition of 'Killing me Softly'. She liked this song and hummed away to it as she waited for the kettle to boil.

Her thoughts turned to this evening, and to David. He'd invited her to his apartment, and was cooking her a meal. How great was that!

She would have invited him before now, but her cooking skills were minimal, and that was being kind. She could burn water.

She was so excited, and yet so very nervous at the same time. She knew tonight was the night, and was sure that is what David wanted too. Why else invite her around to his home for a meal?

***

Carrie being up and about must have stirred Natasha, because she appeared at the doorway of the kitchen, leaned against the doorframe and moaned, "I feel like hell, there's no way ever I am drinking again."
"Yeah sure," Carrie smirked. "Until the next time huh?"

Natasha groaned, and walked over to the sink where she poured herself a large glass of water, and scrambled around in a drawer for some painkillers.

"Why do I always have to go too far?" Natasha moaned. "You should stop me, you know I don't know when to stop, especially when I'm mad," she said, as if blaming Carrie for the state she was in. "Oh come on, you know damn well that there's no stopping you when you're on a mission," Carrie said. "It's your own fault, don't try offloading any of how you're feeling on me."

"Sorry, I know." Tash replied, "I was, still am, fuming, but this headache is killing me, I need to go back to bed but we have to set off to the match soon."

They were due to go and see Sheffield Utd play a friendly against their deadly rivals Sheffield Wednesday, and couldn't wait.
Both girls were mad footie fans, and this match, even though only a friendly, was important to them.

After this, they had the European Championships to look forward to, which started in only a few weeks, and they simply couldn't wait. They were sure England would do it this time, especially as this time, it was held on home turf.

"Well, get a hot shower and some liquid down you, we can't miss this match." Carrie stated.

"I know, give me a few mins, I need a good cup of tea and, like you said, a shower.
Need to wash that man right outta my hair," Natasha said, "who sang that song any way? Whoever it was, knew what she was talking about," she said as she poured the boiling water over a teabag in her cup.

Carrie guessed that Natasha was putting on a big front, she knew her friend too well, and knew she was hurting deeply. But, Carrie decided, she'd not mention the matter.

They'd go to the match this afternoon, and have a great time, hopefully enough to take Tasha's mind away from Marcus.

***

After a much-needed blast from the power shower, the tea, and the painkillers, Natasha was feeling much more like her usual self. She wiped her towel over the steamed up mirror.

The girl staring back was fresh faced, still very youthful in appearance, and with hardly any traces of last night etched in her face, although she noticed once again, the sadness in her eyes.

She wrapped herself in a thick dark blue Egyptian cotton towel, and padded back in to the kitchen for another cup of tea before getting ready. She needed all the hydration she could get, to feel human again.

***

Even in her depressed mood, she knew she'd enjoy this afternoon. Football had a way of taking

her away from her problems, as she hummed
along to The Blade's song 'Greasy Chip Butty.'

Even if it would only be for an hour and a half, she
knew that at least in those precious ninety minutes,
she would not be thinking about that bastard.

The kettle boiled, and Natasha dropped a tea bag
into each mug, and poured the steaming water
over them, giving each a quick stir, and then let
them sit for a minute before carefully removing
each one and putting them on a piece of kitchen
towel, which she put straight in to the fridge (she
intended using these to revive her eyes later).

Adding a spoonful of sugar for Carrie, she carried
the mugs through to Carrie's bedroom, where
she'd already started getting ready.

"You're a bit early aren't you?" Natasha asked,
"We've a couple of hours before we need to set
off."
"I know," Carrie replied, "but I just need to *do*
something! This date with David at his house
tonight is making me so very nervous, I can't sit
still."
"Don't be silly," Natasha smiled, "you know
you'll have the time of your life. Stop
worrying, and enjoy the moment, and if that
doesn't work, just think about us kicking
The Owl's asses this afternoon."

***

Carrie looked at her friend and smiled. Tash had a way of soothing and making you just feel better about yourself. She loved her for that.

Taking the mug of tea, Carrie said, "Thank you, this is much needed. I know I drank way less than you, but I still feel hungover," Carrie conceded. "Mind you, I'm not eating properly, I'm that nervous!"
"We'll get a burger at the match." Natasha said, "You need something on your stomach, not eating will only make your nerves worse."

Natasha knew this too well to be honest, after all her fretting over 'B', who she now referred Marcus as.

***

Going back to the kitchen, Natasha retrieved the now cold tea bags from the fridge, and walked back through to her bedroom, where she placed her mug of tea on her bedside table, laid down, and put the soothing teabags over her closed eyes. Trying to relax and get 'B' out of her mind she took some deep breaths, and allowed the coolness of the teabags to soothe her tired eyes.

***

It was 3pm. Kick off time. The girls were wrapped up in light sweaters and jeans, and the obligatory Utd scarf and hat. The weather may be better, but standing out in it for ninety minutes, you could still get really cold, even at this time of year.

They'd already had a burger each from the food bar, which wasn't really nutritious, but it did the job.
They'd also had a pint of lager each, which had helped both girls' hangovers. Not a great approach using 'hair of the dog' but today they didn't care. They were here to forget their troubles and nerves, and cheer on their team. That was it.

***

Making their way to their usual seats (they were season ticket holders), they waved and smiled at people they'd come to know though coming here so regularly.

After squeezing their way through the already crowded seating area, with more than a few apologies at making people stand up so that they could pass, they eventually reached their seats, just in time for the whistle to blow for the kick off.

This was it, time to kick Wednesday's butts right back to Hillsborough.

***

"Come on Utd!" Natasha yelled. "Kick the bloody ball the other way for God's sake," she said, much to the amusement of the crowd around her.

"*Yes!*" There it was, surely the winning goal. Glancing at her watch, Natasha saw that there were only minutes left. "I only hope the ref doesn't add on too much time," , thinking that, knowing Wednesday, they were likely to sneak in a late goal.

Her heart was in her mouth the whole time, and both her and Carrie were screaming their heads off, "Get past Pressman!" Natasha screamed at her team, willing them on, all her problems forgotten.

As if the God's had heard her, the final whistle was blown, and the girls jumped around like idiots, screaming, "*It's coming home, it's coming home, football's coming home!*"

They didn't care what they looked like, or what ther people thought, their team had
beaten their biggest rivals, and the girls were on a massive high.

***

As they made their way out, pushing though the crowds, and still full of excitement from their team doing what needed to be done, Carrie turned to Tash, flushed from all the jumping and screaming, "Well, that's it," Carrie said, "all we need now is for England to win Euro, then we've done it!"

But Natasha's eyes were focused elsewhere, and her whole demeanour had changed.

Carrie looked in to the direction which seemed to be distracting Natasha, and thought 'Oh no, not again, please God, not again' as she stared straight into the eyes of Marcus.

***

Chapter Fifteen.

Marcus had spotted the girls and was heading their way, but Natasha was quick off the ball, and darted in the opposite direction, leaving Carrie stood in the middle of a massive, moving crowd.

'Great,' Carrie thought, 'just what I need right now', Marcus heading towards me and Natasha scooting off like she's in an Olympic event!'

"Where's she gone?" Marcus asked breathlessly when he finally reached Carrie.
"Don't ask me, she took one look at you and buggered off."
"This is just charming, this is ridiculous, I'm due out on a big date tonight, so the last thing I need is to play Claire Raynor to you two!"

It wasn't often Carrie lost her temper, but she'd just about had enough of this fiasco.

It was like watching 'Groundhog Day' over and over again. Once was enough for that film, given what it was all about, but reliving it day by day was becoming a bit annoying to Carrie.

"I need to see her, Carrie," Marcus explained.
"That's the only reason I'm here. You know I

don't even support Utd (Marcus had had a spell playing for Wednesday), so why else would I be here? I knew she would be, I really need to see her ."

"Well, you know as much as I do, all I know is she took one look at you and dashed off in that direction." Carrie said, pointing to the opposite way out.

"Ok, thanks Carrie." And with that, Marcus disappeared as fast as Natasha had.

'Great,' Carrie thought, 'Now I have to go home alone, which is no big deal I suppose.' But she was worried about Tash. She was being very irrational lately, especially re Marcus, rightly so maybe, but it was becoming a pain in the ass.

***

Natasha ran blindly through the crowds, pushing and shoving her way through, anything to get away from *him*. As she ran, bumping into people and quickly apologising, she had no idea where she was going, or would end up. All she knew is that she had to distance herself from him.

Finally finding herself out on the road, she looked around wildly, willing to see someone she knew to save her, or a taxi to take her to the safety of home.

No such luck, and now the crowds were spilling out even more so, she had no chance of finding a taxi.
There was nothing for it, she ran to her place of work, which was a stone's throw away from the ground.

***

Running in to work on her day off, totally out of breath, her colleagues looked at her with amusement.
"What the hell's happened to you?" asked Andrew, one of the sales lads.
"Don't ask," Natasha replied, and sighed, "I've just come from the match, and needed a quick getaway, the only place I could think of was here."

She walked around to the end of the sales counter, bought herself a cup of, let's face it she thought, crap coffee, but at least it was hot and contained caffeine.

Moving into the sales office, she plonked herself down on a spare chair, put her feet up on an untidy desk, and took a sip of her coffee.

"Eewwwwww," she stated, "this is all my taste buds need after the day I've had."

Tracey walked in to the office, having heard the back end of the conversation, "What am I missing?" she asked, glancing over at Natasha. "Oh nothing believable. Nothing a daily paper would print I don't think," Natasha continued. "Just a mad footballer who is stalking me, and doesn't know what the word 'no' means," she sighed, "sounds like something out of a novel doesn't it? But believe me, in real life, it's not funny, not at all."

She was safe here, he'd not think of looking here, Natasha thought, so went up to her office to while away a couple of hours, just in case he was lingering around.

***

Carrie was ready, and early for a change. As she glanced at her reflection in the mirror, making sure everything looked right and was in place, she took a sip of her wine. She'd allowed herself one glass.
Tonight, she wanted to be alert, and didn't want to be 'half cut' by the time David arrived.

Natasha still wasn't home, but Carrie had spoken to her on her mobile, so knew that she was safe and well, and avoiding Marcus at all costs.

Carrie thought this needed sorting sooner rather than later, for the sanity of everyone, but she'd have to deal with that another day.

***

She'd kept her makeup to a minimum. Her skin was flawless so she didn't need that much. She'd just chosen some shimmering lilac eye shadow, and a black top liner and black mascara to accentuate her beautiful eyes. This she'd finished off with a nude shade of lipstick.

She'd chosen a floaty Lipsy summer dress, in shades of lilac and cream. It was chiffon, with no straps. It clung to her curves nicely, and had two sets of 'V' shapes at the bottom, which came to just above her knees. Very flattering, in quite a classy sort of way she thought.
She finished the outfit off with a matching 'scarf', which came with the dress. She chose to wind it around her neck, so that the long pieces hung down her back, with the front part looking like a matching necklace to the dress. Very 'Audrey Hepburn' she thought as she took another scrutinising look in the mirror.

She didn't bother with much jewellery. The dress spoke for itself.
The only jewellery she wore was some small amethyst earrings which Natasha had bought her

for her birthday, a simple silver ring, and her silver bangle watch. She finished the outfit off with a simple silver clutch bag and matching kitten heels. Very understated, she thought, but so sexy at the same time.

A liberal spray of her favourite Chanel perfume, and she was happy with her overall appearance. Just right for the occasion, and night ahead.

***

A knock on the door a few minutes later announced David's arrival.

One last check around to make sure she hadn't forgotten anything, and she was ready to go.

Opening the door, she was greeted by a smiling David, who said, "God, you look better every time I see you," as he kissed her on the cheek.
"Bet you say that to all the girls!" Carrie replied.
"No, only the special one's." he smiled, and kissed her again, lightly on the lips.
"Is madam ready to go? My parents will arrive in about an hour so we have some time alone first." he said.

Whoa!!!!!!

WHAT?

Parents?

She wasn't ready for this yet. He'd not even mentioned that his parents would be there.

Bloody hell, how to deal with this?

"I didn't realise you'd invited your parents?" Carrie asked, and David immediately picked up on the worried tone in her voice.
"Sorry, I forgot to mention it. It was a last minute thing, and they really want to meet you," he said, looking more than a little sheepish.

Again, Carrie felt way out of her depth. She was nervous enough about tonight as it was, never mind having to make small talk with his parents!

"It's ok," Carrie replied, although it wasn't really, "I'm sure it'll all be fine."
"Thank God for that," David said, "I was worried it would put you off, and don't worry, they won't stay late, so we'll get some time alone together."

Too right it was putting her off, but what could she do about it at this stage? She loved David too much to offend him in such a way, so gritted her teeth and thought 'get on with it girl, it's only one night.'

And with that, she locked the door, took David's hand, as he lead her to the car.

***

Chapter Sixteen.

It was the first time Carrie had been back to
David's apartment, and she was so impressed she
could hardly speak.
The large foyer opened straight into an open plan
lounge, dining room, and kitchen area . She'd
never seen anything like it, except in magazines.

He even had a flat screen TV in the kitchen, how
cool was that?

The lounge was a sumptuous chocolate colour,
with large complimenting plump sofa's, all
arranged so that they faced the massive TV, but
also so one could view the amazing sight of the
city.

The apartment was so high up, Carrie was sure she
could see the whole of Sheffield mapped out like
fairy lights in front of her.

"My goodness, David, I had no idea."
Taking her coat, he replied, "No idea about what,
darling?"
"This place. Well, it's, well, amazing," Carrie
stated in awe.
"It's not bad," David replied as he turned Carrie to
look at him. "But it's lonely, and needs a woman's
touch."

What did he mean? Carrie wondered. Was he
playing with her, or asking her to
move in? She had no idea, so decided to play it by
ear. At the same time thinking, 'do I even want
to?' It's surely way too early to tell.

***

A knock at the door quickly brought Carrie out of
her thoughts.
Shit, shit, and double shit, she thought. David had
come from prime stock, and she didn't think his
parents would approve of her. She was way out of
her depth here, and up the proverbial creek with
out a paddle in sight.

David answered the door, and she heard him greet
his parents in very warming terms.
She didn't expect this, she thought they would be
way more formal than this.

Turning to greet them, she was met with the sight
of a big jovial man. He was older, wider, had a
redness about his face, and was losing his hair, but
she could tell instantly this was David's Father.

"So." he said, "You are the delectable Carrie
we've heard so much about, we've been

dying to meet you, I'm Adam, Dave's Dad." and
with that grabbed her arms and gave her a kiss on
both cheeks.

She was dumbfounded, he was not at all as she'd
expected, and she warmed to him immediately.
She gave him her best smile and said how good it
was to meet him.

Next, it was time to greet David's mother. She
was a totally different kettle of fish to David's
Father, very aloof and obviously thought herself to
be above her station.

"How nice to meet you, Dear, it's always nice to
meet one of David's girls," she said.

What stab in the back sort of statement was that?

For an instant, Carrie was lost for words.   But not
one to be out done, she soon recovered.

"So nice to meet you at last, Mrs Oxton," Carrie
said with the sweetest smile on her face, "I've
heard a lot about you too."
Trying to gain the higher ground, Carrie felt her
confidence growing. "What would
you like to drink, Adam, and Mrs Oxton?"

The referral to them in different terms threw
David's' mother, and she seemed to be

seething about this.

'Oh well, in for a penny, in for a pound', Carrie thought.

"Make mine a Scotch with a dash of water, Carrie dear," Adam replied. "The Scot's
don't like you to ruin a good whisky with anything other than a dash of water," he
laughed whilst taking off his jacket.

Carrie turned to 'Mrs Oxton'.
"What would you like, Mrs Oxton?" Carrie asked, cordially.
"I'll have a G&T with a twist of lime, if you don't mind, dear," she replied condescendingly, still being acutely abrupt.

She was mad with David, surely he'd picked up on his mothers behaviour towards her? If so, he should have intervened, but he seemed too busy in the kitchen.

Typical man, she thought, her anger rising.

'I could murder him for this.' Carrie thought, leaving her to make small talk with people she'd never met, people who she believed were out of her league.

"No probs, Mrs Oxton, I'll be with you in a minute," said Carrie, and grudgingly made the drinks.

Shame she couldn't add a touch of cyanide to the Lady Oxton's drink, Carrie thought wickedly whilst preparing the drinks.

***

Apart from the odd snipe here and there from Mrs snooty pants, dinner ran smoothly, and Carrie found herself really warming to David's Father. He was a jovial man, self made millionaire, but had his feet firmly on the ground and was not at all bigoted, unlike that 'rod of iron up the backside' wife of his. She was a trophy wife, and having come from nothing (as she'd learned from David), had nothing at all to be snooty about.

Still, Carrie remembered one of the things her Father used to say 'it's those who haven't reached the top of the ladder who feel they have something to prove. Those already there are the nicer ones'.

How right he was.

It's as if Mrs Oxton was vying for David's attention, Carrie thought, like it was some sort of

competition as to whom David liked the best, his mother or his girlfriend. So childish she mused, and she was supposed to be the younger, more competitive of the
two. How very silly, Carrie thought smiling to herself.

"What are you smiling at?" David asked, bringing Carrie back to the present.
"Oh nothing, darling, just how marvellous dinner was. Another talent of yours I see."

Another dig at the Lady, Carrie couldn't help herself.

"So, you've not been here before then?" Mrs Oxton asked, jumping at the slightest opportunity to undermine Carrie.
"No, this is the first time. David's been spending most of his time at my house," Carrie said with glee.
"Oh I see. That's unusual," Mrs Oxton replied, "David is usually so quick to bring one of his girls back here," she sniped.

David, having finally picked up on the tension tried to change the subject, but not before Carrie managed to say, "Oh I know, but he wasn't in any rush to bring me
here. My place is good enough and big enough for the both of us."

Mrs Oxton seemed to be seething. Carrie knew she was more than a match for this woman, and knew she would have a battle on her hands if she and David were to progress. She instinctively knew this woman would try to split them up, there was no doubt about that in Carrie's mind.

Even though Carrie knew, she had not done a thing wrong.

***

Chapter Seventeen.

It was now Friday 31st May and the salon was
even more manic than usual.
Annalise had no idea how she'd managed to fit in
all her clients, never mind a lunch break, even
though her stomach was growling at her.

Tony Rich Projects 'Nobody knows' was playing
in the background, but she could hardly hear it for
the din of chattering between stylists and their
clients, and all of the machine's which were
switched on.

"Would you like a drink Maria?" she asked her
current client. Maria was a nice looking woman in
her early 30's, who could have made more of
herself with a little make up to enhance her
features, but it didn't seem to worry her.

"Yes please Anna, a coffee would be great," Maria
replied.
"So, what's it to be today then?" asked Anna.
"Just a tidy up, or will you let me loose on your
locks at long last?"

Maria, one of Anna's long standing clients, was
stubborn when it came to her hair, always insisting
it stay it's natural light brown colour, and only
ever had an inch cut off every three months or so.

This frustrated Annalise, whose creative side was screaming out to do something amazing with it.

Maria seemed to think for a while and replied, "I think I'll let you work your magic on it today, Anna," she said. "I am starting to feel like a frump, and think that a good cut and colour will perk me up."

Blimey! At long last, Maria was allowing Annalise free reign on her hair, which she'd been trying to do for months now. Hallelujah, there was a God, Annalise thought, whilst shouting over a junior to get Maria her coffee.

Annalise gave Maria some colour charts, pointing out some ideas of what she thought would work, and some hair magazines, to see if she could find a style she liked. She wanted to give Maria a severe bob which would suit her small face and soft features immensely, with high and low lights, but was trying also to give Maria the idea that she was in control.

Whilst Maria was making up her mind, Janine shouted Anna over to the phone.
"Hi, this is Annalise speaking,"
"Hey Sexy Bum."
Anna's heart skipped a beat. He had that effect on her, and it had seemed like ages
since she'd heard from him.

"Hey stranger, how's you?" Anna replied, trying to sound cool.

"Great babe. Missing you though. Fancy lunch?" Max asked.

"Sorry, no can do, I'm up to my eyes in it here," Anna said hopefully, "I can make a quick drink after work though, if you can manage it?"

"Pick you up at five then," Max replied in his easy tone.

"Make it five fifteen, just in case I run over."

"Ok babe, no probs. See you later. Can't wait, I've missed your sexy ass."

Anna giggled, and melted at the sound of this, "You too Mr, see you then."

And then she hung up.

***

Anna hadn't seen Max since that awful Saturday at the beginning of May, when they'd driven out to Hathersage and bumped straight in to Suki's parents.

Apart from a snatched phone call here and there, she'd not heard from him and it had started to worry her. But, she thought, at least he'd called now, and looking at her watch which read 1.10pm, realised she would see him in the flesh in about four hours time. Her heart beat faster at this thought, as she returned to Maria, to see if she'd made a choice.

***

Maria was still perusing the glossy pages of a hair magazine.

"Made your mind up?" Anna asked her.

"I thought maybe this sort of style," Maria said, pointing to a sleek bob.

It wasn't what Annalise had hoped for, but at least they were heading in the right direction.

"Okay," Annalise replied, "I can do that, but what do you think of it being a little more dramatic. Don't worry, you're safe with me, I won't shave your head!"

Maria looked a little unsure, so Anna continued, really wanting to use her creative talents to the fullest, "Not too much different to that style, I promise you, you'll love it, else it's a freebie on me, okay?"

With this, it seemed that Maria's mind was made up, "Okay, I'll trust you, go for it."

"And what colours were you thinking?" Anna asked in anticipation. She couldn't believe that Maria had so readily agreed to her suggestion.

"Maybe this shade as a base," Maria replied, pointing to a dark brown, "with these high and low lights," she said, pointing at a deep rich mahogany brown, and a golden blonde.

Perfect, Anna thought with glee. She just knew that this would transform Maria, and give her that much needed confidence boost.

"Hayleigh, can you just wash this Lady's hair for me please? No conditioner, it's going to be coloured."
"No probs," Hayleigh replied, "come this way please," she said to Maria, and with that Maria followed her over to the sinks.

***

Whilst Maria's hair was being washed, Anna allowed her mind to wander.
'I wonder what Max has to say, if anything, about what happened a few weeks ago' popped in to her head. She certainly hoped he'd managed to cover that one up, and not having personally heard from Suki, she was sure all was well in that department.

She only wished they didn't have to sneak around. They'd been seeing each other for a few months now, so surely it was time to make his mind up. She'd press the issue if she felt the mood was right, but didn't want to appear to be rushing him or too pushy, she knew Max hated that sort of thing.

Then she was thinking about Tash and Carrie. The European Championship was to start in a week, and she knew that Tash and Carrie would talk nothing but bloody football for a month, unless England were knocked out early, which was highly likely, Annalise mused.

One thing she knew for a fact, if she wanted to see them, she'd have to endure weeks of football, bloody hell!

Of course she wanted England to do well, but just wasn't interested, and couldn't understand what all the fuss was about. It was only twenty-two blokes kicking a ball around a field for around ninety minutes after all, Anna conceded.

Breaking her thoughts, Maria returned to her chair, ready for the colour to be applied, before the big cut. Anna was so excited.

***

Expertly applying the slices of colour to Maria's hair, Anna made small talk with her.
"So, what does your husband think about this radical change?" Anna asked her.
"He's no idea. It's a surprise for our anniversary. I just hope I haven't gone too far."
Maria replied.

"Well, he's in for a very nice surprise indeed," Anna promised. "You're going to look a million dollars by the time I've finished with you!" she added, although Maria still looked apprehensive.

After the colour mixture had been washed out of Maria's hair, and a conditioner had been applied, it was time to commence on the cut, that would finish this make over off completely. Anna had an expert eye, and just knew this was right for Maria.

Chopping and slicing away, Annalise was in her element. She knew exactly what she was doing, and what would suit her client. That's why she was paid so well.

"So, anything nice booked for your anniversary?" Anna asked whilst slicing in to the back of Maria's hair.

"He's taking me to Avanti, to celebrate," Maria replied.

"Lucky you!" Anna said. She'd not been there herself, but had heard that the Italian restaurant was superb.

"I'm so jealous!" Anna said, "I've never been, but would love to. Some day Mr Right might take me there," she replied wistfully.

"I'm sure there must be a long line of men waiting to take you out!" Maria smiled.

"I wish," Anna replied whilst slicing away. "No, well, if there are, I don't see it, and I sort of have my eye on someone anyway."

"Well, work your magic, and get him to take you. It'll be well worth it I promise you," Maria replied, suddenly full of confidence.

"I'll try," Anna smiled back. "It may not be that easy," she continued. "But that's another story, for another day."

***

Maria stared at her reflection in the mirror.

"My God, Anna, I can't believe it's me, I look like a different person. Why I didn't listen to you before, I don't know. But I'm so glad I finally let you loose on my hair, you've made such a difference to me." Maria said with glee.

Maria's whole features had changed.
What had been a passably pretty face was now a beautiful one, perfectly surrounded
by an array of mid and rich dark chocolate colours, enhanced with slices of honey blonde hair.

The bob style, which was almost shaved into the neck, and much longer at the front, framed her small face and features perfectly. She looked at least five years younger, and had been totally transformed.

"I am almost lost for words, thanks so much Anna."

"Well, better late than never." Anna replied, "your husband is in for a treat!"

"Too right he is!" Maria smiled. "If this doesn't do it for him, God knows what will,"

Insisting Annalise take a generous tip of £15.00, Maria thanked her once again, and walked out of the salon a totally different woman.

Annalise loved that part of her job, giving people that confidence, seeing their reactions when they'd had a total transformation. If you could bottle and sell that feeling, Anna thought, she'd be a millionaire.

***

Chapter Eighteen.

It was 5.20pm, and Annalise was running late.

Bloody hell, why did this have to happen today of
all days?
She was in charge of the Salon for the day, so had
to stay until all was done. All the sweeping up and
cleaning had to be done. And then of course
counting out the money, less the float, and putting
it in the safe.

Glancing at her watch, she knew she'd be another
twenty minutes at least, so decided to give Max a
call.
On the second ring, he picked up, "Hey babe,
what's taking you so long? I'm sat here like a
bloody curb crawler, and am getting some very
funny looks," he laughed.

She had to smile. Hardly anything phased him.
"Give me twenty okay? I promise, no longer,"
Anna replied. "If you like, go up to
Weatherspoons, and I'll meet you in there, save
you from being arrested for lurking with intent!"
she said.
"Okay, see you there then, but no longer?"
"No probs," she replied, and hung up, rushing like
a mad woman, trying to motivate the girls to get
the place cleaned up, whilst counting out the day's
takings.
■ ■

***

Annalise managed to make it to Weatherspoons within time, and spotted Max, sat at the other end of the bar.
He stood up to greet her, wrapping his toned and nicely muscled arms around her
waist.
"Good to see you babe, you're looking good," he said.
"You're joking aren't you?" Annalise replied.
"I've had the busiest day ever and must look like a wreck."
"You always look gorgeous to me, babe," Max replied, taking in the smell of her perfume.
"Here," he continued, "I've taken the liberty of ordering your usual," and passed Anna a large dry white wine.
She took a big sip. Just what she needed after the day she'd had.
"So, Mr, what brings you down this edge of the woods?" she asked him.
Max, taking his time, and staring at her intently, finally said, "I've something
interesting to tell you, I think you may like it."
Annalise was now more than interested.
"What?" she asked, "what's happened?"
Max seemed to be taking his time to reply.
"Oh come on Max, tell me for God's sake!"
"It's over with Suki babe, I'm all yours."

Bloody hell, she'd not expected this.

"What? How? What's happened?" inquired
Annalise anxiously.
"Well, it seems she didn't take well to me taking
you out a few weeks a go. But, to be honest,
things had been on the rocks for a while."
Anna, taking in all of this information, replied,
"Well, no wonder you came looking
for me then."
"What does that mean?" he asked.
Anna took another sip of her drink, "Well," she
said slowly, "If you'd have been sohappy with her,
you wouldn't have looked elsewhere, would you?"
"No," Max replied, "I don't suppose I would've."
And with that, he folded his arms around her, and
kissed her deeply.

He was finally hers. Annalise could hardly believe
it.
She expected at any moment that someone would
pinch her, and tell her it was all a
beautiful dream, about to be shattered.

***

Natasha had been avoiding the phone.

It was now three weeks since that fateful day at the
match, where she'd seen Marcus.
■■

He'd bombarded her at home and at work with phone calls, all of which she'd rejected, and the most beautiful flowers arrived at her home or workplace on a daily basis.

It was becoming embarrassing.

Her resolve was slowly melting though, she could feel it, and she knew she must avoid him at all costs, in order to give her broken heart a chance to heal.

She was at work. She shouldn't be, as it was a Saturday, but she was so overloaded with work, she'd decided to go in for a few hours in the afternoon. She had nothing better to do anyway, until later of course.

It was now the 8th June, and she was due to go out with Carrie later to their local 'The Oak Tree', where the pub were to have two big screens on, one at each end of the room, to watch England's first match in the Euro Championship against Switzerland.

She was sure England would breeze through this match, but one never did know. That was football for you.

***

■■■

Football had always been in Natasha's life. Ever since she was eight years old, and her Dad had taken her to watch Sheffield United, against God knows who, but she remembered the day as if it was yesterday, and had been a mad United fan ever since.

Her Dad had done some building work for one of their players, Les Tibbbot, hence the reason for the free tickets which took her and her Dad to her first match.

She'd been hooked ever since. She'd even been to Les Tibbot's house, and had played with his children, she remembered.

Just her luck, to fall for a bloody footballer. Her Dad would be so mad, if he knew.

She'd hadn't known the pitfalls of dating a footballer, but never imagined in her wildest dreams that she would fall so deeply for one, especially one who would break her heart so badly.

***

Once again, whilst she should be working (she was again on a tight deadline), she was sat at her desk, doodling mini character's from memory, on her plain pad of paper.

Doodling a cartoon of her Dad, which was one of her favourite doodles, she was busy with this when her desk phone rang.

"Hello, this in Natasha Johansson, purchasing department, how can I help you?"
"I hope you can, Tash." was all she heard.

Oh no. Not him. I'm not ready to deal with him, not at all, she thought, 'How on earth did he know she'd be at work on a Saturday anyway'?

"I doubt it," she quipped, sarcastically.
"Please, Natasha," Marcus pleaded. "Just listen to me will you. I've followed you everywhere, done everything I can, but you just won't give me a chance."
"Why on earth should I listen to a lying rat like you?" Natasha spat, making her colleague Gavin look up with interest.

Lowering her voice so that Gavin couldn't hear any further, she said, "You've not a cat in hell's chance with me, Marcus, so I don't know why you're even bothering," she whispered. "You paid me less bloody attention when we were together!"

Marcus seemed to take a while to answer, which was a big risk with the mood Natasha was in with him. "I need to see you, to explain properly. I do have a conscience Natasha, no matter what you think of me," he said.

Biting down so hard on the end of her pen, it actually shattered, scattering tiny shards of plastic pieces across her desk, which she briskly flicked off with a swish of her hand.

"Okay," she agreed against her better judgement, "I'll meet you for one drink, and one drink only," she replied, adamant that she was now in control of her feelings.
She could almost sense Marcus breathe a sigh of relief as he replied, "Thank you Natasha, you don't know what that means to me. Can I see you after work? I could meet you in The Plough if that's convenient?" he pleaded.

The Plough was literally a two minute walk from her place of work, so at least she didn't have to go out of her way. After all, she couldn't be late home tonight, not with England playing.

She was feeling more and more awkward about this. She didn't trust herself to be alone with him, knowing her resolve was low.

Finally she replied, "Fine, 4.30 at The Plough. One drink only, I mean it Marcus."

"I know you do. I promise, no funny business, I just want to see you face to face, to try to explain things to you.," he replied.

"Well, I doubt you'll be able to do that," Natasha retorted. "But like I said, I'll meet you for one drink. You don't deserve any more of my time than that."
And with that, she hung up.

***

Chapter Nineteen.

Natasha arrived on time, but before going into the bar, she checked her refection in the car's mirror. The pub may only be a two-minute walk from work, but why leave the car there, when she needed to get home ASAP? Every second counted today.

Hmmm, definitely dark circles under her eyes, and she did look tired, but she supposed that was only to be expected after the last few months.

Slicking on a bit of light pink lip-gloss, she closed her bag, checked herself once more in the mirror, then locked the car, and headed to the pub.

And to Marcus.

***

He was already there. Sat in the darkest corner.

'How obvious,' Natasha thought, 'he still doesn't want to be seen.'

The pub was already starting to fill up with people who had come in early to get good seats to watch the match, and Natasha wove through the crowds.

■■

She marched over to him with as much confidence
as her esteem would allow.
Without speaking, she took off her jacket, and
flung it on the space next to him.
It was a sign she had no intention of sitting by
him, and she knew Marcus would pick up on this.

With eyes of steel, Natasha looked at Marcus and
asked, "So, what's this all about then? I don't
think we have anything else to say to each other,
do we?"

Marcus looked down at his drink, and Natasha
could sense his uneasiness. He seemed
to be contemplating the best thing to say next.

"I just needed to see you, one last time, Natasha,"
he said, looking up at her.
"What for?" she snapped. "To gloat about what a
fool you have made out of me?"
"No, nothing like that," he replied humbly, "I just
wanted to say sorry, to your face. Whether you
believe it or not, I am in love with you Tasha. I
don't just love you, I am in love with you."
"And what about your little live in girlfriend, who
you conveniently forgot to tell me about?"
"We've finished," Marcus replied, "I want you,
Natasha. I know I lied to you in the worst way
possible, but I wanted you, still want you, and
didn't want to risk losing you."

■■■■■■■■■■■■■■■■■■■■■■■■■■■■■■■■■■■■■

Remembering the excuse about the toiletries, Natasha exclaimed, "Yes, that's all well and good, Marcus, but what sort of sicko says that the toiletries belonged to his dead mother?"

He did look very ashamed at this point.

"Losing my Mum wasn't a lie, I did lose her recently," he continued, "I just didn't think fast enough when you asked me the question. I wasn't prepared for it, and panicked," he continued, "I'm so sorry, it was a really bad thing to say, and if I could go back and do just one thing differently, it would be that. I really am sorry."

Natasha took a sip of her drink and looked up at him. He seemed to be waiting for something special to happen, for Tash to forgive him and jump in to his arms, but he'd hurt her far too much for that to happen.

"I accept that now Marcus. But I can't be with you. I'd always be wondering who the next girl would be. And there would be more, so don't lie to me, or kid yourself. You want me because you can't have me. If you could, you'd soon be on the look out for my replacement, and I just can not live like that," she said, "I love you, Marcus, for some strange deluded reason, but we are finished, for good, I mean it. Please accept that, for both our sakes."
■■

Marcus looked so distressed that Natasha wanted to hug him and tell him that everything would be alright, but she knew that to let her barrier down now, would be fatal.

"I love you Tash," Marcus mumbled, he almost seemed close to tears, "I'm so sorry, so very sorry," he said. "But for me also, because I think I've just lost the love of my life."

Natasha couldn't take any more, she had to get away from him before her resolve crumbled. She finished her drink, thanked Marcus for it, kissed him on the cheek, and after pulling on her jacket, said good bye to him for ever.

Her heart was broken. Again.

Probably for good this time.
How could she ever trust a man again after this?

***

As she drove the few miles home, Natasha felt a calm come over her.
As if she finally had closure.

She'd needed this conversation to finally finish things with Marcus, although she knew in her heart, she would never, ever forget him.

***

As usual, when Natasha walked in, Carrie was at home, having just lazed around for most of the day. Lucky for some, Tasha thought.

Carrie was leaning on the kitchen counter, and was on the phone. It was obviously David she was speaking to. She was so animated and could tell by the tone of her voice that she was deeply in love with her man.

After putting down the phone, Carrie greeted Tasha, "Hi, how's you?"
"Oh don't ask," Natasha sighed, "I've just met with Marcus, and this time it really is the end."
Walking over to her, Carrie gave Tasha a hug "What happened?" she asked, not able to help herself.
"He explained, I listened, and I do understand, in a weird sort of way why he lied to me. But I couldn't ever trust him again, so why put myself through more?"
"I know, sweetheart," Carrie replied. "I just hoped you guys would sort it out, you know me, always wanting the Cinderella ending, but I can totally see what you mean."
Natasha sighed, "Me too, it's just finding my knight in shining armour is proving ▪▪

harder than I thought," she conceded. "I think my expectations are too high, and from now on, for the love of God, please, keep me away from footballers," she said whilst managing a small, sad smile.

"I'll try," Carrie replied, "but you know what you're like when you set your sights on someone!"

Natasha laughed. She knew what her friend said was true. But from now on, she was determined that she would be much more careful where men were concerned.

***

"Any way," Natasha said, looking at the wall lock in the kitchen. "We'd better get a move on, the match kicks off in just over an hour."

And with that, the girls grabbed the bottle of red wine, a corkscrew, two glasses, a pack of cigarettes, and the ash tray, and headed to Tasha's room to get ready.

***

■■■

Chapter Twenty.

The girls had taken no time at all in getting ready.
It was only their local after all, and Tash had just
tied her long tresses back in to a high ponytail,
retouched her makeup, and had chosen some very
daring, very low-riding hipster jeans. This she'd
finished off with a tight England vest, which she
was almost bursting out of in the bust department,
and red stiletto's, in honour of her team.
Carrie was dressed similarly, only her vest was
red, whereas Tasha's was white, and Carrie's
shoes were white. They complimented each other
perfectly.

They certainly looked the part for this exciting
qualifying round for England, who were in group
A along with Scotland (that was going to be *the*
match to watch), Holland, and Switzerland, who
they were playing tonight at Wembley Stadium.

England had been classed as 7-1 to win the
tournament, with their bitter rivals

Germany as favourites to win.

7-1 wasn't bad, but Tasha was sure that they could
do it this time, especially as it was on home turf.

■ ■

The girls were excited, this was the year football was coming home, and even though they'd heard it time and time again, they once again had 'Three Lions' blasting out of the stereo.

***

The pub was already packed.

They'd hoped that they'd left plenty of time before the match in order to get a good seat, but obviously, every one else had thought the same thing too.

They were either going to have to find some friends who were sat near the front, or stand at the back, on chairs, as they were not tall enough to see over the heads of the men.

As they ordered two pints of lager each (it was *the only* drink when watching football, and ordering two each meant they didn't have to leave the match at a crucial point), they turned and scanned the crowds, who seemed to be getting more excited and rowdy by the minute.

"Hey look," Carrie said, "There's Colette, three tables from the front, let's see if we can squeeze through to join her."

■■■

Squeezing through was no problem. They knew most of the people in the pub, and greeted them as they went.

Tasha saw Colette's boyfriend, Paul, stood nearby with a gang of his mates, and waved to him.

Obviously the two of them had chosen to watch the match with their own sets of friends.

"Hey Col," Tasha shouted over the din. "Any room for me and Carrie?"
Colette looked at her table, which was already covered in empty glasses and had five of them squeezed around it already.
"No probs, but you'll have to either find yourselves seats, or sit on our knees," Colette laughed.
Natasha scanned around. Nope, not a seat in sight, not the she'd expected to find one, the place was just too full.
"Looks like we're sat on your knees then" Natasha laughed back. And with that, she plonked herself on Colette's knees, whilst Carrie chose to sit with Trudy. Putting their four pints on the table, it looked ready to collapse.

"Blimey, you've downed a few already haven't you?" Carrie said.
"Not really, other people have been putting their empties on our table too, we've only had a couple

each," Trudy replied. Carrie could see that the other girls had had the same idea re drinks, as there were at least ten full pints on the table now. Very precarious, especially with all the empties.

Carrie, being fussy as usual, gathered up all the empties, making much more room for their drinks, and put them under the table. "Now why didn't I think of that," Colette shouted. "Dozy mare that I am!"

Colette was a very pretty girl, with naturally light blonde hair which was even longer than Tasha's, and beautiful blue eyes, a pert nose and rosebud lips. She was tiny, standing at 5'1" maximum, but had a huge personality, which more than made up for her tiny stature. She was also hilarious, one of the funniest people Tasha knew, and she loved her dearly.

Colette was only a year older than Tash. They had known each other since Tash was three years old, and they had grown up together on the same road, until Natasha's parents had moved them when she was eleven years old. Still, the girls had never lost touch, they had a childhood bond that was so strong, nothing would break it. So many shared memories of lazy summer holidays playing hop scotch or terrorising the younger boys who lived on the same road. Fun days out to the seaside, yet also lost pets buried in their gardens, bruises and tears, tied them together forever.

They got together whenever they could, but it wasn't often enough, Tash thought, and they often said this to each other.

Now sat around the table was Tasha and Carrie, Colette and Trudy, and also three other girls who they had only met on a couple of occasions. Colette introduced the two girls to Clair, Louise, and Mandy, all who were predominantly Trudy's friends. The girls smiled back their introductions, and then they all settled in for kick off time.

***

Natasha was pleased to see that McManaman was playing, she thought he was gorgeous. Not that she'd stand a chance with him, and not that she'd want to, after the fiasco with Marcus, who was in a much lower division, so she could only imagine how arrogant some one of his stature must be.

The players were all now out on the pitch.

Tasha felt bubbles of excitement welling up inside her, "Come on you gorgeous lot!"
she shouted, making everyone around her laugh with amusement.

There it was, the whistle. And so the match began.

***

The girls were so excited, they could hardly sit still.
"Bloody sit still will you!" Colette laughed, "you're killing my knees."
"Sorry," said Natasha, "we'll swap around at half time if you like, give you a break, eh?"

The match was exciting. England were dominating the first half easily, but only managed to score once. Shearer finally managed to end his personal goal drought by receiving a defence splitting pass from Paul Ince and hitting a powerful shot just inside the near post in the twenty-third minute (YAY! SHEARERRRRRRRR!), and the whole pub went into uproar.

The girls jumped up screaming their heads off and bouncing around like idiots, it was
a miracle no one knocked all the lager over.

They sat back down, on the edge of their seats, Carrie and Natasha had to stand up, they couldn't take the tension any longer.

■■

The first half was nearing it's end, and the girls were ready for a quick dash to the loo's and for some more drinks.

"Bloody hell," Tasha said, 'What a match so far?" she shouted above the din, on a total football high.

The half time whistle had been blown, and Tasha, Carrie, and Colette headed for the loo's whist the other girls stayed behind to save their table.

"Bloody fantastic," Natasha squealed. "We're going to do it this time girls, I've got that feeling," she said as she was reapplying some lippy.
"I think you may be right for a change, Tash," Colette laughed. "We still have another forty five minutes, and England are playing well, Seaman is certainly holding his own, I'm sure we'll put away another one in the second half."
"Yeah, and probably let one through too," Carrie replied sarcastically. "You mark my words; England are always the same." she stated, as they headed out of the loos and made their way to the bar.

***

The second half had already started by the time the girls got back to their table, and they sat themselves down again, this time with Colette on Tasha's knees and Trudy on Carrie's. 'Hmmm'

Tasha thought, now she knew why Colette had complained earlier, and Colette was way lighter than she was. No wonder the poor girl was in agony.

Nothing much happened in the second half. England had a couple of near misses, but nothing to write home about, and Switzerland had a near miss, which sent a huge gaspup around the bar.

Then disaster struck.

In the eighty-second minute, a penalty was given for a Stuart Pearce handball and Turkyilmaz scored for Switzerland from the penalty spot to make it 1-1.

"For God's sake, England!" Natasha screamed. "Why do you always bloody do this to us?" She was so mad, she took it personally, as if the England team had done this just to piss her off.

The game ended with a 1-1 draw. Better than nothing the girls agreed.

They could only hope that when they met Scotland on the 15th June, again on a Saturday, they could pull three points out of the game.

■■■

Some of the crowd emptied immediately, but the girls stayed behind for a good natter
and catch up. They were feeling positive about this, as once again 'Three Lions' played on the juke box.

***

Chapter Twenty One.

Carrie was still secretly seething over David's mother, and her snide remarks. She was also that David hadn't stuck up for her more, but he'd seemed indifferent to it all, until it was almost too late.

"Men!" She thought, as she was dusting the lounge.

Housework day was Sunday. Not the best day to choose, because both her and Tash were usually suffering the effects of the night before, but housework seemed to take away the effects of any hangover she may have. Maybe it was the physical work, or the fact she couldn't sit there feeling sorry for herself that did it. She didn't know, but just knew that doing the housework was therapeutic. She was sad like that, she thought, as she reached up with the feather duster to give the light fitting a quick dust over.

Tonight, she was due to go to town with Natasha and Anna.
Sunday's were pretty good in town, and they always took it a little easier than they did on a Saturday night, because of work the next morning.

■■

She'd also arranged to meet up with David later in the night at Dexter's, for a quiet drink with him before home.
She had no intention of going back to his.

When they finally did sleep together, she wanted it to be special, and with 'that night' still freshly imprinted in her mind, was in no rush to go back to his place again any time soon.

'That bloody woman!' Carrie thought again for what must have been the hundredth time. She was going to have to do something about that, else she sensed it would have a serious effect on her relationship with David.

***

Arriving at Harry's bar, for a change from Bellina's, Carrie and Natasha paid the taxi driver, and headed inside. Anna was already there, with their friend Jasmine.

"Hi Ladies," Carrie said, "looking good, as usual."
"Thanks." Anna smiled, "you too, both of you."

Even though it was only a Sunday night, the girls were still dressed up very well and fully made up with perfect faces, and hair that had obviously taken hours to get just right. It was important that they always looked their best. They were only young once, after all.

The girls had arranged themselves around one of the columns in the bar, which had a ledge all the way around for people to put their drinks on.

Carrie and Tasha were heading to the bar, "Can we get you anything?" Carrie asked.
"I'll come with you," Jazz said, and with that, the three of them headed to the bar, to order drinks for them all.

Simply Red's 'We're in this together' was playing quietly in the back ground. Not one of Natasha's favourites, but hey, there was no DJ, so she couldn't complain to one.

As it was a Sunday, and quieter than usual, Harry's, as many bars did, were offering half price on all cocktails.

Perusing the cocktail menu, they all decided on what Jazz and Anna were already drinking, a Strawberry Kiss, which was the most delicious drink they'd ever tasted.
Normally, they wouldn't pay the high prices, but as it was half price night, the girls indulged themselves.

The cocktail was made up of one shot of White Rum, one shot of Disaronno Amaretto, four shots of Strawberry liqueur, and one shot of double cream, all topped off with a fresh strawberry, Yummy.

The method of making the cocktail was to blend all of the ingredients together with ice until smooth. Then pour into a hurricane/wine glass which has a garnish of fresh strawberry on the rim. It was delicious, and they intended having more than one of these tonight.

***

Whilst waiting for the cocktails to be made, Natasha glanced over to where Anna was stood, saving their place, and noticed that she was talking to Chris, an absolutely drop dead gorgeous man, who had a crush on Tasha, and had done ever since Tasha had dated his friend, Anton.

Natasha had been more than tempted on numerous occasions, because Chris really was so good

looking, but also so witty and charming. She'd
avoided him so far though, because she'd ended
her relationship with Anton on fair terms, and
didn't want to upset him by having a fling with
one of his best mates.

Still, she thought, could she hold off forever? She
did find Chris extremely attractive, and thought he
may be just what she needed right now, to get
Marcus out of her head for good.

Suddenly, she had a thought and nudged Carrie,
"Hey, how about we make the longest straw in the
world, and drink Anna's drink from here?"
Natasha said.

"How on earth are we going to do that?" Carrie
asked with amusement.

"Watch this." Natasha replied, and with that, took
a handful of straws from a dispenser on the bar.
She then set about biting the end of each straw so
that it would fit it to another one. She repeated
this until the straw was so long, it could easily
reach Anna's drink. She ensured the last straw's
'bendy bit' was bent at ninety degrees, for
maximum success.

She'd caught the attention of more than a few
people in the bar, who were watching the
girls with amusement.

"Here," Natasha said to Carrie, "Help me out with this."

Carefully lifting the world's longest straw, the girls managed to manoeuvre the straw so that it reached all the way from where they were at the bar, to where Anna's drink was stood on the ledge behind her.

The girls seemed to have everyone's attention now, except for Anna and Chris who were stood close together, engrossed in whatever they were talking about.

Jazz was killing herself with laughter, though trying to muffle it, so as not to alert Anna's attention.

"Here," Tasha said to Carrie, "You have the first sip." And with that, gave the straw to Carrie.

How she managed to take a gulp of the cocktail, Tasha had no idea, as she appeared to be close to hysteria.

"Give it me." Tasha said, and with that, took a large swig of Anna's drink, and then passed the straw to Jasmine "Here, you finish it off."

Jasmine, managing to compose herself, took the straw, and drained what was left of Anna's cocktail.

Withdrawing the straw quickly, and breaking it apart, the girls finally allowed themselves to laugh properly. It seemed everyone in the pub was laughing with them too, it was so hilarious. And still, Anna had no idea.

***

Taking the drinks over to where Anna was still talking to him, Chris noticed them approaching, and smiled that oh so sexy smile at them. 'He's bloody gorgeous', Natasha thought to herself, whilst grinning back at him.

Anna turned to reach for her drink, and looked baffled as to where the contents of her glass had gone.

This caused the girls to once again fall about in fits of laughter, much to Anna's annoyance.

"What the hell are you all laughing at?" Anna asked, suddenly aware that the whole pub was looking at her.

With this, the other girls broke out in to fits of laughter once again, so much so that they were doubled over, tears rolling down their faces. This obviously had a knock oneffect, as others around them were laughing with them too.

"Ok that's it." Anna demanded, "Tell me now, else I'm bloody well going, ok?" she was mad now.

Natasha, God knows how, managed to compose herself, and told Anna
what they'd done. Chris broke out in to peals of laughter, he'd obviously been totally unaware the girls' antics too.

"Oh hilarious." Annalise remarked, but couldn't help but smile, although she was trying her hardest to be mad at them.
"You can bloody well replace that!" she snapped.
"We already have done, here you go." Carrie said, and handed Anna two of the Strawberry cocktails.

"Sorry Anna, but it was just too funny *not* to do it!" said Jasmine, still laughing, her sides hurting from it all.

"It's ok, I see the funny side, you set of idiots." Anna laughed, "my Dad is right when
he says 'It just goes to prove they're not all locked up'."

***
■■

Chapter Twenty Two.

It was going on for 9.30pm before Carrie managed
to drag herself away from her
mates, and walk down to Dexter's to meet David.

Usually, she would have butterflies in her stomach
over the anticipation of meeting him, but tonight
was different.   She was still upset over his
mothers snooty attitude.

Who did she think she was anyway? Carrie
thought.

***

Walking in to the sound of George Michael's
'Freedom" playing, Carrie saw David
sat at one of the end tables, and noticed he'd
already bought her a drink.
He stood up when he saw her, ever the gentleman,
she mused - apart from when it really mattered.

He seemed to pick up on her mood straight away.
"You okay, darling?"
"Fine, thank you," Carrie replied, not looking at
him, but taking a sip of her wine.
"I think that says it all really doesn't it?" he asked,
eyebrows raised.

"I'm fine I told you," she snapped, which she
hadn't intended to do.

It was very obvious she was anything but fine.

How Carrie wished she was still at Harry's,
playing around like a child, and laughing
until her sides hurt.

She realised that this was the first time she'd
thought about not wanting to be in David's
company ever since she'd started seeing him. Was
this the start of the end?
She certainly hoped not.

"Okay, I'm not fine David, and I think you know
the reason why." Carrie finally met his eyes.
"Is this about my mother?" he asked.

'How observant', thought Carrie.

"Yes, in fact it is. She clearly despises me, and
took every opportunity to put me
down," she continued, "and what do you do?
Nothing, that's what, absolutely nothing."
David looked more than a little ashamed. "I'm
sorry about my mother," he said. "She
has idea's above her station, and had no right to
treat you like that," he continued,
"I've actually reprimanded her about it already,
and she say's she's sorry."

Carrie looked dubious. She knew the likes of his mother, and knew that his Mother had probably only said these words to placate her son.

"Well, I'm not in a hurry to meet her again, so don't go pulling any more stunts like that on me again, okay?" Carrie replied.
"I won't, I'm sorry, I can now see it was a big mistake" he said, "I did want you all to myself that night, but as my parents were so eager to meet you, I thought it to be the perfect opportunity. I can now see I was wrong."

Carrie felt her anger dispelling, and felt a little better. Okay, she thought, he's allowed to make a mistake. He is after all only human, and a man at that, she smiled.

"What're you smiling at?" he asked.
"Oh nothing much," she said, "just thinking how stupid men can be, no matter how intelligent some of them are supposed to be!"

He smiled back at her, and they soon fell back in to the easy banter they were used to, and against what Carrie had promised herself earlier, she found herself agreeing to go back to David's home.

***

■■■

Walking in to David's penthouse once again, Carrie was still in awe of the place, it truly was stunning, especially with those panoramic views of the city.

She was feeling very nervous, she knew that this was it, tonight she would be sleeping with David. She was so looking forward to it, but her nerves were on edge.

"Can I get you something, a glass of wine maybe?" asked David.

This was welcome, and Carrie replied that she'd like that very much.

"Turn on some music if you like," he said, as he was getting a bottle of white wine from the refrigerator.

"I don't know how to work your system, I'll wait for you to do it." she replied

Walking through to the lounge, where Carrie sat nervously on the edge of a plump sofa, David offered her the glass of wine, which she took willingly, taking a couple of large gulps to calm her nerves.

"Hey, someone's thirsty, slow down, else you'll be paralytic on me!" he said whilst choosing a classical music CD and inserting it in to the player.

"I am thirsty, could I please have a top up?"

"Of course," he replied, taking the glass off her, and filling it up once again.

The wine was taking effect, and she could feel
herself relaxing, especially with the
soothing music flowing from the stereo.

David walked back over to her, gave her the wine,
and relaxed down beside her.
She put her glass down on the table, and turned to
face him, face flushed from desire and anticipation
at what was to happen.

As Carrie relaxed back, David leaned over her,
and kissed her, slowly at first, and then more
passionately, as his hand moved down from her
shoulder and on to her breast. She let out a slight
moan, and was tingling all over from her arousal.
As his kiss intensified, she lead David's hand to
her groin, whilst she fiddled with his
belt, and released his hard cock from the tight
confines of his jeans. God he was
massive, how am I going to take this? She thought
as she stroked his penis.

This was it, this is what she'd been waiting for,
and deftly, David laid her down, pushed up her
dress, and moving her panties to one side, slid
inside her wetness with ease.

She moaned at the pure ecstasy, and as he moved
in to her, she moved with him, arching her back so
that he could penetrate her deeper.

He pulled the top of her dress down, and licked, sucked, and teased her nipples, 'Oh God' she thought, I am going to come if he doesn't stop this. David seemed to sense her urgency, and started to pump in to her harder, harder, and faster. His breathing was becoming shallow, and Carrie knew he wasn't far off.

"Fuck me David," she whispered, "Fuck me, I'm coming,"

And she was, pure ecstasy pumping in waves through her body which seemed never ending. David was coming now too, deep inside her, and he cried out "Oh my God Carrie, I'm coming, I'm coming."

***

'Wow' Carrie thought.
"Oh my God." David said.

They were laid in the same position, David was still inside her, she held him there tightly with her toned legs wrapped around his waist.

They were both soaked with sweat, and their juices mingled, which ran from between Carrie's legs.

"That was amazing," David said, as he finally looked up at a very flushed, and very satisfied Carrie.

"I know, better than anything I anticipated," she said.

"What's that supposed to mean?" he teased, "that you thought I would be crap in bed?"
"You know what I mean. And we're not in bed, we never even made it that far!"
Carrie replied, "I loved it, it just felt so natural, like we've been together forever and know each other's bodies inside and out."
David smiled, that post-coital smile that only intimate lovers shared, "I know what you mean." he said, then hesitated.

"What is it?" Carrie asked, snuggling in to him a little more, enjoying being in the arms of this man, she felt so protected and secure, and was so glad she'd gone back on her earlier resolve.
"Look at me," David eventually said.
Carrie leaned up on one elbow, looking at him intently.
"I love you Carrie, I really truly love you," He finally admitted.

He'd said it. Those three magic words she'd been waiting for.

She leaned further in to him and kissed him, a slow, languished kiss, before looking at him, and saying, "I love you too, Mr Oxton."

Kissing him again, he stroked her thigh, working his way up, as she began to feel herself become aroused yet again, and before she knew it, they were once again intertwined, making love, as if they'd known each others bodies for a lifetime. Knowing just what to do to one another to make the other quiver with pleasure.

'Yes', Carrie thought before pure ecstasy took over her 'This is the man for me'.

***

Beep. Beep. Beep. Beep.

That bloody awful noise that was the alarm clock, which meant another five whole days of work. Groaning, Carrie clumsily reached over David, still half asleep, to turn the damned thing off.

Trying to focus, she could see the time was only 6.15am.

David stirred, and looked at her lazily, "Morning beautiful, how did you sleep?"
"Wonderfully, just a shame we're back to real life, and I have to get home to get
ready for work," Carrie replied as she snuggled once again under the wonderfully

sumptuous duvet, not wanting this moment, to be over just yet.

She'd not prepared for staying out, and had no clothes, so had no choice but to go home to change before she went to work.

"I know sweetheart," David smiled at her. "But we must earn our bread and butter so that we can continue to live the life we are living."

He was way more sensible than Carrie, which she thought was a good thing, because she was useless at organising herself, and was more inclined to ring in sick than David was. He wouldn't allow that, she knew.

Before she had a chance to get out of bed for a shower, he'd grabbed her, pinned her down, and was once again penetrating her, making wonderful sweet love to her.

***

Laying in bed afterwards, way too late for getting to work as it was, but not even worrying, Carrie languished in the love of David's arms.

Kissing the top of her head, he got out of bed, told her to stay there, and that he'd be back in a minute.

Carrie was a little confused, but stayed where she was.

It seemed forever before David came back, but with him, he'd brought a tray, with freshly squeezed orange juice, coffee, hot buttered toast, and marmalade, and jams.
He placed this on the bed where he had been laid, and said, "two ticks," before he disappeared again in to the kitchen.
■ ■

As Carrie sat up, plumping the cushions behind her, and taking a sip of coffee, he reappeared with a bottle of Champagne and two glasses.
Carrie was now even more confused. What about work?

"I know I said otherwise, but I'm feeling footloose and fancy free, so called in to both our places of work and told them that we're both sick," he continued, "out of character for me, I know, but I just have something to say to you," he said as he expertly opened the bottle of champagne with a pop of the cork, and some of the amber liquid spilled down the sides of the bottle.

Carrie propped herself up again, her interest getting the better of her.

"What do you have to say to me?" Carrie asked, a little worried.

As if plucking up the courage, David took his time in replying "I just wondered if you fancied changing your last name?"
"What to?" Carrie gasped.
"Do I have to spell it out to you woman! Will you marry me, Carrie? Will you make me the happiest man on this earth?"

Oh my dear Lord, she thought, she'd not expected this.

Her instincts took over, as they were very rarely wrong, and she smiled at him, "Yes, I will, David." Before passionately kissing him on the lips, and reaching down to his groin, where it was evident he was already very aroused.David sighed at her touch, and lifted her out of the bed, grabbed the bottle of champagne, and made his way through to the en-suite.

Still kissing her, David managed to turn on the shower, and placed Carrie on the seat inside the cubicle. She remained silent as she watched his beautiful body, muscles ripped in all the right places, as he expertly popped the cork on the bottle.

He walked in to the hot shower, and Carrie immediately took him in to her mouth, teasing him with her tongue. He moaned, but pulled her away, "Here, take a sip of this," and he poured champagne in to Carrie's open mouth, and it trickled over her face, and mingled with the hot water running down her breasts, where David lapped at her, making her nipples harden with excitement.

Taking a mouthful of champagne, and kissing Carrie, he let her drink the champagne from his mouth. 'God, this is so erotic' she thought. Putting the bottle down, David picked her up, pinning her against the tiles, she wrapped her legs around his waist, and he was penetrating her, wet bodies entwined as he once again made love to her.

***

Chapter Twenty Three.

After their shower antics, and a long morning in bed, making love some more and nibbling on delicious hot buttered toast (David had had to make some more, as the first lot had gone cold long ago), and sipping Bucks Fizz, David suggested they drive to Carrie's so that she could get a quick change of clothes.

"Why?" Carrie asked.
"Because I'm taking you shopping for a ring young lady."
"Wow, now?"
"Yes now, we've got the day off, why wait? So hurry up and get dressed, I'm going to throw a couple of months wages on some major bling for my gal."

***

Leaving David sat in the car, and promising to be a few minutes, Carrie ran in to the empty apartment, and took no time in changing out of last nights clothes, changed her underwear for her new black wonder bra and matching thong, she quickly chose a plain black vest top, her faithful jeans complete with gold belt, and some black strappy shoes. She added some simple gold jewellery, grabbed her bag, and was back out of the apartment within ten minutes.

"Bloody hell, I thought you said it took you at least an hour to get ready?" David exclaimed. "To hell with it, I'm clean, I don't want to hang around, now I know where you're taking me, there's no way I'm wasting any where near an hour to get ready!"
"Do I look okay?" she asked, now wishing she'd taken more care.
"You look amazing darling" he said, "now let's get to Manchester before the shops close!"

How exciting' Carrie thought. This is turning out to be the best day of my life.

***

Like David had said, instead of driving in to a nearby city, or even Meadowhall shopping mall, where they may be seen by someone they knew, or even worse, someone from work, David decided to drive them over to the Trafford Centre in Manchester.

He suggested they look around a couple of shops to see if Carrie saw something she liked, then they would find somewhere for a bite to eat.

■■

The countryside flew by. Carrie didn't care about looking at the beautiful Peak District Country views, she just couldn't wait to arrive, so that they could begin to look for her ring.

Pulling in to the vast car park, David found a space near the entrance, and smoothly drove the Mercedes in to the gap.

Not waiting for him to get out to open the door for her, which he liked to do, Carrie jumped out of the car before the engine was even turned off.

"Hey Missy, what's the hurry?" David laughed. "I can't wait, come on, hurry up!" She squealed. He laughed, her enthusiasm was contagious, and David quickly locked the car, and they ran in to the shopping mall.

***

Carrie had not been here before. Shopping wasn't usually her thing, but she was so excited to be here. She couldn't remember ever being this excited. She couldn't wait to get home later and show Natasha her 'rock'.

David had been here before though, and expertly navigated her to the Dome area, and to the first jewellers, Ernest Jones.

■■

Just staring at the beautiful rings, Carrie was overcome with emotion. 'How do I chose one?' she thought.

As if reading her mind, David said, "money isn't a problem, choose whatever you like" he carried on, "or I can help you, if you like?"
"I'd like that very much," Carrie replied.

As they looked at the array of rings, one sprang out at Carrie. A beautiful aquamarine stone, princess cut, with a sizeable diamond on either side, and set in gleaming platinum.

"Oh I love that one, David, but look at the price, there's no way I could ever let you spend that amount of money, not on a ring."

"I told you already, money isn't an issue, you shall have what you want," he replied.

Carrie, airing on the side of caution, said, "well, lets have a look at some other stores, and then we can always come back to this one."

"Whatever the lady wants," David laughed, as he took her to the next Jewellers, Goldsmith's on Regent Crescent.

■■

Carrie loved some of the rings, but nothing compared to the one she'd seen in Ernest

■■

Jones, so on to the next Jewellers they went.

In Beaverbrooks, back in the Dome, there were once again a beautiful array of rings, but nothing struck her like the first one.

She knew now that was the ring she wanted, even if it cost more than a few months of her wages.

"David, I love all the rings I've seen, but the only one that stood out for me was the one in Ernest Jones. I know it's too much money though," she said, feeling quite guilty at not having found a cheaper one.
"Will you not listen to me, God damn it!" he replied, "if I couldn't afford it, I wouldn't buy it, so come on, let's stop dithering and go buy that gorgeous ring of yours."

So off they set, back to the first Jewellers.

***

■■■

The instant she tried it on, she knew it had to be hers. It was as if it was meant to be, it fit her perfectly.

It was so beautiful, the aquamarine stone shone and sparkled and reminded her of David's eyes. The Diamonds themselves would have made a perfectly good ring on their own, with the size of them, but it wasn't them that drew her, it was the aquamarine.

"Oh David," she gushed, "It's so beautiful."
"Just like you sweetie," he replied, and told the assistant that he would like to purchase it.
"Would madam like it wrapping?" Asked the polite assistant.
"*No*! No, I want to wear it now." declared Carrie.

***

Carrie was too excited to eat much, so they chose Carluccio's, which was in the Lower Hall section of the centre.
They ordered drinks. A glass of champagne for Carrie, and just an Orange Juice for David, who had to drive.

Carrie couldn't take her eyes off of the ring, even when the menus were brought.

■■

"Will you stop staring at it and pay me some attention?" David joked, "It's not like it's going anywhere is it?"

"Sorry," Carrie said, "It's just, I can't believe it, I thought today would be a typical day at work, yet here I am, with the most wonderful man in the world, glass of champagne in hand, and the most amazing ring on my finger, "I'm *engaged*!" she squealed, making people around them turn around to look at her in amusement.

Realising she'd been a little over zealous, she tried her hardest to calm down and look at the menu before her, but it was so hard, and she was way too hyped up to even think about eating.

***

The waiter returned to take their order, and Carrie ordered a child's portion of their homemade lasagne, which came with garlic bread and a leafy side salad. David, his appetite obviously not interrupted, ordered seafood pancakes, with a side order of garlic bread with mozzarella cheese, and a bowl of fries.

"How can you have such an appetite at a time like this?" Carrie exclaimed.
"Because I need to eat, and so do you, so just calm down for a moment, and eat your meal when it

arrives!" He berated her, but with an air of amusement about it.

***

Chapter Twenty Four.

It had been nearly a week, and true to his word, Marcus had not been in touch.

Strangely, Natasha sort of missed the attention, though at the time she had found it very annoying.

■ ■

Sitting in the dining room at work, after many hours of hard work (for a change), she'd chosen to have her lunch hour at work instead of having a stroll out.

She'd recently received an endowment from her parents, and not one to save money(she couldn't hold on to it to save her life), she'd decided a girls holiday was just the ticket, and was browsing Teletext on the TV for any offers.

After hearing the fantastic news about Carrie and David, she'd decided to treat Carrie and Anna to a girl's week away somewhere hot.

A pre wedding gift for Carrie, she reasoned, which they could also use as part of her hen night, even though the wedding wouldn't be until next year.

As she browsed through the holiday deals, she did feel a little down to be honest.
Carrie would no doubt be moving out, probably way before the wedding, and the idea upset her. She knew she was being selfish, but would miss her friend so much.

Just as she was feeling sorry for herself, she came across a great offer. Ten nights in Tenerife, in a self catering apartment, which looked fantastic, with three separate bedrooms, air conditioning (very important in such a high climate), and all the mod cons.

The apartments had two pools, one of which had a 'swim up' bar, and a nightclub attached.

But best of all, it was only a few minutes drive away from the fantastic night life that Tenerife offered, in Playa de las Americas. *The* place to party, she thought, excitement bubbling inside her.

Checking the price again, she couldn't believe it. Only £249 per person, all in, for the whole ten nights, including flights. She could easily afford to treat her friends to that, and was sure they could find their own spending money.

Wasting no time, Natasha called Carrie and Anna's bosses, to check those dates were okay for the girls to take a holiday. Luckily, both girls could take those dates, so Natasha asked them to book the dates off for both girls, but not to tell them, she wanted to do that herself.

Natasha then called the holiday company with their details, booked the date for Thursday the 1st of August (Anna's 25th birthday as it happens), for ten nights, for the three of them, and confirmed all the details.

■ ■

That's it. No going back now, she couldn't wait to tell her friends.

***

As soon as she'd booked, she phoned both Carrie and Anna to tell them what she'd done.

They could not believe it, and were so excited.

"What a wonderful, kind and generous gesture" said Carrie, "I just hope that I can get those dates off now you've booked. Trust you to jump in with both feet!"
"No probs," Tasha said, "I've already called your boss, and Anna's, you have the time off booked already."
"Blimey, is there nothing you can't arrange!"
"Doesn't look like it." Tasha laughed.

Both Anna and Carrie had offered to pay her for the holiday, but she was having none of it. "Just find your own spending money," was all Natasha had told them, and she was adamant.

There was no arguing with Natasha once she'd made her mind up.

***

■■

Yes, Carrie would miss David, and Anna, all loved up with the newly available Max, would no doubt miss him too, but what the hell, it was only ten nights, and she wanted this time together with her friends, before it all changed.

Carrie announcing she was getting married had been a shock, but a good one.
It had made Natasha look at herself, her lifestyle, and made her wonder if she would
ever meet the man of her dreams and be as happy as Carrie was with David.

'If only' she thought, as her lunch hour was over, and she returned to her desk.

***

Her phone rang, and she answered it in her usual professional manner.

"Hi sex on legs," was all she heard back. She recognised the voice, but couldn't put a face to it.
"Who is this?" Natasha asked.
"Chris, you fool, don't you recognise me by now?" He replied.
Her heart skipped a beat. Chris. The same Chris who she'd tried so hard to avoid,
because he was Anton's best friend.
Keeping her tone casual she said, "Hi Chris, and to what do I owe the pleasure?"

"I want to take you out for a drink."
Typical Chris, straight to the point.
Without hesitating, Natasha replied, "Okay, where and when, I'll see if I can fit you in."
"Cheeky mare, what about Saturday?"
"No way! England play Scotland, I'm not missing that for anyone, not even you, and I'm out with the girls anyway," she replied.
"See you in the Oak then," Chris replied, and before she had a chance to reply, he'd hung up.

The cheek of him. But, as was her style, she couldn't resist a man with an edge, and was looking forward to Saturday even more so now.

***

Saturday, 15th June, 1996.

A date that would be etched in her mind forever.

Natasha had spent a lazy day, watching mindless daytime TV, and had a shower to wash off the remnants of her spray tan which she'd had done the day before.

And now she was sat here, at 3pm, with a face mask on, fully moisturised from neck to toe, and was busy painting her toe and finger nails, whilst waiting for the face mask to set.

She switched off the TV, and put on some music. Oasis's 'Wonderwall' purred out of the stereo. Perfect, she just loved this song.

Carrie was in the shower. A sound that comforted Natasha, as she knew it would only be a matter of months if not less, that her friend would have moved out.
She would miss her so much, Natasha thought. That statement really was true 'you don't know what you've got till its gone' Natasha thought as she wafted her hands in the air, trying to dry her nails faster.

Anna had already given six months notice on her apartment, but would move in with Tash as soon as Carrie moved out, which was great, as she loved Anna as much as she did Carrie, and it meant she wouldn't be on her own. But she was still so sad this chapter of her life was ending.

***

"Hurry up Carrie," Tasha shouted through to the bathroom.

At least she didn't go barging in like Carrie did when Tash was in the shower. That
■■■

was one thing she wouldn't miss, Natasha thought.

"I need the loo, will you get out of the shower,
before you wrinkle up and disappear altogether!"
Natasha shouted again.
"Ok, I'll be two mins," Carrie finally chirped.
'Ten, more like.' Natasha thought.

Carrie had lost weight recently, Natasha thought,
as she sat in agony waiting for the loo. Probably
due to her excitement over what had happened in
recent weeks, and she was probably living on her
nerves, but she couldn't afford to lose any more
weight.
She was little more than skin and bone as it was,
no matter how hard she worked her muscles in the
gym.

"Well, make sure it is, I'm dying for the loo!"
Natasha replied, not lying either.

As expected, more than ten minutes later, Carrie
emerged from the shower, bright red from the
amount of time she'd spent under the hot water.

"Bloody hell, Carrie, are you trying to burst my
bladder and rupture my bowels?" Natasha asked as
she dashed past and straight in to the bathroom.

Carrie had to laugh, Tasha was so dramatic, she
should have been a bloody actress.
■■■

***

3.30pm, Carrie looked at the clock. Less than four hours to kick off. Time to get ready properly (she was staying over at David's later), and have a bite to eat to line her stomach.
She was just going to prepare her usual, cheese, beans and mushrooms on toast.

Walking over to the stereo, Carrie changed the CD. She'd never liked Oasis, so instead removed it, and put in her favourite Prince CD 'Diamonds and Pearls' and began singing along "D to the I to the A to the M. O to the N to the D, to the pearls of love,"
She settled back on the sofa listening to the music, and was having a little 'me' time before she commenced her culinary delights for tonight's dinner.

***

Natasha came out of the bathroom, looking a lot more relieved than before she'd gone in.
"Thank God for that," she said, "I thought you'd never get out of that bloody shower,"

222

she continued, "I'm having the water supply cut off, no one needs to spend half a day in a bloody shower for God's sake!"

"Drama Queen," Carrie smirked. "I was in there for half an hour max, and if you were that desperate for the loo, you should have gone before I went in, or wee'd in the sink as you've been known to do before," she laughed.

"Oh don't remind me," Tasha groaned, collapsing back on to the sofa, remembering the time she was so pissed, and the toilet was in use, she'd actually pulled down her jeans and pee'd in the sink.

The memory made her shudder, "don't ever let me do that again," Natasha said. "Not that you'll be here much longer," she said with a tinge of sadness in her voice.

"Hey, just because I'm moving out, doesn't mean I won't see you, I'll still see you all the time."

"I know, but it won't be the same as having you here, and I'll miss that," Natasha replied, "I know that sounds selfish, I am so happy for you, really I am, but am feeling sorry for myself, that's all," she said. "Just ignore me."

Carrie leaned over and gave Tash a hug, "you'll never get rid of me, that's a promise."

And one which made Tasha feel a little better.

***

∎∎

As Carrie was preparing the Haute Cuisine dinner of cheese on toast, topped with baked beans, and sautéed mushroom (see, she could at least sauté!), she felt the familiar monthly cramps starting.

'Great' she thought, 'just what I don't need right now'.
Reaching for some paracetamol, and swallowing them whole without water, she was
determined to stop the cramps before they got a proper hold over her. They were crippling if she didn't catch them in time, and had even had to go to bed with a hot water bottle on more than one occasion.

Why did she have to suffer such awful monthlies, when most women seemed to breeze through theirs?

"Dinner's ready," she shouted to Natasha.

"Okay, coming," Tash replied.

Sitting down at the table, Tash smirked, "Mmmm, this looks tasty, I don't believe I've tried this dish before," she laughed, sarcastically.
"Oh hilarious," replied Carrie. "At least I cooked something edible for a change, sothe very least you can do is be grateful for that."
"I'm starting to miss the fire brigade though," Tasha laughed.

"Get stuffed," Carrie laughed with her "Literally!"

***

Chapter Twenty Five.

After the fiasco of the previous England match,
the girls decided to get to the pub much earlier, to
ensure they had a table near the front, with enough
seats for both Tasha and Carrie, but also Jasmine,
Anna, and Colette.

■■■ ■■■

So with that in mind, at 5.30pm on a Saturday afternoon, the girls found themselves sat in the half empty Oak Tree.

The others hadn't turned up yet, but Tash hoped they would soon, she couldn't keep refusing the seats for much longer.
Tasha kept glancing around, "I wish they'd hurry up, people are starting to look
annoyed at us for not giving them the seats."
"I'll call Jazz," Carrie said, rummaging in her bag for her mobile.
"Jazz, where are you, we're struggling to hold on to your seats."
"Look behind you," Jazz laughed, and there they were, just walking through the door, heading for the bar. Thank God for that.

The three girls made their way over to Tash and Carrie, carrying eight pints of lager.
They looked like typical lager louts.
"Here, we've got you each another one," Colette said.
"Cheers." Carrie replied, "how much do we owe you?"
"Nothing," replied Colette, "you can get em in during half time."
"You worked that one well," said Carrie, "that means you bought two and we get to buy you three back!"
"I know," Colette laughed.

The girls chatted for a while, as the pub filled up, and before they knew it, the match was about to start.

Silence now descended on the table as the pre match-commentary started.

"Come on England!" They all said in unison, looked at each other, then fell about laughing.

***

This was it, the teams were walking out onto the Wembley pitch to massive roars from the crowds. Surely all this support would spur their team on, Carrie mused.

They needed three points at this stage, to have a chance of getting through these opening games, and in to the Quarter Finals.

***

After both teams had sung their own national anthems, they clapped to the crowds and ran to their places on the pitch.

"I wish we were there," Natasha shouted to the others over the noise. "There's nothing quite like being at Wembley," she said, having been there several times herself, once to watch Sheffield

United in the FA Cup semi-final showdown against their arch rivals, Sheffield Wednesday, in 1993. With a crowd of over 75,000, most of whom had travelled down from Sheffield, which she knew to be true, because of the state of the M1 that day.

Sadly, the Blades had lost 1-2 to Wednesday, but the day was etched in Natasha's mind forever.

Natasha had been seeing Anton, the footballer, at the time (she seemed like a footballer magnet), hence the reason for getting such great tickets for the match.

Bringing her back to the present was the kick off whistle, and so the match began.

***

Once again, Natasha felt the excitement, but also nerves, building up inside her.
They needed this so much, she could barely bring herself to watch.

Not much happened for most of the first half, and the girls were willing their team on.

"Come of England for the love of God, put the bloody ball in the net will you? And I don't mean your own!" Carrie shouted in frustration.

Typical 'girl' statement re football, and the men stood around them laughed at her.

Half time ended with a disappointing score of 0-0.

***

Waiting at the bar to be served, Carrie turned to Tasha and said, "Bit crap so far, what do you think?"
"Boring if you ask me, all we can hope is for just one goal in the second half and hope that we don't concede, though knowing England, they'll bugger up and let one through," she remarked back.

They carried five drinks back to the table, and settled down to listen to the half time

commentary. "Those commentators do my head in," Colette said. "All they do is state the bleedin obvious, I could do a better job myself."

The others laughed at her, but admitted she may have a point.

Natasha scrambled around in her bag for her lip gloss, and finding it, slicked it over her full lips. "What're you bothering with that for?" Annalise asked. "No one in here's bothered about what we look like right now."

"Well, you never do know," smiled Tasha, having already spotted and waved to Chris, who was stood over the other end of the room, where there was another large screen.

He was looking gorgeous, in his obligatory England shirt and faded denims. Tasha couldn't wait to meet up with him later, almost wishing the game was over.

How bad was that?

***

The second half started better, England seemed much more in control of the ball, and managed to keep a hold of it. "Come on England, do it *now!*" Annalise found herself screaming, which was totally not in her nature. She didn't even like football, but found herself caught up in the excitement of it all, it was certainly contagious, and she found she was enjoying herself immensely.

As if he'd heard her, Alan Shearer scored his second goal of the Championship with a diving header in the 53rd minute to make it 1-0 to England.

The pub went into uproar, everyone on their feet screaming and singing their song;

"It's coming home, it's coming home, football's coming home."

The girls chanted and jumped along, hugging each other.

This was it, Tasha was sure they'd clinched it.

Then in typical England style, they did it again, disaster struck.

In the seventy-sixth minute, Scotland were awarded a penalty for a Tony Adams sliding tackle on Gordon Durie.

"Bloody *hell* England," screamed Colette, "Pull yourselves together."

There was a deadly silence descended on the pub, everyone's hearts were in their mouths as they waited for the penalty to be taken.

It was like a ghost town in the pub now, Tasha thought, and imagined a few tumble weeds slowly weaving their way past her, as everyone waited with baited breath.

"Come on Seaman!" Screamed the girls.

■■■■■■■■■■■■■■■■■■■■■■■■■■■■■■■■■■■■■■■

The penalty was taken, and David Seaman pushed Gary McAllister's penalty up and over the bar.

"*Yes!*" they screamed, and once again the pub was in total uproar. This was fantastic. Football, when good, could make you feel like you were on top of the world, and that's what the girls felt like right now. Even Anna, who usually wasn't that bothered.

From here, England seemed to have gained a massive amount of confidence, as in the seventy-ninth minute, Paul Gascoigne, who was having a great second half, scored an amazing goal from the left wing.
Playing like they'd never seen him play before, he went between the Scottish defence, and just inside the penalty area, he flicked the ball over the head of the last Scotland defender, Colin Hendry, and then volleyed it into the net.

"*Come on!*" the girls screamed again. This was amazing. Surely they'd got it in the bag now, surely the much needed three points were theirs.

The game had been fiercely fought, with Ince and Shearer being booked, and for Scotland, Collins, Spencer, and Hendry having been booked also.

And there it was, the final whistle. England had won Scotland, the result being 2-0.

Just what they needed.

A massive party was going on in the pub, and the girls were a big part of it, Tasha dancing madly on the table, with Colette and the others on stools, singing and swaying along, as the landlord turned up the juke box playing, 'Three Lions' once again.

It must have been on full volume.

Official man of the match was David Seaman, and rightly so, he'd played a blinder.

***

Chapter Twenty Six.

The others were heading into town, to carry on the celebrations, but Natasha had other ideas.

"Enjoy yourselves you lot, but I've got a hot date with the delectable Chris!" Natasha exclaimed. "What!?" Colette asked, "Really? You lucky sod, he's bloody gorgeous. Reminds me of a young Brad Pitt, although, maybe even better looking."

"You're not wrong." Natasha replied, "and I'm going to make the most of it, while it lasts," she laughed. She knew that Chris was not one to be tied down, and right now, that's the last thing she needed either.

No, she was going to have some fun for a change, and Chris certainly knew how to do that.

***

The girls left within minutes, wishing Tasha luck, not that she'd need it they all laughed.
Chris, noticing their departure, sauntered over to where Natasha was still sat, "Hey beautiful, so are we still on for tonight?"
"What do you think I'm doing sat here?" Natasha replied, "waiting for a bus!"
He smiled down at her, "So, what do you fancy doing?"
"Oh come on Chris, let's not beat around the bush, we both know what we want, so why skirt around it?"

Now she had his full attention.

"So, let's go buy some bubbly, and go back to mine and spend the night in bed, doing some interesting things with strawberries, fresh cream, and some Champers, okay?"

■■

No way would any man in his right mind down
that offer, Tasha thought.

"Stop catching flies, and close you're mouth
Chris, it doesn't suit you," she laughed.
"Get in there!" he said, laughing, as he grabbed
her hand and led her out of the bar.

As they walked towards the exit, Tasha noticed
Marcus sat alone at the far end of the
pub. He seemed to be watching her sadly. 'What
on earth is he doing here?' she
wondered. Would she ever be rid of him?

It seemed that he wasn't going to give up so
easily, but Tasha tried to push him to the back of
her mind as she walked out in to the warmth of the
summer evening with Chris.

***

Natasha wasted no time, as soon as they'd entered
the apartment, she grabbed Chris, and kissed him,
her tongue exploring his mouth, whilst her hands
undid his shirt.
Tearing it from him, she dropped it on the floor
and undid the buttons on his jeans.
He was very hard already. She grabbed his cock
through his boxers, and rubbed the shaft with the
palm of her hand.
■■■■■■■■■■■■■■■■■■■■■■■■■■■■■■■■■■

Chris let out a moan as she continued to kiss him,
pressing herself up against him so that he could
feel her erect nipples against his chest.
He tried to take off her top, but she stopped him,
"Go through there, that's my room,
and wait for me,"
Chris tried to protest, but Tasha cut in "Just do it,
get undressed, and get in bed, I'll be two ticks,"

Tasha got the strawberries, fresh cream and
champagne from the fridge, placed them
on a tray, and selected two flute glasses. This was
going to be fantastic she thought, the electricity
between them was amazing, and just what she
needed to stop her pining after Marcus.

She walked through to her bedroom, where Chris
had done as she said. He was laid
in bed waiting for her, so she placed the tray on
the bedside table, and switched the
stereo on low, music to enhance the mood.
She slowly started to take off her clothes, peeling
them away a little at a time, teasing
and tantalising him.
"Come here," he said, his voice full of lust.
"No, you have to wait, I'm doing this my way,"
she continued to peel off her clothes, until all she
was wearing was her red balconette bra and
matching thong.
Chris groaned with pleasure "Come here Tasha, I
want you now,"

"All good things come to those who wait," she
teased, and moved closer to him, taking away the
quilt cover.
God he's gorgeous she thought, as she stared
down at his tanned six pack, and huge erection.

She picked up the cream, and poured it over his
toned chest and stomach, then crawled up the bed,
licking the cream off as she made her way up his
body.
"Bloody hell Tash, I'm going to come if you don't
stop it,"
She didn't listen to him, instead picking a
strawberry, and put it in to her mouth. She
then bent to kiss him, and he took the strawberry
in his mouth.
As she straggled him, she drank straight from the
bottle of champagne then poured
some in to his mouth, and they exchanged
champagne kisses.
"Tash, please, I can't take much more," he
pleaded.

With that, she unhooked her bra to release her pert
breasts, and slipped off her thong.
She then grabbed his swollen cock, and slid it
inside her, riding him slowly.
She moaned as she moved up and down on him,
and he grabbed her hips, trying to make her go
faster, but she was having none of it, she wanted to

tease him to the point where he was nearly coming, and then take him back again.
She did this time and time again, stopping when she felt he was going to come, and
she too felt her orgasm coming.
"For fuck's sake Tasha, let me come!"
So she rode him harder as he grabbed and massaged her breasts. And then they were coming together, waves of ecstasy pummelling through their bodies.

Tasha collapsed at the side of him, taking the bottle of champagne and swigging out of it, before offering it to Chris.

"Bloody hell, that was amazing." he said to her.
"Well, get ready, because that was just for starters." She smirked at him.

'God he was so sexy' she thought, and never imagined sex, especially first time sex with someone, could be so good. Usually it took a few times to get used to the other person, but with Chris, it'd felt like they'd had sex a million times before. She was amazed, and couldn't wait for more.

Everything but the Girls' 'Missing' was playing on the stereo, and Chris leaned back into the pillows, with his hands behind his head.

■■

"Thought we could make a proper start on these and celebrate," she said, pouring
them each a glass of champagne, and placing the tray with the strawberries and cream
on her lap.

Sitting up, Chris said, "Celebrate what?"
Natasha was amazed, "Erm, are you a bloke or what?" she poked fun at him, "We just battered Scotland, and you just bedded me, what else do you need an excuse to celebrate for?" she teased.

She was full of herself, but she had a right to be. She was drop dead gorgeous, intelligent, ballsy, quirky, and so funny. And for the moment, she thought, she was all his, for as long as they both wanted.

***

They giggled as they drank champagne from each others mouth's, and then Tasha
once again poured cream all over Chris, but this time on his groin and erect penis, and took her time licking and sucking it off of him, like a cat lapping up cream. She was so turned on. The first time had been slow, tantalising, mind blowing sex, but this time, Tasha wanted it hard and fast.

■■■

He felt her hard nipples against his stomach as she continued to lick the cream off of him, and he was so hard, Tasha was sure he'd come, there and then.

"Tash, please, let me inside you, I can't bear much more of this," he pleaded.
And so she rolled over, spread her legs, and let Chris slip inside her.

***

Chapter Twenty Seven.

Tasha awoke to beautiful early June sunlight seeping in through the curtains.
Tiny dust particles played in the sun rays, dancing around, and almost sparked, before they were blown away by a breeze from the open window, only to be replaced by new ones.

She lay like this for a while, watching these tiny little specks do their flawless dance in the air, before turning to look at Chris.

As beautiful in sleep as he was awake, she thought.

Carefully removing her arm from around him, she wrapped her dressing gown around her and made her way to the shower.

When she returned to the bedroom, Chris had gone. No sign of him ever being there, apart from two empty glasses at the side of the bed.

Oh charming, Tasha thought, fuck me and then fuck off, how nice of him was that?

She'd obviously misjudged him, and was fuming at him for treating her like a slapper.

How dare he, she was getting madder the more she thought about it.

***

After stomping around in a terrible mood at what Chris had done to her, she made a

quick coffee, and returned to her bed, where she
continued to fume.

Just as she was working herself up in to a real
lather, she heard the door to her apartment open.

Before she'd had a chance to get up again, Chris
peeked his head around the door,
"Morning gorgeous," he smiled.
"Where the bloody hell have you been?" she
snapped.
"I've been out to buy you these," he said, and with
that, emptied the grocery bag on to the bed to
reveal the Sunday papers, a bottle of champagne,
some freshly squeezed juice, some speciality jams,
still warm croissants, and a single red rose.

"Oh, I thought you'd just gone home."
"Not a chance, thought you deserved breakfast in
bed that's all."

She was feeling a little ashamed now, thinking
him so shallow as to just bugger off home when
instead he'd been out buying all of this for her.

"Sorry Chris, this is fantastic, thank you. Get your
ass back in here and help me out with this stuff."

Without having to be asked twice, he was
undressed and leaping in to the bed next to her.

■■

"Let's enjoy these, then enjoy each other," she giggled.

***

They had the most lazy morning. Nibbling on the mouth watering buttery croissants with the delicious jams Chris had chosen, sipping the fragrant coffee which Tasha had made, then sipping at a bucks fizz each.

They had made love slowly after that, exploring each others bodies, and making the wonderful experience last as long as possible. Natasha was in heaven, she could stay here forever, and absently thought about Marcus, and how selfish he was, compared to Chris.

They had then turned the radio on low, easy Sunday listening, and took a paper each, reading side by side, so comfortable, as if they'd been together forever.

***

Tasha knew this was only a fling, but wanted to make the most of it while it lasted, and putting her paper down, she dove under the feather and down duvet, and started to suck, kiss and nibble Chris in all the right places.

■■■■■■■■■■■■■■■■■■■■■■■■■■■■■■■■■■■■■■

Chris gave in to the delights of what Natasha was doing to him. He laid back and allowed her to work her magic on him, with that oh so wonderful mouth of hers.

***

It was inevitable. They had to get up at some point. So reluctantly, at 2pm, they both crawled out of bed, and got dressed.

Natasha agreed to drop Chris off at home as he was playing football later with some of the lads.

As she pulled up outside his house (he still lived with his parents), he promised to call her soon, and turned to give her a lingering kiss. 'A promise of more to come' Natasha thought, as he waved good bye, and drove back home.

***

By the time Natasha arrived home, she'd only been gone fifteen minutes maximum, Carrie had arrived, and she wasn't alone. David was with her.

■■

"Hi you two," she said airily. She'd accepted David as being Carrie's boyfriend long time ago, but he still seemed nervous around Natasha.

"David," she said. "Do us all a favour, and take that rod out of your backside will you!," she continued, "I love the fact you two got together, so stop looking so bloody worried every time you see me!"
"I'm okay about that Natasha," David replied, "I don't feel uncomfortable at all."
"Yeah, sure," Natasha replied. "So stop looking it then!"

Looking at Carrie, Natasha noticed a definite feeling of uneasiness about her friend.

"What's up Carr, looks like you've seen a ghost?" Tasha tried to make light of the situation.
"Nothing. Well, nothing really. It's just that David has asked me to move in, and I've agreed. I'm taking most of my stuff today," Carrie replied, looking more than a little sheepish.

Bloody hell, this was sooner than expected, thought Natasha. She felt like she'd been thumped in the chest.

"Oh, I see," Natasha managed to compose herself. "Sooner than I thought, but I knew it was coming,"

"Look, don't worry, please!" Natasha continued, "I really am happy for you both. Just promise me one thing."

"What's that?" Carrie asked, looking up at her best friend.

"Come to stay here on the night before your wedding, one last single girls night in, okay?"

"Of course I will," Carrie replied, and was so relieved. She'd expected Natasha to take the news much worse than this.

With that, Natasha grabbed both of them in a bear hug, and squeezed them tightly.

David may be her ex, but there was no animosity there, and as he was soon to be more or less her brother-in-law, she thought she'd better let him know of her approval.

"And, if I get you alone later," Natasha said to Carrie. "I can tell you all about my amazing night with Chris."

***

Chapter Twenty Eight.

"So, this is it then?" Natasha said.

"Yes, I suppose it is," replied Carrie. "I'm going to miss you Tash," she said, bursting into tears.

"Hey, stop that," Tash soothed, "this is the beginning of the most exciting chapter of your life, don't cry, you're not losing me, I'll always be here for you."

"I know that," Carrie sniffled. "It's just a little sad….I'll miss our getting ready together, I'll miss trying to burn the apartment down, I'll miss, everything, but most of all, I'll miss *you*," she replied.

"I know, I'll miss all those things too. Well, maybe not the very real fact that one day you would raze us to the ground, but all the other stuff," Natasha continued. "And we'll still have our girly nights, that won't stop, so please, no more tears, this is a wonderful new phase in your life," she said, giving her mate a big squeeze.

***

Natasha had plonked herself on Carrie's bed and sat there with her legs crossed, as Carrie was filling suitcases with her possessions. She had far too much stuff, and it would take more than one journey to get everything over to David's, but she was taking the bare essentials today, and would come back either later on or tomorrow for the rest.

Annalise was due to move in soon, having given notice of six months, but she was going to stand to the penalty, and move in with Tasha as soon as Carrie moved out.

This had upset Carrie a little, feeling she was being replaced asap, but she reasoned, Tasha could do with help with the mortgage. She still felt jealous though, that it would be Tasha and Anna who would be doing 'their' ritual of getting ready, instead of her and Tash. That's only one of the things she'd miss, but at the same time, was so excited to be moving in with David, the man she loved and adored. She still felt so lucky that they'd found each other, and this whirlwind romance was getting better with each and every day.

***

"So, enough of the sniffles," Carrie promised. "What happened with Chris last night?"
"Wouldn't you like to know!" Tasha teased.
"Oh come on, you know you're going to tell me, so you might as well do it now."
"Well, as soon as you left, I dragged him home, stopping off at the Offy on the way to buy Champagne, and we spent the whole night in bed, doing things with strawberries and cream that should never be done, as well as drinking the Champagne." Tasha smirked.
"God, you don't mess around do you!" Carrie laughed.

"That's not all," Natasha continued. "When I
woke this morning, he'd only sneaked
out and bought fresh croissants, some beautiful
jams, fresh orange juice, the papers,
and a red rose, all of which he brought to me in
bed!" Natasha said. "Then he
produced another bottle of Champagne, so we
spent until early afternoon in bed
having wild sex, drinking the Champers!"
"You're insatiable," Carrie mused. "So, what
happens from here?"
"Oh you know Chris, he's not one to be tied down,
and that's not what I want either,
so we're just going to have a good time, while it
lasts." Natasha said, "Plus, we don't want Anton
finding out, it would hurt him, even if it is a
couple of years since we split up."
"Sounds perfect for you right now." Carrie replied,
knowing that this was just what
her friend needed after having her heart broken by
Marcus.

***

It took both Carrie and Natasha to close Carrie's
cases. They had to sit on them both,and even then
it was touch and go as to whether they would close
or not.

■■

"Blimey Carrie, what have you got in here, Ayers bloody Rock?"

"I don't understand why they're so heavy, these cases are only clothes, I've not even started on my other stuff yet," Carrie laughed.

"Well, I think it's going to take you a few journey's, with all this stuff. You're a hoarder, you do know that don't you?" Tasha asked.

"I know, and this would be the perfect time to de-clutter, but I'm not leaving you with a heap of black bags outside your door. The bin men won't collect that amount of stuff, so I'll do that at David's, and anything of any use, I'll take to Oxfam next week."

"Good idea," Tasha said. "Hey, I'll lend you my cases too, so at least you can take as much as possible in one go, save you and David a heap of time and running backwards and forwards." Natasha jumped off the bed and went to get her cases from the large storage cupboard.

This was Natasha's apartment. Her parents had given her a very generous twenty five percent deposit, so all Natasha had to do was find money to pay the mortgage and bills every month, which she did with ease, especially as she always had a flatmate to help towards the bills.

***

■■

Returning with two large cases, Natasha puffed, "Blimey, these are heavy enough on their own, never mind what you're about to put in them!" "And remember, I need these back," she continued, "both of them, for our holiday to Tenerife in a couple of months!" "I know," Carrie smiled. "I can't wait, it'll be like living with you again, which I don't know is a good or a bad thing!" "Oi, cheeky mare," Natasha said, throwing a large scatter cushion at Carrie. "Less of that, else I'm ripping up your ticket." "You'll have a job on," Carrie replied, "I've already found and taken mine." "We should keep everything together. The last thing we need is to lose the tickets or our passports," replied Tasha, knowing how scatter brained Carrie could be. "It's okay Tash, I've given them to David for safe keeping. He's so organised, there's no way he'll lose them."

This made Natasha feel a little easier, though she would have preferred to have kept everything together.

They girls heaved the two packed cases out in to the hallway, making room for the two empty cases, which they placed on the bed, and continued placing Carrie's belongings in to them.

■■

It was a sad day indeed, thought Natasha.

***

Chapter Twenty Nine.

It was now Tuesday, 18th June, and Natasha was in a rush to get away from work as fast as possible, 'as are the rest of England', she thought.

■■

Even though it was only three days since victory over Scotland, tonight, England were meeting Holland, at Wembley.

Tasha thought, 'With four points under our belt already, all we need now is to hold our own, or if possible, win one more match to get through to the fourth round'.

***

Putting her personal belongings into her bag, she was just about to leave work when her boss peeked his head around his door and asked if she had a minute.

'Bloody hell,' she thought 'this is all I need, I want to get home and get ready, surely Paul does too, else, what sort of man was he.'

Grabbing her jacket, to ensure her boss knew she was going as soon as she'd seen him, she walked over to his office and closed the door behind her.

"Take a seat Natasha," Paul said.

'Bloody hell' she thought, 'this must be serious, he's using my Sunday name.'

■■

She sat there, staring at him expectantly, and wishing he'd get the hell on with it so she could dash off.

"I've arranged a buying trip to Florence, and thought it was time you got a chance to visit some of the factories we purchase from, and meet the people you talk to daily." he said.
Oh my Good Lord! This was excellent news.
'Did it mean that long awaited promotion?' Tasha thought with anticipation.

"That's wonderful, Paul, thanks so much, when is it?"
"It'll be for two nights, flying out on Wednesday 7th August, two days after your birthday, if I remember correctly."

Oh No.

Why did these things keep happening to her? On those dates, she would be in Tenerife with Carrie and Annalise.

"Oh no, Paul. I'm on holiday then, I go on the 1st of August for ten days. I wrote it on the wall calendar, and did clear it with you," she said.
"Bloody hell, I forgot about that," he replied.

He sat thinking for a moment, tapping his pen on his desk, before saying, "Oh well, there'll be

another time I'm sure. Just sorry you couldn't
make this one, it would have done you good."

Natasha wasn't stupid, she read between the lines
and knew what he meant. The promotion was now
even more further away, as she was putting her
holiday before work. She knew exactly what he
was saying.

***

With a heavy heart, Natasha drove home in the
mad rush hour traffic, which was crawling along at
a snails pace. It seemed everyone in Sheffield was
on their way home right now.

She couldn't cancel her holiday and lose all that
money, and she couldn't let her friends down, who
were so looking forward to it. Why was Paul like
this with her?
She worked hard, she was a very popular member
of staff, and was a valuable asset, she knew that.

But she knew deep down, Paul didn't really like
her. She'd always known it, and doubted she'd
ever get that promotion now.

It was time to start looking for another job, she
conceded. She wasn't prepared to be treated like

that any longer, and knew that had she been male, she would have received that promotion a long time ago, when it was due. It wasn't fair, and she'd had enough.

'They could stuff their promotion where the sun doesn't shine.' Natasha thought angrily. They needed her more than she needed them.
She was looking for another job as soon as the papers came out on Thursday and Friday night, that's when most jobs were advertised.

***

Once she'd finally got home after forty-five minutes stuck in a gridlock of traffic, even though she only lived two miles away from work, she stormed in to the house, slamming the door behind her.
She was absolutely fuming, and before even taking her summer coat off, poured herself a good measure of red wine, which she gulped down immediately, before pouring another.

She needed to calm down.

Shrugging off her jacket, and casually throwing it over a chair in the lounge, she turned the stereo on and heard the sound of Edwyn Collins's 'Never Known a Girl Like You Before'. Natasha loved this song, it was one of her favourites, and she

liked to think this song had been written about her.
'Quite arrogant really' she thought, but
she didn't care, she was special, and she knew it.

Taking large gulps of her wine, she made her way
to her bedroom to take off her clothes for a quick
shower, before she began to get ready to meet up
with Chris, Anna and Max, at their local.

The other girls were going to another bar to watch
the match this time, and Carrie was watching it at
home with David.
Tasha didn't mind, she liked the idea of meeting
up with Anna and Max, and hoped that they got on
with Chris, though there was no reason not to.
There wasn't anything to dislike about Chris at all,
she smiled, remembering the weekend.

***

Padding back in to the bedroom from her shower,
she heard her mobile ringing.
She didn't recognise the number.
"Hi Natasha speaking," she said easily.
"Hi Tash, it's David."
Surprise!
"Oh hi David, what can I do for you?" Natasha
asked, and then suddenly worrying
about her friend asked, "Is Carrie okay?"
"Oh yeah, she's fine Tasha. It's just I wondered if
you and Chris would like to come over for dinner

on Saturday night. We're having a little celebration dinner for Carrie

moving in, and the thing is, my parents are coming, and Carrie and my Mother don't exactly see eye to eye," he continued, "I hoped you could come along to help

dissolve any awkward situations which may arise, knowing my mother."

"Charming!" Tasha replied, "I'm only invited as the go between."

"Oh no, I didn't mean it like that," he said. "Sorry if it sounded that way. I'd have invited you anyway as Carrie's best mate. She knows nothing about this by the way, so don't say anything to her will you? She'll only fret if she knows she has to spend the evening with my mother again."

"Ok David, I'll check with Chris, but I'm sure it'll be fine," she said, "I'll get back to

you tomorrow, after I've spoken to him."

David thanked her, and she hung up.

'Just what she needed' Tasha thought 'a night of pretentious pleasantries in order to try to keep his bloody mother sweet.'

She'd met his mother only twice, and did not envy the predicament Carrie would be in

if the oh so royal Mrs Oxton had taken against her.

***

■■■

Tasha was ready in no time. She'd had no choice really, given the fact that Paul had kept her behind, and the grid locked traffic.

She'd had a mad rush on to get ready in time, and had decided to leave her long tresses to dry naturally. Her hair had a slight natural wave to it, but she usually used straightening irons to make her hair sleek, but tonight decided, with time not on her side, to leave it 'au naturelle'.

Working two big handfuls of mousse through her hair (the bottle said use a golf ball sized amount, but what good would that amount do?), she bent upside down and shook her hair to give it some body.
She knew her hair suited her like this, and was sure Chris would find that 'just got out of bed' look so sexy on her.

She'd recently had a spray tan, so just applied a shimmering pink eyeshadow,
matching blusher and lipstick and a couple of coats of mascara, and that part of
getting ready was over with.

Glancing at her watch, 5.30pm, she was only going to be a little late and was sure they'd save her a seat.

■■■

She chose her black wonder bra, red England vest, favourite Naf Naf jeans, which had thin vertical white stripes over the blue denim, she added a black belt. She chose to go commando, that'd give Chris a surprise later!

Slipping on her red Jimmy Choo's, the present from that prat Marcus, and some simple jewellery, and she was almost ready to go.

Just a quick spritz of Nina Ricci's 'L'Air Du Temps', a nice light summery perfume, she grabbed her large red bag, and set off to walk the mile to The Oak, where she was sure, her friends would be waiting.

'Bloody hell' she thought halfway there 'May be a taxi would've been better' as the shoes were not meant for walking any distance, and were already killing her.

She made a mental note to take them off in the pub to give her poor feet a rest, and to get a taxi home.

What she did in the name of fashion!

***

Chapter Thirty.

As expected, the pub was full to bursting by the time Natasha arrived.

■■■

She nudged her way through the crowds, in the hopes that Anna and Max had arrived early and obtained good seats.

Glancing forward, she could see that indeed, Anna had managed to get them the same table they'd sat at for the match against Scotland.

Good. This was a sign. Their 'lucky' table, Tasha thought.

She had a quick glance around for Chris, but couldn't see him yet. Still, he'd know where to find her when he arrived.

Natasha managed to squeeze through the throng of people, and finally plonked herself down on her saved seat.

"Thank *God* for that!" she exclaimed, already lifting a leg to remove a shoe. Her feet were killing her. Was fashion really *this* important, she thought.

"What's up with you?" Max asked.

"Oh nothing, apart from the fact I most probably need feet transplants. These shoes may be the Dog's, but they are killing me!" she moaned.

Anna laughed. Natasha, ever the drama queen.

***

■ ■

Having taken off both shoes and hidden them
under the table, Natasha could almost hear her feet
thanking her for releasing them from their torture
chambers.
Smiling at this thought, she took a big slug of
lager from the pint Max had bought her
before she arrived.

She'd have to take it easy, she thought, she'd
already had two very large red wine's, thanks to
Paul and his offer. She *knew* that he was aware
she was away on those dates, he'd done it on
purpose to torment her, she was sure.
Always that bloody carrot, dangling like a drug in
front of her.
Well, not any more, she thought, as soon as she
found another job, she was out of there, with no
notice.
Stuff them, they didn't deserve her.
Let them try and replace her soon. Some chance,
she thought.
And thinking this, knowing how to get back at
them, made her feel one hundred times better.

***

Before the match started, Max went to the bar to
get more drinks. Chris's drink had
gone flat, so Max had drunk it and was to replace
it, because surely he'd be here soon.

■■■■■■■■■■■■■■■■■■■■■■■■■■■■■■■■■■■■■■ ■ ■

"So," Tasha turned to her friend, "How's things with you and Max now that Suki is out of the picture?"

Anna smirked wickedly, "We're having the time of our lives. It's all sex, sex, sex,and more sex. Oh and sometimes we have sex!" she laughed.

Natasha saw a glow about Anna, which only came with being so in love and lust, and envied her friend that.

"I'm joking of course." Anna continued. "Of course the sex is amazing, but having him full time, and not having to sneak around any more is the best thing ever."

"I bet it is," Tash replied above the growing noise, "but have you encountered Suki yet?"

A shadow fell over Anna's face. "No, I've not seen her yet, and I'm not looking forward to it."

Suki was a fire ball, and Natasha almost winced at the thought of her and Anna coming to blows. She had no idea who would win.

"Well, try to steer well clear for as long as possible. Give her time to cool down, you know what she's like," Tasha replied.

"I know," said Anna, "I'm not looking forward to it, but it'll only be a matter of time. We know too many of the same people remember?"

Tasha knew this only too well, and felt a little sorry for her friend. When the confrontation happened, which it would, there would be hair and nails flying everywhere.

***

Totally shocking her, Chris had crept up behind, grabbed her, and nibbled on her ear.

"Oi, who the hell are you, get off of me you creep!" Tasha spat.
Hearing the familiar laughter, she relaxed.
"Ha bloody ha Chris, you do realise that you were very nearly in mortal danger don't you!"
"Not from you Missy, you can't resist me."
"But I didn't know it was you did I, you muppet, so be careful, remember I do after all, have a black belt in Karate."
"So kill me." he laughed, hugging her and then sat down beside her.

He smiled his greetings at Anna, and as Max was now back with the drinks, shook his hand, "Good to meet you mate, I've heard a lot about you."
"All good, I hope?" Max laughed, winking at Anna.
"Sure, Anna loves you man," Chris teased her.
"I so do not," Anna protested.

"Kidding you Anna, take a chill pill," Chris smiled.

And with that, the pre match banter continued easily between the four of them.

***

And there they were again, sat at what Natasha had now dubbed their 'lucky' table, and the whistle had been blown to signify the start of the match.

"Come on *Englaaaand*!" Tasha whooped, nearly knocking all of their drinks over.

"Will you stop it," Anna laughed, "you're embarrassing us!"
"Oh shut up little Miss Prim, I'm here to enjoy myself, so stick a sock in it!" she replied, whilst sticking her tongue out.

'Hmmm' thought Anna, 'I wonder how many drinks she had before she came out.'

***
∎∎∎∎∎∎∎∎∎∎∎∎∎∎∎∎∎∎∎∎∎∎∎∎∎∎∎∎∎∎∎∎∎∎∎∎∎∎∎

The excitement was there in the air again, you could almost reach out and touch it.

The game against Holland was one of England's most feared games, and had them all on the edge of their seats throughout. There were more than a few expletives shared, at lost opportunities, or when Holland looked like scoring.

Holland were one of the favourites and had won the European championships in 1988, so England had to be on their toes.

England started very well and after twenty-three minutes, McManaman (Tasha's favourite) received the ball and ran up the right wing.

"Come on England, put one in the back of the net now!" Tasha shouted.

McManaman waited for Ince to arrive and passed to him just inside the box. Ince cleverly flicked the ball in front with his right heel and blind fouled him.

PENALTY FOR ENGLAND. The pub was once again in uproar.

Then there was silence. Everyone waited with baited breath. Could we do it? Tasha thought.

Shearer took the penalty and hit the ball hard and accurate to the goalkeeper's right to make it 1-0 to England.

YES. Uproar once again. *COME ON ENGLAND*,
Chanted everyone.

Before they knew it, it was half time.

***

"Blimey," said Tash. "That was amazing. Is it just
me, or are England looking stronger with every
game?"
"I think you're right Babe," Chris said kissing the
top of her head. "I'm just off to get the drinks in,
Max, will you give me a hand mate?"

And with that, the lads disappeared to the bar.

"You two so suit each other," Tasha remarked.
This seemed to surprise Anna, "Do you really
think so?"
"Yes, I do. I'm so pleased it worked out for you
guys."
"Me too," Anna grinned, "I knew my patience and
aloofness would pay off eventually. Oh and the
fact we were caught out by Suki's parents
probably had something to do with it!" she said.
"Yep, I guess so, just make sure you listen to me,
stay out of her way, for as long as possible," Tasha
warned.
"I'm not stupid, I'm avoiding her at all costs.
We're not even going into the city, we tend to stay
on the outskirts so we don't bump into her, but I

miss our girly nights, so can't avoid the city forever," Anna conceded.

"You're right, but we can always arrange a girly night to Nottingham or Leeds. They're not that far, and it's better than risking a bitch fight in the middle of town, don't you think?"

"Yes, I do. Lets arrange something, and soon, I miss you Tash."

"Hey, you're moving in next week, then you'll be sick of the sight of me." Tasha laughed.

***

The lads had managed to make it back before the second half, but were pissed off that they'd missed the commentary.

"You didn't miss a thing, they all talk a load of shit." Anna shouted. "And anyway, who can hear them above this noise?"

She was right, the pub was in chaos, you could hardly hear yourself think.

"Hey," said Chris, "shut up, here it is."

And with that, the second half began.

***

England were on top form (watch out Brazil and Argentina in the World Cup come 1998, thought Tasha).

The second goal came after fifty-one minutes, a good cross by McManaman was well defended by Reizinger who then cleared the ball over his own crossbar.

Gascoigne took the corner and Sheringham headed the ball in at the far post. Holland only had a player at the near post for the corner.

"*EN-GER-LAND!*" they shouted.

"This is bloody amazing," screamed Tasha as she was picked up and twirled around by Chris. "I think we're going to do it, I think we're going to win this time!"
"Hope so babe, it's been too long coming," he replied.

The third goal was the best of all, and once again the pub was in total uproar.

In the fifty-seventh minute, Gascoigne received the ball from McManaman before passing a Dutch defender on the left wing. He passed the ball back to Sheringham who unselfishly passed across the box to an unmarked Shearer. Shearer then blasted the ball into the back of the net unchallenged.

"Bugger me, this is the match of the Century," Anna said.

"I think you're forgetting 1966," Max laughed at her limited knowledge of football, and she looked annoyed at him for spoiling her comment.

"Shut up Max, I'm having fun, so belt up or else," she said whilst slapping his head.

He grinned back at her.

Back to the match.

Anderton had a speculative long range shot from outside the box. The Dutch goalkeeper, Van der Sar, saved the ball, but it came loose. Sheringham got there first putting the ball to the goalkeepers right and straight into the net.

Unbelievable to everyone in the pub (and everyone in England most probably) in the Sixty-second minute, England were 4-0 up.

"Does anything get better than this?" Natasha shouted.

"Only sex with you babe," Chris whispered in her ear. She couldn't help but smile.

In the seventy-eighth minute, the substitute Kluivert brought the score line back to 4-1 by running through the England defence, receiving a good pass from Bergkamp, and firing into the net through Seaman's legs.

Bloody hell, a set back, but everyone was sure Holland couldn't recover from England's three goal lead at this point in the game.

However, that goal was good enough to put Holland through to the quarterfinals at the expense of Scotland (on goals scored as goal difference was equal).

The fight had been fierce, with bookings for Sheringham, Ince, and Southgate, and for Holland, Winter, Blind, and Bergkamp.

Teddy Sheringham was officially Man of the Match.

The night belonged to England though, who qualified top of their group.

By the end of the game, the whole of the country was celebrating and believing that on home turf, England could go all the way and lift the cup, least of all Tash, Chris, Anna, and Max.

***

"Come on Babe," Tasha said to Chris, grabbing his hand, "We're going home to celebrate in style!"

Saying their goodbye's and promises to meet up again very soon, the couples parted company, and both sets headed to their separate abode's, with more than football on their minds.

***

Chapter Thirty One.

Tasha woke early, 6am, and nudged Chris awake, "Sorry babe, but I've got to get ready for work. Fancy a coffee before you go?"

■ ■

Chris yawned and turned to look at her. Her mass of hair was tangled wildly, from the massive sex session the night before, *and* she had smudged make up around her eyes.

But to him, stood there with only his England shirt on, which was sizes too big for her, he didn't think he'd seen anything quite so beautiful.

"Go on then Sexy Ass. Any chance of a quickie before I leave?" he asked cheekily.

He had to ask, what bloke wouldn't?

"Nope, sorry, I have to be in by eight sharp, I'm on a mission," she stated.

He knew when not to argue with her, so accepted the offer of a coffee, and laid back down, snuggling down under the covers.

***

Returning with two steaming mugs, Natasha said "Shit!"
"What's up?" asked Chris.
"Shit, Shit and double Shit!"

'Charming', he thought.

■■■

"I told David we'd go over for dinner on Saturday. They're having a little celebration for Carrie moving in. He wants me there as back up for Carrie, as his mother is a bitch."

"So what's the problem?"

"What's the problem!" she replied in amazement. "We play Spain on Saturday, *that's* the problem!"

"Oh. Shit."

"What do I do?" Tasha asked, "I've already said we'd most likely make it, and I should be there for Carrie, but how can we miss the match? It's *Spain* for God's sake, it's the Quarter Finals, anything could happen!"

She had a point.

He'd never met a girl so clued up on football before. She could explain the off side rule better than any man he knew, and the more he learned about her, the more he wanted her. She was so sassy, yet streetwise and intelligent. Put that together with drop dead gorgeous looks, and you had a lethal weapon on your hands.

"No idea," he said, "it's up to you. A boring night in with David's bitch of a mother, or another fantastic night of footie. You can't have both darling." ●●

"How could David have forgotten," she snapped.
"He loves football as much as we do."
"Well, until last night, we weren't sure we were
through, so look at it that way."
"Oh come on, we all knew we were through," she
replied haughtily. "Bloody typical, now what the
hell do I do?"
"Hey, calm down, no need to take it out on me, I
wasn't the one who agreed to this. And if you're
so clued up, you should have known the fixtures."
he snapped back at her, a little more than he
should have.
"Thanks a lot, what use are you!" she snapped
back, and turned and stormed out of the room.

'Great' Chris thought, 'just what I need, Natasha
in a mood like this, at 6.15 in the morning'.

***

Even after her shower, she still hadn't calmed
down, and he had a feeling there was
more to it than Natasha was making out.

"I'm sorry babe, I didn't mean to snap at you, but
you are so annoying when you're in that mood,
and it's not my fault you double booked us."
"No," Natasha said, "I'm sorry, I'm the one who
buggered up, and now I have to try and sort it.
There's no way I want to miss the match, but

Carrie is my lifelong friend, how can I let her
down?"
"I don't know babe, but do something today, don't
leave it until it's too late."
"And what with bloody work, and the nightmare
I'm having there…Oh God, I just can't bloody
stand it," she replied, a little less scathing this
time.

'There it was,' Chris thought, 'she's got work
problems, it explains a lot about her mood now'.

Not wanting to rile her any further, he didn't push
the work issue. She'd tell him in her own time.
And knowing Tash like he thought he did, it was
better to let her figure this out. If he tried to help,
she'd only snap his head off again, and he'd
already had enough of that for one day, and it was
still only 6.45am. Great start to the day.

Little did they know, that the decision about
Saturday's dilemma was about to be
taken out of their hands.

▪▪▪

▪▪▪
Chapter Thirty Two.

▪▪▪

Carrie was on a total high. It might only be early days, and she'd only 'officially' moved in a few days ago, but everything felt so natural, just being here with David.

He'd made her feel more than at home, by giving up most of his wardrobe space for her vast array of clothes and shoes, and told her if she wanted to change anything, to re-decorate, it was up to her, as long as she felt at home, that was all that mattered to him.

She'd managed, by some miracle, to stuff all of her clothes into his wardrobe, but was going to order some new furniture, including a futon, for the spare room, which she'd decided she'd use as her dressing room cum guest room, if any one wanted to stay over.

She loved the décor as it was, but intended to add a few more feminine touches, vases of flowers, some abstract paintings, and some interesting ornaments she'd seen in the local craft store.

Apart from that, she was happy with how things were. And she was more than happy with how things were going with David.

***

■ ■ ■ ■ ■ ▪ ■ ■ ■

They'd wasted no time, and had booked, of all places, the Cathedral, for their wedding. Nothing less for Carrie, David had insisted, although she secretly thought that his Mother wouldn't expect anything less for her precious son.

It was to be on the 14th June 1997, a Saturday, and gave her exactly one year to get things sorted.

She could hardly believe it. She'd gone from footloose and fancy free, to being an engaged lady, with a wedding booked, all in the space of three months. What a whirlwind, but it felt so right, she had no doubts whatsoever she'd made the right choice.

***

David had left for work over two hours ago, after making love to her for over an hour.
The delicious memory was still with her, and she could still smell him on her skin.
She didn't care that she smelled of aftershave, she wasn't washing his smell off her
for anyone.

Glancing at her watch, she realised she was running late, so after grabbing her bag, and a quick check on her appearance in the mirror, she set off for work.

■■■

***

The decision about Saturday night, and what to do about it, was effectively taken out of Tasha's hands.
It was only 9.30am, where she was at work mulling over some shipment contracts, when the call came.
She didn't even take the time to tell her boss, she just grabbed her things and left work, no matter the consequences.
Carrie had been in a head on collision with another car, and apart from knowing that
she was in intensive care, knew nothing else.

***

Even though not a good idea, Tasha phoned Anna's mobile whilst she was driving to the hospital.
"Anna, oh my God, Anna. Carrie's been in an accident. She's in intensive care."
"Where is she?" demanded Anna.
"At Chesterfield Royal."
"I'll meet you there, I'll be as quick as I can." And with that, they both hung up.

■■■

■■■

■■■

David was already there, pacing the corridor
outside the ITU, when Anna and Tasha
arrived. He looked so distraught and beside
himself.

"It's all my fault," he said, "I delayed her this
morning, so she was in a rush for
work." He held his head in his hands, and broke
into tears.
God, if anything happened to her, he'd never
forgive himself, Tasha thought.

***

The three of them hung around in the corridor, not
being allowed in yet. Coffee after coffee, they
became more anxious as they time went by.
Surely, they should know something by now.

Anna had called Max and told him the bad news,
as had Tasha with Chris. Tasha had also called
work and explained her quick departure, it was the
least she could do, she couldn't afford to lose her
job before finding another.

Carrie's mother and sister had been alerted, and
were already on their way from
Burton-on-Trent.

***

■■■

"Why all this waiting?" Natasha snapped, as Doctors and Nurses entered and exited the room, without a word to them.

"Calm down, Tash," said Anna. "We love her, but we're not next of kin. They're probably waiting until her Mother gets here."

"Damn it!" David said in an outburst which was so out of character. "She's my wife-to-be, surely that stands for something!"

"Where's your Mum and Dad?" Natasha spat, "I know your darling mother can't stand Carrie, as she couldn't me, but at a time like this, you'd think even she'd have the decency to be here." she glared at David.

"Hey, hey, you two. Stop it! Stop in now! This in *not* what Carrie needs, us at each others throats, so give it a rest and get some perspective." Anna shouted, rousing the attention of more than a few of the Nursing Staff.

"You're right," Natasha said, "I'm sorry David, I shouldn't have said those things, I was out of order. I'm just so frustrated, we all are."

"It's okay," David said grudgingly, "no apology needed, I shouldn't have shouted either," he said, not looking at anything but the blue-checkered flooring.

***

■■

It seemed like hours, but couldn't have been more than twenty minutes, before a doctor came to talk to them.

She ushered them in to a side room, where it was more private.

"Okay, who's the next of kin?" the doctor asked looking at each of them in turn.
"I am," David replied, "She's soon to be my wife, but her mother and sister are on their way too."
"Right," the doctor said, quickly glancing down at her notes. "It seems that Carrie has sustained a chest injury. One of her ribs has punctured her left lung, but we've got that under control," the Doctor continued, looking at David, "We've managed to stabilise that, but she's also suffered a slight head injury, what's termed as a Cerebral Edema which in layman's terms means a swelling of the brain, and we are keeping her sedated in order for her to heal, so you won't be able to talk to her for a day or two at the least. Don't worry, it sounds worse than it is, I am sure Carrie will be okay,"
she concluded.

At this news, all of them broke into tears, the frustration and fears of the last few hours finally surfacing.

"Will she, will she have brain damage?" David managed to ask between sobs.

"It is unlikely, but at this stage, we can't rule it out," the doctor replied. "She's in the best possible hands," the doctor reassured. "She is stable, and we will keep her sedated as I told you. If there is improvement in the next day or two, we'll hopefully look to move her from ITU to a normal ward. I assure you, we are doing the best we can, and just hope that the swelling subsides soon."

And with that, the Doctor excused herself and was gone.

***

Chapter Thirty Three.

■■■

The next three days were living hell for everyone who cared for Carrie. Carrie's family had arrived, and David was kindly putting them up at his and Carrie's home.

All of them – David, Tasha, Anna, Carrie's Mum Paula and Sister Mollie, spent every waking hour at the hospital, willing Carrie to improve.

Other friends had either come to the hospital, phoned, or sent flowers. So many people cared about Carrie, it was such a devastating time for them all, and they lived on nothing but coffee, cigarettes, and nerves. None of them had the stomach for food.

David even slept at the hospital. They had kindly provided a type of Z bed, and he slept at her bedside, holding her hand, willing her to get better. He didn't know what he would do if anything happened to his Carrie. He already felt that his world had collapsed, he couldn't even begin to imagine how he would feel if Carrie didn't pull through this.

***

Details of the accident were now unfolding.

■■■■■■■■■■■■■■■■■■■■■■■■■■■■■■■■■■■■■■■

Carrie had stood no chance. She'd been travelling on a dual carriageway when a car coming in the other direction had veered onto the wrong side of the road, and had hit Carrie head on.

It hadn't been her fault.

The other driver, who had sustained minimal injuries, was charged with being over the limit, from alcohol consumed the night before, and was also charged with causing serious injury by dangerous driving and being under the influence.

David only hoped it stayed at this charge, and not onto the more serious charge of 'death by dangerous driving'. God, he couldn't even think about that.

He simply could not lose Carrie. She was the love of his life.

***

It was now Saturday, 22nd June.

The date of the Quarter Final match between England and Spain.

Not that this was even at the forefront of their minds, all Carrie's friends and family were doing was taking it in turn to sit with her.

Earlier that day, after a CT Scan, the doctors decided the swelling had subsided enough for Carrie's sedation to be stopped. The Scan had also shown there was no permanent damage, thank God.

A huge sigh of relief was breathed all round.

All that they were waiting for now, was for Carrie to wake up.

She would be groggy, and the doctors did warn she may suffer some amount of amnesia, but everyone was willing Carrie to wake up, with no long term effects.

***

It was early afternoon, 1.30pm.

David, who had been snoozing, with his head laid on Carrie's bed, and still holding her hand, noticed a small squeeze from Carrie's hand.
He looked up, she seemed to be asleep.
"Carrie. Carrie Darling, can you hear me?" he willed her to open her eyes.
Again, but stronger this time, she squeezed his hand.

"Doctor!" David shouted. "Doctor, quick, over here. I think she's waking up."

***

The Doctor rushed over, checked Carrie's vital signs, and was just about to open one of her eyes to shine a torch in to it, when she opened them for herself.

"Oh thank you God!" exclaimed David.

Carrie looked confused, and winced in pain. She seemed to take a while to adjust to her settings, then slowly, and obviously very painfully, turned to look at David.

"Hey beautiful," he smiled at her.
"Hey back." she managed to mutter, but it was obvious she was in a lot of pain, her
voice was little more than a whispered rasp.

***

After a thorough check up, it was thought that Carrie would fully recover with no lasting effects. There certainly weren't any signs of amnesia, thank God, David thought.

She was due for one more CT Scan later that day, to ensure the swelling was still going down, and to ensure they hadn't missed anything, but the doctors were positive she'd make a full recovery.

***

Carrie fell back asleep after what must only have been twenty minutes awake, but David used this time to go outside for some fresh air, and to call everyone to tell them the good news.

Carrie's Mum and Sister were due in at 3pm, but he needed to let them know the good news before that. He was so excited, and so very relieved that he had his Carrie back.

The thought that he'd nearly lost her made him shudder once again, even in the summer heat.

The hot summer's day was made bearable by a light breeze, and David took in lungfuls of the fresh air, as if he'd never experienced it before.

The days spent in the stuffy hospital seemed more like months, and he took a moment to enjoy the warmth of the sun on his skin, and the breeze on his face.

***

Putting the phone down, Natasha shouted, "Fantastic!" through to Anna, who was sat in the lounge.

Anna had been due to move in properly, but that had been put on hold due to Carrie's accident.
However, neither of them wanting to be alone, Anna had packed some essentials, and had been staying at Tasha's ever since Carrie's accident.

"What?" Anna asked expectantly, looking up.
"Carrie, she's awake! It looks like there's no lasting damage. What a relief."

Both girls burst into tears.

***

Everyone raced to the hospital, but as there were so many of them, they had to take it in turns to go in to see Carrie two at a time. There was a lot of waiting around in the corridors once again.

Carrie was still groggy and very sleepy, mainly due to the pain medication she was on, but she managed a few words and a smile with Tasha and Anna.

That was enough for them, that was all they needed to see. Their Carrie back, and on the mend.

They left her when she fell back asleep, and were
replaced immediately by Carrie's Mum and Sister.
David had taken this opportunity to pop back
home for a much needed shower and change of
clothes, before returning to the hospital.

***

"There is a God after all," Tasha remarked to
Anna, on their way back to Tasha's car.
"There certainly is, and I just thank Him for Carrie
being okay," Anna replied, "What a terrible few
days it's been for everyone, especially Carrie."
"I know, and David, I thought he was going to lose
his mind, he was that distraught."
"He loves her like I've never seen any one love
someone before," Anna said. "To
finally find your soul mate, and then to nearly lose
them, must have been the shock of his life," she
continued. "they really do have the fairytale those
two, they were meant to be together, and I am so
relieved for David, for *all* of us, that she's going to
be okay."

'I want a love like that' Natasha thought, as they
climbed in to her XR2, and headed for home

***

■■

Chapter Thirty Four.

Even though Carrie was on the mend, the girls
didn't feel like going out to watch the match.
They chose to stay at home with a bottle of wine
and a Chinese instead.
Chris and Max understood. How could they not?
Hopefully, if England beat Spain, the girls would
feel up to going out to watch their
next match.

Both Tasha and Anna had changed in to their
pyjamas, and with the lounge window
and back door wide open, to allow the wonderful
summer evening breeze to blow
through the apartment, they settled back to watch
the match.

It wasn't the same, not having the atmosphere of
the pub, but they just didn't feel up
to going anywhere after what had happened.

Tonight, they wanted to chill, safe in the
knowledge, their best friend was on the mend.

***

The match was due to start any minute, and the
girls were huddled up on the comfy

sofa, with a nice chilled glass of wine each. They would order a take out once the match was finished.

Strange, but even though they'd hardly eaten over the last few days, they weren't that hungry. They supposed that's what living on your nerves did to you.

The whistle was blown, and England started their fight to get to the Semi Finals.

■■■■■■■■■■■■■■■■■■■■■■■■■■■■■■■■■■■■■■

The girls couldn't muster up that much enthusiasm, but watched their team all the same. They still wanted England to win more than anything, but they were just both physically and emotionally shattered after the last few days.

The match was pretty uneventful, but with each team holding their own.

The girls willed for that one precious goal for England, but it never came.

Even in the thirty minutes of extra time, that precious goal eluded England, but at least they didn't concede one either.

With two great keepers on show, the match ended 0-0 after extra time.

"Oh no." Tasha exclaimed, "look at England's track record with penalties. That's it, we're out."
"Oh don't say that Tash," Anna replied, taking a sip of her wine. "It aint over till the fat lady sings, remember."

Tasha laughed, a much needed belly laugh, that was so welcome.

"Who're you calling fat, you skinny mare?"
"I'm not bloody skinny, but I've lost weight, we both have, after everything that's happened," Anna replied.
"At least we can settle now, knowing she's okay. I'll call the hospital later, just to check."
"Good idea, I'd not thought of that," Anna replied.

***

And so it was here. Penalty time, and the girls didn't know if they could bare to watch. Natasha got up, and was pacing around like a caged lion.

"Will you sit down, you're making me even more nervous," Anna said.

"I can't. I'm too wound up, I can barely watch."

And it was painful to watch, Tasha was sure they were out now. What an awful end to the worst week of her life. She'd really hoped for something to lift her spirits, but could feel that slipping away now.

However, Shearer, Platt, Pearce and Gascoigne all scored their penalty for England, which lifted the girls spirits no end with each goal, they even managed to shout a

"Come on England!"

Hierro missed and Nadal had his penalty saved by a wonderful move from Seaman.

Stuart Pearce seemed especially happy with his penalty after missing the one in the World Cup 1990 semi final.

***

That was it, England had only gone and done it, they'd won 4-2 on penalties!

The Official Man of the Match was once again avid Seaman, and rightly so, saving

those penalties, he'd played his little heart out.

The girls were elated, forgetting their worries for a moment, they jumped up and hugged each other.

"I can't believe it," said Tasha, "England winning on penalties, hardly ever happens." she laughed and they hugged again.
"Bring on Germany or Croatia!, though I hope it's Croatia, I hate it when we play Germany, we never seem to deliver the goods," she said whilst chewing on a fingernail.
"Have faith will you! Look how far we've come already!" Anna said.
"You're right," Natasha replied. "Pour me another wine, I'm going to phone Chris then the hospital to see how Carrie's doing, then we can order a Chinese."
"And anyway," Anna shouted through to the kitchen, where Natasha had gone to use the phone, "how come you know so much about football?"
"What sort of a stupid question is that?" Natasha laughed, "Where've you been the last few years, I made dating footballers an art form!"

***

Tasha spoke with Chris briefly about the match and Carrie. He was so relieved to hear the good news re Carrie, he really was. Before hanging up, they promised to meet up again soon, hopefully before the Semi final, which was to take place in only four days, on Wednesday the 26th of June, again, at Wembley Stadium.

Natasha then called the hospital, and was relieved to hear that Carrie had perked up, and had even managed some ice cream. All positive steps, she just hoped that Carrie was out of hospital soon, and back with David. He'd look after her better than any nurse could.

Fantastic news, now she felt so much better.

"Carrie's definitely on the mend," Tasha shouted through to Anna. "She's eaten Ice Cream!"
Anna laughed, "That's bloody brilliant!, now get the Chinese Menu, I'm starving."

***

Chapter Thirty Five.

Just over a week after the accident, Carrie had made a good enough recovery to be allowed home. A small miracle, that girl sure had a Guardian Angel watching over her. She was still feeling a little fragile, and was on strong painkillers as she seemed to have a constant headache, and as for her neck, it was absolutely killing her.

***

"Come on Babe," I'll walk us to the apartment, get you settled, and then come back down for your bags" David said, so relieved to have her home.

What a week it had been.

"Thank you, I'm bushed, I think I'll just have a bath and then watch TV in bed if you don't mind?" asked Carrie.
"Of course I don't," he replied. "I'll join you in fact. But I'm warning you lady, no sex for you tonight, you need to build your strength back up."

Carrie burst out laughing, "Stop it, laughing makes my head hurt, and as if I'm up to that, I wish!" she continued to laugh, wincing at the same time.

Walking in to the apartment, she was overcome with the aroma of flowers. Entering the lounge, it was absolutely packed full of possibly every single type of flower you could think of.

"Who bought all of these?" she asked, amazed.
"Well, I bought some, but your friends bought some too. Even my mother managed to buy you some," he said, pointing to a beautiful arrangement of Fuchsias. "I ran out of vases, and had to go buy a few more from John Lewis on my way to the hospital yesterday."
"But you all bought me flowers in the hospital."

She'd left those behind for the Children's ward though, to brighten up the place for the poorly children.

"I know, but we all know how much you love flowers, so bought you a load more. Stop complaining, and make the most of it!" he said, kissing her lightly on the lips.

She was overcome at what people had done for her, and in her emotional state, burst in to tears.

"Hey, what's up sweetheart, these are meant to make you happy, not sad."
"I'm not sad, David, it's just everything I've been through, I'm just a little emotional, and now all of these glorious flowers. Sorry, I'm just feeling a

little overwrought, that's' all."
"No need to apologise babe, I understand." he
replied, hugging her lightly so as not to hurt her.

***

'It was good to be home' she thought. Even
though she'd sustained a punctured lung, and what
had turned out to be only minor head injuries, she
hated hospitals at the best of times, and as she got
better, she was almost chomping at the bit to get
out of there, but the hospital insisted she stay in, to
be on the safe side, which she'd resented. She
wanted to be home for God's sake. She knew that
she would get better a lot faster being at home and
with David. She'd missed him so much, even if he
had spent most of his time with her, it wasn't the
same as being at home with him.

"Don't try getting in the bath until I'm back up
here," David warned her. He was so protective of
her, she felt so loved and safe with him.
"I won't, I promise," she replied, before David
headed back to the car to collect her belongings.

***

The bath had been a struggle to get into. It seemed
that every muscle in her body ached, and she felt

so weak. But the hot water soothed her bruised body, and instantly she felt soothed.

"No falling asleep in there, do you here me?" David shouted to her.
"I won't, I promise. In fact, will you pass me the phone, I think I'll surprise Tasha and Anna."

Tapping in the numbers, Carrie waited for someone to answer.

"Hi!" Anna answered after the third ring. "It's me," said Carrie, "I'm home at last!"
"Oh thank God for that. Are you okay? Do you feel alright?"
"I'm fine. I ache a little and my head and neck are killing me, but I'll mend," she smiled. "Anyway, I only phoned to see if there was any gossip I've missed out on?"
"Charming," laughed Anna. "No, you haven't. The only drama of this past week was you. Even football took a back seat, and for Tash to do that, must've meant she was really worried."
"Well, I'm okay, home safe and well, and am just going to take it easy for a couple of weeks. Work don't expect me back anytime soon, and they're letting me have the time off on full pay, aren't I a lucky girl?"
"Lucky, After what you've just been through!" Anna replied, "Lucky you got out of it alive I suppose, but I don't see the accident as being

lucky, do you?"

"I see what you mean," Carrie replied, wriggling her big toe up the hot water tap. "I miss you guys, will you pop over some night, maybe next week, when I'm a little stronger?"

"Of *course* we will," exclaimed Anna, "you try keeping us away."

"And, thanks for the flowers by the way, they are beautiful, you shouldn't have. Please thank Tasha for me as well won't you?"

"You're more than welcome, the least you deserve, and yes I'll tell her. You look after yourself okay, or make sure David does or he'll have us to answer to, and he really doesn't want that experience." Anna laughed.

"He's doing great, don't worry, he's clucking around me like a mother bloody hen!"

"Good to hear it, see you soon, okay? And we'll call you in a couple of days, see how you're getting on, and arrange when to come to see you."

"Okay, thanks Anna, see you soon." And with that they hung up.

***

"That was Carrie," Anna shouted to Natasha, who was in the bath with Chris.

■■

Jumping out of the bath, and peeking around the door, Tasha asked, "is she alright?"

"Yes she's fine. A little fragile, and she still hurts, but is glad to be back home," Anna said. "She wants us to go over one night next week, for a proper catch up."

"That's great," replied a wet Tasha, who was covered in bubbles from the bath, "Shows she's feeling a bit better at least, and I suppose the only good thing to come out of this is that we didn't have to spend Saturday night with *HRH* Oxton!" she laughed.

"Oi Lady, get back in here or lose me forever," Chris said from the bath.

"Gotta go," Tasha said. "Got a God calling me!" and she closed the door.

All Anna could hear were squeals of delight, and water slapping around. 'Honestly', she thought.

***

Laid in the bath with Chris was fabulous. The bath was bigger than the average tub, and there was plenty of room for at least three people (not that she'd want a threesome, even she wasn't that adventurous, she thought).

They were sipping chilled white wine, had Sade's CD playing softly in the background, and had the window open, letting in a beautiful Summer evening breeze. Perfect.

"This is the life," Chris muttered as she turned to kiss him softly, and then slowly worked her way down.

He groaned with pleasure as she teased him with her tongue and then took him in her mouth. He was so aroused, he didn't know how long he could last, and stopped Natasha, to kiss her once again, drawing the moment out.

"Turn around, I want to take you from behind" he muttered, his voice thick, and full of lust. Quickly putting on a condom, before he entered her, he parted her legs, and slowly licked and sucked her. She moaned with pure ecstasy, and sensing this, Chris moved up and entered her with ease. She was so wet, and not from the bath water.

Grabbing onto the taps, Natasha moved with him, faster, then faster, until they were both coming at once. Pure, unadulterated lust pumping through their whole beings.

"God Tasha, you're so good, I can't last more than a few minutes with you," Chris muttered. "You're doing that part of my ego no good at all." he smiled at her, laying back, completely sated, once again.

"Well, find someone who doesn't turn you on so much," she replied.

"Not a cat in hell's chance, I'm enjoying you too much, thanks."

Sipping her wine, she knew what he meant. She knew how good she was, and that was one of the reasons Chris kept coming back for more. He was amazing too, she thought. That body, that six pack, he was a stunning creature.

"Ditto," she smirked back at him.

***

'Bloody hell, it sounds like the Titanic is sinking in there!' Anna shouted with amusement through to the bathroom, as she was sat in the lounge. She was just glad *she* wasn't the one who had to clean it all up afterwards.

***

Max was running late. He'd been pulled over by the police and asked to produce his documents.

This happened often because of the car he drove, and how young he was.

Okay, so he had the Vanquish at his disposal most of the time, but the fact was it belonged to his Dad. Not that he'd admit it to anyone. As far as anyone knew, it was his. Even though they must wonder how he'd afforded it, as well as the hefty insurance and upkeep. He had a decent job in IT, which was very well paid, but not enough to cover the price of this type of car. No one ever asked him though, but if they did, he'd lie.

As far as he was concerned, the car was more or less his anyway.

***

After the police let him go, he rang Anna, who'd now moved in with Natasha full time.

"Hey babe, sorry I'm running a bit late, just got pulled by the cops again. They must be jealous bastards to see someone my age with this baby," he said.

Arrogant Git! She thought.

"No probs, I'm just enjoying the end of Titanic."
"What?"

"Never mind, I'll tell you later," she smiled. "See you in a bit," and hung up.

***

Chapter Thirty Six.
■■

Max wasn't that late, only twenty minutes, and as it was hardly his fault, she didn't say anything to him.

"So, where are you taking me?" Annalise asked. "I thought we'd have a run out to Holmesfield, pop in the Travellers, and the Angel. It's a beautiful night, be a shame not to have a drive out, what do you think?"
"Sounds fine by me," she replied, secretly pleased at spending time in that fantastic car, and all the looks they got when they pulled up somewhere. She felt like Royalty!

Plus, staying away from the city was delaying seeing Suki. Not something she was looking forward to.

Shouting bye to Tasha and Chris, who were still in the bath (God, they must look like prunes by now, Anna thought), they made their way to the car, where Max held the door open for her.

"Bloody hell, have you been talking to David?" she laughed, "I thought he was the only gentleman left on this earth."
"Charming girlfriend I have," he laughed. "Don't open the door, I'm thoughtless, open it for you and

I still get berated. It's true what they say, you can't win with women!"

Anna felt goosebumps all over her, he'd called her his girlfriend, the first time he'd done that, she felt amazing, and wasn't about to spoil the moment with some sarcastic remark.

Instead she leaned over and kissed him deeply, not worrying about her carefully applied lipstick.

"Blimey, what was that for?" Max asked.

"Nothing, but there's plenty more where that came from, if you're a really good boy," she teased.
"In that case, I'm on my best behaviour for the rest of the night at least!" he replied.

Revving the engine, to alert the neighbours as to his presence, he set off towards Holmesfield, and hopefully a wonderful night with his girl.

***

As it was a beautiful Summer's evening, people were out in droves. As they pulled into the car park of The Traveller's, Anna noticed more than a few people admiring the car. How she loved this. Yes, she knew it sounded so superficial, but she loved the attention the car brought.

Grabbing her around the waist, he kissed her cheek, and they walked in to the bar.

***

It was almost empty inside, instead people were making the most of the weather. In England, you had to do that whenever you could.

Without asking her, he ordered a bottle of champagne, and two glasses. He'd allow himself one, then Anna could finish the rest. A tipsy Anna was even more naughty than a sober one, and he intended making the most of it tonight, as tomorrow it would all be about football.

***

The crucial match. They'd drawn Germany in the Semi Final.

***

Walking back outside, Anna put on her Gucci shades, to shade her eyes against the still bright sunshine. They found a spare table, and sat down to enjoy the summer sun and the evening together.

"You're looking as gorgeous as ever babe," Max said.
"Thanks, this is new," she said about her outfit. It

was a Lipsy number (okay, not exactly designer, but she liked their style of clothing, which suited her toned body beautifully), an A Line dress, halter neck, which came to just above her knees. It wastie dyed in the most glorious shades of blues, lilacs, and soft lemon. So simple, but sostriking, especially against her hair. She'd finished the outfit off with some strappy blue sandals, matching bag, and some silver jewellery, oh, and of course a spritz of XS perfume.

"I've got something for you," Max said, and with this, he had her full attention. He reached inside his jacket (so warm outside, but the jacket was a compulsory fashion statement) and pulled out a long jewellers box.

'Oh! What could it be!' Anna thought excitedly.

Tentatively, she opened the box, and staring back at her was the most beautiful charm bracelet she'd ever seen.

"I've bought you the first few charms. A little heart, a cute bear, an eternity hoop, and a little silver handbag," Max said. "But you can add more, or get people to buy you them as presents."
"Oh Max!, it's gorgeous, I love it, I love you!"
She threw herself on to his lap, leg straddling either side of him, and kissed him with a such passion. She didn't care that the dress was now

barely covering her bottom, and that her toned legs were exposed to the top, she was just carried away by the moment.

"Wow, I'll have to buy you presents more often," he laughed, then back tracked,
"Did you just say what I think you said?"

Anna knew what she'd said. She'd not meant to say it, she'd wanted him to say it to her first, but in the heat of the moment, and with this beautiful gift, she'd forgotten herself, and the words had slipped out.

Thinking for a while, she finally looked up at him, not sure if he was ready for this yet, but not wanting to lie either, especially as she had now said it, "Yes Max, I did say it. And yes, I do."

Waiting for his reaction was like waiting a lifetime, but in reality it was only seconds.

"I love you too, Annalise. Have done for a long time, but didn't want to say it if you didn't feel the same."
"Me too." she said sheepishly.

They grinned at each other like they'd just got married, or something just as wonderful, and then she kissed him again.
■■■

"Please, put it on for me, I want to wear it now," Anna said.

Deftly, Max unlocked the clasp, wound the bracelet around Anna's dainty wrist, and locked the clasp again. She stared at it in awe, she couldn't believe he'd chosen such a beautiful present, just for her.

***

Driving the short distance from the Travellers to the Angel, Anna felt the effects of the Champagne. It was her favourite drink, always made her giggly and flirtatious, and she wished she could afford it all the time. Still, she thought, if she managed to hold onto Max, surely she'd get to drink it all the time.

As they pulled in to the Angel's car park, they got the same reaction to the car as they did everywhere they went. And as Anna got out, she got more than her fair share of admiring glances from the males, and glares of envy from the females.

She loved the attention, and head held high, she sashayed over to a spare table outside once again, whilst Max went for drinks.

***
■■■■■■■■■■■■■■■■■■■■■■■■■■■■■■■■■■■■■■■

"What the fuck are you doing here?"

Oh No. She knew that voice, and didn't have to turn around to know that it belonged to Suki.

'How to deal with this?' Anna thought, and where was Max when she needed him?

She turned slowly, and looked up at her enemy. She was at a disadvantage, being sat down with Suki towering over her, but she didn't want to make the confrontation worse by standing up.

SHIT.

"Having a drink, like everyone else here," Anna replied, without a note of malice in her voice. She wanted to try and displace any argument before it built up to something much worse.
"Like fuck you are," Suki spat, "I see you're here with Max," she said, glancing at the car.
"Yes, I am," Anna was trying to pick her words carefully, "I'm sorry Suki, I really am."

But Suki wasn't about to let her off that easily. "You lying cheating whore!" she spat. "You have the cheek to nick my man and then sit there like butter wouldn't melt."

Anna didn't know what to say. She wasn't going to argue. She was in the wrong, and she knew it.

Just then, thank God, Max appeared with the drinks, and didn't look too pleased tosee Suki standing over Anna.

Marching over, he said, "What the hell do you think you're doing Suki?"
"Telling this bitch of a whore what I think of her, that's what," she spat with venom, her dark eyes sending daggers straight through Max.
"Have some decorum will you? You're embarrassing yourself," he replied, noticing that more than a few people had turned around to see what was going on.

"You've some need to talk, choosing this hooker over me!" she snapped back.

By this point, they had the attention of the entire beer garden, and Anna was feeling more than a little uncomfortable.

"Just listen to yourself," he replied. "I don't see Anna talking like trailer trash.   The

only one doing that around here is you."
"Oh fuck off Max, you're a player, always were always will be."

Then she turned on Anna, "Don't you worry you bitch, he'll do the same to you too, it's only a matter of time."

Anna was too dumfounded to reply.

And then Suki noticed Anna's bracelet.

"I see you've given you're new trophy *my* bracelet you heartless piece of shit!" she sneered at Max, then turned on Anna, "Hope it brings you all the luck in the world you conniving whore, you're going to need it."

And with that, Suki was gone, marching back over to her friends.

***

Anna thought she was going to throw up, "Max, take me home, *now*!"
"Don't let her get to you, you knew you'd have to face her sooner rather than later."

Didn't he get it? It wasn't about Suki, or her stinging remarks. It was about the bracelet. Obviously, it had been Suki's, and he'd had the cheek to say he'd bought it just for her.

"Max, I am warning you, take me home. Now."

She got up and marched over to the car and waited for him to follow.

***
■■■■■■■■■■■■■■■■■■■■■■■■■■■■■■■■■■■■■■■

Suki sat watching, seemed delighted with what she'd achieved. Anna was fuming and wished she could muster the strength to go over and wipe that smug grin off Suki's face, but she could find no words, Suki's revelation over the bracelet had left her reeling.

***

They drove home in complete silence. Any conversation Max tried to strike up was met by a wall of silence from Anna.

"She was lying!" Max had tried to tell her, "Anna, listen to me, the bitch was winding you up and you bit."

Still, Anna did not speak.

"I might have bought her a bracelet at some point, but not yours," he continued, "I'm no cheapskate, Anna, I bought that for you yesterday."

Again, Anna did not speak. Her face was set in stone, and there was no way she was going to believe a word Max said, no matter how hard he tried.

Pulling up outside her apartment, he tried once again to talk to her, to regain some of what they'd had earlier in the evening, but before he could say anything to change her mind, she was taking off the bracelet, and threw it at him.

"The next time you buy one of your trophy girlfriends a gift, make sure it's not had one careful owner beforehand." she spat.

He tried to explain, but she'd slammed the door, so much so that it literally shook the whole car, and was marching back to her apartment.

Shit.

What was he supposed to do now?

***

Chapter Thirty Seven.

Max was not one to pursue a woman, but over the last few days he couldn't stop thinking about Anna, and realised he had fallen for her much more deeply that he had thought.

Trust bloody Suki to bugger things up for him. He wouldn't mind, but it was a total lie.

Okay, he may have bought Suki one similar, but certainly hadn't given Annalise Suki's bracelet. Even he wouldn't stoop that low.

He didn't know what to do. She wouldn't take his phone calls, at home or at work, he'd even tried calling to her apartment, but she didn't answer the door, even though he knew she was in.

As he sat at his pc, working from home, he decided one last thing, even though it went against his nature. He'd write her a letter, heartfelt, and add a few 'girly' references, about how he couldn't live without her etc. He cringed at the thought, but he'd try anything to win Anna back.

He missed her so much, and it had only been a couple of days.

Reaching for a pen and pad (a word processor typed letter wouldn't do, it'd have to be

hand written for maximum impact), he started his letter to Anna.

***

It was now Wednesday morning, the 26th of June.

The date England met their arch enemies, Germany, in the Semi Finals.

She should have been going out with Max tonight to watch the match, along with Natasha and Chris, and they were also supposed to be meeting up with Colette and Paul. It would've been a right laugh, but it was all ruined now, Anna thought, as she lay in bed, listening to her favourite Prince CD. The track playing 'When Doves Cry' was one of her all time favourites.

Annalise had a day off. Her day off was always Wednesday, unless someone called in sick. She was Manageress, so didn't have much choice in the matter. She was glad of the break after the last few days.

Max had been bombarding her with calls at the shop and at home, and she was trying her hardest to resist, but it wasn't easy. You just didn't stop loving someone because they were a total git, did you?

She had to keep reminding herself that he'd given her Suki's bracelet. That way, it kept her mad enough to keep him at bay. For now, any way.

***

She dragged herself out of bed at around 10am. She'd not been sleeping well, so the lay in had done her good, and she felt better than she had in days.

Grabbing her dressing gown, she decided on a quick shower, then out in the garden for a spot of sunbathing to top up her all year round tan, with her portable CD player, so that she could carry on relaxing to the sounds of Prince.

Yes, she knew the dangers of the sun, and that she'd probably look old before her time, but at this point in her life, who worried about what the future held?

Hell, she couldn't even think a day ahead right now, never mind years ahead.

***

After a long lukewarm shower, Anna felt invigorated, and her black mood had lifted a little.

Coming out of the bathroom, she had to walk through the hallway to get back to her bedroom, and it was then she noticed the plain white envelope on the door mat, with only one word written on it. Annalise.

Intrigued, she picked it up, turning it over and over, and even holding it up to the light to see if she could view the contents before opening it.

Padding back through to the bedroom, she sat on the bed, made herself comfortable with plump scatter cushions behind her, and slowly, oh so slowly, opened the letter

***

'*My Darling Anna*', she read.   And it was then, she knew it was from Max.

Wanting to tear it up there and then, but also intrigued, she couldn't help herself, she had to keep on reading.

'I realise you don't want to see me or talk to me, you've made that quite evident, but I just needed to get a message to you, in the hopes you will not tear this up (am I right, you're thinking of doing that right now aren't you?) and read on and listen to me, at least give me a chance.

Suki lied to you my Darling, and I don't blame you for believing her, she is conniving, and I understand why you would be so upset.

Your bracelet was bought for you, it never belonged to Suki, and to prove this, even though you probably don't want to see it, I enclose a photo of Suki wearing her charm bracelet. Similar to yours I admit. I am a mere man, I just bought you something beautiful, as I'd seen it before, I knew I wanted you to have something nearly, but not quite, as beautiful as you'.

'Oh please!' Anna thought, but so intrigued, she continued to read.

'Please look at the photo of Suki and her bracelet now Darling, before you read on'.

With that, Anna reached in to the envelope, took out the photograph, and looked in to the beautiful smiling face of the girl who'd once been her friend, but was now her worst enemy. The photo had been torn down the middle and a male hand was over Suki's shoulder, so she presumed that Max was in the other half of the photo, which only added fuel to the fire within her.

However, She looked further down the photograph, to Suki's wrist.

Max was not lying to her. Suki's bracelet was different to hers. He'd not given her second hand goods, as Suki had stated.

She read on.

" 'I hope you've now looked at the photo my Darling, and now realise I'm not lying to you. I bought you that bracelet, it never belonged to Suki. If you believe her, she has won, hasn't she?'

She read on, feeling butterflies in her stomach.
■■■

'I've never lied to you Sweetheart. I know you may mistrust me because of what I did to Suki with you, but I promise you, I love you more than I've ever loved any one, and that is the God's honest truth'.

'I wish you'd given me a chance to explain sooner, my life has been hell for the last few days, I miss you Sweetheart, please, I'm begging you, come back to me. Don't let her win'.

Her heart was beating so fast now, she was sure she was going to have a heart attack, but she carried on reading.

'If you trust and believe me, meet me outside The Oak at 4pm. If you don't turn up, I promise never to bother you again. But please remember this my Darling, I love you with all my heart, and all this has been a misunderstanding, all thanks to Suki, who is so bitter that we were, and hopefully can be again, so very happy. Love Max xxx'.

She believed him.

She'd read the letter over and over again, and had studied the photograph. Her bracelet was different to Suki's, only slightly, but it was different.

'Typical man' she thought, buying similar gifts had been his downfall, but now that she could see he'd not given her Suki's cast off, and had indeed bought her a bracelet of her own, made everything different.

'Suki would not win' Anna thought, and with that in mind, forgot about her sunbathing, and set about getting ready to meet Max outside The Oak Tree.

If all went well, they could stay there, and watch the match with their friends, she mused.

***

Chapter Thirty Seven.

Annalise took her time getting ready. She wanted to look like she'd not made too much of an effort, which was in fact more of an effort than looking like she *had* made an effort.

Already showered, she smothered herself in a shimmering body lotion, so that when the light caught her skin, especially her shoulders, she shimmered delightfully.

She'd made an effort with her make up, but kept it light. She had flawless skin, so only added a little powder to get rid of any shiny areas. Then she added a dash of sparkling blue eye shadow to enhance her beautiful blue eyes, just to her top eye lids, and added a black top liner and two coats of Mascara. She didn't need any blusher, she was tanned enough, so just added a clear lip gloss to finish her look.

She tied her wild black curls back in to a high ponytail, letting a few tendrils hang loose, for a very sexy 'haven't tried too hard' look. Her hair was so unruly it maddened her at times, but also knew it was one of her best features, and made the most of it.

She chose her faded denims, which were so worn, they now had holes in them (real ones, not like the jeans you could buy now, which came to you complete with holes), and a tiny halter neck top which tied around her back and neck. It was multi-coloured in blue, pink, yellow, and white horizontal stripes, and just sat nicely below her bust. No chance of wearing a bra with this number, but her breasts were still full and pert, so this didn't bother her.

She added a cute diamante Fairy belly bar, which made her toned stomach look so sexy.

Fastening her hipster jeans, she added a blue belt to compliment the top. It had the word "sex"

written in diamante on the clasp. Just enough
sexuality to keep Max on his toes.

Slipping on blue pumps, and choosing a bag to
match, she was just about ready, and it was still
only 3pm.

She chose a long silver chain and matching
earrings, and a chunky silver ring. Then she
headed through to Natasha's room, to pinch a little
of her Lou Lou perfume, which she loved. It was
a little heavy, so she used it sparsely.

Checking her appearance in the mirror, she
decided she looked casual enough for her meeting
with Max, but dressed up enough to stay out all
evening, if it all went well, which she so hoped it
did.

Reading the letter again, and looking at the photo
one last time, she went through to the kitchen
where she wrote a quick note for Tasha, who
wasn't home yet. A quick explanation, and saying
she hoped to see her in the pub later, and adding a
few kisses, she walked out in to the hot late June
Sunshine, and strolled the mile to The Oak.

And to Max.

***
■■

He was waiting. Sat on the bonnet of his car with his Police shades on, and casually sipping a drink, he was getting more than a few admiring glances from the females.

As Anna approached, she knew that this charade was for her benefit, she was no fool, not by any one's standards.

"So," Max smiled.
"So," Anna replied.
"You believe me?" Max asked, hopefully.
"Yes, I do," Anna stated, "I'm sorry," And with that he grabbed her and kissed her passionately, much to the chagrin of the females who'd been eyeing him up.

"No need to apologise. Suki is poison, and I can see why you reacted the way you did, I would probably have done the same," Max said, still hugging her, her head nuzzled in to his shoulder.

"But you sure know how to give a guy a hard time, I've done nothing these past few days apart from try to contact you, you're more elusive than Shergar!" he laughed.
She looked up at him and grinned, "well, I had to make you work for it didn't I?" And kissed him again.

***
▪▪

Walking hand in hand towards the pub, Max took off his shades, and they headed to the bar, ordered a lager each, and went to their 'lucky' table, where they would try and hold onto seats for Natasha, Chris, Paul and Colette.

It was only 4.45pm, but the pub had already started to fill up.

England vs. Germany in the Semi Finals.

This was make or break time, and even Anna, who wasn't really into football, had caught the 'England Bug' and was nervous about this match.

***

Chapter Thirty Eight.

As promised, the others arrived early, Colette and Paul first, soon followed by Natasha and Chris. Both couples were secretly pleased to see Anna and Max here, their problems obviously resolved. The pair were made for each other, it would have been a huge shame for them to split up.

The lads went to the bar, leaving the girls sat around the table.

"So," Tasha asked, "What's happened to change your mind?"
"Well you know I've been ignoring him," Anna said. "But today, as I walked out of the bathroom, I saw an envelope had been put through the letter

box with my name written on it." And so she continued to tell the other girls about the wonderful words he had written to her, and also of the photo, proving that her bracelet wasn't Suki's cast off after all. She promised to show them the letter and photo when Max wasn't around.

"That poisonous bitch!" Colette spat, "you nearly lost each other because of her lies."
"I can't say I blame her though," Anna replied, "I did pinch Max off her after all, and I think, if I'd been in her position, I may have tried something similar."

The other girls conceded that she was probably right, though it was still a bit below the belt what Suki had said.

***

The time flew by, as the three couple's sat there gossiping. Carrie and David should be here they all mused, but Carrie was nowhere near ready to be out and about just yet, and she couldn't drink, because of the strong painkillers she was taking.

Before they knew it, the pre match commentary (the usual crap) had started, and they made sure they had enough drinks to get them through the first half. There was so much tension in the air.

England and Germany were bitter rivals, and no one was sure which way this match would go.

One thing they all agreed on though, if England managed to win this match, they would surely win the Championship, and bring Football home, where it belonged.

The footballers had sung each of their national anthems, and the England supporters at Wembley were taunting the Germans with The song *'Two World wars, and one world cup.'* People in the pub were joining in and singing along. The atmosphere was electric.

Clapping to the crowd once again, the players ran to their spots, and waited for the first whistle to blow. You could hear a pin drop, the atmosphere was that tense.

And there it was, the whistle, and so the match between the bitter rivals began.

The streets of England were deserted.

***

The group had only just settled into the match, when unbelievably, England scored after three minutes.

"Unbelievable!" Tasha shouted. Surely this was the sign, the sign that England were going to lift the trophy!

Everyone was jumping as if as one enormous person, and the pub floor literally shook.

Natasha couldn't hear what Chris said, but she grinned at him, from ear to ear, as he grabbed her and swung her around, before plonking her back down.

Gascoigne's corner had been headed on at the near post by Tony Adams, and Alan Shearer then headed the ball in for his fifth goal of the championships.

It didn't get better than this!

Seaman was playing his heart out, and made some crucial saves. Natasha sent him a kiss to the screen.

Then again. It happened. Disaster struck once again. England were haunted by bad luck, it seemed.

It was in the sixteenth minute that Germany levelled the game with a Helmer cross on the left wing which enabled Kuntz to get behind Pearce and made the score 1-1.

"Bloody Hell England," shouted Chris, "why the fuck do you always let this bloody well happen?"

Both teams held their own through out the rest of the match, and it was going to extra time.

'Oh no' Tasha thought, please, *please* score England, *do not* let this go to penalties, not against Germany. 'Please, if there is a God' she thought 'give England the luck they need.'

They'd long since run out of drinks, but no one was prepared to go to the bar, in case they missed that crucial goal.

***

In extra time, Darren Anderton hit the post. "Bloody Hell Anderton," cried Colette. "You're better than that, put it in the bloody net!"

Then Kuntz put the ball in the England net for Germany. Oh no, this was it, England's dream was over.

However, by some miracle ('there is a God' Natasha thought, and silently thanked Him) this potential golden goal was ruled out because of a push on Adams.

A sigh of relief came from everyone in the pub.

In the ninety-eighth minute, Gascoigne was less than a foot away from scoring when he slid in to try and reach a Shearer cross from the right but it wasn't enough, and the game ended 1-1.

It was to go to those dreaded Penalties.

And against Germany.

This was not good.

***

Everyone seemed to hold their breaths, not a sound could be heard as it was decided who would be taking the penalties.

It was decided that Shearer, Platt, Pearce, Gascoigne and Sheringham would take the penalties, with Southgate as one of those on standby if the scores were equal by the end of the penalty shoot out.

All five England men got their penalties, but so did Germany's. The score was 5-5.

"This is unbearable," Natasha shouted over the din to the rest of her crowd, "I can't watch." And with that she put her hands over her eyes, but was peeking through her fingers, which sort of defeated covering her eyes up in the first place, but she didn't think of that.

Southgate was next up to take a penalty.

It seemed to take forever for him to walk up to the ball and kick it, and it seemed as if everything was happening in slow motion.

Oh no, please no.

Southgate's penalty was saved by Koepke.

Surely now, that was it.

And it was.

Germany scored all of their penalties, and won the game 6-5, and went through to the final.

England were out of the Championship, beaten by bloody Germany yet again.

The girls couldn't help it, they all burst in to tears, and there were more than a few men in the pub crying too.

People were sat around with their heads in their hands, sobbing out loud, not caring who saw them.

All this build up, all the excitement. All the agonising over games, and the sheer delight when England won.

It was all gone. It was over.

***

Just four days later, on the 30th June 1996, it was with heavy hearts that the group watched the final at Wembley.

Germany vs. the Czech Republic.
■■

Germany beat the Czech Republic 2-1 to win the Euro 96 competition.

Berger scored for the Czech's with a fifty-seventh minute penalty, but substitute

Bierhoff replied in the seventy-third minute to make it 1-1.

In extra time, Bierhoff scored again five minutes in for a golden goal to end the game.

German captain, Klinsmann, collected the trophy from the Queen.

Natasha had never felt so defeated. At least they'd hoped that they could draw back some credibility if the Czech Republic won, but no, it had to be the bloody Germans, didn't it?

Always the bloody same.

***

The dejectedness of the crowd was instantly evident, as if a great big balloon had been deflated.

People were crying openly yet again, others were sat hunched over, head in hands.

'Not again', Tasha was thinking, and not to Germany of all Countries.

***

"Come on Babe," Natasha heard Chris say, "let's go home, it's like a cemetery in here now, only more depressing."

They said their good bye's, and walked solemnly out of the pub.

"I can't believe it Chris."
"Me neither," he replied, "I was sure we were going to do it this time, I feel like my guts have been torn out."

"I know the feeling," she mused, and snuggling in to him as he put his arm around her, they walked slowly back to Natasha's apartment.

***

The phone was ringing as they entered Tasha's apartment. Running to it she picked up just in time.

"Hello?" she answered, a little out of breath.
"It's me," Carrie said, "I'm gutted."
"I know Carrie, I am too, I just can't believe it, not to Germany again," she continued. "All those glorious matches, all this build up, I was sure we were going to do it this time."
"And to lose the *them* of all people."
"Don't mention their name, I can't bear it," Natasha said.
"So, what now? If we'd have won, we could have dragged this on for weeks, right up until us going away."
"We'll get over it I suppose," Natasha said. "We should be used to it by now after all."
"You're right on that one. Oh well, swallow our pride and get on with it, as is our usual English resolve."
"We'll get them back in Tenerife," Natasha laughed. "We'll get up early, and go and throw all of their early morning 'towels on sun beds' in to the pool!"

Carrie burst out laughing. Natasha could be hilarious when she wanted to be.

"Stop it, it still hurts a little when I laugh."
"Sorry, and I'm so sorry too, I forgot with all this hit, how are you feeling?"
"A whole lot better," Carrie replied. "I've stopped the strong painkillers and just have the odd paracetamol when I need it, so am starting to feel human again. Those painkillers made me feel like a zombie."
"Yes, but they were necessary, and you sound fantastic now, back to our Carrie. Can we come over to see you, just me and Anna, early next week?"
"Of course you can, I miss you guys, can't wait to see you!" Carrie replied.
"That's a date then, I'll call you over the weekend to make arrangements."

They chattered for a little while longer, just general girly stuff, and then hung up.

***

Natasha walked over to Chris, who'd been leaning against the kitchen doorframe, waiting patiently for her. Folding her arms around his neck and kissing him, she lead him through to her bedroom, where they could forget the terrible night they'd had at the hands of Germany.

***

Chapter Thirty Nine.

It was now Saturday 20th July.

Natasha woke early, feeling a little nauseous. 'Probably excitement at the prospect of a big girly night out' she thought, as she got up and padded in to the kitchen, where she boiled the kettle for her morning cup of tea.

While waiting for it to boil, she searched in a drawer for some Rennie's. She knew they had some somewhere, but it had been ages since she'd taken any, and it took a good rummage around in the messy drawer before she found them. Checking they were still in date, she took two out of their blister pack, and allowed them to melt in her mouth. Hopefully these would get rid of this awful feeling of sickness and heartburn she felt.

***

A big girls night out was planned for tonight, all for Carrie, who hadn't been out since her accident.

All the girls would be there. The ones who mattered any way.

Natasha, Annalise, Carrie, Jasmine, Mel, Colette and Trudy. Lucy was not on the invite list.

To everyone's surprise, Jazz had stood her ground this time, and was still awaiting an apology before speaking to Lucy again. And Lucy being Lucy, was being just as stubborn, and had not been in touch since that fateful night in Dexter's.

Not that any one would miss her. She was a pain in the ass, and once she'd got a few drinks down her, had got the girls in to a few scraps in the past. No, they wouldn't miss her.

They were all to meet at Quincy's for a change, and go straight to Euphoria after that. Less chance of bumping into Suki that way, they had agreed.

Even though they were running late, Natasha and Anna were surprised to see they were the first one's there.

Natasha had had her long hair cut in to a sleek bob, a la Victoria Adams from the Spice Girls, and it suited her features. It gave her hair a new lease of life, and was shiny beyond belief (thanks to using Anna's products from the salon). She did miss her long mane of hair, but this style was so much more maintainable.

She was wearing 'that' dress again, the one Carrie had bought her. She knew Carrie would be pleased to see her in it. She thought she'd put a little weight on, as her belly seemed to protrude a little more than usual, but put that down to her monthly being due. She'd kept her face makeup to a minimum except around her eyes, which she'd smudged with a sultry dark grey sparkling eyeshadow, into the sockets, and had heavily lined them with black liner, top and bottom, before apply layers of mascara, and a very nude lipstick. Such a sexy 'come to bed with me' look.

Annalise was wearing a skin-tight black cat suit, with matching black killer platforms. She looked wicked, and she knew it, especially with her jet black hair having recently been retouched with electric blue highlights.

The two girls walked into Quincy's which wasn't too busy just yet, and ordered a bottle of lager each. And straws, two each (as was Anna's style). At least this looked a little more ladylike than swigging out of the bottles!

They found a good vantage point for viewing the talent, and awaited the arrival of the others.
■■■

Natasha was once again a free agent. She knew things with Chris were only casual, and it had run it's course, so she was okay with that, and they were still mates. That was important to her, as long as they remained mates, she could live with that. It hadn't been the love affair of the Century after all.

She was still awaiting her 'Rhett Butler', but given her recent man troubles, was seriously thinking she'd never find him.

Anna was still all loved up with Max, and had managed to avoid Suki again so far, so she was in an excellent mood. She was still eyeing up the talent though, as they were her, which made her confidence soar. Hey a girl could look right? As long as she didn't touch.

***

Colette and Trudy arrived next. Colette had her hair flowing free, she looked like Rapunzel, it was so long. She was wearing a beautiful white, flowing cross over dress, which just skimmed her knees. It was very similar to the 'oh so famous' Marilyn Monroe dress, the one where she was having to hold it down because of an air vent. Colette had finished off the outfit with matching strappy heels and bag. Her tan was amazing too having just returned from Jamaica. Her tan was even more stunning against the pureness of her dress.

Trudy, with her long auburn hair tousled in to the most glorious waves, was wearing a baby blue trouser suit, hipsters, as was the style, and a waistcoat type top, which showed off her midriff and pushed her amazing breasts up. 'What man in their right mind could resist those babies', Tasha thought.

Colette spotted them, and after saying something to Trudy, walked over to where Natasha and Anna were standing.

"Hey, nice to see you, it's been too long." Colette said.

They always said this to each other, Tasha thought, even though they meant it, life in general just always got in the way, and they didn't get around to making arrangements as often as they'd liked to.

Before Trudy had a chance to get over to them, Carrie sauntered through the door, followed by Jazz and Mel.

Carrie saw them immediately, and instead of going to the bar, ran over to them and gave them a big hug, 'more like a scrum', Natasha thought, with how Carrie was holding on to them.

"So good to see you guys," she gushed.
"And you," replied Anna, "you look stunning, Carrie. I can't believe it's not even a month since the accident."
"Well, I had to get better quickly didn't I? I've got a holiday booked in less than two weeks, and need to get back on form," Carrie continued, "God I've missed this and you two so much."

Natasha thought Carrie had never looked so good. Engaged life was obviously suiting her, and it was obvious David was looking after her, as she'd put the much needed weight back on, and was no longer skin and bone.

She was wearing a long, horizontally striped dress, in blues and white, with a daring slash up each side. The stripes showed off her new curves to perfection. Her golden blonde hair was taken up, with just a few tousled strands having been teased down, and she looked like she'd never had an accident in her life. Amazing.

She was being careful with drinking though, having had the head injury, and not long off the pain killers, she made a resolve to only have a couple of drinks tonight, to 'test the water', so to speak.
■■■

Jazz and Mel walked over, and said their 'Hi's' to everyone. They'd even bought Carrie a drink, noticing she'd not gone to the bar but had headed straight to Tasha and Anna.

As usual, Jazz was looking her usual sassy self with her white crocheted dress on (the one which Lucy had thrown lager and black over), and she still had a nice tan, thanks to a top up every week at her local salon. No bra again, and the dress was slightly see through, 'she was so ballsy', Tasha thought.

Mel looked more demure, with her short white blonde hair cut to within an inch of it's life, she looked like a very young, very pretty Brigette Neilson. She never dressed as sexily as the rest of them, but tonight was wearing black hipsters, with a matching top.

She was showing a bit more flesh, and her midriff and most of her back was on show. If only she'd make this effort more often, she'd be a show stopper.

"Thanks Jazz, Mel, just what I need," said Carrie, as she took a small sip of her small dry white wine spritzer, "Mmmm, just what the doctor ordered."

And so they all toasted Carrie and her amazing recovery, and spent the next hour catching up, and eyeing up all the eye candy. There was plenty of it on show, and the girls made the most of it.

***

A song came on which they all loved, but couldn't for the life of them remember what it was called or who sang it.

It didn't stop them singing along to it though, Carrie at the top of her voice, after being stuck inside for weeks on end, made the most of it. "My lovers got no money, he's got his tumbleweeds." she sang.

The others fell about laughing, Tasha was literally doubled over with laughter, and as her laughter was so contagious, the other found they couldn't stop laughing either.

"What's so funny?" Carrie demanded.

Which only made them laugh even more.

"Is someone going to tell me?" She'd not had enough to drink to see the funny side of things, especially when the fun was being poked at her, and she had no idea why.

"Sorry," Anna managed to splutter. "It's just what you sang that's all. You sang, 'My lover's got no money, he's got his tumbleweeds' when the words are actually 'My lover's got no money, he's got his *strong beliefs*!"

Carrie laughed out loud, a real laugh, that came from deep within her, and she couldn't stop. 'How stupid of her!' she thought 'And how many times had she shown herself up like this!'

"How was I supposed to know *that*," she exclaimed. "It sounds like tumbleweeds to me."

To which everyone burst out laughing again, much to the amusement of a group of lads stood nearby.

"How I've missed this" Carrie said, 'even if the laugh *is* on me!"

After they'd managed to compose themselves, the girls walked out of Quincy's and had to hail two taxi's as there were too many of them to get in to one.
■■■

And off to Euphoria, to dance the night away, they went.

■■■

■■■

■■■

Chapter Forty.

The bouncers outside Euphoria, Shayne and Dan, recognised them straight away and opened up the rope to let the girls straight in so that they didn't have to queue.

"Thanks guys," smiled Natasha, flirtatiously, and they winked back at the group.
"Looking good tonight ladies," Dan remarked, and the girls all grinned their appreciation back at him.

They paid, and walked straight in to the heaving throng.

***

Colette and Trudy had lost the toss of the coin, and had to go to the bar to get all the drinks, whilst the others made their way up to the top end of the club, which was up a few steps, so that they could get a better view of what was going on. They always stood here, one of their many 'girls night out' rituals.

"David wants me home by 1am," Carrie shouted to Natasha.

"What? Why?"

"He doesn't want me overdoing things, that's all, but I'll see how I go, may stay later if I'm up to it."

"Don't you go letting him lay the law down," Natasha said firmly, remembering only too well how David liked to be in control. "Keep true to yourself Carrie, don't hone yourself to what you believe someone wants you to be, always be the person you are, don't ever change for any one," she continued. "Remember, he fell in love with you for who you *are*, not for what he wants you to be."

"You're right, I know, that's why I'll go when I'm ready and not before."

De Lacy's 'Hideaway' was playing. A favourite of theirs, so they took their drinks, and placed them on the shelf at the side of the dance floor, and made their way on to the floor.

"I need a hi-hi-hi-hideaway," they all sung as they allowed the music in to their souls, and they danced along to the track. They were all great dancers (well, they should be with the amount of times they came out dancing), and were getting a few admiring glances from the surrounding males.

This track was followed by another they loved, Tori Amos's 'Professional Widow', so they continued to dance, totally absorbed by the music, going mad on the dance floor, most people moved out of the way to make way for their moves.

Carrie, who was facing the bar as she danced, noticed someone she did not want to see, and Natasha, having registering the look on Carrie's face, turned to look in the same direction.

Marcus. But he was not alone. He had a girl with him.

The girl was as different to Natasha as chalk was to cheese, so surely this couldn't be the live in girlfriend. She was tall, slightly overweight, mousy brown hair, with passably pretty features, but she was certainly no stunner.

***

Marcus was watching Natasha, had been ever since he'd first spotted her enter the club, and the girl, as if sensing this, looked over to what was capturing Marcus's attention.

"What are you looking at those slappers for?" Cindy asked her boyfriend.
"I'm not," he replied, "I'm just scanning the crowds."

"No you're not, you're staring at those slappers, which one is it Marcus?" she asked.

Cindy had known that Marcus had had an affair, and even though she knew this, she'd still begged him to stay when he'd left her.And she'd welcomed him back with open arms when he'd returned to her.

He always returned to her.

"I told you Cindy, for God's sake, I am not staring at anyone, will you just drop it," he replied with frustration. He needed her in a bad mood like he needed a hole in the head.

Seeming to sense that he was becoming mad with her, she backed off, but watched him carefully without him noticing. He was definitely watching one of those girls, but which one?

***

Natasha's face registered shock, and she felt the room close in on her. She was finding it hard to breathe, and stumbled backwards, only to be caught by Colette.

"Hey, how many have you had?" Colette laughed. "Not enough," Tash replied, and quickly moved away from the dance floor and headed to the top bar.

Carrie, sensing her friend needed her, quickly followed, telling the others she wouldn't be a minute.

She found Natasha at the top bar, with a large glass of red wine already in hand, which she was consuming as if she was some sort of Alco.

"Hey Tasha, slow down, you'll end up in a right state, and he's not worth it."
"Too bloody right he's not," she replied taking another large slug of wine, "I wonder if that's the girlfriend?"
"Probably," replied Carrie, "you know what they say, men like to flirt with gorgeous women, but only settle down with average looking one's, that way they know their women won't stray."

This statement was totally out of character for Carrie, who was such a good natured soul, but she must have sensed Tasha needed some boosting, and said this to placate her.

Natasha gulped down the rest of her drink, excused herself from a very worried Carrie, and marched in the direction of the loos.
■■■

It was then he caught a hold of her arm, and
literally dragged her into a dark corner.

"Hey, what the hell do you think you're doing?"
she spat at him.
"I still love you, Tasha," he said urgently.
"So what're you doing here with her, I take it
that's the girlfriend?"
He looked down at his shoes, as if studying them,
"Yes," he looked up, "That's her. She's gone to
the toilet so I took my chance to talk to you."
"Doesn't exactly look your usual type, Marcus, I
imagined someone much more glamorous."
"Don't be bitchy, Tash, it doesn't suit you. And
it's not her fault I'm a total shit, is it?"
"You have a point," she replied vehemently. "So,
why bring her here tonight, knowing I'd probably
be here. Don't you think that's risking it a bit?"
"Yes, it is, but I just wanted to see you, even if it
meant not being able to talk to you."

Natasha was silent. She didn't have a lot to say to
him.

"Are you still seeing that young Brad Pitt look-a-
like?" he asked her.
"How do you know about him?"
"I saw you together, on a couple of occasions," he
said with a hint of sadness.
"Well, not that it's any of your business, but no,
I'm not. Me and Chris are mates now, that's all."
■■■

He seemed so relieved to hear this.

"Will you come back to me, Tasha, please, *please*. I miss you so much and can't stop thinking about you."

Typical Marcus, she thought. Out with his live in girlfriend, who he'd conveniently forgotten to tell Natasha about for months on end, and now he's out with her, yet asking Natasha to go back to him. Unbelievable.

How arrogant could one get?

"I could hardly come in here alone so I had to bring her, the lads are all away. But it's you I want Tash, surely you can see that by now?" he pleaded.
"I told you before Marcus, and I'll tell you again. I loved you, still do, but I will never come back to you. I can't trust you, and I can't, won't live like that, no matter how much I love you."

Cindy had reappeared as if by magic, and had heard the last few exchanges between Tasha and Marcus. If looks could kill, Tasha would have dropped dead on the spot.

Staring straight at Natasha, but talking to Marcus, Cindy snapped, "This is the bitch, isn't it?"

Wrong footed, and feeling as if his back was against the wall, he denied all knowledge of what Cindy was talking about.

"I *heard* you, you bloody idiot! Do you think I'm *that* stupid?" she fumed.

And with that, she grabbed Marcus and dragged him out of the club, Marcus managing one last glance back at Natasha before he disappeared.

'Well' Natasha thought 'That saved me any further hassle'.

But seeing Marcus again had sparked the feelings she had for him, feelings she'd hoped has disappeared forever.

'Obviously not' she thought, sadly, as she watched him disappear once again. 'Would she ever shake this man out of her life? She didn't even know if she wanted to any more.

***

Jazz had met up with Simon, her squeeze from the bar next door, and was all over himlike a rash. The others were amazed. Jazz's 'boyfriends' did well to last more than a few weeks, so there must be something special about this one.

"Must be the horse theory," Colette laughed, and Carrie caught herself looking at his groin, hoping to see if what Jazz had told them was true, but it was far too dark in the club.

Not surprisingly, Jazz walked over to them, "I'm off now if you don't mind, got an offer I can't refuse," she smirked wickedly.

"Shame we didn't have bets on how long that would take!" Carrie said to the others "I'd be quids in!"

"Oi cheeky," Jazz smirked, "see you all soon I hope, I'll fill you in when I see you, and in the meantime, I'll be getting filled in!" she laughed, and with that she grabbed Simon and literally frog marched him out of the club.

***

Chapter Forty One.

It was Wednesday 31st July, the day before their holiday, and the girls were excited beyond belief. Carrie had made a full recovery, so was safe to fly, and more importantly, let her hair down properly. Just what she needed after the last couple of months.

Anna, Tasha, and Carrie were sat in their local, The Oak, waiting for Max and David, who they'd arranged to meet for a drink before they went away. Carrie was staying at Tash and Anna's tonight, as it was an early flight, the taxi was due to pick them up at 4am.

"I've not had any luck on the job front," Natasha said, taking a sip of her wine, "It's a nightmare, there's nothing out there, nothing that will pay what I'm on at present."
"What, there's nothing at all?" Carrie asked, sipping her spritzer.
"Nope, not a thing, I wish I could afford to take a break and re-train, I'd like to do something creative instead of all the paperwork and deadlines I have to work with now," Tasha conceded.
"Can't you get a grant or something for that?" Anna asked, "I'm sure there must be something you can do, to help you with the mortgage and

bills whilst you go back to college?"

"I don't know," Tasha said, "I'll look in to it, but I doubt it, I'm nearly 26, so I don't think I qualify to be honest, so I'll just have to bide my time and hope the right job comes along soon. The longer I stay there, the more I resent it."

Things at work had certainly been strained since Paul had put her in that predicament. Probably not helped by her attitude. Once she got a bee in her bonnet, she was stubborn, and she was now working to rule, arriving bang on time and leaving bang on time. No more overtime for them, no more freebies. They couldn't fire her for working hard and for working her normal working hours, after all.

When Paul had mentioned a deadline had not been met, Natasha had simply replied that she needed an extra assistant, as there was just too much work for her and her assistant. Of course the company were not about to fork out, and they couldn't complain if she worked her guts out, but didn't reach deadlines within normal hours.

Paul, her boss, should be doing more to help anyway. That was in the contract, but he was always smooching off to lunch with some supplier or client. Lunches that often took up most of the afternoon. Still, there was no one to reprimand

him apart from the owner William, who was far
too laid back to even know what a reprimand was.

***

Natasha knew he didn't like her, but had no idea
why. She'd never done anything to offend him,
and had always been a hard worker. Enough was
enough though, as soon as she was back from
Tenerife, even if it meant moving to a similar job,
even to one of their competitors, she'd do it, just to
get out of that place.

Bringing her back to the present, Carrie asked her
if she had anyone on the scene at the moment.

"No, no one," Tasha replied, "Not since Chris, and
then bumping in to Marcus. To be honest, I can't
stop thinking about Marcus, he's got a way of
getting under my skin."

At this remark the others groaned. This was all
they (and Natasha) needed, another fiasco with
Marcus, because that is what it would be, a fiasco.

"What's up?" Natasha asked.
"You know what's up," said Anna, "don't give in
and go back to Marcus for God's sake, look at the
state you were in not so long ago, and how far
you've come since. Let sleeping dogs lie, Tash."
"I wish it was that easy," Tasha replied.

***

The lads had arrived, and they were all sat outside enjoying the last of the summer sunshine.

"This time tomorrow, we'll be in the bars in Playa," Carrie said excitedly.

"Ok, no need to rub it in," David laughed, "Whilst we'll be stuck here working, you'll be having the time of your lives, charming, thanks for the invite, ladies."

"You know nothing comes between a girl and her friends," Carrie continued, "This is my last official 'singles' girls holiday."

"Hey, less of the 'singles'!" David said, "no funny business Carrie, I mean it."

"Nice to know I'm trusted," she snapped.

"I didn't mean it like that, babe, sorry, it's just I'm gonna miss you," he said, trying to regain some ground.

"Well, it sounded like it to me! You've got to trust me. I wouldn't be marrying you if I didn't love you, there'll never be another man for me."

This seemed to pacify David, whilst Natasha was gesturing throwing up, by pretending to put two fingers down her throat.

"Hey, I saw that!" Anna said, "You've some need to talk. When you're all loved up the whole world gets to know about it!"

"Only messing, sweetie, I know how easy you bite." She smiled a genuine smile at her friend.

"I'll miss you too, babe," Max said to Anna, "be a good girl, and don't do anything I wouldn't do."
"In that case, I can pretty well do as I please!" Anna retorted, to which everyone burst out laughing.

Tasha was feeling a little left out. She wanted some of what Anna and Carrie had, but she attracted the wrong type, or more likely she went for the wrong type.

Deep down, she was really softening towards Marcus. She didn't know why, because her resolve had been so good for so long, but she missed him (what little she'd seen of him anyway). 'Was it worth giving him a chance?' she wondered. She made a mental note to give it serious consideration when she got back home. He did seem genuinely sorry, and had proved his commitment by pursuing her endlessly for months. Surely that stood for something?

***

The night was growing old, it was 10.30pm, and the girls needed to try to get a couple of hours sleep before getting up at around 2.30am ready for the taxi.
■■■

Natasha hung back as Anna and Carrie said and hugged their goodbye's to their partners, saying how much they'd miss each other, and delaying, not wanting to leave them.

"Come on you two, we'll never get any sleep at this rate!" Natasha said, and with that the lads gave Tasha a hug too, and wished them all a great holiday away together.

***

Chapter Forty Two.

They were at East Midlands Airport, ready for
their flight, which if on time, would be taking off
in around an hour.

Natasha hated flying, and saw it only as a means
to an end. She tried to avoid it, having had a crash
landing in a two seater aircraft when she was an
Air Cadet in her teens. She hadn't been hurt, but it
had been enough to scare the living daylights out
of her.

The other two saw it as part of their holiday, and
were so excited. They were in the twenty-four
hour shop, looking for some light reading, but
Natasha couldn't concentrate, she was always a
tightly wound coil before flying, and couldn't
concentrate on anything.

The bar wasn't even open so she couldn't have a
drink to calm her nerves, but she had a hipflask in
her bag with brandy in it, in case of emergency.
The last thing she wanted was a bloody panic
attack in front of a couple of hundred people.

Excusing herself, which the girls barely noticed,
she nipped to the loos, where she took a couple of
gulps of the brandy. It burned the back of her

throat, but she could feel herself relax almost instantly. There, that was better, and there was still enough left for on the plane, if she needed it.

Making her way back to the other two, she popped some chewing gum in her mouth to mask the smell of the brandy, both from the girls and the staff. If they thought she was drunk, she wouldn't be allowed on the plane, and she just thanked her lucky stars that Customs had not checked her handbag.

Natasha found the girls, still browsing through the book section, but Natasha was looking at magazines, and having chosen a few, went to look at the sunglasses, she fancied a new pair, even though she'd already packed a black pair and a brown pair. Both fake Gucci's, but good fakes, no one would guess.

Picking up some silver ones with large mirrored shades, she tried them on. Hmm, yes, they suited her face perfectly. Price tag? £79.99. Blimey, but what the hell,

she'd put it on her credit card and worry about that later.

***

■■

Forty-five minutes later, as the girls were sat reading through their purchases, their flight was called, and Natasha felt that rush of nerves again. Still, it was too late to go to the loo now, so she picked up her handbag, and carry-on bag, along with the other two, and headed towards departures.

***

Excusing herself as soon as they'd got on the plane, Natasha said she needed the loo again.

"Bloody hell, have you got the runs or something?" Anna laughed.
"Something like that, I hate flying," she replied.
"God knows why I put myself through it." she pretended to laugh, but was a bag of nerves.

Locking herself in the tiny loo, she fiddled in her bag for her hipflask again, and shakily opened it to take three big gulps of the brandy. Allowing it to absorb, she started to feel more relaxed once again, and wondered why all toilets on aircraft were so bloody small. 'No chance of a mile high experience in this one' she thought ruefully as she popped more gum in her mouth and made her way back to her seat.

She'd insisted that they have the curtain down on the window, she couldn't bear to look out just yet. She knew that most accidents happened on take off or landing, so didn't want to see anything until they were well on their way.

She wasn't so much scared of flying, the heights didn't bother her, it was the possibility of crashing that worried her so much.

***

Four hours and twenty minutes later, with the sun already up, promising a scorching day, the plane was turning to land on (what looked like) the air strip. Grasping her seat handles so hard, her knuckles almost opaque, Natasha gritted her teeth for the landing.

***
■■■■■■■■■■■■■■■■■■■■■■■■■■■■■■■■■■■■■■■

"You see," Carrie said, "Nothing to be worried about."
"Easy for you to say, you didn't have a crash landing in a plane when you were sixteen," Natasha mused.

The others grinned at her, and Natasha felt herself relaxing as the plane rolled to a halt on the runway.

Chapter Forty Three.

■■■

Arriving at their apartment at the Hacienda Del
Sol, the girls got out of the coach to blistering
heat, and it was still only 10am.

"What will it be like come 3pm?" Natasha said.
"It's bloody boiling already!"
"We're just off the top coast of Africa," said
Carrie sarcastically. "What did you expect?
Snow!"
"Hilarious - not!" Natasha laughed.

The apartments looked even better from the
outside than they did in the brochure. They were
based on three floors, and from what the girls
understood, theirs was on the ground floor, which
meant that they could simply walk straight out to
the pool. Perfect.

Once the driver had unloaded their luggage,
Natasha tipped him 800 pesetas, just under £5.00
in real money.

"What did you do that for?" Anna asked. "He's
already being paid to do his job."
"Well, I just thought it would be a nice gesture
that's all," she replied.

"You're too soft," Carrie replied. "You'll never be rich!"

Natasha said she never wanted to be, to which the other two burst out laughing.

"Come on then, let's go and check in."

***

"Wow," stated Carrie as they walked into their apartment. "This is better than I expected, just look at this place."

She was right, the rooms were light and airy, thanks to air conditioning, with cool terracotta tiled floors throughout. They had a bedroom each 'which was good' Natasha thought 'If they pulled!'

The kitchen was fully functional, complete with a nice long breakfast bar for them to sit around. It also had an oven, sink, fridge and freezer, dishwasher and microwave. No washing machine though, so they'd either have to hand wash their clothes, or take them to the 'lavandería'.

The airy lounge, which was at the back of the apartment, and from where you gained access to the sumptuous gardens and pool, had a large TV with English channels. 'Not that they'd be watching too much TV' Tasha mused.

The bathroom was larger than expected too, with a corner bath and separate shower unit, in white, with complimenting shiny white tiling from floor to ceiling.

They'd brought their own stereo, as they didn't think there'd be one in the apartment, and they were right, there wasn't, but apart from that, the apartment was perfect for them. They set this up in the lounge, so that they could hear the music wherever they were in the apartment.

They'd also brought around ten cd's, mainly dance music 'Ministry of Sound' kind of albums, to get them in the mood whilst they were getting ready, but also some softer music for them to listen to whilst lazing around the pool or at the beach.

***

They didn't squabble over bedrooms, all were just as nice as the next one, so they quickly unpacked, arranging their clothes and shoes into wardrobes and drawers. Natasha then took all of the important documents, like passports, return flight tickets, and excess travellers cheques, and locked them away in a safe which was stuck solid to the wall inside Natasha's wardrobe. She always aired on the side of caution when it came to things like this.

Before heading to the local supermercado to stock up, Anna put away what they had brought with them. Coffee, tea bags, sugar and milk powder, as well as tea towels and dish cloths, and of course some fairy liquid. She then put the small amount of washing up powder (good job customs hadn't seen that, it could have been mistaken for some other type of white powder, they'd laughed) and fabric conditioner, all away in to different cupboards.

They wouldn't be eating in much, but it would be nice to have some fresh milk, mineral water (drinking out of the taps here was a big no no) cereals, orange juice, bread, butter, cheeses, fruit, and snacks, for if they wanted a snack or breakfast.

Carrie, being fussy, immediately emptied the cupboards of their contents, and all dishware, cutlery, and mugs, cups, and glasses, were placed in the dish washer.

"I'll stay here and give the kitchen a clean over, hilst you two nip to the shop," Carrie told the others.

They had to smile, Carrie was so finicky about cleanliness, she'd have cleaned out all the cupboards, drawers and sides, long before they got back.

"Just make sure you get a small pack of dishwasher tablets, some cleaning fluid, and bleach too. Oh, and some painkillers, I forgot to pack any," she shouted after them as they were strolling out of the front door.
"No probs, Carrie, see you in a bit," Anna shouted back.

"What's she like!" Anna said as the two girls strolled towards the shop, "I mean, we're here to relax and have the time of our lives, and the first thing on her mind is doing a bloody spring clean!"
Natasha laughed, "You know Carrie, everything has to be just so, and more importantly *clean*!.
I'm not complaining, we get the easy job of doing the shopping."

***

Carrie decided she wouldn't wait for them to get back from the shops with the dishwasher tablets, instead pouring a big blob of fairy liquid in the dishwasher instead, and setting it on it's hottest setting. 'There, that'll clean that lot up whilst I clean the kitchen' she thought, as she set about filling the sink with hot soapy water.
▪▪▪▪▪▪▪▪▪▪▪▪▪▪▪▪▪▪▪▪▪▪▪▪▪▪▪▪▪▪▪▪▪▪▪▪▪▪

Carrie was bent over with her bottom in the air, halfway through cleaning out the cupboards, when she heard a strange noise from behind her.

Looking around, there were masses of suds coming out of the dishwasher.

Oh no! 'What's wrong with it?' she worried.

At that point, the other two returned, and walked through to the kitchen, and to the sight of Carrie stood in a sea of bubbles.

"What on earth's happened here?" Natasha asked.
"I decided not to wait for you, and put a load of fairy liquid in the dishwasher instead. I think that's the problem."
"Oh no!" Anna exclaimed. "Everyone knows you don't put washing up liquid in to a dishwasher, Carrie you nutter!"
"What are we going to do?" asked an embarrassed Carrie.
"No probs, I'll stop the cycle, and reset it to rinse mode, then we'll use one of these tablets," Natasha said, pointedly holding up a dish washer tablet.

"In the meantime, pass me the mop, and I'll get this floor cleaned up," Anna said.

Before anyone had a chance to clean up the mass of bubbles, Tasha ran to her roomand got her camera. This was definitely one for the album.

"Honestly, we've been here for less than an hour, and look at what Carrie the Calamity has done already," Natasha laughed. "Can't wait to see what the next nine days bring!"
"How was I supposed to know that'd happen?" Carrie said. "Fairy liquid is for washing dishes, so I just presumed it would be okay for the dishwasher."
"You muppet," Tasha laughed. "If washing up liquid was okay to use in a dishwasher, why did they invent dishwasher tablets?"

Carrie finished off cleaning out the kitchen, before moving on to the bathroom with the right product this time, all-purpose cleaning fluid. She wouldn't settle until these two (already sparkling) rooms were cleaned to her standards.

***

Chapter Forty Four.

■■

It was now midday, on the first day of their holiday, and also Anna's birthday. The other two had pretended they'd forgotten, much to Anna's chagrin, but they weren't about to let on just yet that they'd remembered.

Later, they would take her out for a celebratory meal and give her their gifts. Let her fume about it, they'd agreed. She would be delighted later, when she'd found out that they hadn't forgotten.

***

Anna had excused herself from the other two, who had found a perfect spot by the pool, and were already working on their tans, whilst listening to Misunderstood (Don't Let Me Be) by Eve Gallagher.

She made her way to her bedroom, and gently closed the door behind her. Listening to ensure she hadn't been followed, she opened her wardrobe door, and carefully took out her presents and cards from her parents and siblings, and of course, Max.

Placing them carefully on her bed, she settled down to open them. She was tinged with sadness though, as with the excitement of the holiday, the other girls seemed to have forgotten her twenty-fourth Birthday.

She opened the card from her parents first, it was a lovely card, her Mum always managed to buy her a card which had a beautiful verse. This one made her cry, though she had to admit, that was probably something to do with her friends having forgotten her big day. She then opened cards from her brother Rob and his girlfriend Amanda, and then one from her Sister Gabrielle and her partner Andy. Both of her siblings had put money in her cards, and she knew this was because they knew how hard she was to buy for.

She then opened the card from Max, which also had a beautiful verse, and he'd added that he missed her but hoped that she would have a wonderful holiday. She missed him already, she thought to herself.

On to the presents, there were only three. One from her parents, and two from Max.

Carefully opening the one from her parent's, she discovered a small box. Strange, her parents didn't usually buy her jewellery. Opening the box, she saw there was a note, and a car key! Quickly opening the note, she read it hastily.

■■

*"Hi Darling, seeing as we're not with you to give
you your gift this year, we thought we'd send you
on your hols with part of it. The other half is
waiting outside your apartment for when you get
home. Love you loads our little Anna, Mum and
Dad xxx."*

Wow. What a gift, she was so excited. Looking at
the key, she could tell it was a Fiat, but what type,
she had no idea, she'd have to wait until she got
home to find out. Bum. She was wishing her
holiday over before it even began.

Moving on to Max's presents, he'd clearly marked
them 'gift one' and 'gift two'.

Strange, she thought.

Opening the first one, she noticed it was a
jewellery box too. She tentatively opened it, to
see the most beautiful love heart charm, with the
words 'I Love You' inscribed on to it. It was for
her charm bracelet, and she couldn't wait to put
this new charm on to it, it was exquisite.

Opening the second one, there was another
jewellery box, but this one was empty apart from a
note.

She unfolded it, and all it said was "Will you?"
■■

'Oh my God!' she thought, 'Could this mean what I think it means?' She couldn't wait to find out. She tied a sarong around her middle, grabbed her purse, she dashed out to phone Max to find out.

Looking at her watch, it was 4.20pm English time. Max would still be at work, so she rang his direct dial number. On the second ring he answered, *"Hi, IT Consultancy Team, Max speaking, how can I help you?"*

"Thank you darling, for the beautiful charm, I love it!" she said to him.

He laughed *"You're welcome sweetie, I hoped you'd like it."*

"I do, I love it Max, thanks so much!. But your second gift, the note saying 'Will you'? Does it mean what I think it means?"

"Well, put it this way, I'm now down on one knee, so read the note again."

"Really Max? You're not pulling my leg are you?"

"Babe, even I couldn't be that callous, so will you?"

"Of course I will! Oh my Lord, this is turning out to be the best birthday *ever*, and I'm not even with you, I wish I was Max. Will you propose properly when I get back?" she asked him, with an urgency in her voice.

"If that's what you want babe, sure I will. I've already got the ring, I wanted to give it to you myself, but thought this would be a unique way of proposing."

"Too right it is, I've never heard of anything like it before!"

"I love you Annalise. Can't wait for you to come back to me, even though you've only just gone."

"Me too," she said, and she meant it.

She then went on to tell him about her new car from her parents, which he thought was great, and then told him that the girls had forgotten, and how bad this was, because she certainly wasn't going to remind them.

"But what the hell, I am over the moon with my birthday gifts and of course you asking me to marry you, I can't believe it!"

"I don't think they've forgotten," Max said,
*"they'll be making you wait, you know what
they're like."*

"I doubt it, it's nearly half past three, and there's
no sign of a card, or anything. I just think they've
forgotten, what with the holiday and everything."

"Just wait and see, I bet you I'm right."

"I hope you are," she said, "it's going to be a crap
night out if they have forgotten."

They spoke a little longer, and then said their 'I
love you and miss you's,' Anna thanked him again
for his gift and wonderful proposal, and hung up.

She then rang her parents, "Mum, thank you *so*
much! What a wonderful gift and card, I can't
thank you enough!" Anna gushed.

*"You're welcome love, are you having a nice
time?"*

"I'm having a lovely time," Anna replied. "Apart
from the fact that Tasha and Carrie seem to have
forgotten it's my birthday."

*"I'm sure they haven't love, I bet they're just
keeping you waiting."*

"I hope so Mum, else it'll put a right dampener on this holiday, I mean what sort of friends forget your birthday?" Anna said, "but I've also some fantastic news, Max has asked me to marry him, how great is that?"

"I know all about it love," her mum replied, *"he asked our permission first."*

"Blimey, he did it the old fashioned way, I wouldn't have pegged him down as that,"

Anna said, "What do you think?"

"We think it's fantastic news, and couldn't wait to hear from you. What a wonderful birthday surprise for you darling, I bet you wish you were with him now!"

"I do, I miss him so much, and you too Mum, thanks again for the wonderful pressie."

"You're welcome love, you just enjoy your holiday, the girls will be playing games,

you mark my words, they won't have forgotten your big day."

"Hope you're right Mum, can I have a quick word with Dad?"

"He's right here, see you soon love, and enjoy your hols,"

"Thanks mum, see you soon."

"Bye love, take care, love you."

"Love you too."

The phone was passed to her dad.

"Hi love, Happy Birthday, are you having a good time?"

"Yes thanks Dad," not wanting to moan at him too about Tasha and Carrie forgetting her birthday "Thank you so *much* for my present," she gushed. "You've made me want to come home Daddy, thanks for such a wonderful present. By the way, what is it?"

Laughing, her Dad informed her it was an N Reg Fiat Punto in a deep metallic red colour. N Reg, it was nearly new Anna thought, and was even more excited.

"Wow, can't wait to get home to give it a test drive Dad, thanks so much for such a generous gift."

"Well, we figured you deserved it, and are old enough now to be allowed out on the roads by yourself, though your Mum and I aren't so sure the rest of England are quite ready for it!"

"Charming, but thanks Dad, I really mean that. Love you, and I'll see you soon."

"You have a great time, lovey, and we'll see you when you get back."

"Can't wait!" Anna replied, and hung up.

It was with a heavy heart that Anna made her way back to their apartment. All this exciting news, and no one to share it with, because Carrie and Tasha seemed to have forgotten about her special day.

***

Chapter Forty Five.

After an afternoon in the hot Tenerife sun, the girls were already sporting healthy glows. They were being careful though, with factor twenty-five sun lotion, as they didn't want to look like chilli peppers on their first night out on the town.

After a couple of hours of siesta time, the girls started getting ready at 7pm, each in their own bedroom, but with the doors open so that they could chatter and listen to the music as they were getting ready. The nights out here started much later, so the girls were in no rush to get out as they would have been back home.

Anna heard a 'pop', and walked through to Carrie's room. No sign of her, so she went in to Tasha's room. No sign of her either.

Confused, she walked through to the lounge, where the girls shouted "*Surprise!*

Happy Birthday Anna!"

The room was decorated with balloons and ribbon, and the girls were stood by the breakfast bar, fully dressed and ready to go out, with a bottle of

Champagne and three glasses of the amber liquid fizzing on the counter top in front of them, as well as cards and presents.

"Oh my God!" Anna exclaimed in delight, "I thought you'd forgotten."
"As if!" Carrie laughed.
"We were just seeing how long you could take it before you gave in and gave us a good talking to about forgetting your big day," Natasha said, "but it seems your resolve is better than ours, so I'd say that's one-nil to you!"

Anna rushed over and hugged her friends, "What a wonderful surprise. How did you blow up all of these balloons and get them all up without me even knowing?"

"We enlisted the help of the lads next door," Carrie said. "They blew up the balloons for us this afternoon, and we just rushed to put them all up in the hopes that you wouldn't catch us at it!"

"Typical," Anna said, "You're already friendly with the men next door, I should have known," she laughed.

"Hey, it's all in good fun," said Carrie. "I'm nearly a married woman, and Natasha is behaving, for a change!"

■■

"Oi!" Tasha said, "I always behave. Well, until the second date that is!" to which they all laughed.

"Anyway," Tash continued, "grab a glass," and they cheered Anna again, wishing her a very Happy Birthday.

She opened her cards, which were bordering on pornography with pictures of bare male torso's from behind on the fronts of the cards 'No surprise there then' Anna smiled.

She then moved on to her presents.

"These are from both of us," Carrie said, "we couldn't decide who should buy what, knowing what a fussy bugger you are, so decided on a joint purchase."
"I'm not that awkward, thanks very much." Anna laughed, delighted the girls had done this for her.

She opened the first present. It was a bottle of 'Nina' by Nina Ricci, one of her favourites, and she thanked them for it, so pleased with her gift.

She then moved on to the last gift, and opened it carefully. Another jewellery box! How many of these she'd already had today.

■■

Opening the box, staring back at her was the most beautiful charm, a little silver envelope, but shaped like a box. The little charm opened as there was a little clasp at the back and the charm appeared to be held together by a magnet as it snapped shut. Inside there was a little piece of paper rolled up. She carefully unrolled it to read the words; "Best friends forever, Anna, Carrie, and Tasha. Tenerife, 1996 xxx."

She felt herself well up, but tried to hold back the tears in fear of ruining her make up.

"What a thoughtful gift, I can't believe it, you've spoiled me," she said, still staring at the beautiful charm, and all that it meant.
"Shut up and drink your Champers before it goes flat." Natasha laughed at her.

Then suddenly, Anna remembered her other gifts, and the proposal. Running through to her bedroom, she brought them all in and put them on the counter top for the girls to see.

***

"I can't believe it, you lucky mare," said Carrie, "a car *and* a proposal, you are *so* lucky!"

"I know, I am the luckiest girl alive!" she squealed, and went on to tell them about her conversation with Max, and how he'd proposed.

The girls thought it was the most romantic gesture, and were so pleased for her.

Natasha did feel a little bit jealous, two of her friends were now engaged, and she'd not even got a boyfriend. 'What was up with her?' she thought. As if reading her mind, Anna said, "Hey Tash, you're young, beautiful, intelligent, and very sexy, you've just not met your soul mate yet, but don't worry, you'll meet him when you least expect it, or you may already know him, who knows?"

"Don't mind me, honestly, I'm fine," she replied, "I'll know when I meet him."

Carrie made a mental note to make Natasha feel special this week, especially as it was because of her kind gesture, that they were all here together.

***

After finishing the Champagne in no time, the girls took one last look at their appearances, checked all the windows and doors were locked, and headed out for their first night on holiday.

Firstly, they grabbed a quick burger and chips from the buffet, not nutritious, but they were in a rush to see the nightlife of Tenerife.

Not having been here before, they wandered aimlessly until they happened upon a small bar called the Pink Pig, of all things. Sauntering inside, they noticed that it was fairly quiet, even though it was past 10pm, but they decided to have a drink, and ask where the action was.

Natasha went to the bar, whilst the others found a seat by the open window, so they could feel the warm nights' breeze on their faces. The sunbathing earlier had made them warmer than they normally would have been, but it would all be worth it when they went home with amazing tans to show off.

Natasha recognised the barman. She'd seen him before, but for the life of her, couldn't think where.

"What'll it be?" he asked Natasha with a warm smile. She liked this man immediately. There was something about him, but she couldn't put her finger on it.

"I'll have three bottles of Stella please." Natasha replied, still wondering where she knew his face from.

As if guessing her thoughts, he said, "You're wondering where you've seen me before, right?" Natasha blushed, 'had her staring been that obvious?' "Well, as it happens, yes I was." "You're probably too young to remember, but I'm Chris Quinten, I played Brian Tilsley in Coronation Street for a while."
"*That's* where I've seen you before, I thought you looked familiar," Natasha said, "I thought I knew you for a minute!"

He laughed, an easy laugh, and said that's what most people said to him.

Natasha went for her purse to pay, but he said, "No, these are on me, thanks for stopping by. I own this bar with my sister, it's always nice to have a pretty face in here."
"Thanks, that's very kind of you." Tasha smiled.
"You're welcome. Where are you from by the way, I recognise your accent?"
"We live near Sheffield, South Yorkshire."
"Ah," he replied. "That's why, my sister lived there for a while, no wonder I recognise your accent."
"That's interesting, whereabouts in Sheffield did

she live?" asked Natasha.

"Somewhere called High Storrs, I think."

"I know it," Tasha said, "my friend used to work near there. Come over and have a chat with us if you like, if you're not doing anything else of course."

He said he'd like that, and with that returned with Natasha to where the others were sat.

"Don't I know you from somewhere?" Carrie immediately asked him, to which Chris and Natasha both laughed, and he explained where they knew him from.

Natasha retrieved her cigarettes from her bag, and offered them around. Everyone apart from Carrie accepted one. Carrie had given up a couple of months before, and Natasha had wondered since if it was anything to do with David. 'Probably' she thought, knowing how he'd tried to get her to stop.

They all fell into an easy banter, and when the girls asked him where the best nightlife was, he even offered to drive them to 'Veronica's' as it was known, and show them around. How great was that! To be shown the best places, by a celebrity.

He had a quick word with his sister, and then drove the girls into town, where he took them to

Lineker's, Rooftops, Bobby's, Soul Train, and too many more to mention.

The girls had the time of their lives, especially being with Chris, who was loads of fun, and as he seemed to be well known, they got into many places free of charge, and got to drink whatever they liked for free.

The music everywhere was amazing. They heard all of their favourites…Born Slippy by Underworld, Hideaway by de Lacy, Macarena by Los del Rio (still corny!), Make the World go Round by Sandy B, Insomnia by Faithless, Keep on Jumpin by The Lisa Marie Experience, and so many more…

What a great start to their holiday.

It was 5am by the time Chris dropped them back at their apartment, and he made them promise to visit his bar again soon, which of course they agreed to.

Thanking him once again, they staggered in to their apartment, and to their much needed beds.

***

Anna's last thoughts before sleep overtook her were, 'This has been the best birthday ever, I just wish Max was here to experience this with me.'

■■
***

Chapter Forty Six.

■■

Waking at 10.30am to a sharp knocking on the door, Natasha managed to drag herself out of bed to answer it.

Who could it possibly be at this time? She checked her appearance in her bedroom mirror, 'Oh dear, some maintenance will be needed to lick me in to shape' she thought, she looked and felt awful.

The knocking continued.

"*Alright!*" Natasha snapped, "I'm coming!"

She opened the door to sunlight so bright it hurt her eyes, and made her head bang with fury.

"Good morning!" the lady chirped, "I'm your Rep for this holiday, and I'd like to invite you to our meet and greet at Anthony's across the road. It'll be at 4pm, and will be in your best interest to come along so you get the most out of your holiday. There'll be free cocktails too, so I hope to see you then?"

'How could anyone be so bright and cheerful at this time in a morning?' Natasha thought, and the last thing she needed was more alcohol.

"Okay," she found herself agreeing. Anything to get rid of this annoying woman.

Padding through to the kitchen, each footstep painful to her poor head, Tasha opened a drawer and retrieved the painkillers. Releasing two from their capsule, she swallowed them with a large swig of fresh orange, straight from the bottle.

God she felt awful, her head was pounding and she felt so sick too. 'No more overdoing it' she thought, it would only spoil their holiday.

She poured herself a pint of mineral water and headed back to bed until her headache and nausea subsided a little.

***

"Wake up sleepy head, we need to grab a bite to eat and then sunbathe!" Natasha looked up to see a very bright and perky Anna peeking around her door.
"How come you look and appear to feel so great?" Natasha moaned, pulling the covers over her head.

Not one to give in easily, Anna walked over and whipped Tasha's sheets off her.

"Oi!, give me them back," she protested.
"Nope, it's noon, and time to get a move on, so get
a shower, get some water down you, and get
dressed so we can grab a bite from the buffet.
Fifteen minutes, then I'm coming back to get
you!"

"Bloody hell," Natasha moaned, "I feel like shit,"
even though she must admit she felt hundred times
better than she had an hour and a half before.
"Some grub, sunshine and a swim will do you
good, so get a move on," and with that Anna
disappeared.

Natasha took a few moments to come around, and
then tentatively sat up in bed. Yes, she was
feeling a lot better. 'I'll have that shower' she
thought 'and then head outside'. The last thing
she wanted to do was go home as pale as she was
when she left.

The shower revived her even more, and covering
herself in a luxurious white fully towel, she went
back to her bedroom to slather herself in sun
protection, factor twenty-five.

She roughly towel dried her hair, and tied it up and
out of the way. She'd left conditioner on it to
protect it from the damaging rays of the sun. She
then chose her favourite bikini, an aqua blue one,

which tied at the sides, and was covered in tiny silver dots, which shimmered beautifully in the sunlight. Her breasts seemed bigger than usual, 'that's a good thing' she thought, but she must be careful, she'd put on a bit of weight recently, and didn't want to put on any more.

Quickly making her bed, she grabbed the sun lotion, a magazine, her shades, and headed out to the poolside, where the other girls were already settled.

"Bloody hell, it's alive!" laughed Carrie.
"Don't, I feel like crap, I'm being careful from now on, I don't want to ruin the rest of our time here."
"Here," Anna said as she passed Tasha a plateful of fresh fruit and a bagel, "I got this for you from the buffet, get it down you, you'll feel heaps better."

Taking the plate, Tasha asked, "do I look like I've put weight on?" she turned around so they could have a better look.
"May be a little, but it suits you," said an always honest Carrie, "who wants to be skin and bone?"

"You know men prefer a little meat on a woman."
"Yes, but I'm not doing anything differently, I don't understand it."
"Well, we are getting older," Carrie conceded,

"our metabolisms may be slowing down, there's no denying you need to be more careful about what you eat and drink as you get older to maintain your figure."

"And your breasts are looking particularly spectacular in that bikini!" Anna added.

"Hmm, I'm going to be careful though, don't want to put any more weight on."

Natasha concluded, not happy at the news that her friends had noticed her weight gain too. That meant she definitely had put weight on, and she wasn't happy about it.

Plonking herself down on the sun bed they had saved for her, Natasha said, "Did you hear that knocking on the door at half ten?"

"No, who was it?" Carrie asked.

"Our bloody holiday Rep. She says there's a meet and greet at 4pm today at Anthony's across the road, and said it's in our best interests to go to get the best out of our holiday," she continued, "more like a way to get us to sign up to one of those nights out and part with even more money."

"Sounds like we should go though," Anna said.

"I suppose so," Natasha agreed grudgingly, she didn't like anything eating into their holiday time. "There's free cocktails too apparently, so that's a reason to go, though I don't know if my poor system will stand it."

"Oh stop moaning," Carrie said, "it'll be a laugh, and a way of getting to know some other people."

With that it was agreed, they'd spend until 4pm in the sun then go straight to the bar for the meet and greet, and then return to the apartment to shower and have a little sleep before getting ready to go out later.

***

They spent a lazy day around the pool, chatting, reading, going for the odd dip to cool down, and having a little snooze.

The Apartment block gardens and pool were so sumptuous, lush green palms dotted around, giving shade to those who needed it. The pool was split in to two, making it almost as if there were two pools, and there was a whirlpool at one end, where people could sit and enjoy the whirling and pummelling of the water as they relaxed back with a drink or a book, or both. There was also an area of tables with parasols near to the apartments' Eaterie, for yet more shade for those who didn't want to sit out in the hot Tenerife sunshine.

The pool also had a swim up bar, which the girls thought was cool. They'd make use of that later in the week they'd agreed, when they weren't suffering hangovers.

■■

They had already aroused the interest of more than a few groups of men, who were doing their best to get the girls attention with great displays of perfect dives, pool volleyball, and generally puffing up their chests and strutting past the girls at every opportunity. The girls found this highly amusing, and were languishing in the attention they got wherever they went.

Natasha had already thought she may have a holiday fling, if she spotted someone good enough. She knew the other girls would look, maybe even flirt, but they wouldn't touch. They were way too loved up to do anything like that.

***

At ten to four, they grudgingly gave up their sun beds, dropped their things in their apartment, wrapped a sarong around their waists, grabbed their bags, shades and large floppy sun hats, and headed to Anthony's.

The girls were boiling hot from all the sun, having caught much more of the sun in one day than they intended, and were looking more red, than the brown they'd been trying for.

"Too much sun today ladies, we'll have to keep hydrated and well moisturised else we'll look like prunes by the time we get home," Carrie said. "I know, I'm pacing myself tonight and from now on, I way overdid it last night, and it spoiled it for me this morning, " Tasha agreed, still feeling a little queasy.

Entering the bar was absolute bliss. The air conditioning was on full blast, and it was much appreciated, Tasha thought. She was feeling more human by the minute, and her hangover and nausea seemed to have subsided, enough for her to accept a free cocktail or two anyway.

Tasha noticed the Rep who had so rudely awoken her this morning, standing over in a corner of the bar, surrounded by at least thirty people already, all sitting around her in a semi circle. Noticing the girls arrival, she waved them over. "So glad you could make it!" the Rep said. This one was larger than life, 'trust us to get a Rep like this, someone who was so giddy and over the top, it was almost sickening' Natasha thought.

Looking at her name tag, clipped to her jacket, Natasha noted she was called Lydia. 'Giddy Liddy" Tasha thought, yes that name suited her completely.

"Thanks for inviting us," Carrie stepped in, "we're looking forward to hearing what's on offer."

■■

The girls took a cocktail each, Tequila Sunrise they looked like, but no explanation was given as to what they actually were. Taking a sip Tasha decided it was delicious, and would probably grab another freebie before the meeting was over. The girls saw the lads from the apartment next to theirs, and waved as they made their way over to some spare seats near to them.

"Hi, nice to see you here," one of them greeted the girls, "I'm Nicky," he said with a thick Scottish accent, "This is Oliver, and Tom." he said, pointing at each man in turn. "Hi Back," Tasha replied, "I'm Natasha, Tasha for short. This is Annalise, Anna for short, and Carrie" she said, also pointing the girls out. "So, you're from Scotland," she continued, "Whereabouts?"
"Prestonpans, near Edinburgh," Nicky replied.
"What about you?"
"We live in Chesterfield, near Sheffield in England."
"Well, I gathered you were from England, I know Sheffield though, worked there a few times."
"Funny you should live in Prestonpans, I was up their visiting a friend at the beginning of the year, we stayed at the Rockville Hotel on the coast, do you know it?" Tasha asked.
Nicky laughed "Do we know it? It's our local!"
"Well, it is a small world," she smiled back at him. She liked him she decided. He was attractive, but

not in a drop dead gorgeous sense, not like
Marcus, but there was something so very likeable
and attractive about him.

Yes, she thought, I'll have to try to get to know
him better.

Lydia had started talking, they'd missed some of
what she'd said as they had been chatting to the
lads, but as expected, this 'meet and greet' was
just a way of getting the group to buy one of the
'day or night out' packages.

At the end of her speech, Giddy Liddy, who had
got giddier and more animated the more she talked
(was this girl on speed? Tasha thought), finally
finished and passed around folders so that the
group could decide if they wanted to book one of
the packages.

"I'll just get us another cocktail each," Carrie said
standing up, "they're delicious, might as well
make the most of them, eh?"
"Ok," replied Anna, "We'll have a quick look
through this," pointing to the folder in front of her
on the table "and see if there's anything we may
like."
"No probs," Carrie replied as she walked over to
where a queue was already forming, to get some
more of the free drinks.
■■

"This one looks good," Tasha said, pointing to a 'Medieval Night'. "We get a coach up to an old castle type thing. There are free drinks which we get to drink out of old silver goblets, and we get to rip up chicken and eat it like Henry the Eighth," she laughed.

Anna took a closer look, reading through the information. "It looks great, they put on a Knight's display, complete with horses and charges, sounds great," she continued to read, "Oh and look, The Drifters are playing live afterwards, fantastic!"

"They won't be the original Drifters, there's been that many of them," Tasha replied.

"But I bet it'll be a laugh, how much is it?"

"Erm, let's see. It's 45,000 pesetas, which is around £25.00 in English money I think," Anna said, doing the quick calculation in her head. "That's not bad for a night out, we'd spend more than that on the Veronica's strip, especially with taxi fares as well, we'll book it if Carrie agrees."

Carrie agreed straight away, "Sounds fantastic she said, I'm just glad you didn't want to go on one of those bloody day trips where they have you all sat on one of those stupid banana things."

■■■

They laughed at her, "No, we didn't fancy that either," Tasha replied.

Nicky looked over and asked them if they were going on any of the trips.

"Yes, we've decided on the Medieval Night," said Carrie.
"Us too, we'll have to sit together," he said, pointedly looking at Tasha, "We'll have a right laugh."

So, as the meeting came to an end, and they booked and paid, the girls said their goodbye's and headed back to the apartment for showers and a quick nap before their night out.

***

Chapter Forty Seven.

■■■

It was 11pm, and the girls had just arrived at
Bobby's Bar, which was more like a club, as it
stayed opened well in to the earlier hours. Along
with Lineker's and Soul Train, they'd decided this
was one of their favourite bars. The music was
good here, great dance music, and as they'd
already popped in the previous two bars, had
decided they would stay here for the rest of the
night.

"I can't believe this is only our second night,"
Carrie shouted over 'Fire Starter' by the Prodigy,
"Feels like we've been here forever."
"I know," Anna shouted back, dancing along to
the track, "I could stay here forever, if Max was
here too of course."
"Hey, no talk of boyfriends," Tasha shouted. "This
is for girls only, remember!"

The humid nights, and the heat of the bars and
clubs was almost unbearable. So, the girls wore as
little as possible. Tonight, they'd all opted for just
a bikini top, Tasha's was red, Anna's was azure,
and Carrie's was gold. This they'd teamed up
with denim cut off shorts, and shoes to match their
bikini tops. Their hair was tied up, it was just too
warm tonight to wear it down, and Tasha's hair
especially frizzed up terribly if she got too hot.
They'd already started tanning nicely, but were
still a bit too red for their liking, after too much

sun earlier in the day. Still, at least it was dark, so at least they just looked tanned, rather than baked.

'Children' by Robert Miles was now playing, another of their favourites, and the girls danced as if their lives depended on it. They were still young, and were having the time of their lives, on what would be their official last girly holiday.

Natasha and Anna were now dancing along to Livin Joy's 'Keep on Jumpin', and were really going for it, dancing like idiots, when out of no where, came Carrie, flying across the floor, arms by her side, and skidded straight through them.

They stopped dancing and just stared in amazement at Carrie as she continued her horizontal journey across the dance floor. She looked like some sort of stealth missile. As she continued along the floor, her bikini top came unfastened unbeknown to her, and as she finally came to a stop, she stood up, with the top dangling loosely around her neck, with her breasts on show for all to see. By the time she realised, it was too late, she'd flashed the whole club her ample breasts, and was receiving a standing ovation.

Laughing their heads off, Tasha and Anna walked over to her, and helped her fasten her top.

"Trust that to happen to me!" Carrie said, totally embarrassed.

"Well, you've made our night, and that of every bloke in here," Anna laughed.

"Well, I've never done that before," she said, whilst brushing herself down. She was now filthy all down her front from the dance floor.

"Well, I can honestly say, we've never seen anything like it before," Tasha laughed, "what were you doing?"

"I don't know, all I remember is falling, and then someone giving me a push."

"Why keep your hands by your side though?" Tasha asked, still laughing at the antics of her friend.

"I've no idea, at least now I've some idea what it must feel like to be superman!"

"Why, he always had one arm up!" said Anna. "And he was usually flying, not doing a horizontal slide across the floor!"

***

Wandering out of Bobbie's, totally shattered from dancing for what must have been hours, the girls immediately took off their shoes. Their feet were killing them, and they decided to walk barefoot along the promenade, and head to a small café bar near to the beach, for one last drink before heading back to what was their home for the next week.

"God, I'm bushed," said Natasha, pulling her untidy hair back up in to a ponytail.

"Me too," Carrie agreed, "can't wait for a sit down, don't I sound old?"

Glancing at her watch, Anna said "Well, it is 4am, I don't think age has anything to do with it, anyone who's danced as much as we have tonight would surely feel the same," she continued, "plus, we don't take drugs to keep us awake remember, whereas a lot of people do, that's the only way they can carry on."

Reaching the Café Bar, they each ordered a bottle of water. They'd had enough alcohol to drink for one day, Natasha thought.

As they each sat back in comfy chairs around a table outside the bar, Chris drove past, and noticing them, slowed to a standstill and wound down his passenger window, "Blimey," he said, "looks like someone's been busy."

"We've danced all night, are baked from too much sun and are knackered," Tasha replied, "you should have been there, Carrie was hilarious, and flashed everyone in the club!"

"Why am I never there when things like that happen?" Chris laughed, as Natasha regaled him with the story of Carrie's horizontal manoeuvres. "Do you fancy a lift back?"

"That'd be great, Chris, thanks," Carrie said, "We were going to walk on the beach for a while, but if

you're going now, we'll come with you."
Chris climbed out of the car, and locked it, "I'll walk with you if you don't mind, I've lived here for so long, but never seem to get near the beach. Could do with some cool sand between my toes."

With that, the girls collected their bags, shoes, and bottled water, and followed Chris down on to the beach. The sun was just rising, and it was casting a wonderful ruby haze over the horizon.

"What a sight," Tasha sighed.
"I know," Chris replied. "I suppose I take it for granted now, but it still never ceases to amaze me when I see it."
"You're so lucky, living out here," Carrie said. "Will you ever come back to England?"
"Someday, yes. But I'm enjoying it out here for now. I think I'll give it a couple more years, then head home."
"If I had a choice, I don't think I could ever leave," said Tasha, who was already smitten with the Island.
"Oh, you would. England is where the heart is, you'd want to return eventually," he replied.

Walking along the beach, in silence now, they enjoyed the cooling early morning breeze, and the feeling of the cool sand beneath their feet was so soothing after all of that dancing. 'Utter bliss' thought Natasha.
■■

Chris dropped them back at their apartment by
5.30am, and Tasha knew they'd be bushed later.
'A snooze in the sun will do us good' she thought
sleepily, as they got out of the car, and thanked
Chris for the lift.
"No problems ladies, I hope to see you in my bar
soon, take care."
And with that he drove off.

"I wonder what he wants from us?" Carrie mused,
"He takes us on a tour of the best hangouts, gives
us free drinks and lifts, and hasn't made a move on
any of us. I wonder why?"
"Carrie, are your eyes painted on?" Anna laughed.
"Can't you see he's smitten with Tasha."
This was news to Tasha, "I've not noticed that,"
she replied genuinely.
"Oh come on," Anna replied, "surely you've seen
how he looks at you?"
Tasha thought for a moment, and then said, "No,
really, I haven't noticed a thing. He is a dish
though," she laughed, "but I bet he gets the pick of
the girls who come here in search of some fun.
I'm not interested in being a notch on his
bedpost."

The other two burst out laughing. "Since when
did you find some morals, and how much did they

cost you?" Anna said.
"You cheeky cow, you know I can keep my knickers on when I want to!" said a hurt looking Tasha.
"I know sweetie, we're only joking with you."

Saying their good nights, they fell into a deep, much needed sleep. Tomorrow, they would be doing exactly the same as they had done today. Sleep, sunbathe, eat, drink and dance. That's what they were here for, after all.

***

Tasha was up first for a change, she felt fresh and wide awake, which was strange as she'd only had about four hours sleep. No sign of a hangover, but then again, she'd been careful not to over do it last night, especially having overdone it in the sun.

She sat up in bed and stretched her lithe limbs, and climbed out of bed. It was then the nausea over came her, totally out of the blue, she'd felt great only minutes earlier. Running to the loo, she wretched, and threw up just water and bile. There was nothing else in her stomach.

Anna must have heard her, because she appeared in the bathroom doorway, "Are you okay Tash?"
"I was," Tasha replied, "I woke up feeling great, stretched, stood up, then felt so sick.

I don't know what's up with me."

"Did you drink any of the local water, or even use it to brush your teeth?"

"No, I'm always careful, and I've only eaten the same as you, so can't imagine what it could be."

"It could be a bug you've picked up. Either that or your pregnant." Anna laughed.

WHAT?

Natasha looked up at her wildly, "Pregnant? I've not even thought of that, Anna. What if I am?" she said, whilst trying to remember when her last period was.

"Are you always careful?"

"Yes, well, no. Twice with Marcus, we didn't use anything, but that was months ago, surely I'd have had signs before now."

"Not necessarily, not everyone gets the same symptoms at the same time, and it could be the reason you've put on some weight."

Natasha put her forehead against the cool wall tiles. 'Oh no' she thought 'Surely she couldn't be'.

"I can't be Anna, I just can't be!" and with that she was retching again, but this time it was with nerves. Nerves of thinking that she may be

pregnant, and as she'd always been careful with
Chris, it had to be Marcus's.

Anna stayed with her, soothing her, as she
continued to retch, "There's nothing else for it,
you have to know, Tash, we'll buy a test today."
"I just can't be, that can not happen to me, Anna, it
just can't."
"Look, go back to bed for a bit, I'll bring you
some Rennies to settle your stomach, and a glass
of water, and then I'll get ready and go to the
Farmacia across the road to get you a test, you
need to know."

Natasha groaned, she did *not* want to know. There
was no way she could be pregnant. No way, it
must be a bug, that's all, she thought.

Quickly doing her sums, she realised, that if it was
the very worst, and she *was* pregnant, she would
be about three months gone. The last time she'd
slept with Marcus had been at the end of April.

But, she reasoned, she'd had no symptoms until
recently, so she couldn't be pregnant, it just wasn't
possible.

***

■■■

■■

Chapter Forty Eight.

Natasha was in her bedroom, curled up in bed in the foetal position, hugging her knees to her chest. It was a smoulderingly hot day, but she couldn't feel it, all she felt was cold. She lay there shivering, worrying about what was about to happen.

A light tap on the door announced the arrival of Anna and that dreaded kit. Without waiting to be asked, both Anna and Carrie entered Tasha's room, and walked over and sat down on the bed beside her.

"Here it is Tash," said Anna, "you need to know love,"

Natasha started at the little white paper bag, which contained something which could change her life forever, and she didn't think she could bear it.

"I can't do it Anna, I just can't,"
"Yes, you can. You have to know one way or the other, so come on, get up and go and do the test,"

Tasha felt as if this was happening to someone else, almost like an out-of-body experience.
■■

In a robot like fashion, she got out of bed, took the bag from Anna, and made her way to the bathroom where she locked the door behind her.

She sat for a long time, just sat there on the toilet lid, staring at this little piece of plastic that had the ability to shatter her whole world as she knew it, into little pieces.

Finally, she plucked up the courage, and peed on the little stick. Then she sat waiting the required two minutes, which to Natasha, had been the longest two minutes of her life.

She tentatively picked up the stick after what seemed like an eternity, and looking at the results window through half closed eyes, as if this would some how make a difference to the result.

And then she saw it. Two vivid blue lines in the little window. Checking the box again, she was sure this meant it was negative?

But no, two blue lines were positive. She was pregnant. With Marcus's child.

She burst into tears, uncontrollable tears, so much so that she'd ended up heaving yet again.

Her whole world had fallen apart, all in the space of two little minutes.

***

The girls had heard her and were knocking on the door, "Tasha, Tash, let us in, please," Carrie said.

No reply, all they could hear were racking sobs coming from the other side of the door.

Carrie fiddled in her purse for a peseta, and using that, she unlocked the bathroom door. Taking one look at her, sat down at the side of the toilet in a heap, they knew straight away, Natasha was pregnant, and not happy about it.

***

It was now Monday 5th August.

Two days since Natasha had found out she was with child.

It was also her birthday.

Some birthday, she thought, as she opened her eyes to the glare of the mid morning sun.

She was still trying to come to terms with it.

■■

What would she do? What could she do? She'd
sat for hours with the others, talking and trying to
come to terms with what had happened, and what
to do about it.

How stupid she was. Not using contraception on
those two occasions, the idea of getting pregnant
had not even entered her head.

And now she was paying the consequences.

Still laid in bed, still in shock, and mulling it over
in her mind, it was all she couldthink about. It had
ruined her holiday, that was for sure. Even if she
decided she wouldn't keep the baby, she wasn't
going to do it any further harm by drinking any
more alcohol. After all, she thought, it wasn't the
baby's fault she was a complete idiot, was it?

***

A tentative tap on her bedroom door marked the
fact that the others were up and around, "Come
in," Tasha said.
"Happy birthday sweetheart," they both said in
unison, "how're you feeling?"
"Like my whole world has collapsed, and I'm
stood on the edge of a crevice, not knowing
whether to stand and weather the battle, or jump in

and make it all go away," she replied as she sat up slowly.

The girls had prepared her a simple breakfast. Some juice, a little bit of toast, and a coffee. They'd also thoughtfully added some ginger biscuits, knowing that ginger can take away morning sickness.

They'd also brought in her cards and presents, which they placed on the bed beside her.

It was not the fun filled birthday which Anna had had, only four days before, it was a much more sombre affair, because of Tasha's news.

Oh how she wished she could go back to Anna's birthday, when they'd just arrived here, and was so excited about that, but also Anna's news of her new car and proposal from Max.

No such look for Natasha. Her parents' card would be back home in England, and she had no boyfriend to lavish her with gifts. Instead, she just had her two friends, and a baby she didn't think she wanted.

"Thank you," she finally said, and managed a small smile as she picked up a biscuit to nibble on, hopefully to stop any nausea before it started. "You're more than welcome," Carrie said, "hurry up and open your presents!"

"What are they," Natasha asked. "Booties?"

The others didn't know whether to laugh or not, but aired on the side of caution, and didn't laugh until Natasha said, "Oh for goodness sake, crack a smile when I joke will you? No one died, I just got myself in to a big mess that's all," she smiled.

The tension was broken, and forgetting her breakfast, Tasha opened her cards, which were as expected, rude one's. She didn't expect any less from the others.

The gifts were beautiful. A bottle of Jean Paul Gaultier's Classique, a heady perfume, and one she loved. Her second gift was an exquisite silver heart locket on a chunky silver chain. She loved longer chains, and this one had to be twenty-four inches at least, it was beautiful. She carefully opened the locket, and saw that inside, the girls had cut out and put a photo of the three of them, she thought from earlier in the summer, outside the Oak Tree, all smiling, carefree and having fun.

'How times change so quickly' she thought.

On the left hand side, inside the locket, instead of another photo, they'd had the caption "The Three Amigos, Forever x." typed in small print…similar to the idea her and Carrie had had for Anna's present, it was a beautiful gift, and a wonderful keepsake, of a time when things were so much simpler.

"Thank you, thank you both so much," Tasha said, with tears rolling down her face (she found herself crying at almost anything and everything these last few days.) "What beautiful gifts, I don't deserve you two."
"Why ever not?" asked Carrie. "You're one of the sweetest, kindest, warmest, funniest people I know, who'd *not* want you as a friend?"

This only made Tasha cry more, and they all huddled together in a group hug.

***

Later that night, they were due to go on the Medieval night, but the girls had said that if she wasn't up to it, they'd be happy to do whatever she wanted. The last couple of nights, they'd spent at quieter bars, choosing to eat late, lingering over their meal, rather than go clubbing. Natasha needed this time to get her head around things, and going clubbing wasn't a great idea until she'd decided what she was going to do about her situation.

As they lounged around the pool in the hot mid afternoon sun, Tasha found herself running her hands over her once flat toned stomach. 'I've got new life growing in here' she thought 'how can I give it up?'

It was a gesture that had not been missed by the others and they knew there and then that Natasha had made her mind up, she was keeping the baby.

Chapter Forty Nine.

The Medieval night was been brilliant, a great distraction for Tasha. She'd opted for lemonade instead of wine though, yet another sign she was going to keep the baby, although she'd not told the others yet, and they weren't going to push her on the subject, she would tell them in her own time.

The fake fights between the knights on horses were amazing to watch in the arena of the large castle, and the girls were sat next to their Scottish neighbours, who had made sure they'd been seated next to the girls. It was great fun.

The castle and event had such a sense of history and nostalgia about it, and Natasha couldn't help but think they were back in the days of Tudor, and were absorbing every minute of the experience, as they sat there, drinking out of old silver goblets, and using their fingers to tear apart their chicken. Wiping their hands and mouths on a napkin provided still didn't remove the stickiness of the succulent chicken from their fingers, and they found themselves sucking their fingers several times in a bid to rid them of the stickiness.

Nicky, who Tasha had quite fancied before her news, was now in her mind, just a friend, and as if sensing this was so, Nicky had treat her as one.

They danced along to The Drifters, letting their hair down, and having a great time dancing to the oldies but goodies. Tasha slow danced with Nicky, as Anna did with Tom, and Carrie with

Oliver, but there was nothing in it, it was all harmless fun. The girls made it clear from the word go, that they were off the market and the lads had accepted this, and had treat them as friends only ever since.

Still, Natasha felt a sense of excitement as Nicky held her close, with his arms wrapped around her, she lay her head on his shoulder and took in his wonderfully masculine smell. 'Trust me to get myself in a mess, and miss out on a chance with this man' she mused, as she moved slowly in time to the music, wrapped in Nicky's arms. When he bent down to kiss her cheek, how she wished she could turn to kiss him on the lips, but knew that wouldn't be fair on him. The baby had changed everything, but she enjoyed her time with Nicky and their flirtations, while it lasted.

At the end of the night, the coach came to pick them back up for the twenty five minute journey back to their apartment. It was early by Tenerife standards, only twelve o clock, but the girls decided to take up the offer from Nicky and his friends, to have some drinks on the patio, at the side of the pool.

***

"Tasha, hey Tasha, wake up, we're back," Anna said, trying to rouse Tasha from her sleep.

"What? Where are we?" she asked.
"On the coach, we're back at the apartment now, come on sleepy head, get up, we've got to get off."

Natasha pulled herself up. God she was so tired, she could go to bed right now, but it was still her birthday (even though it had gone past midnight) so she made herself stay up for a few drinks with the lads next door.

The girls quickly changed into their bikini's and a sarong, ready for a midnight swim in the pool, even though there were signs saying no night swimming, who was around to stop them?

Moving outside, the lads were already sat around two tables, and had made space for them. There was at least twelve bottles of beer of the table
"God, you're not thinking of going to bed any time soon are you?" Carrie laughed.
"Not a chance, we've only a few days left before home," Tom replied. "Time soon flies out here."
"Here," said Anna. "We've brought a couple of bottles of wine, help yourselves."

And so they fell into easy banter with the lads, poking fun at each other, especially each others accents, and when Carrie had tried her Scottish accent, everyone had broken in to fits of laugher, "That's the worst Scottish accent I've ever heard," laughed Oliver. "You sound American!"

■ ■

"Ok clever, you try our Yorkshire accent," she challenged.

As much as they tried, the lads simply could not do it, and this had the girls in fits of laughter.

Anna got up to go to the loo, and taking their chance, the lads grabbed her arms and legs. Screaming and trying so hard to wriggle away from them, she had no chance, they had too firm a grip. She protested loudly, but before she knew it, she was being hauled through the air, and was thrown in to the pool. She came up gasping for breath, hair plastered to her head, mascara running down her cheeks, and she did not look happy. Swimming over to the ladder, she scrambled out, and marched over to where they were sat, "right, that's it, all out war," and threw a bottle of lager over Oliver and Tom.

They jumped up, and squealing, she ran away again, as fast as her wet feet would allow.

They were too quick for her though, and soon had her in a firm grip once again. Yelping "No, No! not again!" the two lads tried to get her back over to the pool, but she struggled harder this time, and when they went to throw her in, she kept a hold of their shorts, and pulled them both in with her.

Resurfacing, they were all laughing like idiots, least of all Tasha who was sat back watching their antics. Much to Tasha's surprise, Carrie jumped in to join them, and they splashed around, splashing water all over each other, it was hilarious to watch them under a bright moonlit sky.

Natasha felt all the tension leave her, and for the first time since finding out her news, felt truly at peace with herself. She was even beginning to get a tiny bit excited. The lads hadn't noticed she wasn't drinking, so there was no awkward questions. Anna had noticed thought, and all she was waiting for now was for Tasha to tell them for herself.

It had better be quick too, because what they'd arranged for the day after tomorrow, would give Natasha the shock of her life.

Everyone had returned to the tables, after a few shouts from annoyed neighbours that they were trying to sleep, so they tried to keep it as quiet as possible, but it was proving impossible after the pool antics and yet more lager spraying at each other.

"Oh for God's sake," Tasha laughed, "will you all grow up!"

"Listen at you, any one would think you're our mother!" laughed Oliver.

Anna and Carrie's heads snapped around to see Natasha's reaction to this remark, but it didn't seem to faze her, she just poked her tongue out in Oliver's direction.

When Tasha was distracted by Nicky, Anna whispered to Carrie "God, I hope we've done the right thing,"
"I'm sure we have, she has to face him, and can't avoid him here. At home she could, so even if she doesn't thank us for it straight away, I think she will in the long run."
"Well, we'll soon know, won't we?" Carrie replied.

***

Anna and Carrie awoke early on the sixth morning of their holiday, still giddy from the events of the night before. They stood talking it over in the kitchen whilst waiting for the kettle to boil.

"Last night was brilliant, the best one yet," Anna said.
"I know, they're such a scream aren't they, and it's so nice to find a group of lads who are mates and don't expect anything from us, that's got to be a first."

"Do you think their gay?"

"Don't be stupid," Anna laughed, "Nick had the right hots for Tasha, until she made it clear she was a no go zone."

"Well, the other two could be," replied Carrie.

"I doubt it, my Gaydar says they're not. They're attracted to us, I can tell, but they know that we're taken so I think they've accepted we only want their friendship. To be honest, I was expecting them to still try something on, but they've been true gents, we should make the most of it."

Moving on to a more important subject, as Carrie buttered toast whilst Anna was pouring boiling water in to three cups, Anna said, "How do you think she will take it? Do you think we've done the right thing? I mean, she's not even officially told us yet."

"Well, it's too late for that now isn't it? She's feeling vulnerable and alone, no matter how much we fuss around her. She's covering up, you know Tasha, always put on a sassy front," Carrie continued, "this is make or break time, and for that reason, even though she might not thank us for it immediately, I am sure we've done the right thing in the long run."

***

Taking a breakfast tray through to her, they found her already sat up in bed, "Morning you," said

Carrie, "we thought you were still asleep."
"No, I've been awake a while, but have been taking my time getting up, I don't want to be sick again, am fed up with it." Tasha yawned and stretched, her hair a tangled mess, and last night's make up still smudged around her eyes.

"Well, here's a little breakfast and of course your ginger biscuits, let these digest before you get up, they've been helping you haven't they?"

"Sit down please," Tasha said to them both, "I've something I need to tell you."

Sitting down with Carrie, Anna knew, well hoped, what was coming.

"I don't know how I'll cope, I don't really know what I'm doing or what I'm going to do. All I do know, is that I am keeping the baby."

With this the girls jumped up to hug her, only just managing not to knock over her breakfast tray. This is what they'd been waiting for.

"That's fantastic news Tasha, we were secretly hoping you'd choose to keep the baby!" said Carrie.
■■■■■■■■■■■■■■■■■■■■■■■■■■■■■■■■■■■■■■

"Yay!" said Anna, "I've just realised, we're going to be Auntie's!" and they hugged Tasha to them once again.

Hearing them say this, made Tasha not feel so alone. She had loads of acquaintances and friends, but her family were in Sweden, and she had no man at her side, so she was feeling a little scared and lonely.

As if sensing this, Carrie said, "don't you worry, we're going to be the best Aunties' in the world we promise, we'll be with you every step of the way, before and after the baby is born, that's a promise, you'll never get rid of us."

With this news, Tasha sighed a huge sigh of relief, and felt as if a huge weight had been lifted. She wasn't going to be alone.

***

Chapter Fifty.

Later that day, as Carrie lay fast asleep on her sun bed, Tasha and Anna quickly dressed in mini summer dresses over their bikini's (they were going to be as quick as possible, not wanting to miss out on too much sun), slipped on some sandals, and walked out of the front of their apartment, and hailed a taxi.

Once in town, with her limited Spanish, Tasha asked a local where the nearest   Joyeros

(Jewellers) was. They were directed to a little side street, about a quarter of a mile's walk, which they didn't mind. The exercise would do them good, and there was a lovely breeze from the ocean, so the walk would be lovely, almost a welcome from all the lazing around they had done.

Even only six days into their holiday, they were sporting the most magnificent tans, and now went without face makeup at night, just opting for a touch of lip gloss, highlighter on their cheekbones, and some mascara. That was all they needed, their skin was glowing from all the sun.

It was with reluctance that they had to turn off the main road, and on to the much hotter, claustrophobic side street, which was so narrow, you could reach your arms out and nearly touch either side.

"Blimey, it's hot in here, let's get this done with so we can get back to the beach road as soon as possible," Anna said.
"How do you think I feel?" asked Tasha, "I feel constantly hot nowadays, so this is a killer for me!"

Trust Tasha, she was certainly going to use this pregnancy to her advantage, that was for sure.
■■■

Entering the tiny Joyeros, which they had found easily thanks to Tasha understanding a little Spanish, they were relieved to find it air conditioned.

"Thank goodness for air con," said Tasha. "I don't think I could have stayed in here long without it."

Anna agreed.

Hearing the tinkle of the door opening, the owner came through to the front of the shop where the girls stood expectantly.

"¿Hola, puedo ayudar yo?" (Hello, can I help you?) said the owner.
"Yo no hablo muy bueno español, disculpe." (sorry, I don't speak very good Spanish) said Tasha in her very basic knowledge of the language.

"That is no problem Madam, I speak some English," replied the owner.

Thank God for that, Tasha thought.

"We would like a silver bracelet, with a chunky silver heart, with these words inscribed on it please," Tasha said pushing forward a small piece of paper.

The owner read it, and said, "No problemo, I can do. Please, choose bracelet." and with that, the owner brought to them two displays, one of bracelets, and one of charms.

The two girls knew straight away which one's they wanted. A beautiful, shiny silver bracelet, not too chunky, but not too small either, in a Prince of Wales link chain. The heart was the perfect size for the bracelet, bulbous, and the words 'Friends forever, Carrie, Anna and Tasha 1996' would fit perfectly, with the 'Friends forever' on one side, and the words 'Carrie, Anna and Tasha 1996' on the other side.

Then they would not only each have a memento of this holiday, but of their ever lasting friendship, forever.

Tasha pointed out the two items, and the shop owner carefully took them from the display, "One hour, is ok?"

"That's fine, thank you, will we pay you now?"
"No, you pay when happy," the owner said with a smile.

The girls thanked him, and left the shop.

"What'll we do for an hour?" Anna asked, "Carrie will surely notice we've disappeared by the time we return."

"It doesn't matter, we'll give it to her as soon as we get back, I want her to have it straight away, so that we all have something similar as soon as possible."

"You're right, and it was such a good idea, Tash, she's going to love it."

"Come on, let's go back to the beach road, and find ourselves a little café where we can have a cool drink."

***

'Feel the Sunshine' by Alex Reece was playing in the background. "How apt." said Anna, as she sipped at her mineral water.

"Hmm, this is bliss," said Tasha, leaning back, closing her eyes, and wriggling her toes out of her sandals, "the breeze is even cooler now, I feel wonderful."

"Me too, but I can't wait to see Carrie's face when she see's our gift!"

"I know, she's going to love it. A memento of the most glorious holiday, even if the presence of another person did make an appearance, though albeit through the translation of only two blue lines," laughed Tasha.

Anna was so pleased that Tasha had decided to keep the baby. Just coming to terms that she was pregnant was a huge shock, so to have decided in a matter of days that she was going to keep the baby was a miracle. But then again, if Tasha was already three months gone, she didn't have much choice, apart from adoption. Could Tasha part with her baby she wondered?

Still, Anna thought, things are different out here, I wonder how she'll feel when we get back to reality? Being back on home soil, may give Tasha a big wake up call.

Anna knew Tasha wasn't happy with her work, but to have any chance of decent maternity leave and pay, she'd have to stay there now. Had she even thought of that? Anna wondered.

'But,' thought Anna, 'the biggest shock is yet to come. Tomorrow, at around 10am Tenerife time.'

***

The girls had been whiling away the hour sat in exactly the same spot. They were sat in the sunshine, so they were still getting their tans topped up, but at least it was bearable here.

"Good job we brought some suntan lotion," said
Tasha, "I didn't realise how long it would take."
"It's time now though, we should be heading back
to the shop," Anna replied, glancing at her watch.

With regret at having to leave such a lovely spot,
the girls quickly made their way back to the
Jewellers, and into the bliss of the air conditioned
shop.

The owner appeared once again from the back
room, bringing with him a long thin blue velvet
box. "Open, you like?" he asked.

"Oh my goodness," said Tasha, turning the heart
over and over in her hand, "It is beautiful, how
they say, exquisito, hermoso, muchas gracias,
Senor. The writing fits perfectly, our friend will
love this!"

Anna was now looking and feeling at the bracelet,
and she agreed, it was perfect for Carrie "Muchas
gracias, Senor," Anna repeated Tasha's words.

The shop owner looked very pleased with himself
at this news, and took the bracelet back, gave it a
little polish, and placed it back in to it's velvet
box. He then placed this in to a beautiful little
jewellery bag, the same colour as the box, and

439

tying it with a velvet ribbon, presented it to the girls.

This man was obviously very proud of his work, and took his time to create perfection.

Paying him, and thanking him once again, the girls left the shop, and hurried down the narrow street and once again on to the beach road, where the welcoming breeze remained.

***

Carrie was awake, and wondering where the hell her friends had gone. She'd looked in the apartment, no sign of them, and their bags were gone. Charming, she thought as she huffed around waiting for them to return.

To work off some of her frustration, she dived expertly in to the pool and swam a few laps, the soothing coolness of the water was so welcome against her hot skin, and she dove underwater, fully submersed, several times, so that her whole body felt refreshed and cool.

She swam a few more laps, which wasn't easy given the shape of the pool, and the amount of people in it, but she was determined to get some kind of exercise.

Getting out, she reached for her towel to dry herself off and she noticed Tom, sat on his Terrace. "Hey Tom, have you seen Anna or Tasha? They've gone *awol* on me."

"Saw them head out of the front about two hours ago at least," he replied.

Charming, two bloody hours, and not even a note of explanation.

Then she started to worry, 'what if something was wrong with Natasha?' No, they'd have woken her surely if that was the case. But it was still worrying and very annoying that they had abandoned her like this.

Just as she was putting on some clothes to go in search of them, the front door opened, and the two of them breezed in as if nothing had happened.

"Where the bloody hell have you two been?" Carrie snapped, "Tom says you've been gone over two hours!"
"Stop shouting at us and you may find out," smiled Tasha, holding out the bag for Carrie.
"What's this?"
"Open it and find out," said Anna.

Carrie sat down on the sofa, carefully unwrapped
the little bag, and tentatively took out the beautiful
box. Looking up at them both, as if questioning,
she held the box, turning it over in her hand, and
then slowly opened it.

Staring at the beautiful bracelet in awe, she
noticed the inscription on the heart, turning it over
to read the other side, she was overcome with this
beautiful gesture.

"Oh, what have I done to deserve this? And I just
snapped your heads off, I'm so sorry, this is
beautiful, so very beautiful, thank you," she said
as she got up to hug her friends.
"We wanted you to have something like we do,"
Tasha said, pointing to her own charm, "as a
memento of this, let's face it, momentous
holiday!"
"And because of the year we've all had, and your
accident and all that, we just thought it would be
nice for us all to have something to remember this
year by."

Carrie was almost speechless, "But you already
paid for me to come here Tasha, there was no need
to do this too."
"Because there wasn't a need, that's why we did
it," Tasha replied.
"You can wear it later," Anna said, "just have a

bite to eat here, and a quiet drink at the Pink Pig, and an early night for a change, we all need one day with at least eight hours uninterrupted sleep."

"What, you don't want to go down to Veronica's?" asked Tasha.
"No, just a quiet night tonight, we'll get up early tomorrow and browse the shops before we sunbathe," Anna said knowingly to Carrie.

"We have to get Natasha to bed early," said Anna, out of Tasha's ear shot, "She's going to have the shock of her life when she see's him."

***

Chapter Fifty One.

Tasha had no choice in what time she got up, Anna was in her room at eight with a cup of tea and three ginger biscuits.

Tasha, still half asleep, even though she'd had over eight hours, looked up through bleary eyes, "What sort of time is this? We're supposed to be on holiday," she protested.

"Come on, eat these and drink your tea, we want you up, looking gorgeous, and ready by 10am, we've some serious shopping to do."

Still protesting, Tasha took the tea and biscuits, which were helping her nausea immensely, and immediately started nibbling on the biscuits and sipping at her tea. She liked being looked after like this, and could get used to it, she thought.

Then sadly remembered, she had no one but her friends, who would be married before she knew it, and it would then be her and the baby, alone.

***

By 9.30am, Natasha was showered, hair washed and dried, and tied up casually to look like it had taken a few minutes when in fact it had taken nearly half an hour. She'd let a few tendrils hang down to frame her face, and had applied a little lip gloss and mascara. She squirted on a little Escada Sport, her favourite perfume of the moment, as it was so light and fresh. She'd then chosen a very flattering white floaty summer dress, with her gold roman sandals and matching bag, she looked like a Greek goddess....the sun, the pregnancy, or both, were certainly suiting her, she thought.

"Come on then!" she shouted to the other two. They hadn't bargained on Tasha being ready so quickly, and were now stalling for time. It was 9.40am, and they had at least twenty minutes to go.

"Sorry Tash," Anna shouted through, "I'm having a bad hair day, just give me a few more minutes."
"In that case, I'm going over the road to have a browse in the shops, I'm ready and I don't like hanging around, won't be long."

Before they could protest, she had gone.

Great, now what to do?

***

10.10am. Still no sign of Tasha, and the girls were pacing, wondering how to get her back here without it looking suspicious.

"I could go and get her?" Carrie asked.
"No, it won't work, if she knows we're both ready, she'll expect us to both go over the road, and then head off in to town to go shopping. We've got no choice but to wait here for her to return."

Then there it was. A knock at the door. No going back now.

Opening the door, Carrie looked up in to the eyes
of the man Natasha adored.

"Hi Carrie, you're looking fantastic, that tan suits
you," Marcus said.
"Thanks Marcus, you're looking well yourself,
where did you go for pre season training?"
"The south of France," he smirked, "not been back
for more than a couple of weeks before I got your
call."
"Well, the climate suited you, you're looking
really good."

And he did, with a casual T shirt, cut offs and
loafers on, he looked drop dead gorgeous, Carrie
thought.

"Thanks, so where is she then, and why the big
mystery? It'd better be good to dragme thousands
of miles away, when the season starts in a few
weeks, I got a right bollocking off of the boss, but
he's allowed me three days, that's it, then I have to
get back."
"We go home in three days anyway, so you may
even be on the same flight."
"No, I'm allowed three days as of today, so I'll
have to leave the day before you, so please stop
skirting around the issue, Carrie, where is she, and
why am I here?"
"She was sick of waiting for us, so she popped

over to the shops. I have to tell you Marcus, she doesn't know you were coming, and we had to lie to her to get her up and ready. She thinks we're off to town shopping."

"She doesn't know I'm coming?" Marcus asked incredulously, running his hands through his tousled dark brown hair, "Why not? what's the big secret Carrie?"
"You'll find out soon enough," Carrie replied. "Look, me and Anna will make an exit now, it will be for the best. You make yourself comfortable here, she'll be back soon."
"You can't just leave me here!" Marcus exclaimed. "The shock of me being here could kill her!"
"I doubt it. Help yourself to anything from the kitchen, but keep out of our knicker drawers," she laughed, "I'll know if you've been prying!"
"What do you take me for, some kind of perv!" he laughed back.
"Look, we must go, it's for the best, you'll find out everything when Tasha gets back."
"Ok, but only cos it's you," he smiled.

God, she could see once again why Natasha kept being drawn back to this man. He may be weak at times, but he was simply drop dead gorgeous.

"Come on Anna, we'll escape through the back way, less chance of bumping in to Tasha," and with that, they were gone, leaving Marcus in their apartment, wondering what the hell was going on.

***

Tasha made her way back to the apartment, sucking on an ice lolly, enjoying the coolness in her mouth against the blistering heat of the sun. Seeing Nicky and the lads coming out of their apartment, she waved as she walked over to them, "Hi you lot, where are you going?

"Just to town to get some last minute duty free," Nicky replied.
"That's what we're doing, may be we can catch you for a drink at the little café next to Bobby's, a good bye drink if you like?"
"That'd be nice Tasha, see you around one-ish then?"
"Great Nicky, see you then."

Tasha walked in to the cool apartment. Strange, no music could be heard, and no chattering of the girls, "Hello, you two, where are you?" she shouted as she made her way to their bedrooms. No sign of them, 'this is strange' Tasha thought, as she walked out of Carrie's room, and made her way through to the lounge.

She let out a scream when she saw who awaited her.

"God, what the hell are you doing here?" was her first instinct, "you gave me the fright of my life!" "Hello Natasha," Marcus finally spoke, "I got a call from your friends, they said it was urgent that I see you, so much so that I had to travel out here." Natasha stared at him in disbelief. "Well they had no right,"
Well, they obviously thought there was a good enough reason Tash, else why would I be here?" Inside she was seething with her friends. It wasn't their decision whether Marcus should know or not, how dare they put her in this position? She was fuming, and was sure Marcus could see steam coming out of her ears.

"Let's go for a walk," she finally said, "There's something I suppose I ought to tell you, seems as you're here."

They walked along in silence, Marcus following her lead. The silence was like a great crevice between them, which Tasha did not know how to fill.

Eventually, after what must have been a twenty minute walk, Tasha turned in to a side street, and entered a café. He followed her in."What would you like to drink?" Marcus asked her.

"I'll just have a mineral water with lots of ice and a twist of lemon, thank you," she said, courteously.

"Not like you," he said glancing at his watch, "thought you may want a white wine spritzer, being on holiday and all that?"

"No, water will be fine thanks," she insisted.

Marcus ordered the drinks, and followed Tasha outside, to where she had sat at the table furthest away from the Café.

"You look good, Tasha, the sun suits you, but then again, you always look good, with or without a tan."

Tasha was trying to appear composed, but felt far from it, her nerves were so on edge, she was sure he could see her shaking.

"Thank you, I feel good, this break has done me the world of good."

***

She wondered how she would break the news. She could murder her friends, and would easily have done so had they been anywhere in sight. She *had* to tell him now, they'd left her with no choice.
▪▪

"Marcus, I am sorry that Carrie and Anna dragged you all the way out here. What I am about to tell you, you may not want to hear," she continued. "If I'd have been at home, I doubt I would have told you to be honest, but it seems those friends of mine have left me with no choice."

She could see that she had his full attention now. He was staring at her intently, leaning forward, elbows on the table, head in hands. He did not speak, he seemed to be allowing her all the time she needed.

"The thing is Marcus, oh for the Love of God, how do I say this?" she paused, and looked down.

Seeming to make her mind up, she looked up and staring straight at him, she said "Marcus, I am pregnant. And you are the Father."

***

BAM!

He'd not been expecting this, and in his confusion and initial panic, he said the very last thing he should have said, "Are you sure it's mine?"

As soon as he'd said it, he knew he'd made a big mistake. Her eyes were like steel daggers,

piercing in to him "How dare you?" she asked
menacingly, "how the hell dare you ask me that!"
"I'm sorry, Tash, I.."
But she cut him off. "I am not some two bit
slapper who sleeps with just any one. There has
only been you and Chris in the last four months,
and I took precautions, apart from with you."
"I'm sorry Tasha. I don't know why I asked you
that, I know you're not a slapper, I wouldn't have
travelled here to come and see you if I thought that
would I?"

"I'll allow you that, Marcus, but I could and will
strangle Anna and Carrie when I get my hands on
them. It should have been my decision whether to
tell you or not, but they took that decision away
from me didn't they? How could I not tell you
seeing as they've dragged you over here?"
"You could've told me when you got home, it's
only three more days."
"I think that's why they called you, because once
back home, I most probably wouldn't have told
you."
"But I have a right to know, Tash, no matter what
you think of me, I am the baby's Father."
"I know," she replied. "It's just I would have
preferred to do this my way, and not have it forced
on me. One thing I will tell you is, I don't expect
anything from you. Nothing, not a thing."
"Don't you understand, Tasha? I love you, I

worship you, I'd do anything for you, and want to be with you, even more so now."

This seemed to have her attention, "What about your little girlfriend?"
"I finally found the guts to leave. I don't love her, and would rather be alone than with someone I don't love," he continued, "I love you Tasha, will you give me, us, a chance?"
"How can I trust you? You'll only do to me what you did to her."
"But that's where you're wrong Tash. I made a mistake in not telling you of my circumstances, and I have paid a very high price for that ever since. I lost you, and I've never known a pain like it," he took a deep breath and continued, "I've *never* felt like this before, ever. You are in my every waking moment, from the moment I wake up until the time I fall asleep. You're even with me in my dreams. I can't stop thinking about you Tash, you're the one for me, they'll never be any one else, I swear. I'll swear on anything Tash, just please, I'm begging you, give me a chance?"

***

Tasha sighed. She so wanted to believe him, but didn't know if she could trust him, and couldn't bear her heart being broken by him again.

"I don't know Marcus, you've really hurt me, there is no trust, and without that, what do we have?"

"I love the bones of you. I've hounded you for months, so much so that it became embarrassing, and I've just travelled all this way to see you just because your friends asked me to, doesn't that count for something?"

He did have a point.

"And now we have a bond that will tie us together forever, a baby! Tasha, all I want is you and our baby, please darling, please, give us a chance."

And with that she got up, walked around the table, sat on his knee and kissed him deeply, letting her true feelings, which she had tried so hard to fight, come to the surface.

***

When the girls arrived home, they very carefully, and more than a little warily, walked in to the apartment.

Tasha in a mood was not one they wanted to mess with. They only hoped that what they'd done had paid off. There was no way she could avoid him here, she would have to have had it out with him, it would be make or break for good.

If she'd gotten home without Marcus knowing, she could have avoided him, avoided this, and the girls knew that would have been a mistake.

Yes, granted, Marcus had not been straight with Tasha, but his actions since proved beyond all doubt how much he loved her.

***

The apartment was silent.

They looked in the lounge, no one there. They looked in Tasha' bedroom, no one there either.

And then they looked out on to the terrace. And there they were, Marcus sat on a lounger, with Tasha curled up at the side of him, her head in his lap, his arm around her, protecting her.

"Yes," whispered Anna. "We did the right thing."

***

▪▪

Chapter Fifty Two.

The four of them went out to dinner that night, in celebration of Tasha and Marcus being reunited. Anyone who looked at the couple just knew that they were meant to be together.

Marcus insisted on going to one of the best places to eat, the restaurant at the Hotel Sir Anthony Grand Luxe, a five star hotel, with a Haute Cuisine menu.

Tasha was like a different person, she was glowing, even more so than before, and so animated. She looked like a woman in love.
▪▪

"So, what are we drinking?" Marcus asked.

"Well, in respect for Natasha's current disposition, we should really have water." Carrie said.

"Don't be so bloody stupid," Tasha laughed. "Champagne all round, I'll allow myself one sip and that's it. I don't see why you should all suffer just because I couldn't keep my legs closed!" to which they all laughed.

"Champagne it is then, and a Jug of Iced Water for my baby, well, my babies!" Marcus said, waving for the waiter's attention.

Marcus couldn't keep his eyes off his girlfriend. Not only was she the most beautiful woman he'd ever met, she was also sassy, outspoken, intelligent, witty, and always bloody right! Which he supposed, was a typical woman.

And now she was his, she was really truly his, and there was no way on this earth he was letting her go again. And to complete the fairytale, she was having his child, life didn't get any better than this, thought Marcus, smiling to himself.

"What're you grinning at?" Anna asked from across the candlelit table.

"Just how I'm the luckiest man alive," he replied. "She's finally mine, and we're going to be a family, I can't believe it, and it's all thanks to you two, you little devils!"

"In fact, Tasha, will you marry me?" Marcus turned to her.

"Wow, didn't see that coming!" she replied. "No, I won't, not yet, but I will have your baby!"

Everyone laughed at the irony of it all.

"And, I should berate you two," Tasha said to Carrie and Anna. "But, I have to thank you, you've made me see sense, which I wouldn't have done back home. Thank you for bringing Marcus back to me," she then turned to Marcus, "and thanks for not giving up on me." She smiled then leaned in to kiss him.

"Eewwwwww, get a room will you!" Carrie laughed. "And anyway, you're not the luckiest man alive, David is."

"I think you'll find that Max is," Anna cut in.

"Of for the love of God, so all three of us are, okay?" Marcus said, shaking his head at these three amazing women.

The waiter arrived with the Champagne and four crystal flutes. He offered to pour, but Marcus said there was no need.

Instead, he poured three flutes for himself, Anna and Carrie, and just a drop for Tasha. "Here's to the seven of us!" he toasted.

"Yes," they replied in unison. "Here's to the seven of us."

***

The menu's were brought. Thick cream folders embellished with gold leaf, so lavish Tasha thought. They befitted the hotel restaurant perfectly, she could certainly get used to living like this, she thought.

"I think I'll go for the Courgette Flowers, stuffed with Langoustine Mousse and

Truffles, served with a Wild Mushroom sauce and spinach salad, followed by the Organic Chicken Breast with Green Asparagus and Wild Mushrooms, with a Herb Cream Sauce for main," Carrie said.
"Mmmm, sounds good, I think I'll have the same," said Marcus, still perusing the menu.
"I'm going for the same starter, got to be careful now," said Tasha, patting her stomach, "and for main, I think I'll go for the Fillet of Turbot, pan-fried with Jamaican Pepper, Fennel Puree on Basil Butter."
"I don't know!" Anna stated, "they all sound so scrumptious." She concentrated on the menu and finally decided on the Terrine of Rascasse Fish with Plum, Lemon and Cucumber Crème Fraîche, served with a Mixed Leaf Salad, followed by

Cutlets and Medallion of Sisteron Lamb, herbs crust and a confit shallots sauce.

Seeing that they had made their choices, the hovering waiter came to take their order, where Marcus also ordered another bottle of Champagne and turned to Tasha, "Would you like something other than water darling?"
"No, iced water is fine, if I could just have a few more slices of lemon please?" She politely asked the waiter.
"Certainly madam," he replied, and walked away.

"Will you stop sucking those, you're making me cringe," Carrie said to Tasha, who was sucking and nibbling on her fourth lemon slice.
"Sorry, I think baby likes," Tasha replied with a glint in her eye.
"Blimey, we've got months of this, you do realise she's going to have you running around in circles, don't you Marcus?" Carrie remarked, rolling her eyes in exasperation.
"I don't mind, what the lady wants, the lady gets."

Tasha grinned, she was going to make the most of this, that was a certainty.

"I must phone Mum and Dad when I get home, tell them the news," Tasha said.
■■■

"I'm going to call my Dad later," Marcus said, "this is just what he needs after us losing Mum like that."

They all agreed this was a good idea, perk the old chap up no end, knowing he was going to be a Granddad. "Just a shame my Mum isn't here," Marcus said sadly, "she'd have loved you, Tash, and would've been over the moon at being a Grandma, such a damn shame, I really miss her, you know?"

"I can't imagine not having my Mum around," said Anna. "It must be hard for you, Marcus, she wasn't that old was she?"

"No, she wasn't. But I don't want to be maudlin tonight, she wouldn't want us to be, so enough of that now, okay?"

"I'm calling David as soon as we get out of here, can't wait to tell him the news," said Carrie, "he'll be over the moon for you both."

"I'm phoning Max, too, this is just so great not to share with him, even if he is in bed, which I doubt, knowing him, he'll be living it up and have forgotten all about me by now," said Anna.

"I very much doubt it, it's so obvious how he feels about you, Anna, so stop saying stupid things," Tasha replied.

Anna grinned back at her, she knew what Tasha said was true.

■■■
***

Before they knew it, it was day nine of their
holiday, and Marcus had to go home. He had
insisted they didn't accompany him to the airport,
that they enjoy their last day in the sun and their
last night alone in Tenerife, and promised to be at
the airport to meet Tasha when she got back, "No
matter what the boss says, but I'll be on the bench
for the whole season at this rate," he joked.

***

"Well, what a week it's been," Tasha stated as she
sat down on her sun bed, beside the pool, "I can't
believe how much has happened and so far from
home as well. Thank you, you two, you've done
me a huge favour. You took a massive risk, but it
paid off, and I'll always be thankful to you for
that."
"We could see something you couldn't, that's all,"
said Carrie, "that you and that rascal are meant to
be together, so all we really did was give fate a
helping hand."
"Well, fate or not, thank you." She smiled at her
friends, as she rubbed in more lotion.

Looking at her tummy, she now wondered how
she'd not seen it before. She'd not put weight on
anywhere else apart from there, and her breasts

were fuller. All the telltale signs apart from early pregnancy morning sickness. She thanked her lucky stars she'd only been sick a few times, and had only mild nausea, compared to some of the horror stories she'd read.

Suddenly worried, she said, "You don't think I've harmed the baby do you, with all the partying and all this sun?"

"I doubt it Tash," replied Anna. "You read stories of women who drink and smoke all the way through their pregnancy and have perfectly healthy babies. I know it shouldn't be done, but some women don't care. Then there are those who carry on with their lifestyles as normal, with no idea they're pregnant, and their babies are alright too. At least as soon as you found out, you cut out the alcohol and cigarettes."

"But I could still murder a cigarette," Tasha replied. "The drink doesn't really bother me, although it would've been nice not to have had to drink mineral water for most of the holiday, just my luck huh?"

"You've been wanting to stop smoking for ages now, at least this has made you do something about it," Carrie said.

"True, but I still want one. Stop talking about it, it's making me crave. Rub some lotion on my back instead will you?"

Sitting up, Carrie muttered, "God, what did the last one die of?"

■■

■■■
***

Chapter Fifty Three.

The girls, having spent yet another full day in the
sun, were now all a deep golden brown, Tasha and
Carrie, being naturally blonde, had not gone as
brown as Anna, but all the same, they'd got
excellent tans from their nine days of sunbathing.
That's all they'd done, all the time they'd been
there. Sunbathed, took a siesta, had dinner, then
gone out. Apart from the Medieval night, they'd
not seen anything of the island, apart from Mount
Teide, a large dormant volcano, the third largest
volcano in the world the girls had been told by
their Rep Giddy Liddy.
■■■

The volcano was quite visible on a clear day, from the front of their apartment building. Not surprising, as it stood nearly 3,800 metres about sea level.

"At least it's dormant." Tasha had said on numerous occasions when they had looked up at the giant beast.

They all knew what dormant meant though, and weren't all that comfortable knowing that the thing could blow up whenever the fancy took it, even though their Rep had assured them that the volcano would rumble and give enough warning to get everyone, including the locals, off of the island safely.

The volcano was also why the beaches on Tenerife were termed as 'black sand', because of the remnants of the volcanic ashes from when it had last erupted in 1909, scattering it's burning ashes down and over the island.

New 'pale yellow' sand had been imported in to make the beaches look more appealing, but you could still see the black sand, a constant reminder that the volcano could blow again any time it wished.

So apart from viewing Mount Teide from a distance, they'd not seen a thing of the island. They'd wanted to go to the aqua park which was supposed to be a great laugh, but with everything that had happened in such a short space of time, the girls found themselves on the last full day of their holiday, and they intended to make the most of it.

After sunbathing, they would skip a siesta, and get ready to go out early for a bite to eat, and then go dancing on the Veronica's strip, and say their goodbye's to the island.

***

It was 5.30pm, and Anna was knocking on the bathroom door, "Tasha, will you please hurry up in there, I need a shower, Carrie's almost ready, and I'm still stood here covered in sun cream."
"Just getting out now, won't be a mo."
"Good, else we'll never get out."

Carrie was ready by 6pm, whilst Anna had only just got out of the shower. She was wearing a short black dress, with little cupped sleeves, and with a cut out piece on the front and back of the dress. It was held together by two thin bits of material on each side, and showed off her toned stomach and back to perfection. She'd added some black strappy heels, and silver jewellery, of course including the gorgeous bracelet the others had purchased for her. To finish, she'd sprayed herself liberally with her signature perfume, Chanel No.5, and was pacing, ready to go.

"Will you sit down Carrie, you're making me nervous," said Tasha.
"Well, I'm ready, and Anna will be ages yet."
"That's your fault for being in the bloody shower so long."
"Hey, you took as long as me!"
"I guess Anna just drew the short straw," Tasha replied, "I suppose we could've saved time by one of us having a bath, whilst another had a shower, but it's a bit late to think of that now isn't it?"

"Yes, the best idea's from you always come at least two hours too late," Carrie laughed. "I'm going next door, see if I can nick a bottle of Bud from the lads."
"There's some wine in the fridge."
"Nah, I fancy a beer and a natter with the lads, it'll probably be the last time we see them properly."
"Get their numbers," Tasha said. "I'm often up in Scotland as you know, it'd be nice to have a drink with them in the Rockville if they're around."
"Will do," Carrie replied as she waltzed out of the door. ▪▪

Natasha had chosen to wear her white floaty dress again, with the flat gold Roman style sandals for comfort. She added some gold jewellery, just a ring, necklace, and hoop earrings, and a gold bag to match. Having arranged her now white blonde hair, which had been bleached even further by the sun, into a messy 'just got out of bed look', piling it on top of her head with lots of tendrils hanging down, she took a final look in the mirror and liked how she looked. Her tan was glowing, and was a drastic match against the colour of her hair.

A squirt of her new perfume which was one of her presents from the girls, a touch of flattering pink sparkly eyeshadow, highlighting blusher, lip gloss, and a touch of black mascara, and she was ready to go.

Shouting through to Anna that she was just popping next door for a chat with Nicky and the lads, she walked out of the patio doors, and walked around the little wall which separated the two apartments, and without knocking, she walked straight in.

"It's a bloody good job we're dressed," said Tom, "Girls popping in without even a knock, we could have been starkers," he smiled.
"That's what I was hoping for," laughed Tasha.
"Now you don't mean that, we saw you with your

boyfriend. What a surprise for you, him turning
up like that."
"A nice one though," she replied, "Carrie and
Anna arranged it, I had no idea."

Deciding to tell them her news, she continued,
"We've been having a rough time, long story so I
won't go in to that, but since we've been here, I've
found out that I'm pregnant." She paused for
effect.

"Wow, that's bloody fantastic news, isn't it?"
Oliver asked as he sauntered in to the room.
"It was a big shock, but now I've come to terms
with it, I am so happy, so yes, it is good news,"
she continued. "They dragged Marcus out here,
because they knew I'd have to face him and tell
him the truth, and also face my feelings for him.

They know me only too well, because had I got
home, I doubt I'd have contacted him."
"Well, he's one lucky sod if you ask me," Nicky
said swigging out of a beer bottle "I'd have flown
all this way too for news like that too."

She smiled at him. To think that only days ago,
she was considering a fling with him, it seemed so
long ago now.

Carrie had perched herself on their sofa, and
looked comfy, with a bottle of Budweiser in her

hand, "You soon got yourself comfy," Tasha
mused.

"For some reason, I feel comfy with this lot," she
smiled at them.

"Oh that reminds me," said Tasha. "If you like,
give me your numbers, I often visit Scotland to see
a friend, and usually stay at either The Rockville,
or the Laird and Dog in Lasswade, so we could
meet up for a drink, if you like?"

"That'd be great," Nicky replied. "I know you're
spoken for, but it'd be nice to be mates, stay in
touch if you like," he said as he was scribbling
down his number.

"I'd like that very much too," she replied.

***

Anna, alone in the apartment, was nearly ready,
and was singing along to 'I'll be there for you' by
the Rembrants. She loved this song, the theme
tune to her favourite series 'Friends', and turned
the volume up higher. She had the front and back
doors wide open, to let the wonderful dusk breeze
blow through the apartment.

She'd applied light make up, a silvery eyeshadow,
highlighter to enhance her tanned cheek bones, a
black top liner, mascara and a pink lipstick. Her
hair, she'd left loose, and her jet curls cascaded
down her back, the electric blue streaks not so
noticeable now, thanks to the sun, but they didn't

look that bad. Still, she made a mental note to get
them touched up as soon as she got home.

She'd chosen simple jewellery also. Silver charm
bracelet, the one Max had bought her, which
included the beautiful charm from the girls, small
diamond stud earring (another present from Max),
a silver strapped watch, and a chunky square silver
ring, which she wore on the middle finger of her
right hand. She was saving her left hand for her
new engagement ring waiting at home.

She'd missed Max immensely, and had called him
a few times, but it wasn't the same. She'd be sad
to leave here, it was so beautiful, but had so much
to look forward to when she got back home.

As she stood there, with just her bra and a tiny
thong on, something caught her eye from the front
of the apartment. Not many people passed by, so
she'd felt safe having the doors open, and the rest
of them were only next door.

She focused, and in the darkness, she noticed a
man in the bushes outside the apartment. Though
shocked, she focused a little more closely. He was
playing with himself!

'Oh my God' Anna thought, and without even
thinking, screamed at the top of her voice, and ran

out of the back door and around to the lads apartment.

"Fuck, Anna, what's wrong?" Tom asked, true concern registering.
Out of breath from her dash, and the shock, she breathed heavily as she tried to explain "There's a man, a man out there."
"Out where?" Tasha asked.
"Out front, in the bushes," she gasped. "He's playing with himself."

With that, the lads got up and ran out of the front door. They ran up and down the street several times, checking behind bushes and walls, etc., but couldn't see any one.

They eventually made their way back, but went in through the girls apartment's front door, locking it, and checked the apartment was clear, before leaving by the back door, locking that too behind them.

"There's no one there, not now any way," Nicky said, "What were you thinking Anna, the front door wide open, and you, standing there like that?"
She looked down, forgetting she only had her underwear on, and was suddenly very embarrassed. She grabbed a towel, and held it around herself "I never thought, we always have the doors open, it was just habit, I just never

thought."

"Well, it's not the best idea to be in your apartment on your own, with all the doors open, and no clothes on, is it?" Tom said.

"Like I said, I never thought, and Tash had only been gone a few minutes."

"Well, no harm done, thank God," said Nicky, "but I can't believe you strut around like that with the front door open, anyone could be watching."

This disturbed the girls. They'd spent every night doing that, and had often walked around naked. How stupid had they been?

"Oh my God," said Carrie, "he could've been here before, but we just didn't see him, he could've been watching us every night for God's sake!" The thought made her shudder.

"You know, you should really report this to the Police," Oliver pointed out."I can't, it's too embarrassing," said Anna, still feeling creeped out that a man could have been watching them and playing with himself in the bushes for over a week!

How gross was that?

"Well, it's up to you, but I'd tell the Police. The next girls may not be so lucky."

■■

Nicky backed up what Oliver had said.

"He's right Anna," said Tasha. "We'll pop in to
the Police Station on our way out later."
"They'll think I'm stupid," Anna protested.
"They'll think we're *all* stupid, but this needs
reporting, who knows what he'll do next, would
you want that on your conscience, if he actually
went further, and attacked a girl?"
"No I wouldn't, you're right, I'll report it."

With that, the girls said their goodbye's and said
they hoped they'd bump in to the lads later for one
last drink.

"Here, drink this," Tasha said, passing Anna a
large glass of white wine.

Anna took it gladly, and finished it in three gulps
"God, I'm shaking like mad, that really freaked me
out," she said.
"I can imagine, it would've done us too," Carrie
butted in.
"How long has he been watching us? He could've
been there every night, the thought really gives me
the creeps," Tasha said.
"What do I say to the police? I didn't even get a
good enough look at him, all I saw was a
silhouette and saw his arm was moving in a way

that could only mean one thing, gross!" she shuddered at the all too clear memory.

"Just tell them what you saw, at least they may put patrols up here, that may be enough to scare him off doing this again," Carrie conceded.
"True, I'll do that. Just let me get dressed, and we'll go there first, get it over and done with before we go out. This is *not* going to spoil our last night here," Anna replied, "just one thing, please don't tell Marcus or David about this, if Max finds out he'll bloody kill me for being so stupid."

The girls agreed, this was best kept a secret.

Chapter Fifty Four.

Anna had dressed quickly, in an azure tie-dyed halter neck dress, which was A line (her favourite cut, it was most flattering, she thought) and just skimmed her knees. She added some matching platforms and shoulder bag, and then added some silver jewellery, and a spray of Carrie's Chanel. She'd taken a liking to the perfume, and would get herself a bottle on the way home from the duty free shop, as well as something for Max, she thought.

▪▪▪

All ready, and more than a little flustered, they locked the back patio doors and were just about to head out when Anna realised she didn't have her camera. All of them had been taking a camera out every night and day, so they had as many memories as possible of this holiday.

Anna was sure she'd left it on the kitchen counter top, but it wasn't there, so the three of them set about searching for it.

After twenty minutes, and a thorough search, they still hadn't found it. "When was the last time you had it Anna?" asked Tasha.
"This afternoon, out by the pool, but I brought it in and put it there next to my book and sunglasses," she said, pointing to where the book and glasses were still stood on the counter.
"I'll have a quick look outside, hang on," said Carrie, who unlocked the patio doors, and went out to the terrace and had a look around. Not seeing it there she stepped down to the sun beds where they had been laid earlier. It wasn't there either.

Feeling uneasy being outside by herself, she quickly made her way back indoors, locking the doors behind her.
▪▪▪▪▪▪▪▪▪▪▪▪▪▪▪▪▪▪▪▪▪▪▪▪▪▪▪▪▪▪▪▪▪▪▪▪▪▪▪

"Nope, can't see it anywhere," she told the others.
"Oh my God!" Anna exclaimed, "you don't
suppose that man has been in here do you, and has
taken my camera?" she once again shuddered at
the thought.
"I never thought of that," Tasha said. "It's a
possibility, you ran around to Nicky's leaving all
the doors open, it could have happened."

The three of them were now seriously freaked out.

"Well, I don't see any other explanation," Anna
said, "I definitely put it there with my stuff, I
know I did."
"Let's check to see if anything else is missing,"
Tasha said. And so the three of them had a search
to see if anything else was missing. They

checked everything, even in the locked safe, but
everything was there as far as they could see. Not
even the portable stereo system had been taken.
Just Anna's camera.

"I had some fantastic photo's on there, I just know
I did," she said miserably. "And now it looks like
creepo has a lasting memento of us all, now that
seriously bothers me."
"Don't worry about the photo's, we'll get
duplicate's of ours done for you, but you need to
report this to the police too, so that you can claim

insurance and also the cops can maybe alert any photo shops, so that if he tries to have the film developed, the police may catch him that way," Tasha reasoned.

"Good idea," said Carrie. "But I'm not looking forward to being interrogated by the police, they're going to think us a right set of idiots."

"We'll just have to bite the bullet," Tasha said, "it won't be the first time something like this has happened, I'm sure, and I'm certain it won't be the last."

With that, the girls picked up their bags, walked out of the apartment, and made sure their front door was locked firmly.

Walking as quickly as possible to the brighter area of the main road, they were seriously shaken by what had happened, and now Tasha thought, she was glad to be going home, she didn't think she could stand another night here after this.

***

Once at the Police Station, the girls explained as well as they could, what had happened to the Officer on duty. He said, in fragmented English, to take a seat and that someone would be with them shortly.

It seemed like hours, thought Anna, as they sat waiting, even though it was less than half an hour. This was bad enough as it was, never mind having to wait all this time.

Eventually, a female Officer called them through, and they were shown into the first room off to the right in the long corridor. The room was sparse and smelled of old farts. It was painted a light blue colour, which was cold and intimidating. The room only contained an old scuffed table, and Anna noticed there was some graffiti on the wall at the side of the table. It was in Spanish, Anna didn't understand it, but was sure it contained expletives. The only other things in the room was a tape recorder on the desk, and there were four chairs, two on each side of the table, and a window, which the Anna presumed was a one way window. People could see in, but no one could see out.

Taking one of the chairs, the Officer moved it to the other side of the table, so the girls were all sat in a row.

"So," the Officer said whilst turning on the tape recorder, and stating her name, the time, and then the names of the girls, "I understand you wish to make a statement about a stalker?" she said, glancing down at her notes.

Her English was very good, as was her accent, and Anna wondered if she'd spent any length of time in England. Then she thought 'what am I thinking that for? How is that relevant when we're here to report a serious crime?'

Anna cleared her throat nervously, and explained to the Officer exactly what had happened, including her missing camera.

The look on the Officer's face showed nothing but contempt for these foreigners. Her look told Anna she thought that they'd brought this on themselves, and were nothing but little slappers. This made Anna feel very stupid, and very small indeed.

"You do realise how stupid that was, don't you?" the Officer stated. "On your own in an apartment, with all of the doors open, and just your underwear on?"

Put like that, it sounded funny, and Tasha and Carrie let out a nervous laugh.

The Officer quickly turned to them, "What, you think this is funny? This is not funny, tis serious."

This only made the girls laugh even more, though it was their nerves doing this to them, not the incident.

■■

"That's it," the Officer snapped. "If you do not take this seriously I will charge you with wasting Police time."

The Officer looked like she was about to explode, it was evident she was absolutely fuming with them.

So, stifling their laughter, they apologised, said they were just nervous, and that it was their nerves making them laugh. They didn't know if the Officer fully understood what they'd said, but she seemed to accept it.

So, they listened as Anna continued to explain, but they were shaking, trying so hard not to laugh any further.

The Officer had been making notes throughout, in English Anna noticed, and once she had asked them a few more questions about whether they'd seen anything suspicious before tonight, and was satisfied she had all the information she needed, the Officer finally asking them to read through her notes, and if all was correct, and there was nothing missing from her report, to each sign it.

The girls took it in turns to read the report, and signed their names at the bottom of the sheet. When it got to Anna's turn, she read through it, and it once again took her back to the moment when she'd first noticed the man in the bushes. It made her shiver, even though it was very warm and stuffy in the small room. She finally signed her name at the bottom.

Finally, the Officer said, "I doubt we'll find him, but will put patrols in the area over the next few nights, and we will advise all of the photo shops in the area to watch out for a man bringing in a film for processing, especially if the results are photo's of you three," she continued, "I'll take your photograph's before you leave so that we can compare, should he be stupid enough to try to have the film developed."

After having their photo's taken, which made them feel like convicts, the Officer took their home addresses and phone numbers, and said they would be in touch if they found the man, or Anna's camera.

Thanking the Officer, the girls walked out into the balmy night air.

***

"Thank God that's over," said Anna with a deep sigh. "What was so funny anyway?"
"Nothing, I don't know, it was nervous laughter, that I couldn't stop once I'd started," said Carrie.

"It wasn't helped by the fact that Tasha was laughing too, it was contagious."

"Hey, don't blame me, you started it!" Tasha said.

"Well, it doesn't matter now, at least we've reported it, and it's over with, even though you two nearly got us arrested for wasting Police time!" said Anna abruptly, but she had to smile, their laughter had helped to calm her, and she could see why they would have laughed, she had found it hard at one point not to join in.

"Come on, let's go and enjoy our last night here, and at least when we get back to the apartment, we'll know the Police are patrolling," said Tasha. "Still freaks me out to think he's been in our apartment though, I'm checking my knicker drawer when I get back, I bet he's taken some," Anna replied.

■■■■■■■■■■■■■■■■■■■■■■■■■■■■■■■■■■■ ■ ■

■■

Chapter Fifty Five.

They had the most amazing night, starting off at
Lineker's, they were greeted by the barmen like
old friends. "Hey girls, any news?" asked Jamie.
"Nothing much," replied Anna, "apart from having
a peeping tom, having my camera nicked by him
we think, and nearly being arrested for wasting
police time," she laughed.
"Blimey, when you do things, you certainly go the
whole hog don't you?" he laughed, "So, what
happened?"

Anna, being the one it had happened to, found
herself telling Jamie all about it, and warming to
her story, made it sound even more bizarre than it
already was.
■■

"This is going to end up like Chinese whispers," Tasha quietly said to Carrie. "The story will get bigger and better the more she tells it," she continued, "we'll end up having been kidnapped, tortured, held at the peeping tom's mercy for weeks on end, and us ending up in jail for drug dealing, or something similar."

Carrie laughed, "I know what you mean, this should be fun watching it pan out, but I don't see how we can keep this a secret from David, Marcus, and most of all, Max. Especially as we may be getting a phone call from the police. They're not going to be impressed with us flaunting about with nothing on for all to see, and for getting ourselves into what could have been, a very serious incident, but it'll be a whole lot worse if we don't tell them about it straight away."

"I know, I'll have a word with her," said Tasha, "I don't like secrets, and these things have a way of getting out. Best to tell the lads straight away, and get it over with, than them find out later, which will make things much worse."

Anna had finished telling Jamie about the whole fiasco and he was berating her for being so stupid, "The locals don't like foreigners at the best of times, even though you provide them with a very good income with what you bring to the Island, but you were stupid to do that, there are some dodgy characters about, you need to be much more alert and aware when you're in a foreign country, even more so than if you were at home."

"I know that now, I just wished I'd have known before. This is our last night here, but in future, I'll not be making that mistake again," Anna replied.

Jamie, like a lot of the bar owners or workers, was also from England, Hitchin in Hertfordshire to be exact, but he'd been out here working the bars for a few seasons now, and knew what he was talking about. He'd told Anna this, and once again, told her you couldn't be too careful, the locals resented foreigners descending on their Island, taking over and flaunting over every bit of flesh they could, having sex on the beach for all to see, and basically misbehaving. Even if the locals made a good living from those same foreigners, they still resented them.

***

Anna, having been well and truly told off by Jamie, finally ordered their drinks, large Vodka and Tonics for her and Carrie, and a fresh orange and lemonade for Tasha. Jamie didn't ask why Tasha was on the soft stuff, which Tasha was glad for, enough stories had been told for one night, one year in fact, she mused.

'Boom Boom Boom' by The Outhere Bros. was playing. Tasha liked this bar, it played an eclectic mix of music, both old and new, which she found refreshing, instead of the constant din of dance music. 'God, I'm beginning to sound old' she thought as she realised what she'd just thought. Oh well, it had to happen sometime, and it was about time she grew up, she was going to be a Mum in six months time.

"Oh my God," Tasha exclaimed, "I've just thought, it's only six months, and then I'll be a Mum."

"Erm, hello!" said Carrie, "you've only just realised that?"

"No, well, yes. But it's just dawned on me how fast six months will pass before my life changes forever."

"But in a good way," Anna said, "this will be the making of you Ms. Johansson."

At the mention of Tasha's surname Carrie asked "Which reminds me, why did you turn Marcus down, when he popped the question?"

"Because a) it was very unromantic in front of you two, b) I'm in no rush, c) we've only just got back together, we've not had any proper time together, and d) I'm making him wait. He needs to ask me at least six more times before I'll say yes, if indeed I decide to," Tasha concluded.

"Of course you'll marry him, you're having his baby, that's much more of a commitment than getting married," Anna said. "But you're right, it wasn't very romantic, make him sweat it out, he deserves it!" she laughed.

"Too right he does," Tasha replied. "I'm going to make the most of this pregnancy, then make him sweat some more. I think I'll wait until the baby is a toddler, that way he or she can be either my pageboy or bridesmaid!"

"What a great idea," Carrie said. "If Marcus will wait that long."

"Oh, he'll wait," Tasha said. "If he wants us, he's got no choice in the matter."

Finishing their drinks, they walked over to where Jamie was stood chatting to some girls, and each of them gave him a hug, and wished him well, as this would be the last time they'd see him. "It's been my pleasure Ladies, you take care now, and try to avoid peeping toms and close arrests from now on, you hear me?"

The girls laughed with him, gave a quick wave, then walked out of the door.

***

The rest of the night was pretty much the same, walking in to their usual haunts, having a drink,

Anna telling her tale, which as Tasha had predicted, was getting bigger and bolder the more told it, and the more she drank.

Then, they'd hug their goodbyes to the barmen or women, and move on to the next bar.

They ended the night at Bobby's. Their favourite place.

They ordered the drinks, V&T's for Carrie and Anna, a mineral water with lots of ice and lemon for Tasha.

They moved over to the side, and watched people dancing and having a good time "I'm going to miss this," Tasha said, "it seems we've been here forever, but at the same time, only a couple of days. It'll never be the same again, just us three."
"No, in future it'll be us seven," Carrie replied, "you can join in all the Mother and Baby groups whilst we get pissed," she laughed.
"Charming, thanks a lot Carrie."
"Now you know that isn't true, we'd never ever leave you out, especially Marcus, he's going to be fawning over you both, I can just tell. He's so pleased you agreed to have him back, I've a feeling he's going to stick to you like glue."
"I bloody well hope not," replied Tasha, "I can't stand needy men!"

Underworld's 'Born Slippy' was playing, and the girls drained their drinks to go and have their last dance in Tenerife.

Straight after 'Born Slippy' came on another of their favourites N-Trance's 'Stayin Alive', so they stayed on the dance floor, making some moves, some almost silly in places, but they didn't care, this was their last night, and they didn't give a hoot what people thought.

"Hey," shouted Tasha over the noise of the music, "there's Nicky etc. over there, at the bar, let's go buy them a drink for keeping a look out for us while we've been here."

The girls had grown very fond of the group of Scottish lads, and would miss them. It would be hard staying in touch, as the girls doubted their men would approve, but if ever Tasha was in the area, she would give them a call, it would be nice to meet up again, she thought.

Weaving through the masses, the girls eventually made it over to where Nicky, Tom and Oliver were stood at the bar. Tasha noticed once again how attractive Nicky was, especially tanned, but then gave herself a mental slap, she was a taken woman now after all.

"Hey Nicky," she shouted, "What're you having?"

He turned at the sound of her voice and smiled, a great big grin "You're offering to buy us drinks, bloody hell woman, what do you think this is, equal rights!"
She poked him in the ribs, a little too sharply than she'd intended, and he winced "Hey watch it, just cos you're preggers doesn't mean I won't put you over my knee and smack that cute little ass of yours."
"Now now, you know you can't do that," she teased.
"I know, I wish," he smiled back at her.
"I'll get the drinks in though, thanks for the offer. What're you having?"   "V&T's for those two, and a mineral water for me, lots of ice and slices remember," she replied, "just my luck to find out I'm pregnant on holiday, I really could do with a drink right now, and a cigarette. I can't believe it's going to be at least six months before I can have either again. Probably longer if I breast feed."
"Too much info Tasha, thanks for that," Nicky laughed, and turned to order their drinks.

Having made their way back to their vantage point, the lads joined them, Nicky said, "Fancy going to sit outside on the terrace? We can't talk properly in here."

Everyone agreed, and they managed to weave their way through the crowd again, and out into the blissfully warm night air, "Oh, that's better," said Tasha, enjoying the light breeze on her skin.

"So, back home tomorrow," Nicky said, "are you looking forward to it girls?"
"Yes, and no," said Tasha, "we'll miss this place, and this is our last official girly holiday, so that's sad, but I can't wait to get back to Marcus, and phone my Mum and Dad with my news."
"You haven't told them yet?" asked Tom
"No, I want to be home and settled before I do that. I'm sure they'll be delighted, but just in case, I didn't want to tell them while I'm out here and have it spoil my holiday."
"What about you two? Are you looking forward to home?" asked Tom again.
"Same as Tasha, but we'll be pleased to get back to our men, sad as that sounds," said Carrie. "Plus Anna has a new car and engagement ring waiting for her back home, so she's looking forward to that, and I have a wedding to start planning, so I need to get on with it, as it's next June."
"Surely it doesn't take ten months to plan a wedding?" Oliver butted in.
"You'd be surprised," replied Carrie, "Some people plan at least two years in advance."
"I had no idea, that's put me off straight away."

"You say that now, but wait till you find 'the one', then you'll feel like I do," she smiled at him.

The easy banter continued, until it was time for the girls to head back. The lads were staying out a little longer, so said their goodbye's and that they'd see them tomorrow, they were after all, on the same flight home.

Standing on the pavement, trying to hail a taxi, which tonight for some reason, was proving more difficult than usual, they saw Chris across the road, coming out of Lineker's. "I'm glad I've seen Chris," Tasha said, "it would have been sad to go home not having thanked him for how kind he's been to us."

"Chris," shouted Tasha. "Hey, Chris, over here."

He looked in their direction. Noticing who it was, a big grin spread across his face, and he ran across the road, dodging cars, to greet the girls.

"Hey trouble," he smiled at Tasha, and then greeted the others. "I guess it's your last night?"
"Yes, it is. We're sad to leave but it'll be nice to be back home again." Tasha replied.
"I'll grab a taxi with you if that's ok? We're going in the same direction after all."
"No probs," said Tasha. "We wanted to see you anyway, to thank you for your lovely welcome,

and for showing us the best haunts, and for well, just being so nice to us."

"Hey, no thanks necessary, it was my pleasure, believe me," he grinned back at her, perfect white teeth showing.

Either it was his tan, or he'd had them whitened, Tasha thought, and wondered why she'd not noticed before.

The taxi had dropped them off way too soon, Tasha had enjoyed meeting Chris, and his company. "So, this is it then," she said to him.

"I guess it is," he replied, and then grabbed her and kissed her on the lips. Sorry, I've been wanting to do that for days, glad I got a kiss off of you before you leave me."

"Hey, naughty, you kissed me!" she laughed, but she wasn't offended. He was just one of those guys you couldn't help but like.

Hugging their goodbye's and saying the usual 'take cares', they left Chris outside The Pink Pig.

Glancing back once, Tasha saw that he was watching them walk away, and she waved at him. 'If only...' she thought, and they walked the short distance to their home of the last ten days, locking the door tightly behind them.
■■

■■
***

Chapter Fifty Six.

Day ten, and home. The girls were excited, but so sad too, as they were packing their suitcases.

"Do you think we ought to buy some aftershave here or at Duty Free at the airport, I think it'll be cheaper here," said Carrie.
"Cheapskate," shouted Anna from her bedroom, "but you're right, I think it will be cheaper here. Once we're packed, we'll get a taxi into town and go in search of some, but talk about leaving things until the last minute!"

It was a stiflingly hot day, the breeze, which had been with them throughout their holiday, seemed to be taking a holiday of it's own.

"God, is it me or is it even warmer than usual?" Tasha asked, as they were sat in the taxi, being driven into town.
"No, it's not just you, it is warmer, too much so to

be honest, glad we're going home now, I couldn't stand this sort of heat for ten days," Anna replied.

The taxi dropped them off at the shopping mall, and paying the 400 peseta fare, they thanked the driver, and got out of the car. "It's so cheap here isn't it, just over £2.00 for a taxi into town. That's one thing I will miss for sure," Carrie said.

They didn't have a lot of time, their coach was due to pick them up at 4pm, and as it was past noon already, they wanted to get their shopping done, and get back to the apartment in good time.

They wasted no time in finding a Perfume Tienda, and went in to make their choices.

Carrie chose Joop for David, a nice gift set, which included a 100ml Eau de Toilette spray and a shower gel. It was a steal at only 33,000 pesetas, which was around £18.00. Anna chose Jean Paul Gaultier's 'Male' for Max, another gift set, which cost just over £20.00 and a bottle of Chanel No.5 for herself. A little treat after the shock of last night. Tasha chose Nino Cerruti's 1881 for men, another gift set, this time with a 125ml spray and shower gel, for the same price as Carrie's choice for David.

Happy with their purchases, the girls left the shop in the hot midday sun.
■■

■■

"I think I may get Marcus a necklace, one of those leather chains with a silver charm on it, I've seen them before, and I love them, I think that would be right up his street," Tasha said.

"Good idea, we've not spent much have we? I might get something similar, if you don't mind?" Anna asked.

"Why should I mind? He's your fiancé!"

Quickly, as fast as the heat would allow at least, the girls made their way to the little jewellers where only a few days earlier, Tasha and Anna had bought Carrie her bracelet.

Entering the shop was once again total bliss, the air conditioning must be on full, it was almost a shock to the system. "This is better, I could stay in here all day," Carrie mused.

"I think that's the idea, so you buy more," Tasha replied. "These shop owners aren't stupid, anyone who wants any real business knows air con is a must, else people just won't hang around in this heat."

Hearing the tinkle of the door, the owner appeared from the back, just like before. "Hello Ladies, nice see you again."

"So this is where you got my bracelet from, you little minxes," Carrie smiled.

"Yes, and because it's such a lovely shop, and because of the air con, that's why we came back here." "How can I help today?" the owner asked.

Tasha tried to explain what they wanted, in broken Spanish, "Querríamos cadena de cuero con encanto de plata, por favor." (A leather chain with silver charm on it).
"Blimey," said Carrie, "your Spanish is much better than mine, I can stretch to asking for two beers or glasses of wine, that's about it."
"I studied at A level remember, plus took a home learning course after that, so I've remembered a lot of it, but am still way from fluent."
"Better than us two though, which is a good job really isn't it?" Anna said.
"Not really, this gentleman speaks English, don't you?"
"Si Señorita, I do!"
"I like him!" said Tasha, "he's just called me Señorita, which only really applies to young girls."

The girls laughed, along with the shop owner.

"Well, he wants a sale doesn't he, so of course he's going to flatter you," said Carrie.
"Cheers for that Carr, not!"

The owner brought over a large display of silver charms. The leather chain was standard black or brown with a little silver clasp, and either eighteen or twenty inches in length, so that wasn't going to be a hard choice. But the array of charms was. There were so many to choose from, Carrie and Anna couldn't decide.

Tasha saw what she wanted straight away though, a sharks tooth, encased in silver. It was stunning, and she knew instantly that Marcus would love it. "I'll take that one," she told the owner, pointing to the charm, "with a black, twenty inch leather chain please." (she said this in Spanish, so the other girls didn't have a clue what she was talking about). "Si Señorita, no problemo." And he set about wrapping it for her in dark blue tissue paper, which he then placed in to a matching box, and then put it in one of those beautiful little blue bags, which he tied with a blue velvet ribbon.

"He pays such beautiful attention to detail, I think the wrapping is all part of a gift, and this is just perfect," Tasha stated, and the others agreed.

By this time, Carrie had chosen a silver crucifix, pointing it out, and asked Tasha to explain she'd like a twenty inch brown leather chain. Anna had also made her mind up, a simple silver chunky eternity hoop on a twenty inch black chain, which was perfect for what she was going home to.

The owner took the same care wrapping each of the necklace's, which he'd already expertly tied each charm to the leather, so that when worn, the charm would sit perfectly on the chest.

The necklaces were all the same price, 55,000 pesetas, around £30.00 pounds each. Perfect, now the girls felt they had spent enough.

Thanking the owner, they left the shop and were once again hit with the heat of the day, "Boy, I'll be glad to get on that plane, and that *is* saying something," Tasha said.

"I'm so pleased with our purchases, I think they'll be chuffed to bits, don't you think?" Carrie asked. "They sure will, or at least, they'd better be!" Anna replied.

They ran down the hot little street, and hailed a taxi straight away. Back to the apartment, then home.

***

They arrived back at the apartment by 3.30pm, only half an hour to spare. They cleaned out the fridge and cupboards, and threw any perishable's away, taking home with them anything that would be used. Then one last check around to make sure they'd not left anything behind, and checking

Tasha had their documents safely in her bag, they sat out on the terrace for the very last time.

"God it's been great hasn't it?" Anna asked.
"Fantastic, the holiday of a lifetime, I'll never forget this time, not ever," Carrie replied, "Thanks so much for making this possible, Tasha."
"Hey, stop it, I didn't do it for you to keep thanking me, just you two being here with me, and everything I've been through, is thanks enough for me."

They heard a knock on the door, and knew it was their ride to the airport. Taking in the lush green gardens, the pool, just everything, and saving it to memory, the girls left the apartment, locked the patio doors, and said good bye to Tenerife.

***

■■■■■■■■■■■■■■■■■■■■■■■■■■■■■■■■■■■■■■■

Chapter Fifty Seven.

The flight was uneventful. They shared a few
laughs with the lads, but soon fell asleep. They
were all absolutely exhausted from the ten days of
late nights and partying, and were so looking
forward to their own beds, snuggled up with their
men.

"Tasha, Tash, wake up, we're about to land,"
Anna said, softly nudging her.
"Blimey, that time soon flew, so to speak. I'm
bloody freezing, do you have a cardi or something
I could borrow?"
"Here, have this," said Carrie, passing Tasha her
cream cashmere cardigan.
"Thanks, but what about you?"
"I'm fine, not cold at all, you hang on to it until we
get in to the car."

She knew David would be there to meet her, he'd
promised when they'd spoken on the phone the
day before. She'd tried to tell him that Marcus
was coming, but he'd insisted. It wasn't a

problem though, as it was a Saturday, so no work tomorrow for any one.

***

It was just past 11.30pm, and walking off the plane was a shock to the system. It was mid August, but the change in temperature was amazing, "God, it feels like winter," Anna remarked. "I can't believe the difference."
"I know," Tasha said, "I've got Carrie's cardi, and I'm still bloody freezing." She shivered.

Going through Customs was a breeze, they only stopped Carrie to check through her carry on bag, and that was it. Their cases took a while to arrive though. Tasha said "Why am I always the last to receive my case? I am never one of the lucky one's who gets their case straight away, oh no, I'm always last."

After twenty minutes of waiting, their cases arrived, and they picked them up ready to walk through to arrivals, anxious to see their men again. "Here, give me your case, and carry my bag instead." Anna said to Tasha.

Tasha tried protesting, but Anna was having none of it, so she took Anna's relatively light bag, and they walked through to arrivals.

∎∎

Seeing Marcus straight away, Tasha squealed his
name. He heard her before he saw her, and
looking in her direction, came running over to her,
and picking her up as if she was as light as a
feather, he kissed her and swung her around,
"God, have I missed you!" He murmured in to her
hair, which smelled of sweet coconuts.

"But it's only been a day!" she teased.
"No, I mean since we split up. I'm never letting
you go again."

She was delighted to be back in his arms, and
couldn't wait to get back home and snuggle up in
bed with him. "Will you stay over with me
tonight?" she asked.
"Of course I will, I have no intention of leaving
you now."

She could not wait to get home. The unpacking
and giving of presents could wait until tomorrow,
all she wanted was something hot to drink, and to
snuggle up in bed with Marcus.

David, who'd been looking out for Carrie, came
charging over and hugged her like she'd been gone
a century, not just ten days, "I've missed you
honey. The next holiday, I'm coming with you,
like it or not."
"Like," she replied, and kissed him. Only now

was she truly realising how much she really had missed him. The holiday had been so busy with birthdays and the shock discovery of Tasha's pregnancy, she hadn't had much time to dwell on the fact David was so far away, but now she was back, here in his arms, she never wanted to leave him again.

***

Anna was feeling disappointed. She hadn't expected Max to be here, and had told him that she'd got a lift home with David, but she had hoped that he'd still come to surprise her.

Tasha noticed Anna looking so miserable, "What's up sweetie?"
"Oh nothing. It's just, well, I told Max not to come as I'd got a lift with David, but I was hoping he'd still be here."
"He may be waiting back at our apartment, he does have a key remember?"
This seemed to perk Anna up a little, "but I still wish he was here," she said.

And then he was, as if out of nowhere, he appeared in front of her, down on one knee, holding up to her an open box, with the most exquisite diamond ring in it. 'God,' she thought, 'that's got to be half a carat at least.'
"Yes, I will!" she squealed, and bent down to kiss

him. Not expecting this, Max lost his balance and they both ended up lying sprawled out on the floor, much to the amusement of people around them.

"This isn't exactly what I had in mind when I met you from the plane!"
"It's perfect to me," she said, not even attempting to get up, "put that ring on my finger, I've waited ten long days and nights for this moment!"

And with that, he did as she asked. The ring was a little loose, but that could be rectified, and she stared at it in wonder. She was engaged! It had taken her ages, but all her waiting had paid off, she finally had her man.

Saying their goodbye's to Carrie and David, who were to travel home alone, the girls hugged, and tears sprung into Tasha's eyes "I'm going to miss you, again."
"Me too," Carrie was openly crying. "Thank you for the most wonderful time, and for this," she said, pointing to her bracelet "I'll never forget our holiday, not ever. And we must meet up soon, a girly night to exchange and look at photo's."
"Yes, we will." Tasha said, wiping away her tears.

Anna had walked over, and the three girls hugged together, as if in a scrum once again. "Thanks for the Summer of '96." Anna said to them both, and they thanked her the same.

"Come on you two, you'll be together again in a few days, let me have her back for a while at least," David laughed.

With that Carrie hugged and thanked Anna for the bracelet too, promising to get her a copy of the photo's seeing as Anna's camera had been stolen.

***

And then they were gone, leaving Tasha and Marcus, Anna and Max, to drive home together.

"Max, Marcus, I believe you've met," Anna smirked.
Shaking hands with Marcus, Max said, "Yes, but last time we met he was being shoved out of a pub by an irate Tasha ."
"Don't remind me," Marcus rolled his eyes, "Tasha on a mission is not one to be messed with, believe me,"
"Oh, I do believe you mate, I've seen it first hand more than once!" Max replied.

They loaded the girls' luggage in to the back of the borrowed Landrover. The Lotus would have been no good to carry all that luggage and four people.

■■

They all got into the vehicle silently, no more words needed to be said. Not yet anyway.

Tasha and Marcus were up front with Marcus driving. Tasha, with her hand on Marcus's thigh, stroking it gently. 'This is comforting', she thought.

Anna and Max snuggled up closely in the back, glad to be back together at last.

'Ten days is such a short period of time', Natasha thought, 'but yet so long, look how much has happened in this short period, well, last six months to be honest', she mused whilst enjoying the closeness of Marcus by her side. She was no longer alone.

With the purr of the engine, Marcus put the Landrover into gear and slowly they drove home, together.

And they all lived happily ever after.

Well, that is, until the Summer of '97!

"Wait and see" thought Natasha. "Just wait and see."

■■■

■■■
THE END. (for now!)

■■

Natalie lives and works in Sheffield, South Yorkshire, with her two cats, and too many fish to mention.
■■■

She spent fourteen years working as a Buyer, and has spent the last five working as a Company Secretary. As well as this, she is an artist, and has held exhibitions all over the UK, as well as sales both in the UK and worldwide.

She will continue with her artwork, but is also writing the sequel to this book. She intends to carry on writing, so watch this space!

■■

Lightning Source UK Ltd.
Milton Keynes UK
21 September 2009

144006UK00001B/36/P